Other Books by Jae

Happily Ever After

Standalone Romances:
Paper Love
Just for Show
Falling Hard
Heart Trouble
Under a Falling Star
Something in the Wine
Shaken to the Core

Fair Oaks Series:
Perfect Rhythm
Not the Marrying Kind

The Hollywood Series:
Departure from the Script
Damage Control
Just Physical
The Hollywood Collection (box set)

Portland Police Bureau Series:
Conflict of Interest
Next of Kin

The Vampire Diet Series:
Good Enough to Eat

The Oregon Series:
Backwards to Oregon
Beyond the Trail
Hidden Truths
The Complete Oregon series (box set)

The Shape-Shifter Series:
Second Nature
Natural Family Disasters
Manhattan Moon
True Nature

the
Roommate
Arrangement

Jae

Acknowledgments

As always, I'd like to thank my awesome beta readers. They were my cheering section and my guinea pigs who provided feedback on the first draft of this book and made the writing process less lonely and more fun! A big thank-you to Anne-France, Claire, Danielle, Erin, Laure, Louisa, Melanie, and Trish.

I'm also sending a shout-out to my editor, Robin J. Samuels, and to my fellow lesbian fiction authors Chris Zett and Catherine Lane, who took time from their own writing to join my team of beta readers.

Last but never least, thank you to my loyal readers for letting me keep them up at night because they need to read just one more chapter. I hope you stay up late for *The Roommate Arrangement* too.

Chapter 1

THIS EVENING WASN'T GOING TO end well. Steph knew it the moment Marissa, the comic opening for her, pulled the microphone out of the stand and accidentally whacked herself in the nose.

The rest of her set didn't go any better.

The local country bar didn't have a greenroom, where comedians could wait before going up on stage, so Steph sat at the bar and had a front-row seat to the disaster that was her opening act.

Marissa clamped both hands around the mic as if about to recite a poem. "Has anyone here done a juice cleanse lately?"

Steph stifled a groan. A juice cleanse? Really? That was the material she had chosen for rural Idaho?

The people in the audience looked at Marissa as if she'd asked if anyone owned a pet dinosaur.

Marissa didn't seem to notice and prattled on. "All my friends swear by them. They say it gives them bright skin and a flat belly. But all I got was one hell of a headache when I woke up. How was I supposed to know that mimosas don't count?"

That got her a sympathy chuckle from a woman in the front row. Two of the men in the back got up and returned to the pool tables, and the noise level in the bar rose as people went back to their conversations.

Not even the skin-tight top Marissa wore could keep the audience's attention, despite its plunging neckline. Sweat gleamed on Marissa's brow, and she started to speak faster, rushing through her set and making things worse.

Wonderful. Steph didn't look forward to going up after her. She'd been happy when she had found out her opener would be a fellow female comic.

Stand-up comedy was still such a male-dominated field that Steph was often the only woman—and the only queer person—in the lineup. But now that Marissa was bombing, Steph would have to work harder to show them that women could be funny. Male comedians never have to deal with that. No one judged them by another guy's failure. It wasn't fair, and it made Steph even more determined to prove herself.

"Can I get you a drink…or anything else?" the bartender asked behind her.

Steph turned and regarded the pretty redhead. Was it just her imagination, or had there been a flirty undertone?

"You kinda look like you could use one," the bartender added with a subtle wink.

Yep. Definitely flirting. God knew Steph could have used a drink to make it through Marissa's routine, and flirting was her favorite pastime. At the start of her career, she would have said yes to the drink—and to the implied offer—but her nearly ten years in comedy had taught her a lot. Now she never drank before her set because it slowed her down, and she had learned the hard way to not hook up with employees at the venues where she performed.

Too bad. The redhead was cute. Steph sent her an appreciative grin. "Thanks. I'm good. Depending on how this goes," she gestured toward the stage, "I might have to hightail it out of here right after my set."

"Nah, I doubt it. I remember you from last year. You're good. Now she," the bartender nodded toward Marissa, "is a whole nother ball game."

They both paused and watched Marissa for a few seconds.

"…and then he nudged aside my selfie stick and said—" Marissa took a nervous pace forward and stepped onto the mic cord, pulling it out. Her voice cut out in the middle of the punch line, which might have been a blessing in disguise because their small-town audience wasn't into Marissa's big-city humor.

Come on, read the crowd.

Marissa managed to plug the microphone back in and struggled through the rest of her set.

Steph wasn't sure who was more relieved when it was finally over— Marissa or the audience. With a mumbled "This joke normally goes so much better," she fled from the stage.

The bar owner took the mic and stared after her. "Um, thank you. That was…interesting. Give it up for Marissa Jones, everyone."

The crowd clapped without much enthusiasm.

"Are you ready for your headliner?" the bar owner asked with fake cheer. "Please give a warm welcome to Tiffany Renshaw!"

Steph groaned. He had gotten her name wrong the second year in a row.

But she was a professional, so she smiled as she bounded onto the low stage as if she owned the place. No way would she let them see her sweat. She shook the owner's hand and took the mic from him. "Thanks, but it's Stephanie Renshaw, actually." She gave the audience a conspiratorial grin. "Someone should tell him a man could really get in trouble calling out the wrong name at the wrong time."

"Oh, he already knows that, sweetheart," the owner's wife shouted from the back of the room.

That got them the first real laughter of the evening.

Grinning, Steph launched into her routine and forgot about everything else—her frustration with Marissa, the fleabag hotel where she'd spent the night, and the eight hundred and fifty miles she'd have to drive to make it back to LA. It was always like this for her. Up on stage was the one place where she felt at home. Being a comic on the road for most of the year had stopped being fun a while ago, but this was why she was still doing it.

Before she knew it, an hour had gone by, and she was delivering her closing bit. "Since it's Halloween, let me talk about something really scary: most comedians' love lives. Have you ever noticed how the majority of comics are either single or divorced? Apparently, sarcasm and being gone most of the time are not desirable traits in a partner. Who knew?" She pressed her hand to her chest and acted surprised. "I also found out that Ramen noodles are not considered an appropriate first-date meal and that most people don't find it attractive if you start scribbling down ideas for jokes while they tell you their life story."

A chuckle went through the crowd.

"So, I'm single. I know, shocker, right?" She playfully tossed back her tousled hair.

The audience made fake sympathetic noises.

3

"Oh, don't worry. It's by choice…well, not mine, but anyway." That wasn't exactly true, but it always got her a laugh, so she'd left it in.

"I'd take you, babe," one of the guys who had drifted back over from the pool tables shouted.

"Sorry," Steph answered without missing a beat. "That wouldn't be fair to all my other suitors. Anyway, my parents think I have bad judgment when it comes to the people I date. Well, either that or bad eyesight. I used to have this really buff boyfriend. He wore an ankle weight all the time, and I thought, wow, he's really into keeping fit." She acted it out, hopping around on one foot to show the audience where the weight had been. Then she paused before delivering the punch line. "It turned out it was an ankle monitor. He'd forgotten to mention he was out on parole."

The crowd roared, and a guy in a cowboy hat thumped his beer mug on the bar and doubled over, howling.

The wave of laughter flowed over Steph, and she soared on top of it like a champion surfer. The adrenaline rush hit her, and she couldn't help laughing along with the audience. Nothing could beat the feeling of making a room full of strangers laugh.

When she thanked the audience and left the stage, she caught the gaze of the cute bartender.

Okay, maybe sex could. Too bad one of the few rules she lived by was to keep her hands off venue employees—and people with ankle monitors.

Steph was still buzzing from her stage high when she crossed the parking lot toward her Mini Cooper convertible.

"Stephanie? Wait!" A woman's voice from behind stopped her.

A wide grin formed on Steph's lips. Apparently, the cute bartender didn't intend to let her leave without saying goodbye. She turned, a bit of flirty banter already on the tip of her tongue.

But it wasn't the redhead who'd followed her; it was Marissa. "Are you heading back to your hotel?"

"No. I'm so keyed up I figured I might as well head toward LA and get as many miles in as I can and just crash in some motel along the way."

"Can I hitch a ride?" Marissa asked. "I took a Greyhound here because what they're paying me doesn't even cover the gas money."

Greyhound? Wow. That was true dedication. "Sure. Hop in. There's not much legroom, but my car sure smells better than the bus."

"Thanks." Marissa squeezed her backpack into the trunk next to Steph's duffel bag.

They climbed in and drove the first couple of miles in silence, but Steph felt what was coming, so she wasn't surprised when Marissa said in a near whisper, "That was bad, wasn't it?"

Steph wasn't going to lie, but neither did she want to discourage a fellow comic. "We all bomb every now and then. Part of the job."

"Yeah, but I don't understand it. I did the exact same material in bars and cafés in LA, and it worked every time."

"You're not in Kansas anymore, Dorothy. You can't do the same jokes wherever you go. Those guys back there couldn't relate to juice cleanses, mimosas, and LA rush hour."

"Hmm. You might be right." Marissa pulled her phone from her pocket and started to take notes. "Any other advice?"

Steph threw her a look out of the corner of her eye. When had this turned into a free consultation? But they had a lot of time to kill, so she might as well help out a colleague. She pointed at Marissa's low-cut top. "I'd take a look at your wardrobe if I were you. Bits over tits."

"What?"

Steph chuckled. "Don't get me wrong, it's not that I don't appreciate a good-looking pair of breasts. I definitely do. But if you want people to take you seriously, show them good comedy, not your cleavage."

Marissa blushed and adjusted the neckline of her top. "Does that mean you're gay? All those jokes about your bad taste in men are completely made up?"

"Nope. All true." Steph grinned. "I'm bi, which means I have indiscriminate bad taste in men *and* women."

A giggle drifted over from the passenger seat. "Oh my gosh, you're funny. If you can make me laugh after that disaster, you're really good."

"Spend enough time working the road, and you'll be really good too." *Or slink home with your tail between your legs,* Steph mentally added. That wasn't what she was doing, though, was it?

Marissa sighed. "I know you're right. With the five minutes here and there I cobble together in LA, there's no way to improve fast. I need the longer spots you can get out here, but I've only been on the road for three weeks, and I already hate it. I thought being in a different town every week would be a fun adventure, but…"

"Tell me about it. Except for a week back in LA this summer, I've been on the road all year, bouncing around the country, living out of my suitcase, and eating shitty food."

"So you're going back to LA for good?" Marissa asked.

"Yeah. Let's face it. No one was ever discovered in a country bar in southern Idaho, so I'm aiming for my big break in the city of sunshine and smog. That's the plan anyway—if I can find an apartment without having to sell a couple of organs."

"If you need a place to crash for a while, I've got a sleeper couch," Marissa said.

That was part of what Steph liked about being a comedian. While competition for gigs was fierce, there was an unspoken code among comics. Whenever another comedian needed a place to stay for a couple of days, you provided it, no questions asked.

"Thanks, but luckily, my sister lives in LA. She's offered me her guest room for as long as I want it."

"Oh, I bet that'll be nice."

"Yeah, kind of. My sister's a neat freak, so it'll be like living with my parents." Although, truth be told, Claire had gotten more relaxed since she and Lana had become a couple for real. That was one of the reasons Steph liked her future sister-in-law so much.

"I know what you mean," Marissa said. "My sister's the same. Oh, hey, wait a minute! She and her boyfriend are moving from LA to New York and looking for someone to take over the lease on their two-bedroom apartment. It's not listed yet. Do you want me to give them a call?"

"That depends on how much the rent is. Like I said, I'm pretty fond of my kidneys."

"It's not too bad, especially considering it's close to Melrose and Sweetzer," Marissa said.

If Steph had been a dog, her ears would have perked up. Finding a halfway affordable apartment that close to two of the big comedy clubs was about as likely as encountering a zebra on the interstate. It was almost too good to be true. "How much is 'not too bad'?"

"Twenty-two hundred, I think."

In other words, highway robbery in most other parts of the country, but pretty cheap for such a central spot in LA. From what little she made as a comedian, she couldn't afford it. But if she got her friend Penny to give her back her old job as a dog walker and maybe picked up a few Uber rides, it might actually be doable. "You know what? Give them a call. If I find a roommate who pays his or her part of the rent on time, I think I can swing it."

Marissa slapped her own forehead. "Oh, shoot. Sorry, forget I said anything."

"What? Why?"

"The landlord doesn't rent to singles," Marissa said. "I'm sure there's a story there, but I never found out what it was. I just know they don't want singles or roommate situations."

Steph frowned. "Isn't that housing discrimination?"

"Only if you can prove it in court, I guess. Too bad. It's a great neighborhood—nice and quiet, but only a few blocks from The Improv and The Fun Zone. It even comes with two parking spots. Plus it's rent-controlled. If I didn't plan on being on the road for most of next year, I'd move in myself."

"Damn." Steph slapped the steering wheel. "For an apartment like that, I'd marry someone, if need be."

"Sorry," Marissa said again.

After that, both kept quiet for a while, with only the radio and the monotonous sound of tires on pavement breaking the silence. The words she'd just said seemed to echo through Steph's mind. *For an apartment like that, I'd marry someone.* She wouldn't go that far, of course; she enjoyed the freedom of sleeping with whomever she wanted too much. But the landlord didn't need to know that. What if she did what her sister had pulled off last year? When Claire's first fiancée had broken up with her, endangering the publishing contract for her relationship advice book, Claire had hired an out-of-work actress to play the role of her loving future spouse.

Maybe Steph could do something similar. In a city like Los Angeles, it shouldn't be hard to find someone who was desperate for a place to live and willing to play her significant other in front of the landlord.

Steph grinned at her idea. It was genius—as long as she avoided doing what Claire had done: falling in love with her pretend partner.

That should be easy since she wasn't the falling-in-love kind. She and her roomie would share the apartment, not the bed. Once the lease was signed, they could each go back to the joys of single life.

Now she just needed to find a person willing to go along with her plan. Craigslist probably wasn't the right place for that. She chuckled as she imagined the ad. *Wanted: roommate to share two-bedroom apartment. Centrally located, comes with a parking spot, on-site laundry, and a fake relationship.*

When they crossed the state line into Nevada, she was still amusing herself imagining the kind of person who would answer an ad like that. She couldn't wait to meet him—or her.

Chapter 2

RAE SQUINTED INTO THE DARKNESS beyond The Fun Zone's front door, trying to keep watch on the people waiting in line. The glare of the flashing neon signs bothered her. She was already dreading driving home after the late show, but public transportation in LA was as shitty as her night vision, so there was no other option.

Damn, she really needed to find an apartment within walking distance of the comedy club.

Not gonna happen. Stop whining and focus on work.

"Hey, newbie."

The sudden voice seemingly out of nowhere sent her pulse skyrocketing, but she did her best to not let on that he had taken her by surprise and merely turned her head.

One of her colleagues, Brandon Zimmerman, came into her field of vision. He had taken up position at the door right next to her.

Shit. She couldn't miss things like that and show weakness while on the job.

Brandon crossed his bulky arms over his chest and regarded Rae with a toothy grin. "Want me to take over here while you keep an eye on the ladies' room? Last month, some girl drank too much and passed out in there."

Was that all he thought Rae, as the only female doorperson on staff, was good for—checking the ladies' room?

Rae looked him straight in the eye, even though her five foot ten couldn't quite match his impressive height. She fixed him with a glare that had made even the most hardened criminals tremble in their boots. "Let me make one thing clear: I've been hired to do the same job you're doing. If you think I'm here to play the getting-the-puking-girls-out-of-the-restroom brigade, you—"

A commotion from inside the club interrupted her.

The early show wouldn't be over for another ten minutes, so it couldn't be patrons jostling for a selfie with the comedians.

"You can't kick me out, asshole," a slurring voice shouted in the lobby. "I've got a ticket. I paid, man."

"So did everyone else, and they are here to hear the comics, not your blabbing," Carlos, one of the doormen, answered. "I warned you three times to shut up."

"That's the guy who wouldn't stop complaining about the two-drink minimum," Brandon said to Rae.

She snorted. The blabbermouth was drunk as a skunk, so he clearly hadn't limited himself to two drinks. He was just looking for a reason to cause trouble. "You know what? I changed my mind. You can take over the door. I've got this." She nodded toward the lobby.

"You sure?" A wrinkle of concern formed on Brandon's forehead.

"Affirmative." After two relatively uneventful weeks at the new job, this was her chance to prove that she could handle unruly customers—to her colleagues and to herself. Not waiting for further protests from Brandon, she pushed past him, into the club, and strode toward Carlos, who had grabbed hold of the patron's arm to escort him outside.

God, the guy was massive, even towering over Carlos, who wasn't exactly tiny either. This could get ugly fast.

Rae reached out to put her right hand on the holster of her Beretta, but her fingers encountered only air. A sense of loss pierced her chest. Even after eight months, she still missed the familiar weight of her duty belt and what it represented.

Stop feeling sorry for yourself. This is your job now.

As she crossed the lobby, she tried to tell herself that she'd been in situations like this a thousand times before, and she had never needed a weapon. She had always managed to talk down even the most aggressive opponent. Well, except for—

Don't think about it. You can do this.

She took a steadying breath and calmly walked up to them, careful not to get between them or crowd the red-faced man, who looked as if he was about to deck Carlos.

Sweat trickled down her back, dampening the black shirt beneath her suit jacket, but she knew her face was an impassive mask. At least she could still rely on her poker face. "What's going on, sir?"

"This fucking asshole wants to kick me out!" The guy tried to break free of Carlos's grip, throwing him against a column with a poster of the comedians who'd perform today, but Carlos hung on.

Rae knew she had about five seconds before fists would be flying. "Let go of him, Carlos."

Her colleague looked at her as if she'd sprouted horns.

Damn, had no one taught him how to de-escalate a potentially dangerous situation? She'd have to talk to him when this was over.

"I'd like to have a word with him, to hear his side of the story," Rae said.

The drunk guy stood taller, even though he was swaying, and gave Carlos a haughty look.

"Let go, Carlos," Rae repeated with more force.

"If this blows up, it's on you." Carlos finally let go.

The guy stumbled and nearly fell.

Quickly, Rae grabbed his elbow—or rather, she wanted to—but missed. She gritted her teeth and managed to take a hold of his arm on the second try. "It'll be getting really loud in here once the show ends, so let's step outside and talk."

The drunk guy threw Carlos a triumphant glance, then trotted after her like a well-trained lapdog.

Since dozens of people were lined up out front, waiting for the late show, she led him to the back door. There was no sense in dragging other people into this mess.

Once they were outside, she let him ramble about the two-drink minimum and the overpriced buffalo wings. When he started complaining about the cost of parking, she raised her hand to interrupt him.

"Sorry you had such a bad experience tonight, sir. Probably best if you don't come back." Without waiting for a reply, she slipped back inside, closed the door between them, and bolted it. By the time he realized she had no intention of letting him back in, she was halfway across the lobby.

11

"Damn," Carlos muttered. "Didn't think we'd get him out of here without at least a broken nose or two—one of them mine. Where'd you learn that trick?"

"LAPD."

"Fuck, you're a cop?"

"Was."

"Wow." Carlos looked at her as if she were a superhero in a red cape. "I tried to get into the academy myself, but…" He shrugged. "Why did you leave the department?"

Rae ignored his question and walked past him back to the front door.

The adrenaline that had pumped through her slowly trickled off, and a slight tremor went through her hands, which had been rock-steady during the confrontation. She shoved them into the pockets of her black slacks so Brandon wouldn't notice.

By the time the club owner signaled them to let in the late-show crowd, her nerves had settled. "You handle this line." She pointed to the people who had purchased their tickets online. "I'll take that one." She gestured toward the patrons who were hoping to get tickets at the door.

The corners of Brandon's lips twitched as if he couldn't decide whether he wanted to frown or give her an amused grin. "Are you always this bossy?"

It reminded her of what her partner, Mike, had always said when she had insisted on driving, and for a second, she nearly smiled. "Yeah. Better get used to it." She stepped forward to check the ID of the first person in line and to do some random pat-downs for alcohol, drugs, or weapons.

Over the course of the last two weeks, she'd gotten pretty efficient with the door checks, so it didn't take too long before she'd herded her part of the crowd inside—minus a butterfly knife and two flasks someone had tried to smuggle into the club.

Just when Rae was about to help her colleagues seat the audience, another customer—a woman in her late twenties—jogged up and tried to squeeze past with a "hi" and what she probably thought was a charming grin.

Unimpressed, Rae blocked the door with her broad shoulders. "I'll need to see an ID, and the ticket for the show is twenty dollars, ma'am."

"I'm not here to see the show," the woman said. "I'm a comedian."

Rae's gaze went to the poster behind her, then to the slender woman in front of her. Blonde hair tumbled onto her shoulders in uncontrolled waves, and a zigzag part made it look even more tousled, as if she had just gotten out of bed. Her admittedly pretty face wasn't on the poster. "You're not in the lineup."

"Not tonight, but one of my friends is. I just want to say 'hi' for a minute." The blonde stretched her five-foot-seven frame so she could point over Rae's shoulder at one of the headshots on the poster. "Gabriel Benavidez."

That name was on the poster, which was probably how the blonde knew it. Rae wouldn't fall for such a cheap trick. "ID and cover charge, please."

"Oh, come on. Comics always get in free of charge at The Fun Zone." A mischievous glint entered the blonde's eyes. "Want me to tell you a joke to prove I'm a comedian?"

Rae crossed her arms over her chest. She wasn't in the mood to stand here for the rest of the night and argue with this troublemaker who thought she could charm her way inside without paying just because she was cute. "No, thanks. I'm sure you're hilarious," she said without even the hint of a smile, "but I'm a doorwoman, not a talent booker."

"Everything okay over there?" Brandon called.

Rae gritted her teeth. She hated that he thought he needed to come to her rescue. "Everything's fine."

A sudden touch to her left shoulder nearly made Rae jump out of her skin. She whirled around and caught sight of Brandon, who had taken up position only inches behind her. *Stand down,* Rae told her battle-ready body and struggled to unclench her fists. "For fuck's sake, Zimmerman. Back off. I told you everything's fine."

"Um, guys...and girls, can we all relax?" the blonde said. "I just want to say 'hi' to Gabe."

"Steph, is that you?" Brandon craned his head around Rae.

The blonde gave him an easy grin. "Yep, the one and only. Missed me?"

Brandon laughed. "Yeah. Probably not as much as the boss did, without you showing up here every week, begging him for a spot in the lineup."

"Hey, I don't beg." The blonde winked at him. "Well, not unless some hottie with very talented fingers is involved."

Brandon roared with laughter and reached around Rae to pull the blonde past her. "Let her in. She's one of the comics. Totally harmless."

Rae glared after them, not liking the way Brandon had encroached on her turf. *Harmless, my ass.* She would watch the blonde closely anyway.

Steph walked past the framed headshots of famous comics who'd performed at the club. A few had been added since she'd last been here, and she vowed to one day have her own picture on The Fun Zone's wall.

Brandon slowed his steps. "You still know your way around, right? I want to check in with Carlos before the show starts. He's new and still getting used to how things are run here."

"Sure, go ahead. Thanks for getting me past Ms. Doberman." She pointed over her shoulder. Amazing how much had changed in just a few months. The club hadn't had any women on the door staff last year or when Steph had been here for a week in June. Usually, Steph was all for more women in male-dominated jobs, but while Ms. Doberman with her broad shoulders and lean waist definitely looked hot in the black suit-and-tie uniform that doorpeople at the club wore, Steph wasn't so sure she was a good addition to the team. She hated people who abused what tiny bit of power they had, and to her, that was what the doorwoman had been doing.

Brandon chuckled. "No problem. She's new too, so I guess she's trying to prove herself. I wish I could say her bark is worse than her bite, but I'm actually not sure. She's a hard-ass." It sounded like a compliment. "I'd better go. Talk to you later."

When he walked away, Steph continued past the bar, through a curtain, and then down a narrow hallway.

In the greenroom, nothing had changed at all. Two comics sprawled on the worn couches, trying to best each other with stories about bombing on stage, while another sat in a corner and recited his material to himself. A fourth stared up at the framed covers of comedy albums lining the wall as if they were the most fascinating things he'd ever seen.

Was he high on something? Steph shook her head. While she had smoked weed every now and then in the past, she knew that getting high before a show was never a good idea.

The fridge door thumped closed, and Gabe appeared from behind it, a beer in one hand and his set list in the other. When he saw her, he quickly set them on the counter before crossing the greenroom and engulfing her in a hug. "Steph! You're back!"

The familiar scent of his aftershave greeted her, and she could even detect a whiff of butter, cinnamon, and sugar from his mother's homemade *churros*.

After a few seconds, he let go and stepped back to study her. "Wow, you look like shit."

Steph laughed. "Such charm. Must be why I broke up with you."

"Breaking up?" He elbowed her, but his tone was light, without a hint of bitterness. "Is that what it's called when you sneak out the next morning without even leaving a note?"

"Oh, come on. Like you wanted to take me home to meet your mother."

"You have met my mother."

Steph rolled her eyes. "You know what I mean."

"Yeah, yeah. But seriously, you do look like shit. Don't people sleep in Iowa?"

"Idaho," Steph said. "I didn't stay after the last gig. We made it one-third of the way to LA before crashing at a motel."

"How long are you staying this time?" Gabe asked.

"I'm back for good. My clock is ticking, you know?" She made tick-tock-tick-tock sounds.

Gabe's jaw gaped open. "You wanna have a baby? Seriously?"

"God, no!" Steph laughed. "Can you imagine me as someone's mom? I'd probably kill the poor kid the first time I try to feed it my cooking."

"What's up with the tick-tock-tick-tock, then?"

"I wasn't talking about my biological clock," Steph answered. "I'm talking about my professional clock. Back when I tried stand-up for the first time and everyone kept telling me you can't make a living from it, I gave myself ten years to prove them wrong. I promised myself I'd have my big break by my thirtieth birthday."

Gabe counted the months until March on his fingers and let out a low whistle. "That gives you four months. No pressure or anything. So I guess that means you want to get back into the LA game right away and hit some open mics with me tomorrow?"

"I'd love to. But first I need to find a roommate who'll pretend to be the love of my life," Steph said with a grin.

Gabe stared at her. "Um, what?"

"Long story. I'll explain the details later. Basically, I have a chance at an apartment right around the corner, but I can't afford it without a roommate."

Gabe sighed. "Story of my life. Between Yolanda and our two roommates, the last time I got to use the bathroom without someone knocking on the door, hurrying me along, was…well, never."

"Seriously, I want that apartment. Can you imagine hitting two or three clubs in the same night without spending hours stuck in traffic?"

Gabe gave her a dreamy look. "Man, that sounds great. I'd move in with you myself, but Yolanda probably wouldn't like it."

No, she definitely wouldn't. Gabe's girlfriend wasn't a big fan of their friendship, even though their one-night stand had been long before Yolanda had been in the picture. "Guess I'll have to play the roommate roulette on Craigslist." She groaned. The last time she had put out an ad for a roomie, one potential roommate had shown up with enough pets to populate a zoo, and another seemed to have confused her ad with the *casual encounters* section.

"Hey, wait," Gabe said. "I think Ray is looking for a place closer to the club."

"Ray?" Steph repeated.

"Yeah, one of the newbies on the door staff." He pointed toward the club's entrance.

"Might not be a bad idea. The club does a background check before hiring anyone, so at least I would know I'm not moving in with an ax murderer."

"At least not one who got caught," Gabe quipped.

"Right. If he's clever enough to evade the police, he's hopefully got his shit together enough to pay his part of the rent on time. So where do I find this Ray?" Steph asked. "Is he working tonight?"

"Yeah, but Ray is actually—"

One of the club's assistant managers popped his head into the greenroom. "Benavidez, you're up."

Outside, Steph could hear the MC give Gabe's intro.

Gabe grabbed his set list and took a step toward the short hallway that would take him from the greenroom to the stage. Then he paused and looked back at Steph. "Ray is—"

"Don't worry about it. I'll find him." Steph made a shooing motion. "Go out there and kill it!"

Gabe grinned. "Will do. Call me tomorrow—but not before noon."

Then he was gone. Applause from the showroom drifted over as the audience gave him a warm welcome.

Steph wished she were out there instead, making people laugh in one of the biggest comedy clubs in the city. Well, she would get there, but first she needed to secure an apartment. Time to go talk to Ray.

When Steph left the greenroom, the lobby was empty except for Brandon.

"Hey, Brandon, can you point me in the direction of your new colleague?" Then, remembering that there were several, she added, "Where's Ray?"

"Outside, calling a cab for some girls from a bachelorette party who drank a little too much," Brandon said.

Steph wrinkled her nose. Bachelorette and bachelor parties were the worst audience ever. They often showed up drunk and expected the night to be about them, not about comedy.

Well, if Ray could handle a group like that, he could handle a little fake romance to convince their future landlord they were worthy of his apartment.

"Thanks. See you next week." She gave Brandon a friendly wave and pushed through the glass doors.

Ms. Doberman stood at the curb, keeping vigil over a cab that was pulling away, but there was no sign of Ray anywhere.

Then Steph looked more closely. In the orange light of a neon sign forming the words *The Fun Zone,* she could make out a bulky figure leaning against the building. The black suit almost blended in with the near darkness, but the glowing tip of a cigarette gave away his position.

Ugh. Ray's a smoker. Steph decided she could deal with it, as long as he smoked only in his own room. But French-kissing to fool their landlord was definitely out.

She walked over to him and cleared her throat.

"Oh shit." He tossed away his cigarette and frantically waved his hand to disperse the smoke, like a teenager who'd been caught smoking. Then he blew out a breath and slumped against the wall. "Man, I thought you were the boss. He doesn't like it if we're smoking on the premises."

"Nope, just little ol' me. Sorry, I didn't mean to scare you."

"You didn't. But I'm new, and I don't wanna get in trouble my first month here." He ran a hand over his crew cut and produced a pack of smokes from somewhere, which he held out to her. "Want one?"

"No, thanks," Steph said. "I came out here because my friend Gabe said you're looking for a place closer to the club. I heard about an unlisted two-bedroom apartment we could share. Interested?"

He froze with the lighter raised halfway toward the cigarette dangling between his lips. "Uh…"

"It's only a couple of blocks from here," Steph added. Why was he staring at her as if she had offered her services as a hit woman?

"Not sure that'd be a good idea," he mumbled around the unlit cigarette. "I've got a girlfriend, and I don't think she'd like me moving in with another chick."

"Oh." Steph chuckled to cover her embarrassment. "Sorry, Ray. Gabe failed to mention that."

Now he stared at her again, his jaw so slack that he was close to losing his second cigarette too. "Looks like he failed to mention something else too."

"What?"

He finally took the cigarette out of his mouth. "My name's Carlos."

What the fuck was going on here? Steph blinked up at him. "Then who the hell is Ray?"

"I am," a deep but unmistakably female voice came from behind her. Steph whirled around.

Ms. Doberman stood in front of her, strong arms folded over her chest. The neon sign threw flickering lights across her striking face, which carried a don't-mess-with-me expression.

"Y-you…? But…but I thought…" Steph glanced back and forth between Ms. Doberman and her male colleague. "You are Ray?"

"Looks like it." Ms. Doberman tapped the name tag pinned to the lapel of her suit jacket.

Earlier, Steph hadn't paid it any attention. Now she squinted to read it in the dim light.

Rae, it said. With an *e*, not a *y*.

Oh shit.

Ms. Doberman—Rae—observed her with an impassive gaze. "Problem with that?"

Steph lifted both hands, palms out. "Oh, no, no, I just…" God, she was going to kill Gabe as soon as she got her hands on him. Slowly. Painfully.

"Um, I think I'll go see if Brandon needs any help keeping an eye out for hecklers." Carlos squeezed past them and hurried inside.

Rae didn't move. She kept fixing Steph with that cool gaze of hers. In the near darkness in front of the club, Steph couldn't make out her eye color, but something about her eyes seemed off somehow, though Steph couldn't put her finger on what it was. Maybe the low light was playing tricks on her.

"You were looking for me," Rae said. "You found me. What did you want?"

Jeez, she wasn't one to mince words. Steph hesitated. Should she still go through with her plan? She took a deep breath. Yeah, why not? She and Rae had gotten off on the wrong foot, and they'd probably never sit on the couch and watch Netflix together, but that didn't mean they couldn't be roommates, right? Break-ins had been on the rise in Beverly Grove for the last couple of years, so if they sold Rae as someone who worked in the security industry, they'd have a better chance of getting the apartment.

But this time, she'd approach it a little differently so she wouldn't embarrass herself a second time, as she had with Carlos. "Do you have a girlfriend?"

"Pardon me?" It sounded like a growl.

"Or a boyfriend," Steph added quickly. With her chiseled features, her swimmer's build, and the cut of her black hair—short on the sides and back, but longer on top—Rae looked like a lesbian or a queer woman, but Steph didn't want to stereotype. There were plenty of tough-looking straight chicks after all, or Rae could be bi or pan.

"If that's your attempt to tell me a joke, you're bombing." Rae turned on her heel and headed toward the door with a powerful stride, no doubt intending to close it after her, leaving Steph outside.

"Wait!" Steph rushed after her and grabbed Rae's arm to stop her.

Rae froze. The muscles of her forearm seemed to turn into a block of concrete beneath Steph's fingers. Slowly, she turned her head and looked down at Steph's hand. Her gaze had the intensity of a laser beam.

Steph wrenched her hand away as if she'd been burned. "Look, I know I started this all wrong, but please hear me out."

Rae's stance didn't soften, but she gave the tiniest of nods, indicating that she would listen.

Okay, here goes nothing. "My friend Gabe said you're looking for an apartment closer to the club."

Rae turned so she was facing Steph, who bit back a smile.

Gotcha! She had Rae's full attention now, but she had to reel her in carefully. "I just heard about a great two-bedroom apartment not too far from here. The tenants are moving out, and they are looking for someone to take over their lease."

"What's the catch?" Rae asked.

Steph tried not to shuffle her feet under Rae's probing gaze. "Well, the rent is over two grand, so I'm looking for a roommate."

"Roommate." Rae tilted her head. "You mean, you and me...living together?"

Steph quirked her lips. The way Rae had said that, as if it was an entirely foreign concept to her, was almost cute. "That's usually what a roommate arrangement implies."

Rae's brows bunched together. "If I said yes, would you always be such a smart-ass?"

"In the interest of full disclosure...yeah, probably. My family says I don't have an off button." Steph tried out her most charming smile on Rae, but the woman's expression gave nothing away. "So are you interested?"

"How close to the club is the apartment?"

"Walking distance."

Rae's brooding expression lightened. She rubbed her strong chin. "And I'd get my own bedroom?"

"Of course," Steph said. "Even though it would officially be a guest room or a home office."

"What?"

Damn. She'd nearly had her, but now Rae looked at her with that suspicious expression again. "The landlord is a bit of an asshole. I mean, not that I know him, but he insists on renting to couples only. So you and I—"

"Forget it," Rae said.

"Thank you very much. Has anyone ever told you, you're killer on a girl's ego?" Steph reached out to nudge her but then pulled back. She playfully puffed out her chest and fluffed her hair. "Just so you know, there are dozens of people all over the country who'd love to be my significant other."

Rae arched her brows. "If you're such a hot commodity, why aren't you asking one of those plentiful people to move in with you?"

"Because I'm not the relationship type, and I don't want them to think otherwise," Steph said. "You and I, we'd just pretend to be a lovey-dovey couple when we're around the landlord. As soon as the lease is signed, you can go back to scowling at me."

Rae stared out into the darkness or maybe at the flickering neon lights of Melrose Avenue.

Steph waited, bracing herself for rejection.

Finally, after what seemed like an hour but was probably only a few seconds, Rae directed her attention back toward Steph. "All right."

"All right?" Steph hopped up and down. "You'll do it?"

"Only if I like the apartment—and if you abstain from hugging me."

Steph froze because she'd been about to do just that. "No hugging. Check. Um, well, I might have to hug you or hold your hand in front of the landlord. We wouldn't want him to think we're about to break up, right?"

Rae sighed. "Right."

"Great. Glad we're on the same page." Steph beamed at her. "So want to give me your name and number?"

Rae just looked at her.

"Jeez, I'm not trying to chat you up. I need your number so I can call you once I set up a meeting with the landlord, and we won't be very believable as a couple if we call each other 'hey, you.'"

"Your family is right. No off button," Rae grumbled. She took the phone Steph handed her and added her name and number to Steph's contacts, then sent herself a text so she'd have Steph's number too.

Steph took the phone back and checked the small screen. "Pleased to meet you, Rae Coleman. I'm Stephanie Renshaw." She held out her hand, but Rae just gave her a nod. "Wow, so I guess we're really doing this."

Rae shrugged. "Guess so."

"Okay, then." Steph decided to get going before Rae could change her mind. "I'll call you as soon as I set something up with the landlord."

Rae gave her another nod.

When Steph walked toward her car, she felt Rae's gaze following her.

"Stephanie," Rae called.

She turned and grinned. "Steph, please. If you call me Stephanie, I'll think I'm in trouble."

"Somehow, I get the feeling that happens a lot," Rae said.

"What, now you're a comedian too?" Steph asked.

Rae let out a huff. "God, no. Just wanted to answer your question from earlier."

"What que—?" Then it occurred to her. "Oh, the girlfriend…or boyfriend question?"

"Yeah," Rae said. "I don't have one."

"See, that's where you're wrong. You've got a girlfriend now, babe." Steph blew her a kiss and sauntered off.

Chapter 3

WHAT THE HELL HAD SHE gotten herself into? Even hours later, Rae still couldn't believe she had agreed to Stephanie's...Steph's bizarre plan. She had enough complications in her life, so why hadn't she told her no?

The thought of sharing space with someone, especially someone who seemed as different from her as night and day, was already making her uncomfortable. She had grown used to living on her own and handling things her way. On top of that, she would also have to pretend to be happily in love with Steph.

Happy. In love. She'd forgotten what either felt like. What on earth made her think she could pull this off?

With a heavy sigh, she climbed into her Subaru.

Just as she turned the key in the ignition, the first raindrops hit the windshield.

Great. Rae sent a glare up at the night sky. *So much for "It never rains in Southern California."*

In the past, she would have welcomed the sporadic light showers LA sometimes got in November, but the rain made driving in the dark even harder.

Sweat beaded on her forehead as she slowly backed out of the parking space.

God, she hated that such a simple task was now giving her trouble. She had spent the past eight months trying to adapt and only looked for a new job once she could make it through the day without spilling drinks and bumping into doorways. But her depth perception was still dodgy, especially at night, without any shadows to help her judge how far away objects were. Her brain screamed at her that she was about to hit the bumper of another car, even though the Subaru's camera and security features told her it was farther away than it appeared.

Finally, she managed to navigate the SUV onto the street and tried to ignore the glare from oncoming headlights as she drove to her apartment in Silver Lake.

This. She nodded grimly. This was why she had agreed to Steph's outlandish plan.

If they could convince the landlord to let them rent the apartment, she'd no longer have to drive at night. She could walk to the club and back, and that would be worth all the silliness that came with this arrangement.

But Rae didn't let herself hope for too much. Maybe the apartment would turn out to be an overpriced dump with a leaky roof, a broken AC, and more drug dealers than she'd ever arrested as her next-door neighbors. Or, with the luck she was having, Steph would turn out to be the roommate from hell. After all, how normal could a woman who came up with such a bizarre plan be?

On Sunday morning, Steph hurried toward the café where she'd told Rae to meet her. "Sorry, I can't talk long," she said into her phone. "I'm meeting my girlfriend."

For several seconds, only the sound of a dog's barking filtered through the phone.

"Your…what?" her friend Penny nearly shouted. "Okay, what happened to you in Idaho? Drugs? Brainwashing? Some weird cult?"

Steph laughed. "All right, I admit it. We're faking it."

"Faking *it*?" Penny repeated. "Um, you know, Steph, I'm not sure I want to know that much about my best friend's sex life. Not that I don't already know all the details, since you're not exactly shy about oversharing."

Steph huffed playfully. "You're just jealous."

"Ha! You know I prefer dogs to women." Penny paused. "Ugh, that sounded pervy, didn't it? You know what I mean. A dog will never break your heart or drive you up a wall during PMS."

"Exactly what I'm always saying. Give me a dog over a relationship any day." The one time in her life when Steph might have been interested in being someone's girlfriend, she'd made a big mess of things and ended up hurting everyone. "Speaking of dogs…" She had reached Blue Bottle Coffee and lingered in front of the door to finish her conversation before going in. "Do you think your canine customers would appreciate a good-looking, friendly, not to mention modest dog walker?"

"I'm sure they would. But I thought Gabe was allergic to dogs."

Steph could almost see the big grin on Penny's sun-kissed face. "Hardy-ha-ha. You know I was talking about me. So can I have my old route back? Pretty please?"

Penny didn't answer immediately. "You know you left me in a bit of a lurch when you spontaneously decided to hit the road in January. That's not fair to the other dog walkers—and especially not to the dogs. They can't understand why you just don't show up one morning."

Steph winced and tried not to imagine how poor Moose might have felt when another dog walker had come to pick him up. "I'm sorry. I promise I'm sticking around for longer this time. Who knows? If I'm not on TV or headlining in the big clubs in four months, I might even come work for you full-time…if you'd have me."

"I'd love that." More softly, Penny added, "But I'd love it even more if the comedy biz would finally realize how hilarious you are and you would achieve all your dreams."

Aww. For once, Steph struggled to come up with a joke to hide how touched she really was. "Tell me again why you don't have a girlfriend."

"Better yet, why do you suddenly have one?" Penny countered. "Seriously, what's up with that?"

"I'm on my way to look at an apartment. I talked to the current tenant, and she agreed to let me take over the lease if the landlord agrees, but apparently, he has this thing about not renting to singles, so I found myself a fake girlfriend."

A couple with a stroller stared at her as they walked by.

Penny blew out a noisy breath. "I swear, the ideas you come up with sometimes…"

"Hey, don't judge. Remember that little detail Claire let slip when you got her drunk on her birthday last year?"

"For the hundredth time, I didn't get her drunk. She was a bit tipsy at best, and all I did was to get her a bottle of red for her birthday because I had no clue what else to give her. How was I supposed to know she's such a lightweight?"

"Whatever," Steph said. "But at least now you know that my sister did the same thing."

"Yeah, and she's going to marry her fake girlfriend next year," Penny answered.

Steph chuckled. "I admit she's taking the whole thing a little too far. But don't worry. That won't happen to me, no matter how hot my fake girlfriend might be."

"Is she?" Penny asked.

Was she? Their first meeting last night had been so confrontational that Steph hadn't stopped to think about the way Rae looked. Okay, at least not much. Of course she had noticed Rae's powerful build. Now she peered through the café's floor-to-ceiling window.

Somehow, she wasn't surprised to find Rae already there, sitting with her back to the wall. Gone was the black shirt and tie she'd worn last night. Instead, she wore a pair of black jeans and a white button-up that strained against her broad shoulders. She appeared more relaxed than she had been at work, but her eyes were alert, constantly scanning her surroundings.

Now, in the light of day, Steph could make out details she hadn't noticed last night. Rae was a few years older than Steph had thought—probably in her midthirties—and her hair wasn't actually black, just such a dark shade of brown that it could be mistaken for it. The color reminded Steph of coffee beans. Her short hair emphasized her sculpted cheekbones and her strong jawline. With the permanent near scowl on her face, she was too intimidating to be called beautiful, but she was certainly striking. Only her sensitive mouth and a few unruly strands flopping across her forehead softened her brooding appearance.

As if sensing Steph's gaze on her, Rae turned her head and looked at her. She didn't smile or lift her hand for a wave; she just looked back at Steph with that strange intensity that made a shudder go through her.

"Steph?" Penny said. "You still there? Is she hot or not?"

"Um, I guess she is—if you're into the tall, dark, and brooding type. And you know I'm not. At least not the brooding thing." Steph switched the phone to the other ear, preparing to open the door with her right hand. "Listen, I have to go, but can I give you as a reference to the landlord?"

"Sure. Call me later, and we'll set up a schedule for you."

"Will do. Um, Penny…is there a chance I could have Moose back or at least get to see him? I really missed him while I was gone."

Penny breathed in and out audibly. "You're in luck. I've walked him for the past month because his walker gave notice. If you want him back, he's yours starting tomorrow."

"Thank you."

When they ended the call, Steph tried to rein in her broad grin as she entered the café. She paused to take in the airy room with its white-painted brick walls and minimalistic decor and then walked up to the tiny, round table Rae had claimed and settled on a chair across from her. "Hi. Thanks for meeting me here."

Rae nodded and shifted a little to the side, as if wanting to keep the front door in her sight.

Steph grinned at her. "Are you waiting for someone else?"

"No," Rae said but didn't offer an explanation, so Steph decided to ignore that little bit of weirdness.

She threw a glance at the counter, where an espresso machine let out a gentle hiss that reminded her she hadn't had her morning coffee yet. "I'm getting a latte. Can I get you anything?"

"Coffee."

Steph arched her brows and waited, but again, nothing further came from Rae. Oh great. Was this what she had to look forward to if she lived with Rae? Having to drag every single syllable out of her? "Do you want cream or sugar?"

"No. Just black coffee." After a beat, Rae held out a five-dollar bill and added, "Please."

Steph shook herself at the thought of black, unsweetened coffee. Well, at least Rae wouldn't use up all of the cream and leave the empty container for Steph to find, as one of her previous roommates had done.

It didn't take long for her to return with a creamy latte for herself and a single-origin brew from Guatemala for Rae, which she slid in front of her. "Want half?" She held up the tahini chocolate chip cookie she had splurged on.

"No, thanks."

"More for me, then. These are really yummy." Steph took a big bite and studied Rae while she chewed.

A couple of what looked like pockmark scars dotted Rae's forehead and gave her a hint of vulnerability. Her eyes were a lighter shade of brown than her hair, and the left one didn't seem to move as much as the other. Rae put her cup down and straightened as if uncomfortable with the close perusal. "What?"

"Nothing." Steph didn't want to make Rae uncomfortable by mentioning her lazy eye. "Can't I just enjoy gazing adoringly at the woman I love?" She fluttered her lashes.

No reaction. Not even a tiny twitch of Rae's lips. Rae cradled her mug as she observed Steph across the table. Her hands, which were big for a woman, made the cup seem as if it were part of a tea set from a dollhouse. "Why did you want to meet at ten when we're meeting the landlord at eleven?"

"Well…" Steph gestured, cookie in hand, accidentally getting crumbs everywhere. "I thought we could get to know each other."

Rae regarded her suspiciously. "You're not gonna be that kind of roommate, are you? The type who sticks to me like glue and insists that we go grocery shopping together and share all of our meals?"

"God, no. Way too domestic. But I think we should get to know each other a bit if we want to convince the landlord that we're a couple."

"Fair enough." Rae stiffly tilted her head, her body language screaming out how uncomfortable the situation made her. "What do you want to know?"

Steph decided to keep it simple so she wouldn't spook her any further. "How long have you worked the door at The Fun Zone?"

"About two weeks."

"And before that? Have you worked for another comedy club?"

"No."

Steph sighed and took a gulp of her latte, wishing it contained something stronger. This wasn't getting them anywhere. "Why don't you tell me what you think I should know about you?"

Rae seemed to think about it for a moment before she nodded. "My full name is Raelynn Joy Coleman, I'm 36, and I have no criminal—"

"Wait! Raelynn Joy?" Steph burst out laughing, then covered her mouth with her hand to control her mirth. That name so didn't fit the intimidating woman.

Rae shrugged. "My parents believed in letting the universe choose my name on the day of my birth, and it turned out to be a sunny day, so…"

"So Rae like ray of light?"

"Guess so."

Steph giggled. "Well, considering you could have been a Rainbow or a Cloudy-with-a-chance-of-rain, I think you got off lucky. I actually like Rae."

Another shrug from Rae, but her stiff stance seemed to loosen a bit. "What about you?"

"No Rainbows in my family. They named me Stephanie Katherine, after my mom's parents, Stephan and Katherine. That's the part of the family that was filthy rich."

"Your family's rich, and you are looking for a roommate to help with the rent?" Rae moved her head from side to side while she studied Steph. She did that a lot, Steph had noticed, and it made her look a little like a bird of prey peering at a mouse from all angles. Another little quirk Steph hadn't quite figured out yet.

"It's my mother's money, not mine. I'm not saying I never accepted a cent from her. I've done that once or twice, but only when I had no other choice. Usually, I find another way to rustle up some money. I can do without the lecture about responsible behavior or the reminder that I shouldn't have dropped out of college that comes with the money, you know?"

Rae nodded and, to Steph's surprise, actually looked as if she understood disappointing her parents.

Steph's phone started to buzz in her pocket. She pulled it out and glanced at the screen. "It's Mr. Kleinberg, the landlord. Oh shit. I hope he isn't calling to tell us he already gave the apartment to someone else."

"If he is, this was the shortest fake relationship in the history of mankind," Rae said.

Only one way to find out. With a finger that was slightly damp, Steph swiped the screen and lifted the phone to her ear.

Rae watched Steph as she nodded several times, as if the landlord could actually see her.

"Yes, sure," Steph said. "No problem at all. We're in the neighborhood anyway. We'll be right there."

Okay, that didn't sound as if Mr. Kleinberg had called to tell them he'd rented the apartment to someone else. Rae wasn't sure if she should be relieved or disappointed. The more time she spent with Steph, the more she doubted that moving in with her and pretending to be her lover was a good idea. Not that there was anything wrong with Steph. Aside from her irreverent nature and smart mouth, she actually seemed nice, but God, they were just so different. Could they really live under the same roof without wanting to kill each other?

Steph put the phone away and looked up. For the first time, Rae noticed that her eyes were a pale gray. Maybe the color should have reminded her of cool stone or unbending metal, but with the twinkle in them and the easy grin on Steph's face, they appeared warm somehow.

"He asked if we can make it a little before eleven since he has another couple coming to look at the apartment later," Steph said.

Rae grabbed the leather jacket from the back of her chair and slid her wraparound sunglasses onto her face to protect her eye as they left the café. "So we've got competition."

"Looks like it. Are you ready to impress the hell out of Mr. Kleinberg?"

Rae gave a noncommittal grunt. She couldn't remember when she had last tried to impress anyone, and it admittedly made her a little nervous.

"Let's walk." Steph pointed around the corner, toward Sweetzer Avenue. "It'll be faster. The apartment is only two blocks from here."

Rae nodded and tried to inconspicuously circle around Steph to keep her on her right.

Pain flared through her left knee. Suppressing a curse, she turned her head to see what she'd bumped into and found a square stone planter. She glared at the damn thing.

"You okay?" Steph lightly placed her hand on Rae's arm.

There she goes again with the touching. Rae started walking again so Steph's hand would fall away. "Yeah. I'm fine."

"You sure?" Steph asked. "That looked like it hurt."

"I've had worse." And wasn't that the truth! In the beginning, her left leg and shoulder had looked as if she was someone's punching bag because she'd constantly run into things. "So how do we convince him we're a couple?"

"Just act naturally," Steph said.

That wasn't very helpful advice. Rae gestured at where she was walking with a careful distance between her and Steph. "This *is* my natural."

Steph chuckled. "Not the touchy-feely type, hmm? I figured. Relax. I don't think he's going to expect us to christen the kitchen counters with a hot make-out session. Something simple should be fine."

"Simple?" Rae sent her a questioning look, not sure what that meant in Steph's book.

"Yeah. Something like…this."

For a second, Rae thought Steph might try to kiss her, but all she did was slide her hand into Rae's.

Somehow, that gesture was even more intimate than a kiss, maybe because Steph didn't seem to be in a hurry to let go. Rae stared down at their entwined hands. Steph's slender fingers looked nearly vulnerable in her grasp, yet there was an easy confidence in her secure grip. Her skin was warm and soft against Rae's rougher palm. It wasn't unpleasant at all, but she hadn't held anyone's hand in so long that it felt surreal.

When Rae continued to stare, Steph gave a gentle squeeze. "This okay?"

Rae wrenched her gaze away and tried for nonchalance. "Yeah. Of course."

Steph studied her. "I know you said you don't have a girlfriend, but you've had one in the past, right? I mean, you're into women, aren't you?"

Clearly, she had sensed Rae's discomfort and wasn't sure what to make of it.

Rae gently pulled her hand from Steph's and stuffed it into her pants pocket. "I'm not into anyone right now. But yeah, I'm a lesbian. So don't worry; you won't weird me out or anything."

Steph grinned. "Good to know." She strolled alongside Rae, easily keeping up with her despite the three inches Rae had on her, as if she was used to walking a lot.

Since Steph's attention was on the Spanish-style cottage across the street, Rae could observe her without being caught. Steph's style was an interesting mix of classy and rebellious. Her charcoal gray skirt had deep pockets, like cargo pants, and a pair of attached suspenders that trailed up her formfitting, purple top. Rae would rather have shot herself than worn something like that, but she had to admit that Steph looked cute. It didn't hurt that the above-the-knee skirt showed off her killer legs.

"What?" Steph asked.

"Nothing." Rae directed her gaze back to the street ahead of her. The neighborhood where they might soon live exuded the same relaxed vibe as Steph did. Even though the bustle of Melrose Avenue was only a few blocks away, this area was surprisingly quiet and walkable. Palms and other trees and carefully watered strips of lawn lined the street. A mix of houses from the thirties, newly built single-family homes, and small apartment buildings rose on both sides. "Just wondering… What do we say when he asks how we met?"

"The truth," Steph answered.

"Oh, you want to tell him we met when you tried to con your way into the club?"

For a moment, Steph's mouth moved without anything coming out. "I…I wasn't… Comics really get in free at The Fun Zone. At least it's always been that way in the past."

"I know," Rae said. "But no one told me."

"Is that an apology?" The amused twinkle was back in Steph's eyes.

"It's an explanation." Rae had never apologized for doing her job, and she wouldn't start now.

Steph tilted her head in a faux regal nod. "Explanation accepted. Let's tell him we met at work." She pointed at a two-story building across the street. "I think this is it."

Rae assessed the apartment building with an analytical gaze. Four units faced the street, each one with a balcony, and she guessed that at least the same number of apartments lay on the other side. The sliding glass doors might be a possible entry point for burglars, but all in all, the building and the neighborhood seemed very safe.

Flanked by a couple of palm trees, half a dozen stairs led up to a sturdy front door. A bald man in his sixties waited next to two rows of white mailboxes.

Steph slipped her hand back into Rae's and tugged her across the street.

Rae tried to ignore the feeling of Steph's fingers entwined with her own and focused on not misjudging the height of the curb or the steps.

"Mr. Kleinberg?" Steph asked as they approached.

"Yes." He smiled. If he was surprised to be faced with two women instead of a heterosexual couple, he didn't show it. "You must be Ms. Renshaw and Ms...?"

"Coleman." Rae slid her hand free of Steph's hold and stuck it out for him to shake. It was a trick she had learned early on. If she was the one who held out her hand first, she wouldn't embarrass herself by missing when she tried to grasp someone's hand.

Mr. Kleinberg took her hand in a firm grip. "Thanks for meeting me a little earlier. Let's go in, and I'll show you around." He led them inside and up the stairs, to one of the units on the second floor, facing the backyard.

Steph reached for Rae's hand again, and this time, Rae wasn't sure if she was trying to convince Mr. Kleinberg of their loving relationship or if she needed some encouragement.

Just in case, she kept her hand in Steph's until Steph pulled free to follow Mr. Kleinberg into the tiny bathroom.

It was the only one in the apartment, Rae realized, so they'd have to share. Well, they were adults. They could manage.

The landlord and Steph kept up a constant stream of chatter about the gated parking spots, the AC, and the laundry in the back.

Rae was happy to let Steph do the talking while she wandered through the apartment and looked around. Her gaze skimmed over the gas range in the kitchen, the dark hardwood floors in the living area, and the carpeted bedrooms with spacious closets.

Finally, Steph joined her in the kitchen. Under the pretense of placing a tender kiss on Rae's cheek, she leaned close to whisper in her ear. "What do you think?"

"Hmm?" Heat spread through Rae's face from where Steph had fleetingly placed her lips, distracting her.

"The apartment."

"Oh. Right. Looks good to me," Rae answered. "You?"

A low laugh tickled Rae's ear, making her shiver. "I spent most of the year on the road, so my standards aren't very high. If there's no funky smell and no stains on the carpet that make me think someone has been murdered, it's fine with me."

"If you come in here, you can see the parking spots from the window," Mr. Kleinberg called from one of the bedrooms.

When Steph walked away to take a look, Rae stayed behind and lifted her hand to her cheek. Maybe she should establish some house rules from the start. Rule number one: no touching. In her former job, letting someone close enough to touch had meant inviting danger, and even before joining the police department, she'd never been the touchy-feely type.

But before she could start thinking about house rules, they needed to get the apartment first.

Rae crossed the room to check out the small balcony facing the tree-lined backyard. From here, she could see that the building formed an O around a small inner courtyard with two potted trees and other plants, so there were more units than she had initially thought.

Steph hurried over, wrapped one arm around Rae, and tried to tug her away.

"What are you doing?" Rae whispered. Was there something wrong with the balcony? She gave it another skeptical look but couldn't detect anything out of the ordinary.

Steph tugged again, but Rae didn't budge. "What are *you* doing?"

Mr. Kleinberg joined them. A frown carved the lines bracketing his mouth even deeper. "Something wrong?"

"No, no, everything's wonderful. You'll have to excuse my sweetie." Steph patted Rae's arm with her free hand. "She can't help it, you know? Once a cop, always a cop."

What the fuck? She hadn't told Steph she'd been on the force. How had she known? Even the comedy club rumor mill couldn't work that fast. And why would she comment on it like that?

Steph gave her another loving pat. "Sweetie, you look like you're serving a search warrant."

It was only then that Rae realized she had flattened herself against the wall and was peeking around the doorjamb to gaze through the glass sliding door. *Damn.* Old habits really did die hard. To the landlord, she probably looked more like a police officer searching a suspect's apartment than a potential tenant.

At Steph's words, the confused expression on his face faded. He gave Rae an appreciative look. "Oh, you were a cop?"

Rae consciously tried to relax her stance by leaning into Steph's semi-embrace. The warmth against her side felt the same way holding Steph's hand had earlier—pleasant yet strange at the same time. "Yes," she said as lightly as she could. "Fourteen years."

"Impressive. You must have made captain or something."

She shook her head. "Didn't like the paperwork or the politics. I was always happiest out there, patrolling my beat."

"Well, I'm sure the other tenants will appreciate having someone down the hall who'll keep an eye on the building," Mr. Kleinberg said.

Keep an eye. His wording made Rae suppress a grimace.

Steph sent him a hopeful gaze. "Does that mean we'll get the apartment?"

He smiled at them. "Well, there's another couple coming to look at the apartment later today, but to be honest, I'd really like to give it to you. Provided your credit and background checks and references check out."

"They will," Steph said firmly.

"Well, then let's get the formalities out of the way." He slid a pen from his pocket and laid it down on the breakfast bar, next to an application form.

Within minutes, they had filled out the application and were back outside, with a promise from Mr. Kleinberg that he'd get back to them by Tuesday.

"Yes! I think we did it!" Steph threw her arms around her.

Rae stiffened.

"Oh, sorry." Steph let go and stepped back.

Rae waved away her apology. Her focus was on something else. "How did you know?"

"That we'd get the apartment? I had a feeling. I mean, who can resist this charming face?" Steph pointed at her grinning visage.

"Not that. That I'm a cop." Rae bit her lip. "*Was* a cop." Realizing that she no longer had a right to claim that title still hurt as much as the day she'd had to give up her job.

"Sounds like you're missing it," Steph said. "So why did you leave?"

Rae waited until she had safely navigated down the stairs and stepped onto the sidewalk before she answered. "Long story." That had become her standard answer because it usually got people to back off. Having her story spread all over the newspapers and the Internet had been bad enough; she had no desire to share it with anyone else. "So, how did you know that I used to be on the force?"

"It's kind of obvious when you know what to look for. I used to have a boyfriend who taught me how to spot a cop, and when I saw you checking out the apartment, I remembered how you sat with your back to the wall earlier, watching the front door, and I put two and two together."

Rae raised her eyebrows.

"Yeah, boyfriend. I'm bi."

Rae didn't care if Steph was bi, gay, or straight. That wasn't why she'd raised her brows. "Sounds like you're into bad boys."

"And bad girls," Steph added with a grin.

"Good to know your type. I'm definitely safe, then."

"Yeah, don't worry." Steph patted her arm as they made their way down the street. She didn't even seem to notice that she was once again touching Rae. "I won't try to sneak into your bed at night or join you in the shower."

Rae nearly choked on her own spit and tried to ignore the interesting images those words conjured up. One thing was sure: living with Steph wasn't going to be boring.

Chapter 4

EARLY TUESDAY EVENING, STEPH WAS getting ready to head out to a gig at a bar in Echo Park, where she'd have to compete with the Lakers game on TV and get handsomely paid in wings and beer. But at least it would give her some stage time, which was hard to find in LA. She was just about to grab her T-shirts and some of the other merchandise to make at least a few bucks when her phone rang.

A glance at the screen showed that it was Mr. Kleinberg.

Steph dropped onto the bed in her sister's guest room and accepted the call. "Hi, Mr. Kleinberg. Please tell me you've got good news."

He chuckled. "Good evening. Yes, I do. Everything checked out. The apartment is yours, if you still want it."

"Of course we want it!" Steph didn't bother to sound as if she had a lot of other prospects. "Thank you so much. When can we sign the lease?"

"How about Friday at six? My wife would like to meet you too before we hand over the keys."

"Sure. Works for me." Steph paused. *Damn.* As someone involved in a relationship, she was supposed to take her partner into consideration, wasn't she? *Must be why I'm single.* "Um, I mean, Rae usually works evenings. I'll have to check with her to see if she can get someone to cover for her."

"Just let me know," Mr. Kleinberg said.

"Will do. Thanks again." Steph said goodbye and ended the call. She ran out of the guest room, did a victory dance, and cheered as if she'd won a gold medal. If apartment hunting in LA were an Olympic discipline, she had definitely landed a spot on the winners' podium.

Claire stepped out of the kitchen, an immaculate white apron tied around her waist. "I take it that little display means you got the apartment?"

"Yes!" Steph pumped her fist. "If all goes well, we'll be able to move in this weekend. Then I'll be out of your hair, and you and Lana can go back to having sex on the kitchen table." She loved making her prim-and-proper sister blush, and Claire didn't disappoint.

"We're not...doing that. Lana just loves to tease me about it because one of the chapter headings in my book is *Sex Begins in the Kitchen*."

"Oh, chapter heading. Is that what they call it nowadays?" Then she took mercy on her sister. "Hey, are you and Lana free this weekend to help me get my furniture out of storage and set everything up at the new place?"

Lana appeared in the doorway to the kitchen and traded a gaze with Claire in that silent-communication way they had. "We're free. I'll even make sure Claire is wearing proper moving attire. When I moved in with her, she lugged around boxes in an elegant blouse and a pair of tailored slacks."

Steph laughed. She could see her sister showing up in her shrink costume on moving day. Maybe she should write a joke about it for her routine. "Thanks. I'll let you know as soon as I know more." She grabbed her merchandise from the guest room and glanced at her wristwatch as she walked to her car.

Was Rae already at work? She decided to try anyway and leave a message if Rae didn't pick up.

After three rings, Rae picked up. "Yeah?" The sound of her heavy breathing filtered through the phone.

What on earth was Rae doing? "Hey, this is Steph. Did I catch you at a bad time? Are you at work?"

"No, today's my day off. Just working out." Something metal clanked, as if Rae had set down a dumbbell.

Steph curled her fingers more tightly around the phone as she imagined a sweat-dampened shirt clinging to Rae's chest and shoulders.

"So?" Rae drawled when Steph remained silent for too long.

"Oh, sorry." Steph shook her head to get rid of those images. Of all the sexy, single people in LA, Rae was pretty much the only one she shouldn't be thinking about like this. *Never shit where you eat, remember?* But that didn't mean she couldn't tease and flirt a little. "Are you free for a hot date on Friday evening at six?"

A growl rumbled through the phone. "Stephanie..."

Steph winced and grinned at the same time. "What? You, me, Mr. Kleinberg, and his wife."

"Is this your way of telling me we've got the apartment?" Rae asked.

"Yes. Just got the call."

If Steph had expected her to cheer, she was mistaken. "Good," Rae said calmly.

"Good? That's all you have to say? Hey, you get to move in with me. Come on, show some enthusiasm!"

"Yay," Rae said in the most monotone voice possible.

"No wonder you're single if you think that's enthusiasm." Steph let a teasing tone enter her voice. When she reached her car, she unlocked it but didn't yet climb in. "So, about Friday… Mr. Kleinberg wants to meet at six to sign the lease. Can you make it?"

Rae was quiet for a moment. "I'll make it work."

"Great. Listen, I have to go. I have a gig in Echo Park, and traffic's probably going to be a bitch."

"Good luck. See you Friday." Rae hung up without waiting for a reply.

Steph stared at her phone. Her roommate apparently wasn't one for small talk. Oh well, it didn't matter. Steph hadn't come back to LA to make new friends; she'd returned to break through in comedy. At least Rae wouldn't distract her from that goal.

Was this touching thing contagious somehow? On Friday evening, Rae peered down at Mrs. Kleinberg and tried not to let her dismay show as the landlady hooked her arm through Rae's and led her from room to room, ignoring the fact that they had seen the apartment already.

"Harold and I tend to stay out of our tenants' business, but if you ask me, I'd make the smaller room the bedroom and turn the bigger one into an office or a hobby room. After all, all you're going to do in the bedroom is sleep, so you don't need much space in there."

Steph opened her mouth, a mischievous smile on her face.

Rae sent her a sharp glare. *Don't say it. Don't.*

Still grinning, Steph closed her mouth.

Mrs. Kleinberg patted Rae's arm. "The kitchen would look quite nice with semi-transparent curtains that let plenty of light in, don't you think?"

Christ. Would she have to go through more touching and interior design tips in every room before they could finally sign the lease? She would rather take an entire shift of doing nothing but waiting for speeders or writing reports. Mrs. Kleinberg had taken hold of her left arm, and no matter how much Rae hated having people on that side, she couldn't shake her off without appearing rude.

Mr. Kleinberg gave his wife an indulgent look and didn't seem inclined to stop this torture anytime soon.

Steph walked over. "Oh, honey?"

With a start, Rae realized she meant her. Apparently, Rae was as bad at pretending to be in a relationship as she had been actually being in one. "Yeah?"

Steph slid neatly between Rae and their landlady. "Could you take a look at the bathroom to see if you think my little corner shelf will fit? You're so much better at taking mental measurements." She gave Rae a look so loving that Rae wondered why she was striving for a career in stand-up instead of acting.

"Oh, yeah, sure…um, honey." Rae hurried off, hoping she looked like a dutiful girlfriend and not like an introvert trying to escape an overly friendly woman.

"Want me to help?" Mrs. Kleinberg called after her. "I think we have a tape measure somewhere, don't we, Harold?"

Oh shit. Rae threw a look over her shoulder and forced a smile. "Thanks. I've got it."

Mrs. Kleinberg moved to follow anyway, but Steph hung on and drew her away to the living area. "All I need is a guestimate for now. We'll measure everything later. But I have a question, if you don't mind."

"Of course, dear," Mrs. Kleinberg said. "Ask away."

Phew. Rae fingered her collar and breathed more freely as she hid out in the bathroom for a moment. As relieved as she was to have escaped Mrs. Kleinberg's clutches, now she owed Steph, and that was a feeling she didn't like, just as she hated being the damsel in distress.

That was what Steph had intended, right—rescuing her from Mrs. Kleinberg? Because if she truly needed mental measurements for a corner shelf, she was out of luck. Judging distances and measurements was no longer one of Rae's strengths.

"Ms. Jones, the previous tenant, mentioned that you don't rent to singles," Steph's voice drifted over from the living area. "Not that it matters to us, of course. I'm just curious."

Mrs. Kleinberg sighed. "We had a series of unpleasant experiences—the tenants before Ms. Jones were two roommates who liked to party all night, disturbing their neighbors. We had to call the police several times. Then there was a single tenant in a downstairs unit who brought home strangers who damaged the apartment and another who fell in love with an ex-convict and let him move in without our permission."

Reluctantly, Rae left the bathroom and rejoined them.

Steph immediately wrapped one arm around her as if she had missed Rae during the few seconds of her absence.

"In our experience, couples are usually more settled," Mrs. Kleinberg added. With a smile, she pointed back and forth between them. "I mean, look at the two of you. I'm sure we won't have to constantly check up on you to make sure you're not tearing up the carpets or tossing cigarette butts from the balcony."

Rae slung her arm around Steph too and faced Mrs. Kleinberg with her best reliable-ex-cop expression. "No, ma'am. No need to check up on us at all."

Finally, after what seemed like an eternity, Steph and Rae had each paid half of the first month's rent and a security deposit, and both had signed the lease.

When the door closed behind the Kleinbergs, Rae sank against the kitchen counter. "Wow. I thought she would ask to move in with us."

Steph laughed. "Come on. She was just trying to be nice."

"Yeah. Nice." Rae grimaced. "What do we do if she decides to check up on us after all and discovers that we have separate bedrooms?"

"I'll tell her you snore like a walrus with a bad cold."

Rae glared at her. "I don't."

"But the Kleinbergs don't know that. Come on. Be a sport. At least we've got the apartment."

"Yeah. So now that we do, no more touching or calling me 'honey,' okay?"

"What?" Steph clutched her chest and sniffled loudly. "Now that you got what you wanted, you're breaking up with me?"

Rae groaned. "That's what I get for moving in with a comedian."

"Yep. It's in the contract. You should have read the fine print before you signed it. Now you'll have to get used to it." Steph trailed her hand over the kitchen counter. "I can't believe this is ours now. Well, not really ours, but you know what I mean. Are you going to move in tomorrow, or did you have a hard time finding help to move on short notice?"

"I'll move in before work." Rae didn't have to wait for anyone since she intended to handle the move on her own.

"Me too. Want to grab a bite to eat and coordinate furniture?" Steph asked.

Rae wrinkled her nose. "Coordinate furniture?"

"We might end up with two microwaves, two couches, and two coffee tables, and there's not enough room for that, so we should talk about who's bringing what."

After her encounter with Mrs. Kleinberg, Rae was all peopled out and needed some space. "Bring whatever you want. I don't have a microwave, a couch, or a coffee table anyway."

Steph gaped at her. "You don't have a—?"

"No." Not in the mood to explain, Rae walked to the door. "Like I said, bring whatever you want. We'll make it work."

"Hey, wait," Steph called after her. "Aren't you forgetting something? You might need these if you want to move in tomorrow."

When Rae turned back around, Steph tossed her a set of keys.

Christ, if people would only stop throwing stuff her way. Rae knew she had little chance of catching them, but she didn't want to look like a fumbling fool so she tried anyway—and missed by at least a hand's width.

The keys clattered onto the hardwood floor and slid to a stop in front of her toes.

Steph stared at her.

The heat of humiliation burned Rae's cheeks. Gritting her teeth, she tried to look as dignified as possible as she bent and picked up the keys.

"Are you—?"

"Good night." Rae clamped her fingers around the keys, turned on her heel, and abruptly pushed the door open.

Steph's puzzled-sounding "good night" echoed after her all the way to her car.

Chapter 5

EARLY THE NEXT MORNING, RAE let out a string of curses. Transporting a queen-size mattress on her own was a bitch. By the time she had wrestled the mattress, the bed frame, and some other pieces of furniture into the small U-Haul truck she had rented, she was drenched in sweat.

Next, she stacked moving boxes onto the dolly and wheeled them out to the U-Haul. At least this apartment building had an elevator, making it easy to get things downstairs. The new one didn't, so getting everything up to the second floor would be difficult, but Rae was determined to manage somehow.

She pulled the dolly free from under the boxes and went to get more.

Finally, she loaded the last box and her kettlebell into the truck. She wiped her brow on the back of her arm and paused on top of the loading ramp to take one last look at what had been her home for the past nine years. Memories of things that had happened in those walls flooded her. An image of Mike came unbidden, and she saw him sprawled out on her living room floor the last time he'd been over, his blue eyes twinkling as he tried to wrestle the last beer from her.

Memories from the past eight months threatened to replace happier thoughts, but she thrust them aside before they could fully form.

She jumped down from the ramp, shoved it back into the truck, and slammed down the door, firmly shutting the doors on her memories too.

Just as she was about to climb into the U-Haul, a familiar car pulled up behind it, and Kim got out.

Shit. Of all the times for Kim to pay her a visit, she had to choose now.

Kim's curly hair bounced up and down as she marched toward Rae. Even though Rae had at least half a head and nearly forty pounds on her, Kim took up a threatening stance in front of her. "What's going on?"

Rae didn't try to beat around the bush. "I'm moving to a new apartment."

"You're moving?" Kim echoed. "When were you going to tell me? Did you plan on letting me find out when I came over to see if you're still alive because I never hear from you—and then find your place empty?"

Rae winced at the *still alive* and lowered her gaze to the asphalt. Did Kim sometimes, deep inside, wish that Mike was the one who had survived instead of her? God knew, she wouldn't blame her. "I'm sorry, Kim. That wasn't my intention. It was all very short notice. I only found someone to take over the lease on this place yesterday."

"Still, you could have called me or some of the guys," Kim said. "You know they would have dropped everything to help you move. They aren't just your brothers in blue while you're on the force. It's kind of a life thing, and they take care of their own."

"Nah. They don't spend enough time with their families as it is. I can manage on my own."

"God, Rae. You're more bullheaded than Mike was—and that's saying something because my dear husband could out-stubborn a mule! Asking for help is not a sign of weakness, you know?"

"I know that," Rae said. Still, she hadn't wanted to ask for help, especially from any of the guys. No matter what Kim said, she was no longer part of that close-knit group, and seeing them would only make her feel that loss more acutely.

"Then why not call me? I really don't understand you. How did you plan to get your couch and the other big stuff into the U-Haul by yourself?"

"I don't have a couch. All my stuff is already in here." Rae patted the side of the truck.

Kim stared at her. "You don't have a couch?"

Rae shrugged despite her protesting muscles. Why did everyone seem to find that so hard to believe? "Lise took it when she moved out."

"Lise took it? But that was four years ago! Why haven't you replaced it? Is that why you always prefer coming to our...my house instead of meeting at your place? And why didn't Mike ever mention that you don't have a couch?"

Rae held back a groan. This was part of why she hadn't asked for help. She didn't want to feel as if she had to defend the way she chose to live her life to anyone. "Because stuff like that didn't matter between Mike and me. I'm barely ever home, so I didn't bother getting another."

"That might have been true in the past, but you were practically holed up in your apartment the past eight months."

"I…I wasn't ready." Even now, she had days when she'd rather stay in bed because being out in the world confronted her with her new limitations and reminded her that her life would never be the same. "Anyway, I won't need to buy a couch, because Steph is bringing hers."

Kim sank against the U-Haul as if her knees were threatening to give out. "You're moving in with someone, and I haven't even heard about this woman?" With a stricken look on her face, she squeezed her eyes shut. When she opened them again, unshed tears shimmered in them. "Why are you shutting me out of your life? This feels like I didn't just lose Mike that day; I lost one of our best friends too."

"No, Kim, that's not…" Rae's throat tightened, strangling her words. She leaned against the truck next to Kim and forced herself not to move away when Kim's shoulder brushed her arm. Kim was on the wrong side, her left, but maybe for once that was a good thing. At least she wouldn't have to see the hurt she'd caused. "You're not losing me. I promise. I just… I need some time to myself, to find out who I am now that I can't be a cop anymore."

Kim took her hand and squeezed it. "You don't have to find out alone. You were there for me after Mike…after we lost him. Please let me be there for you too."

"I know you're there for me if I need you. But this is something I need to do on my own," Rae said quietly. "And just so you know: Steph isn't my girlfriend. Well, she is, if my new landlord or landlady are around."

"What?"

"It's complicated. I'll call you tomorrow and explain everything."

"No, you won't. I'm coming with you to help you move in, so you can explain everything in the truck." Kim's tone didn't leave any room for argument.

Rae sighed but knew she wouldn't be able to talk Kim out of it. "Okay. Let's go, then. I need to take the U-Haul back before I go to work."

Kim eyed the large vehicle. "Do you want me to drive? I know it's not easy for you to—"

"It's been eight months. I'm fine." Rae climbed behind the wheel and waited until Kim had gotten in on the other side.

Navigating the U-Haul with its unfamiliar dimensions really wasn't easy, and her neck muscles started to protest because she had to turn her head so often, making sure there was nothing in her blind spot. But thankfully, traffic wasn't as bad as usual since it was Saturday, so she knew she could make it to Beverly Grove without any major problems.

"So," Kim said after a while, "want to explain that girlfriend-not-girlfriend thing? It's been fifteen years since I dated anyone, but I thought you either have a significant other or you don't. That isn't any different for lesbians, is it?"

Rae chuckled. "No. My new landlord doesn't want to rent to singles, so Steph suggested we apply for the apartment as a couple."

Kim lifted one hand. "Wait, wait. I think you skipped a few steps of this story. Who is Steph?"

"Stephanie Renshaw. Struggling comedian, my new roommate, and a bit of a pain in the ass."

"Ooh!" Kim clapped once. "She sounds like exactly the right person to draw you out of your shell."

"I'm quite happy in my shell, thank you very much. I don't need anyone to draw me out, especially not some smart-mouthed comic."

Undeterred, Kim bounced up and down in the passenger seat. "I can't wait to meet her."

Rae let out a groan. This was going to be a long day.

Steph had expected Rae to show up with half a dozen strong and capable off-duty police officers, who would make fast work of unloading everything and setting up the furniture. But when another U-Haul truck pulled up behind the one Steph had rented, only Rae and a woman in her midthirties climbed out.

In a pair of beige slacks and a short-sleeved, cranberry-colored turtleneck, the stranger looked the way Claire probably would have on moving day if Lana hadn't intervened.

What was going on?

Penny climbed out of the U-Haul behind Steph, nearly dwarfed by the floor lamp she carried. "Who's that?"

"That's Rae," Steph said, her gaze on the worn jeans and the cotton T-shirt that seemed molded to Rae's shoulders. "And…um, I don't know who's with her, but I'll find out." She put down the moving box she'd been carrying and walked over to them, giving the woman a curious glance. Rae had insisted she didn't have a girlfriend, and with her average height and a mass of curly chestnut hair falling onto slender shoulders, the stranger looked nothing like Rae, so she probably wasn't a relative either. "Hi."

"Hi." The woman greeted Steph with a warm smile and stuck out her hand. "I'm Kim Lindstrom, a friend of tall, dark, and silent over there. You must be the roommate-slash-pretend-girlfriend."

Steph laughed. "Yep, that's me. Call me Steph, please."

"Great to meet you. I'd say Rae has told me so much about you, but if you've spent any time with her, you'd know that's a lie."

"Hey, I thought you're here to help me move in, not to gossip about me as if I'm not standing right next to you," Rae grumbled.

Kim gave her a playful nudge, which Steph observed with interest. "If I had known I'd be helping you move, I would have dressed differently, so I can gossip as much as I want."

Then the rest of Steph's friends, relatives, and comedy buddies trampled down the stairs, and chaos broke out as everyone introduced themselves.

Rae managed to sneak away from the group, open her U-Haul, and pull out the ramp. Crowds apparently weren't her thing, and Steph had a feeling that Rae would consider any group of more than two people a crowd.

Quietly, so she wouldn't lure over the rest of her friends, Steph joined her at the ramp and peeked into the truck. Rae hadn't been exaggerating— she really didn't have much stuff. But the mattress, the bed frame, and the dresser would still be hard to get upstairs without an elevator, especially in the kind of shoes Kim was wearing. "If you'll take that end, I'll take this one." She pointed at the mattress.

Rae jerked as if she hadn't noticed Steph standing right next to her. "Thanks. I've got this. You probably have your hands full with your own stuff."

"Are you kidding? My sister has this all planned out with the precision of a military operation. She'll pay you to get me out of her hair so I can't mess up her perfect system."

"Yes, I will," Claire called. "And I'll double my offer if you tell me you labeled your moving boxes, because my disorganized baby sister hasn't, so she has no clue where her screwdrivers are."

Steph huffed out a breath. She'd listened to complaints about her labeling system—or the lack thereof—for the past hour. "Just because I'm not following your thirty-two-step packing plan doesn't mean I'm disorganized. I'll find the screwdrivers, okay?"

"She probably tossed them in with the sex toys," Gabe commented.

"No," Penny said. "Those take up a box of their own."

Steph's comedian friends roared with laughter and added their own comments.

"Great," Steph murmured. "That's what I get for being friends with comics. This will probably make it into a few of their routines."

The corner of Rae's mouth twitched as if she was close to smiling. Well, that was a first—and almost worth the teasing Steph had to take from her friends.

Steph squeezed past Rae to get into the U-Haul and lifted up one end of the mattress.

"You really don't have to—"

"I know," Steph said. "But we want the Kleinbergs and our neighbors to think we're a couple, so there's no 'your stuff' and 'my stuff,' just 'our stuff.'"

Rae kept hesitating and shook her head as if wondering when she had lost control of the situation.

Was it really that hard for her to accept a bit of help? Steph let out an exaggerated groan, as if she could no longer hold on to the mattress and could feel it slipping from her hands. "This is getting heavy. Hurry up."

Rae climbed the ramp with two long steps and took up the other end. As she carefully walked backward down the ramp, she looked up at Steph. "Do you really not know where your screwdrivers are?"

"I know exactly where they are." Steph held her head up high. "They're in the box with the brown lid."

"They all have brown lids."

Steph gave her a sheepish grin. "Oops."

Rae started to feel like a mama duck as she walked down the stairs. Steph's sneakers squeaked behind her, and then the rest of the group followed.

Most of them went to Steph's U-Haul, but two of the guys continued on to Rae's. She had seen them at the club, so she knew they were comics, but she didn't remember their names, even though they had introduced themselves earlier. One of them—a wiry Latino with a *careful or you'll end up in my stand-up routine* T-shirt—grabbed a moving box labeled *dishes*.

"Oh, no, no, that's mine." Rae waved at him to put it back down.

"So?" He eyed her. "Doesn't it have to go upstairs?"

"Yes, but…"

Steph walked over before a tug-of-war over the moving box could ensue. "Just let them help. The faster it's all done, the faster they'll leave and you can be alone."

Was she that obvious? Rae rubbed her neck.

Steph gave her a smile and a nudge. "Come on. Help me with the box spring."

Rae knew when she was beat, so she followed Steph up the ramp and picked up one end of the box spring. "Thank you," she said grudgingly.

"No need to thank me. Consider it payment."

"Payment? What are you paying me for?"

"The use of your screwdrivers," Steph said, deadpan.

Rae struggled to keep her face impassive. "What makes you think I know where my screwdrivers are—or that I even own any? You're not going for that lesbians-and-their-tools stereotype, are you?"

Steph flashed her a grin over the top of the box spring. "Nope. But you disassembled your bed, and I don't think you did that with your teeth."

"You've got me there, Sherlock."

They navigated the box spring upstairs, this time with Steph being the one to walk backward.

Just as they reached the apartment, another one of Steph's comic buddies squeezed past them with a box labeled *sheets* and carried it toward Steph's room.

"Um, that one goes into my room." Rae jerked her head to the smaller of the two bedrooms, which she had volunteered to take because she didn't have as much stuff.

The comic stopped and turned. His gaze went from Rae to Steph and back. "Oh. You have your own bedroom?"

Rae frowned. "Of course. Why wouldn't I?"

He laughed. "Man, I thought 'roommates' was some kind of queer code for the two of you riding the bedroom rodeo together."

Claire looked up from the moving box she was digging through, probably searching for the screwdrivers. "Sometimes a cigar is actually just a cigar."

"Thanks, Dr. Freud." Steph turned from her sister to her friend. "And no, we're really just roommates. If I have a rodeo in my bedroom, it'll be with another lucky cowgirl or cowboy."

Rae groaned and marched on to her room. She had a feeling that *what the hell have I gotten myself into* would become a mantra of sorts for her.

Steph had just laid out the parts of her new bookcase when Rae's friend Kim stuck her head through the open door. "Rae said you might need this." She held out a screwdriver.

"Oh, thanks." Steph crossed the room and took it from her. "I still haven't found mine."

Kim chuckled. "I know. Your friends' theories about where they might be are getting wilder by the minute."

"Wilder than the sex toys comments?"

"Kind of. Trust me, you don't want to know." Kim gestured at the pieces of the bookcase. "Do you need some help with that?"

"I'd love some, but doesn't Rae need you? Lana or Penny can help me once they're done putting the pots and pans away."

"Rae is putting up the curtain rods, and your sister already claimed the spot as her helper."

Steph peered through the open door and caught a glimpse of Rae balancing on top of a ladder, a power drill in her hands, while Claire had taken up position next to her with the vacuum cleaner to catch the dust from the drilling before it could trickle down. "Looks like my new roomie is a woman of many talents, isn't she?"

Kim nodded. "There's not much she can't do." Quietly, more to herself, she added, "Other than asking for help."

Steph decided to ignore the muttered words because they obviously hadn't been meant for her ears.

"All right. Then let's tackle the bookcase." When Kim knelt on the floor to hold the side of the bookcase steady while Steph tightened the cam, Steph eyed the beige slacks she was wearing. "Want to borrow a pair of jeans from me? You might have to roll up the legs an inch or two, but otherwise, they should fit."

"No, that's okay." Kim blew a curl of hair out of her face and smiled at her. "I have a feeling by the time you find the right box, we'll be done here."

Steph let out an exaggerated sigh. "Am I that easy to see through, or are you a psychologist too, like my sister?"

"Not quite. I'm a dating consultant."

The screwdriver slipped and scratched along the side of the bookcase as Steph stared at her. "That's a thing?"

"If it isn't, don't tell my clients."

"Not planning on it." Steph finally tightened the screw. "So how do you know Rae? She wasn't one of your clients, was she?"

Kim laughed heartily. "God, no! She'd rather book a vacation on a crowded cruise ship than let me guide her in her search for a soul mate. Not that she is searching, mind you. She doesn't believe in that kind of thing."

Neither did Steph.

"So how did you meet her?" Steph screwed on the top of the shelf, and then they turned the bookcase over so she could nail the back panel in place—or rather, she could have if her hammer hadn't been missing along with her other tools.

"Through my husband. They were partners on the force for twelve years." Kim's smile became wistful, and the cheerful atmosphere in the room seemed to shift.

Even though Steph's family often accused her of having no tact at all, she hesitated to ask more questions. At least a dozen of them swirled through her mind: How had they managed to stay partnered for that long when Rae was obviously as bad at forming relationships of any kind as she was, and why wasn't he here to help his former partner move? Had something happened to him?

Kim nodded as if sensing her unasked question. "He—"

"Looks like you might need this." Rae stood in the doorway, holding out Steph's small, red toolbox. "Your sister found it in the box with your underwear."

Steph stared at her. "Um, why is she unpacking my underwear?"

"Because you didn't label the boxes, and she had no idea what was in there before she opened it up," Rae said.

She had a point there. Why on earth had she stuck the tools into the box with her underwear? "Great. That'll definitely make it into Gabe's stand-up routine."

Rae crossed the room, stepping carefully over the shelves scattered throughout, and handed her the toolbox. Her gaze searched Kim's, and she radiated a protectiveness that seemed to engulf her friend. "You okay?" she asked so quietly that Steph nearly didn't catch it.

Kim nodded and got up from the floor. "I'm fine."

Steph swallowed against her dry mouth as she watched them interact. Clearly, there was some kind of bond between them, and she had a feeling it wasn't only happy memories that tied them to each other. "If you need your helper back, I can manage the rest on my own."

Instead of once again declining any help, Rae nodded. "Thanks. I could use a second pair of hands in the bedroom."

"That's what I always say," Steph quipped because she couldn't stand the sudden tension anymore.

Kim smiled and patted her shoulder as if she knew exactly what Steph was doing.

Rae followed her friend to the door, where she paused, glanced back at Steph, and gave her a curt nod.

Toolbox in hand, Steph stayed behind, not sure what to make of her new roommate at all.

Rae was breaking down the moving boxes she had already unpacked when Steph knocked on the open door. "Hey, it's starting to look like someone lives here instead of a construction zone."

"Yeah, it's getting there." Rae let her gaze trail through the room. Compared to Steph's room, which was crammed full of mismatched furniture, a huge scratch-off map of the world, photos of Steph with half a dozen different dogs, and more pictures of Steph with friends and family, Rae's room looked pretty Spartan.

Aside from her queen-size bed, there was only a dresser, a bedside table, a small desk, a chair, and the shelf with her books. Other than the dumbbells in the corner and the eye drops on the bedside table, she hadn't left out any personal items.

After growing up with parents who had elevated reusing and recycling to an art form, never throwing anything away and hording all kinds of clutter, this was how she liked to keep her home.

Steph pointed over her shoulder. "I'm ordering pizza for the hungry masses. What kind do you want?"

"I'm good, thanks. I'll get something later." Rae opened the next box, hoping Steph would take the hint.

Instead, Steph leaned against the doorjamb. "Oh, come on. Pizza on moving day is a tradition. Don't tell me you're one of those people who act as if eating a few carbs every now and then will be the end of civilization as we know it."

A ball of wadded-up newspaper arced through the air from the kitchen, where several people where unpacking dishes. It bounced off Steph's head and rolled across the hardwood floor.

"Hey, I said I'd eat a slice," Claire called. She walked over and picked up the newspaper ball. "But if you had a job where you sit on your behind for most of the day, you'd have to watch what you eat too."

Steph rolled her eyes. "Just say it, Claire: ass."

Rae watched them banter back and forth. Unbelievable how different siblings could be. If they didn't have the same blonde hair and pale gray eyes, she would have been convinced one of them had to be adopted.

Finally, Claire's fiancée ended the playful argument by interrupting Claire with a soft kiss and drawing her away.

"So?" Steph turned back toward Rae. "Pepperoni okay? Kim said you're not a vegetarian."

"Is she staying and having pizza with you guys?" Rae asked.

"Yes. You're the only holdout." Steph tapped her fingers on the doorframe and sent her an expectant look.

Well, if Kim was staying, Rae didn't want to make it awkward for her by hiding out in her room. She suppressed a sigh. "Double cheese, please."

A grin spread over Steph's face. "Got it." She hurried off, the phone already pressed to her ear, rattling off an order for enough pizza to feed their entire neighborhood.

An hour later, empty pizza boxes littered Steph's coffee table and the moving boxes they'd pushed together to serve as an additional table. One of the comics had even brought a cooler full of beer, but Rae knew she'd have to drop off the U-Haul and get her car soon, so she didn't want to drink.

Besides, being in a room full of so many people chattering like a flock of scrub jays was already giving her a headache, even without any alcohol. She'd never been a people person, but since the shooting, social interaction seemed to have become even more exhausting. Under the pretense of getting some water from the tap, she escaped to the balcony and slid the glass door closed behind her, leaving only a tiny gap.

As soon as the sound of too many voices faded away, the tension in her shoulders receded. Exhaling deeply, she leaned against the balcony railing and watched the breeze play with the leaves of the potted trees in the courtyard.

They had really lucked out with this apartment, even though it was too soon to tell how lucky she'd been in the roommate department.

Laughter drifted through the glass, pulling her attention back to the living area.

Steph sat perched on one of the moving boxes, gesturing with a half-eaten slice of pizza while she regaled her friends with a story of her adventures touring the country. Clearly, she was in her element among so many people, and Rae wasn't sure if she should pity her or envy her.

One of the comics threw a work glove in Steph's direction, which she ducked with a grin.

The good-natured teasing between Steph and her comedy buddies and the slightly twisted sense of humor they shared reminded Rae of the camaraderie she used to have with the guys at the station. God, she missed it.

Steph threw back the glove.

Rae couldn't hear what she was saying, but Claire seemed to nearly choke on the bite of pizza Lana had fed her, and Kim doubled over, laughing so hard that she was clutching her sides.

A reflexive smile curled Rae's lips, and that felt as unfamiliar as the sight of Kim laughing. This was the first time she'd seen Kim laugh so freely since Mike had died. Warmth filled her, and she was glad she'd accepted Steph's invitation to join them for pizza. Still smiling, she turned back around and watched a cat cross the courtyard.

The glass door slid open behind her. The noise of laughter and chatter hit her like a brick wall before the door was closed again, shutting Rae and whoever had joined her off from the rest of the group.

Well, the peace and quiet had been nice while it lasted.

Rae turned.

She had expected to be faced with Kim or maybe Steph, but instead, Claire stood in front of her. Even though she was wearing jeans and a T-shirt, like most of the other helpers, hers were obviously brand-new, and the bottle of beer in her hand looked somehow out of place. She set it on the floor as if she didn't quite know what to do with it.

Claire stepped next to her at the railing and looked down at the courtyard for a while. Just when Rae thought she might get away without having to make small talk, Claire pointed over her shoulder. "I needed a breather. They can get a little rambunctious."

Rae let out a noncommittal hum since she wasn't sure what answer was expected, plus she didn't want to encourage a drawn-out conversation.

"Yes, I know, I know." Claire chuckled. "You'd think a psychologist would be much more of a people person, right?"

"You're a psychologist?" Rae struggled not to take a step back. She knew it was silly, but she couldn't help it. After a couple of mandatory counseling sessions with the department shrink, psychologists were to her what dentists were to other people.

Claire gave her a mild smile. "Don't worry. I'm not going to psychoanalyze you, no matter what my little sister might have said about me in her comedy routine."

"Actually, I've never even seen her routine."

"Ah, so you just don't like psychologists." Claire was still smiling. Even though she and Steph looked a lot alike, her more reserved smile was nothing like her sister's carefree grin.

Rae shrugged. "Don't take it personally."

"I won't. I'm used to it. When I first met Lana, she wanted nothing to do with a psychologist either."

Rae followed Claire's gaze through the glass to where Lana had flopped down unceremoniously on the living room floor. She turned her head as if sensing her fiancée's gaze on her, and a warm smile spread over her face as she gave them a wave.

This time, there was nothing reserved about Claire's answering smile. It transformed her carefully controlled expression into one of unrestrained love and adoration.

Watching them together made Rae vaguely uncomfortable, maybe because it felt as if she was intruding into something very private. "Guess she changed her mind."

Claire laughed, and the rest of her reserve disappeared. "I'd hope so. We're getting married next year."

"Congratulations," Rae said.

"Thank you." With obvious reluctance, Claire took her gaze off Lana to study Rae. "What about you? Are you like Steph, enjoying single life too much to ever consider settling down?"

Rae squinted over at her. This was starting to feel like her fitness-for-duty evaluation. Was Claire being a protective older sister, questioning her to find out if Rae would try to seduce her baby sister?

Before Rae could answer, Steph pushed open the sliding door a bit farther and stuck her head through the widening gap. She didn't step outside as if sensing that the last thing Rae wanted was more company.

But at the moment, Rae was actually happy at the interruption.

Steph narrowed her eyes at her sister. "You're not telling Rae about all the stunts I pulled as a kid, are you?"

"No," Claire said. "Even the abridged version would take us a week, and I doubt Rae has that much time on her hands."

"Haha. And they say I'm the comic in the family." Steph turned toward Rae. "Hey, I was thinking. Why don't we take the U-Hauls back together?

Gabe can follow us in his car and then drop you and Kim off at your old place so you can get your car."

"I can take an Uber," Rae said.

"I know you can, but why would you? We're roommates now."

Oh Christ on a bike. If she added, *That practically makes us family,* Rae would be out of here.

Chuckling as if she knew exactly what Rae was thinking, Steph called over to the living area, "We're leaving to drop off the U-Hauls, guys. That means everyone out!"

Even though Rae didn't like owing her yet another favor, she had to suppress a chuckle at Steph's frank approach. If she'd known it would be so easy to get rid of the crowd, she might have tried it earlier.

Chapter 6

SOMETIMES, BEING A COMEDIAN SUCKED. No health insurance, no retirement plan, no respect from her family, and the pay was shittier than that of a waitress. But stand-up comedy came with one unexpected perk: it was a chick magnet. Most women—and many men—thought it was damn sexy how she could hop up on stage with confidence and make a room full of strangers laugh.

Inviting a date to one of her shows had never failed to work its magic, and judging from the way Allison was nibbling her neck now, it was definitely working tonight.

The show in the tiny room of a comedy club in Burbank had ended half an hour ago, but they were still standing next to their cars in the parking lot, making out like two teenagers.

"God, that was good," Allison said when they came up for air.

Steph trailed her index finger along the curve of Allison's collarbone, which her low-cut top revealed. "Never had any complaints."

"Mm, that too, but I was talking about your show," Allison said. "It's been ages since I've seen any good stand-up, but you blew me away."

Steph gave her a playfully rakish grin. "If I'm that good up on stage, image what I can do in bed."

Allison giggled like a schoolgirl, but the heated look she threw her was quite adult. "Why just imagine it? I'd be willing to find out if you are."

No games. Straight to the point. Steph liked that in a woman. But she wanted to make sure they were on the same page anyway. "I'm game. But I need to make one thing clear before we take this any further. I think you're really great and fun to hang out with, but I'm trying to get my big break in comedy, so there's no room in my life for a girlfriend."

"Good," Allison said. "Because I'm not looking for one either."

Steph beamed at her. "Great. So, your place or mine?"

"Yours. My sister and her two little ones are staying with me right now. Wouldn't want to traumatize them."

For a moment, Steph thought of Rae, who would be right next door if she took Allison to her place. Not that she would be traumatized by hearing two women having sex. A cop's uniform was a chick magnet too, so Rae had probably slept with her fair share of women. Still, it was a weird feeling. *Oh, come on.* Steph had lived with roommates for most of her adult life, and it had never stopped her from taking a one-night stand back to her place. That wouldn't change now.

With determination, she unlocked her car. "Follow me."

It was always the smells that got to her—the smells and the sounds.

Radio static crackled, and her own voice, calm but commanding, cut across the parking lot.

Sirens wailed in the distance, quickly growing louder. Patrol cars screeched to a halt behind them.

"Down!" Mike bellowed next to her.

A thunderous boom, then something hot slammed into her. Searing pain exploded in her head, and she went down.

Someone screamed. Rae thought dimly it might have been her. Or maybe it was the perp who'd shot at them, because the guys from the unit behind theirs were now squeezing off several shots.

The smell of gunpowder stabbed her nose and mingled with the metallic odor of blood.

No gunfire came from next to her. Why wasn't Mike returning fire or calling for an ambulance?

Clutching her head, she rolled onto her side.

Mike was down too. He had dropped his gun and grabbed at his throat with both hands. Blood squirted through his fingers, and he stared at her with wide, panicked eyes.

No, no, no, no. Her vision was hazy, and her head throbbed with pain, but she somehow managed to crawl over to him. Her left side was numb, so she fumbled for her shoulder mic with her gun hand. "Officer down! Corner of Sixth and Archer. We need an ambulance. Right now!"

Blood. There was so much blood, his and hers. Rae clamped her hands over his, trying to hold back the flood spurting through his fingers. It gushed over her hands, warm and sticky, and formed puddles on the asphalt, where it mingled with her own.

His lips moved as he tried to speak, but all that came out was foamy blood that coated his chin.

"Shh, don't talk. Just hold on. The ambulance is en route. They'll be here any second, okay?"

Mike began to shake and flail, his legs kicking out uncontrollably. His face was turning a ghostly blue. Gurgling sounds, interspersed with gasps, drifted up from his throat.

Rae's strength waned, and the pain in her head was so strong now that she thought she would collapse on top of him, but she managed to hold on to the last threads of consciousness and pressed her hands down harder.

Slowly, the flailing stopped, and the wheezing sounds were replaced by deafening silence. He twitched once, then lay still.

An ambulance and more patrol units careened around the corner. Their flashing lights bathed Mike's motionless body in red and blue.

Rae bolted upright, panting, and wildly looked around, not recognizing her surroundings.

Slowly, the images from her nightmare began to fade, and she could make out the unfamiliar contours of her new room in the moonlight trickling in through the half-open shades.

Her fingers ached, and she realized she had balled up the sheets in both fists. She eased her grip and sank back, waiting for the drumming in her ears to subside.

Damn. She hadn't had that dream in a while, at least not the full-length version. Maybe seeing Kim had dredged it up.

What cruel irony. Her nightmares always played out in full 3-D, showing her every little detail with painful clarity, even though she had only seen in 2-D for the past eight months. The faint afterimages lingered even now.

Cursing, she flicked on the light, threw back the covers, and swung her legs out of bed, thankful when they proved to be steady. Running into a wall, waking up her new roommate, and having to face her questions was the last thing she needed tonight.

The corner of the coffee table scraped along her shin as she tried to navigate through the unfamiliar living area in the near dark. *Shit.* She made it to the fridge, pulled the door open, and stood there for a minute, letting the air wafting out cool her overheated body. Goose bumps formed, but she was grateful to feel something other than sheer panic.

The door to Steph's room creaked open, and bare feet padded across the hardwood floor.

Great. Now she had done it. Either she'd screamed out in her sleep, or her collision with the coffee table had woken Steph up. *Interrogation, here we come.*

Rae grabbed a bottle of water from the fridge and closed the door. At least it would give her hands something to do. She unscrewed the cap and took a sip while turning around, aiming for nonchalance. "Hope I didn't wake you."

"Um, hi. No, I was up anyway," someone said from the other side of the living area. The voice was female, but it definitely wasn't Steph's. "I want to make it back to my place before my sister wakes up and sees me do the walk of shame."

Water dribbled down Rae's chin. She stiffened, her body going into defense mode. Why the hell was there some stranger in the apartment in the middle of the night? She flailed her hand around until she found the light switch.

When the overhead lights flared on, they squinted at each other.

The redhead with the freckled nose looked familiar, but for a second, Rae was distracted by the bra sticking out of her purse.

Wait a minute! Wasn't that…? "You're the U-Haul girl." To be more precise, the redhead had been the U-Haul employee who had been there when they had taken the moving trucks back. Steph had flirted shamelessly with her. What a smooth operator! She must have managed to get the woman's number without Rae noticing.

"And you're the roommate." The redhead slipped on her shoes, which she had carried in her hand.

Rae gestured at the apartment. "Obviously, or I wouldn't be here in the middle of the night."

U-Haul Girl blushed and eyed Rae in her sleepwear, which consisted of a pair of boxer shorts and a T-shirt that stuck to her sweat-dampened skin.

Was Steph's conquest checking her out? Christ, this was getting more bizarre by the second. Rae folded her arms across her chest. "The sun will be up soon. Wouldn't want your sister to wake up before you make it home."

"Steph is definitely the roommate with the charm," the redhead muttered.

Rae didn't care what she thought. Unexpectedly coming face-to-face with a stranger, especially after a nightmare, had made her patience run out, and she just wanted her gone—now.

U-Haul Girl marched past her with a haughty look.

"Your bra's sticking out," Rae commented.

The redhead stuffed it more deeply into her purse, opened the door, and walked out without another glance back.

"Hope Steph didn't want a second date." Rae stared after her for a little longer, then turned off the light and went back to bed. She'd have to have a talk about overnight guests with Steph in the morning.

Rae couldn't have slept more than three or four hours, but after her pre-dawn encounter with U-Haul Girl, she hadn't managed more than a restless dozing. A little before seven, she heard Steph get up and come out of her room. Maybe she was looking for her playmate, wondering where she had gone.

When the scent of freshly brewed coffee trailed through the apartment, Rae gave up on sleep. She rolled out of bed, reached for a pair of sweatpants, and went to load up on caffeine.

The living area was an obstacle course of half-unpacked moving boxes that Steph must have opened while looking for something.

Rae carefully stepped around each box and rubbed her left eye, which felt as gritty as if she had weathered a sandstorm. Maybe she'd have to give it a rinse later. But first, coffee.

The counter was littered with clean mugs, and one of the cupboards stood open.

What the hell? Hadn't all of the dishes been neatly put away already? How had Steph managed to create such chaos within minutes of getting up?

Rae firmly closed the cupboard. God, this was like living with her parents again.

The only thing saving Steph now was the fact that she'd made enough coffee for Rae too.

Somewhat mollified, she looked around for her favorite mug, but all of the cups littering the counter had funny slogans and obviously belonged to Steph. She opened the cupboard.

Nothing. Her mug wasn't in there either.

Had it gotten lost in the chaos of moving day, with so many helpers around? Or had someone used it and put it into the dishwasher?

Rae gritted her teeth. Mike had always teased her about being territorial and not sharing well. But now, it was about more than that. The mug she used every morning was oversized and white. The contrast between the white porcelain and the black coffee made it easier for her to judge when she had to stop pouring.

She probably didn't need that little trick anymore, but she had grown used to that mug.

Grumbling, she selected another, reached for the coffee pot, and poured herself some coffee.

A bit of the steaming black liquid sloshed onto the counter. *Dammit.* She hadn't spilled any beverages in quite some time, but if she was tired or distracted, it could happen more easily. *Or if someone steals my mug.* She tore off a paper towel and wiped down the counter. This day was not off to a good start.

Someone else was having a great morning, though.

As Rae passed by on her way to her room, cheerful whistling drifted over from the balcony. Steph sat on one of the two chairs, which was tilted back so she could put her feet up on the tiny table. Despite the cool early-morning November temperature, she hadn't bothered getting properly dressed before stepping outside. Her spaghetti top revealed smooth shoulders, and bare feet stuck out of her sweatpants.

For a second or two, Rae forgot about her missing mug and marveled at the way the rising sun bathed Steph's face in orange hues and made her tousled hair look strawberry blonde. Then Rae's gaze went from the bare skin on display to the large, white mug cradled between Steph's slender fingers. She let out a low growl. *Mine!*

Steph looked up. A welcoming smile spread over her face, as if she wasn't aware of having done anything wrong. "Hey, good morning. I see you found the coffee."

Rae stepped out onto the balcony but didn't return the smile. "I see you found my mug."

"Oh, sorry. Is this yours?" Steph looked at the mug in her hands. "I didn't pay attention to what I was grabbing. I just reached for the biggest mug I could find because I need a bucket-sized coffee after last night." She put the mug down, yawned, and stretched like a cat, which made her top slide up.

Against her will, Rae's gaze was drawn to a strip of fair skin and a pierced belly button, and that annoyed her even more. There was no reason for her to find this mug-stealing comic even remotely attractive. "Next time, I would appreciate it if you used your own mug—and put the ones you're not using back into the cupboard."

"Jeez. Looks like your night wasn't as great as mine." Steph took another sip of her coffee, and the sight of her full lips on the rim of Rae's mug was strangely distracting. "Didn't sleep well?"

Rae grunted something. No way would she discuss her nightmares with Steph.

"Oh shit." Steph slid her legs off the table and sat upright. "Did we keep you up? I'm so sorry. We tried to be quiet, but…"

Truth be told, Rae hadn't heard them, probably because she'd been caught in the grip of the nightmare. But that didn't mean she was fine with having a parade of strangers in her home. "Yeah, about that… I think we should establish some house rules."

"Rules?" Steph repeated as if it were a word in a foreign language.

Rae wasn't in the mood for a confrontation this early on a Sunday morning, but this needed to be said once and for all. She slid out the folding chair and sat across from Steph. "I think it's disrespectful to bring home overnight guests without telling me first."

Steph shrugged. "It was a spontaneous thing, so it's not like I could have asked permission beforehand."

"Well, then maybe next time, you need to spontaneously think of someplace else to take your…um, friends. Because this," Rae placed her hand on the table and spread her fingers apart as if to claim it, "is my home too, and I don't feel comfortable with a bunch of strangers parading through my space with their bras hanging out of their purses."

"A bunch?" Steph rolled her eyes. "I'm not planning on having an orgy in my room, but yeah, I enjoy an active sex life, and I have no intention of living like a nun because you might not like it. This is my home too, so you can't just decide on the rules on your own. If I wanted silly rules about who I can or cannot sleep with, I would have moved back in with my parents."

"I don't care who you sleep with, as long as you don't do it here."

Steph thumped the mug onto the table. "If this is how you want to start this cohabitation…fine."

They sat caught in a stare-down for several moments before Steph picked up her mug—Rae's mug—and stormed past her, muttering something that sounded like, "Way to burst a girl's rose-colored postcoital bubble." The door to her room banged shut.

Rae winced and rubbed her eye. Welcome to life with a roommate.

Chapter 7

"GILLI, NO!" PENNY SAID FOR the twentieth time since they had entered the park and tugged the beagle away from a banana peel before Gilli could gobble it up. "God, I really should ask for more money for walking her. If I let her, she'd eat anything that is lying still for more than a second."

"Yeah, that's what Rae seems to think about me too." Steph kicked a pebble out of the way.

Penny turned toward her, her eyes wide. "What?"

Steph buried her fingers in Moose's tan-and-white fur as the Saint Bernard/Labrador mix lumbered along the paved path next to her. He looked back at her, and the adoration in his gentle brown eyes instantly soothed her. Thankfully, Penny didn't believe in large pack walks, so Steph could focus on Moose and didn't have to handle half a dozen dogs. But since Gilli and Moose loved each other, they sometimes met up when their walks were scheduled for the same time. "Ms. Tall, Dark, and Moody and I had a little disagreement about sleepovers yesterday. I'm all for it; she isn't."

"Thank God, at least one of you has some sense!"

Steph stopped in the middle of the path, so joggers and other people with dogs had to veer around them. That was the last reaction she had expected from her usually understanding best friend. "What?"

"Oh, come on. Even you have to know that sleeping with your roommate would be a really bad idea. It's not like you can just walk out the next morning, like you usually do. If things go sour, one of you will have to move."

"That's not what I meant," Steph said. "You know I don't hook up with club employees."

"Since when?"

A Pokémon Go player with his gaze glued to his phone nearly bumped into Steph, so she continued along the winding path without stopping again. "Since that bartender I slept with a couple of years ago."

Penny frowned. "I don't remember that."

"It was a one-time thing, but when I told him that, it got kind of ugly." At Penny's alarmed look, she quickly added, "Nothing like that. But the bar was in the same room where the stage was, and the bartender is in charge of the blender." She opened her eyes comically wide.

Penny chuckled. "He didn't."

"Oh yeah, he did. When I told him I didn't want a repeat, he turned on the blender every time I said a punch line. Totally ruined my routine."

"And yet you haven't learned your lesson?" Penny tsked. "Doorpeople seat the audience, don't they? What if you end your fling with Rae and she doesn't take it well? She could start seating people in little groups here and there, instead of filling the room from the front. Wasn't that what you complained about last year?"

"Would you listen to what I'm saying? I'm not hooking up with Rae. In fact, if Rae gets her way, I won't be hooking up with anyone ever again."

"Um, can you back up and explain what's going on?"

Steph waited until they had made it past the baseball diamond, where a Little League game was underway. "I met a cute woman at the U-Haul store on Saturday. I invited her to my show, and we had a great time afterward, but the next morning, Rae tore me a new one for letting Allison sleep over."

"Wait, she slept over, only hours after you first met her? I knew you work fast, but that's quick, even for you. Wow, you're incredible."

Steph flashed her a grin. "That's what she said."

Penny lightly smacked her in the arm with the end of Gilli's leash. "Seriously, I'm not judging." She sighed. "Sometimes I wish I could be more like you—sleep with someone without getting my heart involved. But I'm sure you can understand that not everyone is like that."

"I totally get that. If Rae wants to be celibate until she meets the love of her life, that's fine with me. She's the one who's judging me." Steph gripped Moose's leash more tightly.

Penny took her gaze off Gilli to study her. A grin tugged on her lips. "That's a first."

"What?"

"You care. Usually, you don't give a shit about what people think, but you care about Rae's opinion of you."

"Nonsense." Steph couldn't care less about what Rae thought of her... right? But then again, if Rae's opinion didn't matter to her at all, why had she gotten so angry when Rae had confronted her? Storming out of a conversation was not like her.

Penny continued to look at her. Only the soft sounds of her steps—two for every one Steph took—interrupted the silence. People tended to underestimate Penny because of her slim five-foot-one frame and her cherubic face, but she was no pushover. She held Steph's gaze until Steph was the one to give in.

"Okay, maybe I'm not completely indifferent to what she thinks." Steph exhaled. There. She'd said it.

"Why's that?" Penny asked.

"Because...because... I don't know. Maybe because I know she's not completely wrong. I mean, none of my previous roomies cared about me bringing home guests, but as reserved as Rae is, I should have figured that she doesn't want to run into my one-night stands at the breakfast table." Not that most of them stuck around that long.

"Especially not on the first morning in the new apartment, when she's probably just getting the feel of things," Penny added. "You bringing a stranger home when the ink on your lease wasn't even dry... I could understand if that freaked her out a little."

Rae wasn't one to freak out. But yeah, it hadn't been one of Steph's finest moments; she could admit that now. She let out a loud sigh. "Do you think I should apologize or something?"

"Can't hurt. I mean, with how different you are, you two are probably never going to be best buddies, but you don't want this to evolve into a roommate-from-hell situation where both of you feel like you have to hide out in your room when the other is home."

God, no, that was the last thing Steph wanted. "Christ, this roommate arrangement is really cramping my style."

Penny gave her an innocent look. "You have a style?"

Before Steph could answer, she caught movement at the base of a tree. A squirrel hopped through the grass, maybe in search of some lunch. Steph knew what was about to happen. "Oh shit. Squirrel alarm."

Before she could provide a distraction or walk down a different path, Gilli spotted the squirrel too. With a sharp bark, she tried to give chase, dragging Penny off balance. In the ensuing chaos, Steph forgot about Rae and their argument for a while.

When Steph got home from her second walk, this one with three corgis that belonged to the same owner, a rhythmic thumping noise came from Rae's room. It sounded as if the headboard of Rae's bed was banging against the wall, accompanied by the quieter creaking of bed springs.

Steph paused one step into the apartment. *Nah. That's not what I think it is, is it?* Rae wouldn't be having sex with some woman one day after she had nearly ripped Steph's head off for doing the same.

But Steph's overactive imagination wasn't listening to her reasoning. It showed her vivid images of Rae's strong, bare back bunching and the muscles in her arm rippling as she moved against a moaning stranger.

Heat coursed through Steph's body. She firmly shook her head. *Ignore it. Just ignore it.*

But that was easier said than done since the rhythmic thumping continued as she tiptoed toward her room.

Thud, thud, thud. The sounds from the bedroom didn't let up for even a second.

Jeez, her roomie seemed to have great stamina.

Rae's bedroom was right next to hers, so she couldn't help glancing toward the source of those noises.

Uh… She froze on her tiptoes like a burglar who'd been caught. The door to Rae's bedroom was open! Was Rae doing this on purpose to make sure Steph didn't miss the show once she got home? Was she trying to get back at her for Saturday night?

But that didn't seem to be her style. Something else had to be going on…right?

Steph tiptoed closer and peeked around the doorjamb, prepared to withdraw immediately should she find her roommate in the throes of passion.

Rae lay on the bed, with her feet pointing toward the pillow. The muscles in her arm were indeed rippling, but she was neither naked nor with another woman. Nothing sexy going on at all. She was merely tossing a tennis ball against the wall, catching it as it bounced back, and then throwing it again.

Steph wasn't sure if she should be disappointed or relieved. Since she didn't want to be caught lingering in Rae's doorway, spying on her, she softly cleared her throat. "Hi."

Rae didn't answer. She continued to bounce the tennis ball against the wall as if it were the most fascinating thing in the world.

"Hello?" Steph called more loudly. Hadn't Rae heard her over the thudding of the ball?

A probing glance revealed a wire leading from her phone to a pair of earbuds stuck in Rae's ears.

Ah. Steph stepped into the doorway and waved widely to get her attention.

Nothing. Rae caught the ball, then threw it again.

Oh, come on. Rae had to be seeing her, even without turning her head. There was no way she wasn't at least in Rae's peripheral vision. Rae was ignoring her! Steph couldn't believe it. Were they really down to playing childish games already, just two days after moving in with each other? *So much for apologizing! Forget it.*

Steph whirled around and marched to the bathroom for a quick shower before heading out to her gig at a bowling alley bar.

When her doctor had first suggested tossing around a tennis ball, Rae had thought it would be boring as hell. But now she had to admit that there was something almost hypnotic about it. Granted, it wasn't quite as soothing as swimming laps, getting lost in the feel of the water and the rhythm of her stroke, but it would have to do until she worked up the courage to jump into the pool again. Rae challenged herself by throwing the ball faster and faster until it was a yellow blur, then altered the angle to see if her brain could keep up.

When she missed and the tennis ball hit her in the nose, she decided she had practiced her hand-eye coordination enough for one day. She pulled out her earbuds and dropped them into the drawer of her nightstand along with the ball.

Time to get ready for work. She grabbed a fresh pair of black dress pants, shirt, and tie. Except for the lack of a badge or rank insignia, her work clothes weren't all that different from the uniform she had worn for fourteen years, yet somehow it felt worlds apart.

With a sigh, she pushed the bathroom door open—and froze.

She had thought Steph was still out and about, but apparently, she had returned while Rae had been practicing with the tennis ball. Now she was in the bathroom, her clothes strewn carelessly around her, leaving her in only a black bra and a pair of panties that didn't match.

Weird what kind of details Rae's brain latched on to when on overload— and it definitely was. It had been a while since she'd seen a woman in this state of undress, and this one...wow. Her skin was fair despite the California sun, with only her arms and face tanned a light gold tone. Her navel piercing twinkled, drawing attention to her flat belly, and her full breasts rose softly over the cups of her bra as she sucked in a surprised breath.

For several seconds, both stood there, staring at each other.

Then Rae gave herself a mental kick, whirled around, and pulled the door closed behind her. "Sorry," she called through the door. "I didn't know you were..."

"Were what?" Steph asked when Rae fell silent.

Yeah, what? So beautiful? "Home," Rae said. She shook herself out of her strange daze. It didn't matter one bit what Steph looked like. She was a pain in the ass, even though she was kind of attractive.

"Oh, come on."

Rae swallowed. She hadn't said that *beautiful* bit out loud, had she? "Um, what's that supposed to mean?"

"I just stood in your doorway, waving like a maniac for a full minute, and now you follow me into the bathroom because you didn't know I was home? Yeah, right."

Rae clenched her teeth until her jaw muscles hurt. "I didn't see you. I swear." Even she could hear how unlikely that sounded. She knew she should tell her, but something held her back. Maybe it was pride—Kim had always said it would be her downfall one day—or maybe something else. She wanted Steph to see her as whole, not as someone to pity.

Everything stayed silent in the bathroom.

Rae leaned against the door. Why was she even bothering? This roommate thing was so not working out.

Then Steph sighed audibly. "All right. I believe you."

Just like that? It had been a while since someone had taken Rae at her word. The brass sure hadn't when she had told them she could still do her job. Steph's unexpected words made a lump form in her throat. Annoyed, she swallowed it down.

"Um, Rae?" Steph said after a moment. "While you're still dazzled by the sight of my hotness, this might be a good moment to apologize for having an overnight guest our first night in the new apartment. I'll try to be more considerate in the future."

Now she had managed to stun Rae a second time. "Um, thanks. I appreciate it." She stepped away from the door. "I'm gonna go get ready in my room. Bathroom's all yours."

"Aren't you forgetting something?" Amusement colored Steph's voice.

Rae turned around. "Forgetting?"

"You dropped your clothes." The door opened a few inches, and Steph's grinning face peered out. "Here." She passed the bundle of clothes through the gap.

"Oh. Thanks." Rae hadn't even noticed. Her brain really wasn't in full working order today. It had nothing to do with what Steph was—or rather wasn't—wearing. This roommate thing was merely a lot to adjust to.

Steph's chuckle followed her as she walked away. "Cute blush."

Rae stiffened. "I'm not blushing. I haven't blushed since 1997."

"Yeah, right," Steph called after her. "Hey, what happened in 1997?"

"Not a thing," Rae shouted back. "By the way, next time, lock the door."

"Nah. Where would the fun be in that?"

Chapter 8

WRITING JOKES WAS NOT A laughing matter—at least not when you had to come up with material for a gig in a hospital. Sure, she could use some of her usual routine, but she also wanted to come up with some new jokes that were tailored to the hospital setting.

Steph lay on her belly on the couch, dangling her bare feet in the air, and flicked through her joke book, which she used to scribble down ideas or things she'd heard that struck her as funny.

Maybe something about hospital food or the ass-free gowns. Hmm. Should she call Gabe and see if he had time to brainstorm punch lines?

Just as she reached for the phone, the doorbell rang, followed by a rap at the door.

Steph jumped up and made sure the doors to their bedrooms were closed, in case it was the Kleinbergs checking up on them.

When she looked through the peephole, a woman's slightly distorted face appeared before her. All Steph could see was a brown eye and part of the face as the woman leaned close to the peephole, but it definitely wasn't Mrs. Kleinberg.

Steph opened the door an inch and peeked through the gap.

The woman's flowing, rusty brown skirt and her gauzy blouse rustled as she waved at Steph. A smile deepened the laugh lines framing her eyes and mouth. "Hey there. A downstairs neighbor let us in."

Despite the friendly greeting, Steph was sure she'd never seen the stranger in her life. Was she a Jehovah's Witness or a salesperson? "I don't mean to be rude, but if you're here to sell me something, I have to confess I'm a starving artist who considers getting a new toothbrush a high-risk investment."

A low chuckle sounded from behind the woman, and Steph realized that the stranger wasn't alone. The tall man who was with her seemed as unusual as his companion. His graying hair hung over his broad shoulder in a ponytail, and the part of his face that wasn't covered by a salt-and-pepper beard was deeply tanned, looking a bit like a well-worn baseball glove. A dark blue felt beret sat tilted to one side on his head. "Don't worry. We've got nothing to sell. Unless you're interested in a twenty-five-year-old RV."

The woman excitedly clapped her hands. A braided leather bracelet dangled from her wrist. "You're an artist? Raelynn didn't mention that."

"Ah, you know her," the man said. "She never mentions much of anything. Speaks like every word is going to cost her a dollar."

Steph stared at them. "You know Rae?" In the two weeks they had lived together, Rae had never had any visitors before.

"I'd sure hope so." The woman laughed. "We're her parents."

Wide-eyed, Steph looked from the woman's makeup-free face to the flip-flops covering her feet despite the—for an Angeleno—chilly November weather. "You're shitting me," she blurted out before she could censor herself. These two couldn't possibly be the parents of someone as somber as Rae. But then again, most people who met Steph's parents were convinced she must be adopted too.

"Oh, I'm serious. Twenty-three-hours-of-labor serious." The woman pointed at her companion. "This one was about to give up on the home birth idea and take me to a hospital."

Rae's father tried to peek around Steph. "So is our eldest home?"

"Uh, no, but I think she'll be home soon." Rae was definitely a creature of habit. She disappeared around the same time every day and returned home an hour later with her sweat-drenched shirt clinging to her muscular shoulders and firm breasts. Steph always made sure to hang out in the living area around that time. No harm in looking, right?

Belatedly, Steph remembered her manners. "Please come on in." She opened the door wider and stepped back so they could enter. As she led them into the living room, her gaze darted to the three dirty mugs and the empty package of Oreos on the coffee table and her joke book, which she had tossed facedown onto the floor when the doorbell had rung. "Please excuse the mess."

Rae's mother waved her hand. She radiated acceptance, and again Steph couldn't help comparing her to her brooding daughter. "Relax. We're not the cleaning police. I always say a messy home is a happy home."

Despite her reassurance, Steph brushed a few cookie crumbs off the couch. "Please, take a seat, Mr. and Mrs. Coleman."

"Willett, actually," Rae's father said. "We're not married. But please, call me Lonnie. And that's my beautiful partner, CC."

"CC?" Steph repeated. She felt as if her brain was stuck in slow motion.

When she went to take a seat on the worn armchair Rae had contributed to their furniture, Rae's parents drew her down on the couch between them.

Rae's mother shrugged. Her eyes—the same brown color as her daughter's, just less intense—twinkled as she grinned. "Well, it's Celeste, really, but that's a bit of a mouthful to shout out in certain situations, so CC stuck."

Oh God. Was Rae's mother talking about sex? Steph decided she didn't want to know.

CC leaned back on the couch and looked immediately at home. "So you're a painter?"

Lonnie reached across Steph and gently poked CC. "Why would you think that? She said she's an artist. You know there are other art forms out there, right? She could be a poet."

Steph felt as if she had stepped into an old, good-natured argument. Was that what Rae's parents were—a painter and a poet? "Actually, I'm neither. I'm a stand-up comedian."

Silence spread through the living room.

Steph refused to lower her gaze. She had trained herself not to care whether people believed her job was a valid profession or not.

"Wow," CC said. "That must be so rewarding. To create something that makes people feel such strong emotions that they burst out laughing… How powerful!"

Lonnie nodded. "Probably not that different from being a poet. I bet you put as much of yourself into your routine as I put into my poems—or CC into her paintings."

It took a few seconds for Steph to make her vocal cords work. "I guess so." She had never seen herself as a creative artist on the same level as a poet or a painter, but maybe they were right. "The best comedy comes from real life, so you have to make it personal."

CC and Lonnie nodded as if they really understood.

"So is that how you met Raelynn?" CC asked. "Through your work?"

Steph tried not to giggle any time she heard Rae's first name. "Yes. We met in the comedy club where she works." These two were so easy to talk to that she had to cut herself off before she could tell them about asking Rae to be her fake girlfriend to fool the landlord.

"Don't worry." CC patted Steph's hand. "We're not going to judge. So what if you moved in with each other within days of meeting? Love has a way of making time irrelevant."

Steph nearly slid from the couch. "L-love?"

Lonnie laughed. "Or lust."

"No, no, I...we...we don't..."

"No need for embarrassment." Lonnie's beard parted in a soft smile. "Love is love, as far as we are concerned. Doesn't matter if it's between a man and a woman, two women, or two men."

"Or more than two people," CC added. "We're happy that Raelynn found someone after everything she's been through this year."

Steph reined in the impulse to ask about what had happened to Rae. First, she needed to clear up the misunderstanding, or Rae would kill her if she walked in and found her parents basically welcoming her as their new daughter-in-law. "Um, Rae and I, we're just roommates."

"Yeah, that's what she told us when she called to tell us she moved to a new place," CC said with a grin. Then she sobered. "Oh, wait. You mean, you're actually just roommates?"

Wasn't that what she had just said? Steph nodded.

"Oh. We thought..." CC slapped her forehead and chuckled. "Our daughter can be a little...repressed, so when she told us she's moving in with a *roommate*"—she painted quotation marks in the air with her fingers—"we thought it was her way of telling us she had finally stopped keeping everyone at arm's length and had taken a lover."

Even though Steph wasn't one to embarrass easily, her cheeks heated. "No. We share the rent, not a bed."

Rae's parents actually looked disappointed. Finally, CC smiled and shrugged. "Well, as Raelynn's grandma used to say, it ain't over till the fat lady sings. Maybe our daughter will grow on you."

"Um…" For once, Steph didn't know what to say.

Lonnie leaned forward, his checkered shirt stretching over his broad shoulders. "But you're friends, right? You're spending time with each other."

"Kind of."

"So how's our little one?" he asked. "How's she coping?"

Coping with what? Life with a roommate? Or were they talking about something else? Steph wasn't sure how to answer that even if she had known what exactly they were asking. Rae wasn't one for heartfelt confessions. Usually, their conversations revolved around who'd get the bathroom first in the morning or who the last yogurt in the fridge belonged to. "I guess she's all right. She seems to really like the apartment."

"Is she making friends at the new job?" CC asked.

Steph didn't think so. The few times she'd been to The Fun Zone to try to talk the owner into giving her a spot, she hadn't seen Rae talk about anything but work with her colleagues. "She's very well-respected."

Lonnie sighed. "Sometimes, I think we shouldn't have moved so often when she was little. Raelynn never learned to make friends."

"I don't think it would have made a difference," CC said. "There were always lots of kids around, wherever we went. Her brother had plenty of friends."

Laughter shook Lonnie's tall frame. "Oh, yeah, he was Mr. Popular. Remember when we thought he was selling drugs?"

A girlish giggle escaped CC. "We always tried to avoid processed food, even back then." She tapped the empty package of Oreos. "Instead of crap like this, our kids got sunflower seeds and sprouted almonds."

Steph couldn't help making a face. So Rae's parents and her own had at least one thing in common. Steph was the only one in her family who appreciated a juicy burger and syrup-covered waffles.

CC gave her a patient smile. "The kids learned to appreciate it. Or so we thought. Later, we found out that their grandmother, Lonnie's mom, snuck them candy whenever she visited. Darrin—Raelynn's younger brother—established an entire candy-trafficking ring."

"Yeah, until Raelynn busted him." A fond look spread over Lonnie's bearded face. "Always a stickler for law and order, even when she was little. Did she tell you the story about that little incident when she was seven and wanted to play cops and robbers and we wouldn't let her have a toy gun?"

Steph shook her head and tried to imagine Rae at that age. She had probably been an earnest but totally cute kid. "What happened?"

Before Rae's parents could answer, a key jingled in the lock, then the door swung open and Rae strode inside in sweat-drenched running clothes.

Now Steph would probably never find out what the story about seven-year-old Rae and the toy gun was. But the priceless expression on Rae's face was worth not hearing that story. God, if only she could snap a photo! Steph leaned back on the couch and tried to become invisible so she could watch the interaction between Rae and her parents.

Rae stumbled to a stop one step into the apartment.

Even finding the entire team of the Los Angeles Rams in her living room couldn't have surprised her as much as the sight that greeted her.

Her parents sat on the couch, leaning back as if they dropped by for a chat every day. Steph sat between them, looking as if she had thoroughly enjoyed her bonding time with CC and Lonnie.

Oh God. How long had they been here…and what had they talked about? Had they told Steph about the shooting? Rae's stomach twisted into a hard knot. She took a tentative step into the room. "W-what are you doing here?"

Lonnie unfolded his tall frame from the couch. "Hi, Rae-Rae. Good to see you too."

"I didn't mean it to sound like I'm not happy to have you here." As much as she didn't like surprise visits, she was glad to see her parents—and to see that both looked well and neither had lost any of their vibrancy. "It's just… I had no idea you were coming. What if no one had been home? You don't exactly live around the corner." She turned toward Steph. "CC and Lonnie live up in Oregon." Wait a minute! Why was she offering information to Steph? She didn't owe her roommate an explanation. But for some reason, she didn't want Steph to think she was an ungrateful bitch of a daughter.

"We were visiting friends in San Francisco, so we thought we'd drop by and check out your new place," Lonnie said.

Rae knew she shouldn't have been surprised. She couldn't remember a time when her parents had called first; they had always just shown up on her doorstep.

CC got up and opened her arms wide. "Where's my hug?"

Rae walked over and embraced her parents, all the while very much aware of Steph watching them.

Steph got up too and came around the coffee table toward Rae.

What...? For a moment, Rae thought she wanted a hug too, but then Steph walked past her to the armchair, leaving the middle cushion between CC and Lonnie for Rae. *Oh. Of course.* Why would Steph want to hug her, especially as sweaty as she was from her run?

Steph settled down cross-legged on the armchair and gave them a curious look. "You call your parents by their first names?"

Rae shrugged. "That's what they prefer."

"We didn't want to reinforce traditional authority structures with our children, so we encouraged them to call us by our first names." A mischievous smile spread over CC's face. "Plus it makes me feel younger."

"Oh, come on." Steph grinned at her. "You already look like Rae's older sister."

Lonnie chuckled and nudged Rae with his shoulder. "She's a charmer, this one. Better grab her up while you can."

God, how long would she have to sit here and be afraid that every word out of her parents' mouths would embarrass her? "Lonnie, please. I don't want to grab her. Uh, grab her up, I mean." Rae's earlobes grew warm.

Steph leaned forward, her eyes twinkling as she observed Rae. "Oh, look at that. Rae Coleman blushing for the second time since 1997."

"What happened in 1997?" CC asked.

"Yeah, that's what I want to know too." Steph looked back and forth between CC and Lonnie. "Any idea?"

"The *Pathfinder* landed on Mars, Princess Di died, and I think it was the year Dolly the sheep was cloned," Rae said firmly.

Lonnie scratched his beard. "1997... Wasn't that the year Raelynn—?"

Rae jumped up. "How about some coffee?"

Chuckling, Steph got up. "I'll go make some. If you want to go take a shower…"

"And leave you alone with my parents, so they can tell you every single embarrassing story from my childhood?" Rae shook her head. "No, thanks."

Steph exchanged amused gazes with Rae's parents. "Okay, then stay and keep your parents company. I'll make the coffee."

"Thanks." Rae watched as Steph walked over to the open kitchen area, for a moment distracted by the tight fit of her jeans.

CC leaned over and stage-whispered, "She's a keeper."

Rae tore her gaze away from Steph, covered her face with her hands, and groaned. "Let's make a deal," she said through her fingers. "You stop playing matchmaker, and I won't call you *Mommy*."

CC actually winced a little. "All right." She leaned her head against Rae's shoulder—which was easy to do since she was almost a head shorter—and peered up at her with a probing gaze. "So tell me. How are you doing?"

"I'm fine." Rae glanced toward the kitchen, not wanting to get into this topic in any detail while Steph was listening. But she knew her parents expected more than *I'm fine,* so she added, "We really lucked out with this apartment. I mean, it's on the small side, but I don't need much, and the neighborhood is great. Very walkable and the club is just a few blocks away."

"Is there a pool nearby?" Lonnie asked.

"I have no idea. I'm not swimming at the moment."

"What?" The wrinkles on Lonnie's forehead turned into deep furrows. "Why not?"

You know why not, Rae wanted to say but held back.

Steph saved her from having to answer when she returned with a cutting board that acted as a tray. She set down mugs in front of everyone, then placed small jugs and containers in the middle of the coffee table. "I didn't know if you drink your coffee black, like Rae, or take cream and sugar, but this is cashew milk and date paste. I keep some around for when my sister visits me. She's into health food too."

CC clutched her chest. "That's so considerate of you."

It was. Rae gave her a nod of acknowledgment but still hoped Steph would stop being so nice to her parents or they'd never stop matchmaking.

When Steph didn't keep a mug for herself, CC peered up at her with obvious disappointment. "You're not joining us?"

"No. Sorry." Steph looked as if she was genuinely sorry, not only saying so. "I still have some stuff to prepare for when I go to the hospital later today."

Rae paused with the mug halfway to her lips and frowned up at her. "You have to go to the hospital? What's wrong?" Steph looked perfectly healthy to her with her easy smile, relaxed stance, and the glimmer of mischief in her gray eyes. Not that all sicknesses and disabilities could be detected by looking at the person, of course; Rae knew that from personal experience.

"Nothing's wrong. I'm doing a gig there." Steph sent her a teasing smile. "Worried about me?"

Rae kept her face impassive. "Nah. Of course not. I just wanted to know if I'd have the apartment to myself for a couple of days."

"Oh yeah. So you could throw all the wild parties you want. Sure." Without listening to Rae's protests, Steph picked up a battered notebook from the floor, waved to Rae's parents, and disappeared in her room.

CC watched her go, then turned toward Rae and put one hand on her knee. "Now tell me. How are you really?"

"I really am fine."

"Do you like your job?" Lonnie asked.

Did she? Not working had never been an option for her, even if her disability pension had been enough for her to afford not to, so she hadn't given it much thought. "Yeah, I think I do. It's not the same as being on the force, but it's all right for now. It'll keep me busy until I figure out what I want to do with my life."

"At least you don't have to carry one of these horrible weapons and have people shoot at you," CC whispered.

Rae sighed. "CC…"

"What? Is it wrong of me to worry about you?"

"No. But there's no reason to worry, okay?"

"Well, I worry a lot less now that I met your roommate." Somehow, CC managed to make it sound like *the love of your life*. "I think she's gonna keep an eye on you, and from the way you watched her in the kitchen earlier, you've got an eye on her too." She paled under her tan. "I didn't mean to…"

"Relax," Rae said. "It's a perfectly innocent phrase. I don't want you to censor yourself around me, okay?"

CC chewed her bottom lip and nodded.

Rae gulped down the rest of her coffee and slapped her thigh. "C'mon, I'll give you the nickel tour."

An hour later, Rae knocked softly on Steph's door. At Steph's "come in," she opened it a few inches and peeked in.

Steph stood in the middle of the room, facing the mirrored closet doors, a piece of paper in one hand. Had she been practicing her routine in front of the mirror?

"Yes?" Steph tilted her head when Rae didn't say anything.

"Oh, um, my parents are getting ready to leave and want to say goodbye."

Steph let the piece of paper flutter to her bed and followed Rae into the living area. "CC, Lonnie, it was so nice to meet you. You're not driving back to Oregon tonight, are you?"

"No," Lonnie said. "We have friends all over California. With all the visits we have promised them, it'll probably take us at least three weeks to make it back."

"That's great. But still, drive carefully." Steph hugged them both warmly and received sincere embraces in return.

Rae watched with a puzzled frown. How did some people manage to do that...bond so quickly? She'd never understand it. She allowed herself to get pulled into tight hugs of her own and promised to take good care of herself.

Then the door closed behind her parents, and Rae imagined she could hear their RV sputter to life and then race away faster than the speed limit allowed. Finally, she turned toward Steph. "Sorry you had to entertain them earlier."

"No apology necessary. They're great. I wish my parents were more like them."

Rae eyed her skeptically. As a child, she had always wished her parents were more like those of other kids—more normal. Wherever they had gone, Rae had stuck out like a sore thumb with her homemade clothes, her carob-covered birthday cake, and her ignorance of pop culture or anything that other kids had seen on TV.

"Honestly," Steph said. "My parents still think this is a phase I'll eventually grow out of."

"Yeah, I admit I was lucky in that regard. My parents threw me a coming-out party when they found out I'm gay." Rae wrinkled her nose. "Complete with rainbow-colored streamers, dancing to 'I Am What I Am,' and a vegan pride cake."

Steph laughed. "I can see them doing that. But that's not what I meant. My parents are completely fine with me being bi. It's my job they have a problem with. They think stand-up is a silly hobby that I'll give up once I really grow up. But when I told your parents that I'm a comedian... Wow." She shook her head, wide-eyed wonder on her face. "They embraced me as a fellow artist and looked at me as if stand-up might save the world or something. I don't think that has ever happened to me before."

She radiated so much astonished pleasure that Rae couldn't help being proud of her parents. Maybe being different from the norm was a good thing sometimes. "I don't think stand-up is going to cure cancer or solve world hunger, but for what it's worth, I respect the hell out of anyone who bares their soul to a room full of strangers, just to get them to laugh." She shuddered at the mere thought of having to do that.

"Wow, thank you." Steph's gray eyes lit up so they looked nearly silver. "Was that a compliment from Rae Coleman?"

Rae rubbed her neck and looked away. "Yeah, well, don't get used to it. It's probably the full moon or Mercury being in retrograde or something."

Steph chuckled. "Don't worry. I won't get a big head or expect you to dole out daily compliments." She glanced at her wristwatch. "Oops. I'd better get going." She took two steps toward the door, then turned back around. "Wait. How's this?" She lifted an invisible microphone to her mouth. "It probably won't come as a surprise to you to learn that hospital fashion isn't designed by Versace or Armani. If you've ever seen someone in a hospital gown from behind, you know why they call it ICU."

Rae gave her a bland look.

"ICU... I see you. Get it?"

"Yeah, I get it."

A sigh rose up Steph's chest. "So you just don't find it funny. Jeez, tough crowd. It's not that bad, is it?"

There was something funny about it, but Rae usually needed to be in a relaxed mood to laugh at jokes—and it had been quite some time since that had last happened. "It'll probably do fine with the hospital crowd. I'm not the right person to try stuff out on. You know us cops. We have to check our sense of humor at the door when we enter the Police Academy."

Steph snorted. "Said the woman who just cracked a joke."

Rae waved her hand as if chasing away a bothersome fly. "You'd better go and break a leg, or whatever comics say when they wish someone good luck."

"We say go and kill them…or slaughter them."

Rae had heard phrases like that in the club. "God, what are you guys? A bunch of serial killers?"

"Some of us might be." Steph tried for a menacing expression but didn't quite make it.

Rae gave an unimpressed shrug. "I sleep with one eye open anyway." Steph couldn't know it, but that wasn't all that far from the truth since her one eye didn't close all the way when she slept. Now Rae did grin a little, a slow, hesitant twitch of her lips, as if her mouth had forgotten how to do it. She lifted her hand and touched her lips. That was a surprise. Except for the usual dark humor cops were famous or maybe infamous for, she hadn't found much reason to smile or been able to joke about the aftermath of the shooting.

Well, what do you know? Rae stared after Steph, who gave a wave and strode to the door, on her mission to cheer up folks in the hospital. Life with a comic seemed to have its bright sides after all.

Chapter 9

SEEING RAE OUTSIDE OF THEIR cozy little apartment was weird. She looked different towering over the patrons who were lined up in front of The Fun Zone. More intimidating. The sliver of a smile Steph saw at home every now and then was completely absent. But damn, she looked good in her black suit and tie.

What was it about a woman in uniform, even if it was one like this? Steph found her gaze lingering. It had to be the queer equivalent of a Pavlovian reflex.

As Steph approached the front of the line, Rae watched her with a stoic face, as if she didn't recognize her.

Clearly, she was in work mode, so Steph reined in her mischievous streak and greeted her with a friendly but professional smile. "You're not going to make me pay this time, are you?"

"Depends." Rae's expression was unreadable. "Are you on the lineup tonight?"

"No. But I'm hoping to change that. That's why I'm here. I'm trying to convince the club owner to give me a chance at a headliner spot."

Rae raised her brows. "A headliner spot? Wow, you're aiming high."

Steph shrugged. "I've had gigs as an opener at The Fun Zone before. But I won't impress any scout if I'm only doing two minutes of my material here and there. I need to headline a show."

"Good luck with that," Rae said. "Mr. Hicks hasn't hired a female headliner since I started working here six weeks ago."

"Longer than that," her colleague Brandon threw in. "I don't think we've had a female headliner since Mr. Hicks bought the club last year."

A frown made Rae's expression even more intimidating. "I didn't think he'd be so sexist. He hired me, after all."

"Yeah, well, you could probably bench-press him." Brandon chuckled and raised his fist to give her a light punch to the shoulder, but a glare from Rae made him change his mind. "I don't think he's sexist. He just doesn't believe women are funny."

"And that's supposed to not be sexist?" Steph shook her head. "Hasn't he ever heard of Ellen, Tina Fey, Wanda Sykes, or Hannah Gadsby? There are plenty of funny women!"

Brandon held up his hands. "Preaching to the choir. Don't tell me; tell Mr. Hicks."

"I will." Steph braced herself for an uphill battle. Somehow she had to convince Mr. Hicks to let her headline a show. Gigs in hospitals, cafés, and bars were good practice, but they barely paid enough to cover the gas, and they wouldn't turn her into a household name. If she could record herself doing an entire hour of solid material in one of the best clubs in LA and send it to the bookers for comedy networks, she might finally get the TV credits she needed to make her career take off. "Okay, here goes nothing."

But when she went to enter the club, Rae didn't step aside to let her through. "Aren't you forgetting something?"

Steph couldn't resist. She formed her lips into an exaggerated pucker. "Kiss for good luck?"

Rae scowled and rubbed her thumb and forefinger together in the universal gesture for money.

What? Steph couldn't believe it. Her roommate seriously expected her to pay to get in? "You've got to be kidding me."

"Actually...yes. Go on in."

So much for former cops not having a sense of humor—even if it was a really weird one. Steph threw her a wait-until-you-get-home look, which Rae answered with an unimpressed stare. With a shake of her head, Steph marched past her.

She waved at a few of her comedy buddies, who sat at the bar, nursing beers.

The raised stage in the main room was still empty, but a sound tech fiddled with the audio system, the small tables were starting to fill, and waitresses scurried around, taking the first drink orders.

Steph glanced at the mic standing out from the background of the fake brick wall. This was where she wanted to be—but first she had to convince Mr. Hicks that it was where she belonged.

She made her way down the hall and knocked on his office door. With the noise from the bar area, it was hard to make out a reply, so she opened the door a few inches. "Mr. Hicks? I called earlier today…" And yesterday… and the day before. "And you said to come see you next time I was in the club, so…"

He looked up from his paperwork and squinted at her as if he didn't remember their conversation—and didn't remember her from all the other times she had asked him for a spot in the lineup either. Sighing, he tossed his thick pen onto his desk and waved her in.

Compared to the showroom, which seated four hundred people, his office was downright tiny, and every last inch of it was cluttered with papers and promotional material.

Mr. Hicks jerked his chin in the direction of the chair on the other side of his desk, and Steph quickly sat before he could change his mind. "Did you happen to have some time to take a look at the link I sent you?"

He gestured at his desk. "Does this look like I have time for anything?"

This wasn't off to a good start. "Um, probably not. It's a link to a video of me headlining a show at Tickle Me Funny."

Despite the name-dropping, he didn't look impressed. "So?"

"I've put together a very solid show over the past year, and I've had success with it all over the country. I was wondering if you'd let me headline a show at The Fun Zone. It doesn't need to be on a Saturday. The late show on a Thursday would be great."

He reached for his mouse and clicked a few times, probably opening his email. A few seconds later, Steph's voice drifted through the speakers on his desk. "Have you ever noticed how most comedians come from messed-up families? Not me, of course. No, no, really. I'm the only normal one in my family. The others are all psychologists. My sister has half a dozen abbreviations after her name… PsyD, LMFT, PCC… Well, I have a few that people usually tag on after my name too—PITA, FUBAR, and TMI."

Mr. Hicks didn't laugh. Not even a twitch of his lips beneath his goatee.

Jeez, between him and Rae, Steph could really get an inferiority complex.

He clicked around a few times. Was he looking at the other information on her website? He didn't seem impressed by what he was seeing. "No TV credits?"

"Not yet, but I'm working on it."

"Yeah, come back when you've done Colbert or Fallon." He paused. "Um, not done them, done them, but you know what I mean."

Steph knew only too well what he meant. That was her dilemma: she needed TV credits to play bigger rooms like The Fun Zone, but to get network bookers interested, she had to have headlined for some of the popular clubs. Okay, time to put her cards on the table. "You know this business. You managed a club in Denver before you bought The Fun Zone." It didn't hurt for him to see that she'd done her homework.

He had already turned back toward his paperwork, but now he lifted his head. "Yes." He waved at her to go on.

"You know how things work. The comedy boom is over. Really talented people might never get any TV credits—unless someone gives them a chance."

"And you want that someone to be me." It wasn't a question.

"Why not? You didn't get where you are by playing it safe."

He stroked his goatee and regarded her for a while before leafing through a folder on his desk. "I'll tell you what. I'll let you emcee a week in January."

Steph had emceed at clubs like The Fun Zone many times before. At this stage of her career, it wasn't what she wanted or needed. MCs were supposed to introduce the other comics, warm up the crowd, make announcements about any specials, and explain the house rules to the audience. If they were lucky, they could squeeze in a few minutes of their own material, but that was it. "Thank you, but I'm not a newbie. I've been doing stand-up for nearly ten years. I've headlined all over the country the entire year."

"Not in LA," Mr. Hicks said. "Not at my club."

"Not yet." Steph refused to meekly avert her gaze and just accept his decision.

"Damn, I can see where that PITA abbreviation after your name is coming from. You really are a pain in the ass," he muttered. "Do you have any idea what running a comedy club costs? We need to fill every seat to avoid losing money, and you don't have the name to draw a crowd."

"Neither did Amy Schumer, Chris Rock, or Sarah Silverman before they were discovered. I've got to start somewhere. It might as well be your club."

The stroking of his goatee became a tugging. "Forget it. I'm not letting you headline. But…" Steph held her breath while he flipped through the folder again. "If you are as quick-witted up on stage as you are in here, I'll give you a feature spot."

A feature spot… That meant she'd get to do twenty to thirty minutes of material in between the MC and the headliner. It wouldn't pay as much, but if she impressed Mr. Hicks, it would increase her chance of getting a headline spot.

"Deal," she said quickly before he could change his mind. "When?"

Mr. Hicks paused on a page in the folder. "Sunday."

"This Sunday?" Steph squeaked out. That meant she'd be part of the Thanksgiving weekend show that had been promoted heavily all over LA. She barely held herself back from dancing a little jig.

He snorted. "No. The late show on the Sunday after."

Steph's bubble of happiness burst, but she adjusted quickly. Any Sunday would be good since it was often the only day Mr. Hicks would be at the club all evening because he had to be there to sign paychecks anyway. If she was lucky, he'd pop in to see bits of her act, and if he liked what he saw, it might open the door for larger opportunities at The Fun Zone. "That's great. Thanks. I promise you won't regret it."

"I'd better not. I'll have my assistant manager email you the details." He made a shooing motion. "Now get out of here and let me get my work done."

Steph made it out of his office in record time, barely stopping herself from skipping to the door. As soon as she was outside, she jumped up and down like a kangaroo on speed. Yes! She had gotten it—the first of hopefully many big chances.

With a cheerful wave, she rushed past the guys at the bar and out the door.

The line in front of the club had disappeared, and so had Brandon, but Rae was still there, guarding the entrance and letting in stragglers.

When Steph came up from behind, Rae flinched but recovered quickly and sent her an expectant gaze. "What did he say?"

"He's not giving me a headliner spot."

Rae's lips tightened. "Don't take it personally. He—"

"But he's letting me feature next week." Unable to contain her excitement any longer, she threw her arms around Rae for an exuberant hug.

As soon as their bodies made contact, both of them froze.

Rae's arms had come up automatically, and her hands settled on Steph's back, holding her against her even as her body stiffened.

Steph allowed herself to rest against Rae's powerful frame for a moment, then let go and stepped back. "Sorry. I didn't mean to…"

"It's okay."

With only half a step of space between them, they stared into each other's eyes.

Rae's eyes were fascinating. Not only because one of them moved less than the other, especially when she was looking down, as she did now, but also because of their color. From a distance, they looked simply brown. But up close, Steph discovered that they were flecked with amber around the pupils, making them seem to dance like flames.

Yeah, and you could get burned easily if you're not careful, Steph reminded herself. Her roommate was the one woman who was off limits, even for just a night. Not that Rae would ever be interested in a few hours of fun with her.

Rae turned her head away, clearly as uncomfortable with the close scrutiny as she had been with the embrace. Even though Steph's hug hadn't been tight enough to leave any wrinkles, Rae slid her hands over her suit jacket like a bird smoothing down its ruffled feathers. "I'm just not the huggy type."

Steph put on a stunned expression. "No!"

"Smart-ass," Rae grumbled.

Steph sobered for a moment. She wanted Rae to understand what this meant to her. "This is big for me. Really big. Truth be told, I knew he wouldn't let me headline, but a feature spot… It could practically be an audition for the headline act."

Rae gave her an awkward pat on the arm. "Congratulations." She looked sincere. "I'm sure you'll do great. And if you're nice to me, I won't even seat a bachelorette party in the first row on your big night."

Steph laughed. "Thanks, I guess."

In the silence between them, honking and whoops from Melrose Avenue drifted over.

Rae shifted her weight and pointed over her shoulder. "So are you going back in to celebrate with your buddies?"

"No. I'm going home to start preparing. This is my big chance—and I'm grabbing ahold of it with both hands."

Rae gave her a respectful nod. "See you at home, then."

Brandon joined them in front of the club. "At home?" He looked back and forth between Rae and Steph, his eyes going wide. "Holy motherfucker! You two are shacking up?" He let out a piercing wolf whistle. "Man, that's—"

"If you say 'hot,' I'm gonna break your nose." Rae looked fierce, as if she might actually do it.

Steph put her hand on Rae's arm. Tense muscles vibrated beneath her fingers. "We're roommates, Brandon. I bet being on the door staff pays as shitty as being on stage, so we both needed some help covering the rent."

"Ah." Brandon rubbed his nose. "Yeah, that makes sense. This job doesn't pay enough to keep a cockroach alive."

Rae grunted her agreement, and the tension in her muscles receded.

Steph pulled her hand back. *Phew.* Good thing they weren't actually a couple and would never be one. If Rae was already this protective when they were just roommates, she probably would have turned Brandon's nose into mashed potatoes if they had really been an item.

Not that she condoned violence of any kind, but she had to admit that it felt good. She'd grown a thick skin around comedy clubs since most comics had no filter, and she had stopped counting how many less-than-subtle offers of a threesome she had gotten over the years—as if being bisexual meant wanting to sleep with a man and a woman at the same time. But just because she could take it and reply with a witty comeback didn't mean she appreciated those comments.

"Okay, I'm off now. Do you need me to pick you up later?" Steph pointed at the club's parking lot. "I realized you don't have your car."

"Nah, I'll walk," Rae said.

"Are you sure?"

"I can give you a ride home," Brandon said.

Rae firmly shook her head. "I'll walk."

"Jeez, if I didn't know your middle name, I'd think it was *stubborn*," Steph muttered.

"Ooh, what's her middle name?" Brandon asked.

"I don't have one." Rae leveled a threatening glare at Steph, who held up her hands and backed away, laughing.

"I'm not getting involved in this, guys. Good night." With a quick wave, she walked to her car.

Rae reached for a tomato, then looked at a second one and hesitated. Should she make enough salad for Steph too? When they had moved in with each other four weeks ago, she couldn't have imagined doing such a thing since it might set a precedent. One of her unwritten house rules had been that each of them had to get her own food and prepare her own meals.

But Steph had been either in her room, perfecting her routine, or out, working corporate holiday parties or testing new jokes at open mics, since she had gotten Mr. Hicks to give her the feature spot a week ago. Rae had to admit that she had misjudged comedians—or at least this comedian. She had always thought that comics had a pretty cushy job: sleeping in until noon, spending their days watching funny YouTube videos, and then making money by working less than an hour every night.

That wasn't Steph's daily routine at all. She got up around the same time Rae did and usually worked all morning before leaving for her side job. Rae knew because she often heard her talk to herself while she worked on her material. Except for a couple of hours she'd spent with her family on Thanksgiving, Steph hadn't stopped perfecting her set.

Even now the low murmur drifted over from Steph's room.

Rae took the second tomato and weighed it in her hand. Okay, she would do it. But just this one time and only because she didn't want the pizza delivery guy to ring their doorbell late at night, after Steph realized she had skipped dinner.

She washed and sliced the tomatoes, a bit of romaine lettuce, and a red bell pepper before crumbling some feta cheese into the bowl. For a moment, she eyed the olives and onions but decided to leave them out since she had no idea if Steph liked them. With quick flicks of her wrist, she whisked together olive oil and lemon juice and added oregano and pepper.

Just as she was about to pour the dressing over the salad, she paused. Something was missing. Where was the cucumber she'd bought at the farmers market yesterday?

She opened the fridge and rooted through the veggie drawer. Nothing. It also wasn't in the bowl next to the fridge, where she kept the tomatoes so they wouldn't lose their aroma.

What the hell? Had Steph taken it? Since Steph's major food groups seemed to be chocolate, burgers, and pasta, it didn't seem likely. But where else could the cucumber have gone?

Frowning, Rae knocked on Steph's door to solve the mysterious case of the missing cucumber.

The low murmur stopped. "Come on in," Steph called.

Rae swung the door open. "Sorry to interrupt, but have you by any chance seen—" Then she caught sight of the missing vegetable.

Steph held the cucumber in her left hand, raised to her mouth as if it were a microphone. She smiled at Rae as if it were the most normal thing in the world to kidnap a vegetable for comedy purposes.

"Um, what are you doing with that poor cucumber?"

Steph sensually slid her hand up and down the vegetable. "What does it look like I'm doing?" She lowered her voice to a seductive purr.

A shiver went through Rae, and she cursed her body for its automatic reaction. She kept her face impassive and gave her a look.

"Okay, okay." Chuckling, Steph stopped caressing the cucumber. "Don't look at me like I'm some kind of veggie pervert. I'm practicing my set, which means I need a mic."

Rae shook her head. Someone really needed to write a comedy routine about the peculiar ideas comics came up with. "And the cucumber seemed to be the obvious choice to you? Didn't your parents teach you not to play with your food?"

Steph shrugged and gave her a charming grin. "Well, strictly speaking, it's *your* food, and I don't even want to know what my parents would say if they caught me playing with a cucumber. They're psychologists."

"Both of them and your sister?"

"Yep. Pretty much the entire family except for me. Well, Uncle Albert is a psychiatrist."

"Jesus," Rae blurted before she could hold it back. Her head started spinning as she tried to imagine growing up like that. Apparently, they had one thing in common after all: they had both grown up in families that weren't quite conventional.

"Well, it has its good sides too. For one thing, it gives me plenty of material for my routine."

Rae studied her but couldn't tell if she was joking. Did Steph really talk about her family on stage? If she did, was her family fine with being made the butt of jokes?

"So what was it that you came in here for?" Steph asked.

Rae pointed at the cucumber. "The mic."

"Why would you need a mic?" Steph twirled the cucumber. "I thought you weren't the type to go up on stage and tell jokes."

"I'm the type who wants to eat her vitamins. Come on. Hand it over."

When Rae tugged on the cucumber, Steph playfully held on to her end.

"Dammit, Steph!" Rae let out a growl. She wasn't in the mood for a tug-of-war, even though she knew she could easily overpower her more slender roommate. But if she gave a powerful yank, Steph would tumble forward and end up in her arms. That was a big no-no. "Let go, or…"

"Or?" A seductive note seemed to vibrate in Steph's voice.

Heat rushed down Rae's belly. *Simmer down,* she told her traitorous body. Steph was just playing around and didn't mean anything by it. "Or you won't get any of the delicious Greek salad I'm preparing."

Steph let go so abruptly that Rae overcompensated, stumbled backward, and crashed against the door. The doorknob hit her hipbone, and she lost her grip on the cucumber, which rolled along the floor.

Damn. Rae rubbed her hip. *That's gonna bruise.*

"Oh shit. Rae, I'm so sorry. I didn't mean to…" Steph rushed over. "Let me see." Her hands fluttered over Rae's hips, then along her back as she tried to tug Rae's shirt from her pants and pull the waistband of her jeans down a little.

A ripple of sensation washed through Rae as her body reacted without consulting her brain. *Fuck.* She grabbed Steph's hands and pulled them away from her body. "Stop it," she said more forcefully than she had intended. She struggled to soften her tone. "I'm fine."

Steph withdrew her hands but didn't move away. "Are you sure? That looked like it hurt."

"As a beat cop, I've been shot at, kicked in the gut, and thrown against a wall by a guy three times your size. This was nothing."

Instead of reassuring her, the words seemed to alarm Steph even more. "Shot at?"

Every muscle in Rae's body went rigid. *Damn.* Why had she told Steph that? "Yeah." She tried to make it sound as if it were no big deal. "Twice, actually."

Steph paled. "God," she whispered. "And I thought being booed off stage was bad."

"Every job has its pros and cons, I guess."

"That's all you're gonna say about it?"

"What else am I supposed to say? I survived. But I might die of hunger if I don't get something to eat within the next ten minutes." She picked up the cucumber she had dropped earlier, careful not to lose her balance in the process, and strode to the kitchen. Even without peripheral vision on her left side, she sensed Steph following and taking up position next to her.

Steph watched as she washed and sliced the cucumber. Rae's fingers started to ache from clenching them around the knife, in expectation of more questions.

But Steph seemed to sense that Rae had reached her limit. "No olives?"

Rae turned her head and looked at her. She hoped her relief wasn't too obvious. "Wasn't sure you like them."

"I love them." Steph went to the fridge and returned with the jar of black olives. "Toss them in."

When Rae took the jar from her, their fingers touched. Rae's gaze flickered from Steph's hand to her face. For a moment, Rae thought she would tell Steph something unexpected—maybe something about being shot at—but then reason returned and she just nodded at her. "Thanks."

"You're very welcome."

How odd. It felt as if they had been talking about much more than a jar of olives. With a shake of her head, Rae added olives to the bowl and tossed the salad. "No thanks necessary. You're doing the dishes."

Chapter 10

IT HAD BEEN YEARS SINCE Steph had been this nervous before going up on stage. She paced the greenroom with her set list in hand. Should she really do the new bits or rely on the tried-and-true jokes?

Stop it. She knew she was overthinking her set. Her material was good, and she would just play it safe by hammocking the new material—putting it between jokes that always got her laughs.

She stretched and jumped up and down to get the blood flowing and prepare her body for the rush of being on stage.

The headliner glared at her from his spot on the couch. "Can you stop that? This is a greenroom, not a gym."

Christ. Away from the stage, he had the charm and social skills of a constipated bull. She stopped her pacing and peeked out through the curtain covering the short hallway leading onto the stage.

Gabe was the MC tonight. He was out there, explaining the house rules about no videos or photos, and then did a couple of jokes to warm up the crowd. Was it a complete coincidence that he was hosting tonight, or had he gotten the opening spot on purpose to make sure she didn't have to go up to a cold crowd?

If it was the latter, Steph definitely appreciated it. She looked around and tried to gauge the vibe of the audience. It was a good crowd, even though the show wasn't completely sold out. The seating was perfect, with the rambunctious groups sitting in the back, where security could more easily remove them if they caused any trouble.

Thanks, Rae.

As if conjured up by that thought, Rae stuck her head into the greenroom. "You're up in a minute."

Outside, Gabe started to read the introduction she had handed him earlier. "If you've seen *The Tonight Show*, *Comedy Central Stand-Up Presents*, and *Comedians of the World*, well, our next comic has seen these shows too."

The crowd laughed, making Steph smile. So far, so good.

"Please give a warm welcome to Stephanie Renshaw!" Gabe called.

Rae made eye contact once more and gave her an encouraging nod. "Show them what you've got."

"Will do." Steph slid out of the curtain and bounced onto the stage with a broad grin. The spotlight trailed her as she placed her water bottle and her phone onto the stool off to one side, where the recording app could pick up her voice without getting in the way.

After a firm handshake, Gabe handed over the microphone and left the stage.

Now it was her show.

With the mic in her left hand, she stepped closer to the edge of the stage. The glaring lights made it impossible to see past the first row of people, but knowing Rae was likely out there, watching out for hecklers and anything Steph couldn't handle, gave her confidence.

"Thanks so much for coming out on a Sunday night." The pre-show jitters instantly disappeared as she addressed the crowd. "Oh, speaking of coming out, maybe I should make one thing clear right from the start, or you guys won't get half of the jokes about my dating life. I'm bisexual."

Someone in the back cheered loudly.

Steph waved in that direction. "Ooh, thanks. Looks like we've got a bi section present tonight."

The guy who had just cheered shouted something, but with people chuckling all around her, Steph hadn't caught it.

She leaned forward and lifted her free hand to her ear. "Can you repeat that?"

"I'm not bi," the guy shouted, sounding a bit offended. "But my girlfriend is every now and then." Steph knew what was coming even before he added, "So how about it? You, me, and her after the show?"

Steph knew she had to cut him down now, or he would continue to interrupt the show. "Thanks for the offer, but what makes you think you can pleasure two women when you probably can't even satisfy one?"

The guy's buddies howled, and when a wave of laughter from the audience hit her, Steph knew the rest of the set would go well.

Normally, Rae preferred working the door or talking down angry patrons to monitoring the showroom. Once the show started, the house lights went down, so if the door staff had to shush noisy people, they had to find their table in the near dark. With her messed-up night vision, that wasn't an easy task for her.

But tonight, she had volunteered for showroom duty. She had told Brandon it was because the festive music and the holiday decoration in the lobby got on her nerves. The real reason, of course, was that she wanted to catch at least part of Steph's set.

Now she was glad she had. She took up position next to the guy who had just propositioned Steph for a threesome, making sure he could see her as she pointed to her eyes, then to him. *I'm watching you, buddy. One wrong move and you're outta here.*

Even with the laughter bouncing through the room, she imagined she could hear him swallow.

Good. He had gotten the message.

With the room under control, she returned her attention to the stage. Unlike many of the other female comics Rae had seen in The Fun Zone, Steph hadn't tried to appeal to the men in the audience by dressing overly feminine. The formfitting T-shirt peeking out from beneath her blazer sported a painted-on tie. Personally, Rae really liked her style—and not just because the tight jeans showed off Steph's long, slim legs.

"Anyway, when I came out to my parents a few years back, they were actually pretty happy." Steph's tousled hair shimmered under the stage lights. "Yep, you heard that right. They thought me being bi would double the chances of me finally settling down. But it actually doubles my chances of heartbreak."

As Steph relayed the hilarious story of one of her dates, Rae couldn't help marveling at how relaxed she appeared laying her private life bare to the world. She was making herself vulnerable for the sake of entertaining these strangers. How could she stand turning hurtful experiences into something that people laughed at?

Rae's stomach churned as she remembered how it had felt to have her life exposed to the world after the shooting. The story had been all over the news. Not only had each news report made her relive the worst day of her life; the press had also painted her as a hero, and that had been one big, painful joke because she knew she was anything but.

Steph finished the bit about her dating experiences and launched into a different series of jokes. "So as you can imagine, I'm not feeling the urge to move in with anyone. Um, wait, I actually did. Did I mention I have a roommate? And no, in this case, that's not a queer euphemism for dancing the mattress mambo."

What the fuck? Rae's stunned admiration for Steph turned into anger so fast that she nearly grew dizzy from emotional whiplash.

"If you have ever lived with a roommate, you know it's not for the fainthearted, especially if you are so different that sometimes you're not even sure you belong to the same species. For me, a balanced diet means having a chocolate bar in each hand. My roomie, however, is a bit of a dietary overachiever. You know the kind—one of those annoying people who actually enjoy salads and make the rest of us feel bad. She probably gets it from her parents. They're the epitome of modern hippies. I'm sure they pick their kale by doing an aura reading on it." Steph wiggled her fingers around invisible kale leaves as if viewing them through a crystal ball.

Rae's heartbeat throbbed in her temples, and she clenched her fists so tightly that her short nails dug tiny half-moons into her palms. It wasn't the first time someone had made fun of her parents. She had been teased because of their hippie lifestyle a lot as a kid.

The audience laughed at the next roommate joke, but the words didn't register for Rae. She didn't want to hear what else Steph was saying about her anyway, and neither did she want this room full of strangers to know a single thing about her.

A bitter taste coated her tongue. Somehow, she had thought she and Steph were becoming…well, maybe not quite friends, but at least friendly with each other. *Yeah, guess the joke is on me.* That would teach her to keep her distance from people. Any time she let someone close, even in a non-romantic way, she ended up getting hurt, and Steph had just proven that she wouldn't be the exception.

Even with the threesome-guy interrupting the beginning of her routine, this was one of the best sets Steph ever had. Her thirty allotted minutes felt more like ten. Before she knew it, the wrap-up light flashed in the back of the room, and she delivered the last punch line.

"That's it from me. My name is Stephanie Renshaw. Thank you so much, and enjoy the rest of the show." She handed the mic back to Gabe and walked offstage with a spring in her step.

The cheers and clapping only died down long after she had returned to the greenroom.

She had done it!

Her body still buzzed with adrenaline. She felt like spreading her arms wide and soaring all the way home.

But first, she had to stay and watch the headliner since it was considered rude to leave immediately after your part of the show was over. She hung out in the back of the showroom and craned her neck, trying to find Mr. Hicks. She couldn't wait to find out what he had thought of her set. But in the dim light, she couldn't make out the faces of the people around her. Talking to Mr. Hicks would have to wait until later.

A few minutes before the headliner's set ended, Steph snuck out to check on the merchandise table the club had allowed them to set up in the lobby. Her little corner of the table seemed untouched. Not that she had expected anything else with the great security at The Fun Zone.

Speaking of security… She glanced toward the front door to see if she could find Rae, but her roommate's familiar broad back was nowhere to be seen. Instead, Carlos was manning the door.

Did that mean Rae had been in the showroom during her routine? If yes, had she liked her set? A fleeting thought skittered through Steph's mind. Rae hadn't minded her jokes about living with a roommate, had she?

Cheers and applause interrupted her thoughts before she could contemplate it more fully.

The door to the showroom opened, and people began to file out. Several stopped by her table to tell her "great show" or to buy one of her signature painted-on tie T-shirts or a CD of one of her live shows.

An older man walked up to her. "You were very funny."

Steph smiled at him. "Thanks."

"I didn't think you'd be," he added, ruining his compliment, "because you look so cute."

Jeez, what was she supposed to say to that? She barely held herself back from answering, *I didn't think you'd be rude because you look so well-mannered.*

But apparently, he wasn't waiting for an answer anyway. "Let me tell you a story. It's hilarious. You can use it in your act."

Oh no. Steph had encountered people like that all over the country. It usually ended with her being stuck for half an hour while listening to a story that would have put an insomniac to sleep. She looked around for anyone who could help her out of her plight. Her gaze immediately zeroed in on Rae, who was walking toward her.

The crowd around her parted as if a force field of authority surrounded her.

Her face was impassive, and as she stepped up to the table, not a hint of familiarity warmed her eyes.

Damn, she should play professional poker.

"Can I talk to you for a second?" Without waiting for a reply, Rae grasped Steph's elbow and pulled her away from the table.

"Sorry," Steph said to the guy. "Official club business. I'm sure you understand." Once they were safely in the greenroom, Steph sank onto the couch. "Thanks for the rescue. He would have—"

"What the hell were you thinking?"

"Thinking?" What was Rae talking about?

Rae towered over her. "It's pretty obvious you weren't thinking at all, or you wouldn't have made me and my parents the laughingstock of the entire club."

"What are you talking about?"

"Are you being dense on purpose, or do you really think violating people's privacy for your comedy is perfectly fine?"

"Violating people's privacy?" Steph echoed. "Are you talking about the bit on life with a roommate?"

Rae huffed. "That answers that question. You are being dense on purpose."

"No, I'm not. I didn't think—"

"Yeah, we established that already."

Anger sparked alive in the pit of Steph's stomach. She got up but knew better than to approach Rae. "Would you at least let me defend myself?"

The muscles in Rae's jaw bunched. "I didn't have that chance when you talked about me on stage, so why should you get that chance now?"

Steph massaged her temples, where a painful pounding had started. "Listen, Rae. I think you're taking this the wrong way. Those jokes weren't even really aimed at—"

The door to the greenroom opened, and Mr. Hicks stepped inside. "Ah, there you are." His gaze went from Steph to Rae, and his forehead furrowed. "Is there a problem?"

"No, sir," Rae said, her voice even and her poker face firmly in place. "Just checking in with the comics to see if they're happy with how we handled seating."

"Ah. I like an employee who's taking the initiative, but don't worry about it. Most comedians aren't the shy type. They'll let you know if you do something they think is ruining their set." He gave her a pat on the shoulder that made Rae visibly stiffen even more.

"Everything was wonderful," Steph said to draw his attention away from Rae. "I always appreciate working with professionals, and your staff is among the best."

"Good to hear that." Mr. Hicks pulled an envelope from his suit jacket. "Your payment."

Steph took the envelope and opened it. A single one-hundred-dollar bill was tucked inside. That was more than the bar shows paid but still not a lot considering she had spent ten days preparing for tonight. But then again, she hadn't done it for the money but for the chance to prove herself to Mr. Hicks. "Thank you. So what did you think of my routine?"

He stroked his goatee. "I didn't get to listen in, but I'm sure it was fine."

It hit Steph like a punch to the gut. He hadn't listened to her set, not even to a part of it? Had he just used her to fill a vacant spot in the lineup instead of truly giving her a chance to prove herself?

He let out a chuckle and added, "If it wasn't, I'll hear about it. Trust me."

Steph's poker face was nowhere near as good as Rae's, so she struggled not to let her disappointment show. "Um, well, then, maybe next time."

"Sure." He nodded noncommittally and walked out, waving at Rae to follow him.

Before the door closed behind her, Rae turned her head and fixed Steph with a glare that told her the topic of the roommate jokes wasn't closed yet.

Steph flopped down onto the couch and buried her face in her hands. *Shit, shit, shit.* She kicked the pockmarked coffee table. She had worked nonstop for ten days to perfect her set, and to top it all off, she had pissed off Rae in the process—and it had all been for nothing. Her parents might be right after all. Maybe it was time for her to throw in the towel and think about what else she could do with her life.

The door opened. Had Rae come back to finish their discussion, if you could call it that?

"Sorry, Rae," Steph mumbled through her fingers, "but I'm really not in the mood to—"

"Steph Renshaw not being in the mood? That's a first." It wasn't Rae's voice; it was Gabe's.

Steph let her hands drop to her lap. "Very funny. You should be a comedian."

Gabe plopped onto the couch next to her and studied her. "You okay? Why aren't you out there, celebrating?" He nudged her with his shoulder. "You killed it tonight!"

"Yeah." It came out as a sigh. "This was the best set I had in forever. But apparently, it's not enough."

He tilted his head. "Enough for what?"

To make Rae forgive me, was the first thought that popped into Steph's head. What the hell? That shouldn't be what she was focusing on right now. "To convince Mr. Hicks that women can be funny and deserve to headline a show."

"Don't let that ass get you down. You've got more humor in your little finger than he's got in his entire body, including his ridiculous goatee. He'll see that eventually." Gabe stood and pulled her up with him. "Come on, I'll buy you a beer."

"Buy? You know the feature act gets a drink voucher."

"Okay, then you can buy me one." He pulled her out of the greenroom and over to the bar.

It was tempting—a little too tempting maybe. Steph had seen too many comics go down that road, drinking either to get over the pre-show nerves, celebrate a great set, or forget about a bad one. She had enough problems without acquiring another one. "Not tonight. All I want is to go home and crash."

"Man, you've become really domestic since you moved in with Rae." He paused. "You two aren't…?"

"No." Her lips twitched up into a sarcastic smile. "I'm getting all the fighting without the benefits of great make-up sex." She pressed the drink voucher into his hand. "Here. Wish me luck on surviving the night."

"What? Why wouldn't you survive the night?"

She waved dismissively. "Long story. See you tomorrow."

The air was heavy with impending rain as Steph stepped outside. There was no sign of Rae or most of her colleagues; only Carlos was still manning the door.

"Hey, you just missed your roomie." He gestured toward the lights of Melrose Avenue beyond the parking lot, then peered up at the night sky. "But you're just in time to get soaked."

Raindrops started to form patterns on the asphalt. "I'll be fine. I'm parked right here." After a quick wave at Carlos, she dashed toward her car and pressed the fob on her key. She dove behind the wheel and started the car while fishing for the seat belt with the other hand. For once, she couldn't wait to get away from the club.

Luckily, their apartment was only a two-minute drive from The Fun Zone. As she turned left onto their street, she caught sight of a tall figure striding along the sidewalk, hands stuffed into their pockets and head lowered to avoid the rain. Steph didn't need to see the person's face to know it was Rae. She knew the way Rae moved by now, plus her don't-talk-to-me vibes were palpable even from a distance.

For a second, Steph considered speeding past her without stopping. She wasn't up for further discussions. But they shared an apartment, so she couldn't escape Rae. She slowed the car to a near stop and lowered the driver's side window. "Rae," she shouted over the hum of the engine and the drumming of the rain.

Rae swiveled around, instantly on full alert.

"Just me," Steph shouted. "Hop in. I'll give you a ride home."

Rae continued walking. "No, thanks."

"Oh, come on. Don't punish me by punishing yourself."

Rae hesitated. After several seconds, she crossed the street and folded her tall frame into the passenger seat without saying a word.

Once Rae was settled, Steph guided the convertible down the long street. Since there was barely any traffic, she could take her eyes off the road to glance at Rae.

Rae had taken off her soaked-through suit jacket before getting into the car, probably so she wouldn't get the seat wet. Her shirt had become damp too and was clinging to her chest and powerful shoulders.

Stop ogling. You're fighting, remember? Steph redirected her attention to the street. Should she say something, explain why she had made their roommate arrangement part of her routine? Or was it better to wait until they were no longer trapped in the car together?

Before she could decide, they reached their apartment building.

Rae jumped out to open the gate—or maybe to escape her.

By the time Steph had parked the car in its assigned spot and walked around the building toward the front door, she was sure Rae had long since disappeared into her room.

But Rae was waiting outside, one foot in the front door to hold it open.

To protect and to serve. Apparently, Rae could never forget the motto of her former job. She wouldn't leave Steph behind on her own in the darkness, even when she was angry with her. Now Steph was glad she had stopped for Rae instead of letting her walk home in the rain.

They trudged up the stairs in silence, the tension between them rising with every step.

As soon as the door closed behind them, they swiveled and faced each other like two boxers hearing the bell at the beginning of a round.

Not good. This was way too confrontational. To break their adversarial stance, Steph walked to the kitchen to make some coffee. She wouldn't be sleeping tonight anyway. "Want some coffee?"

"I'd prefer an apology." Rae's tone was as cold and cutting as a steel blade.

Steph turned toward her.

Rae's wet hair, which now looked black, stuck to her skull. When she swiped a damp strand away from her forehead with an impatient motion, a bit of hair flopped to the other side, revealing a spot on her scalp where no hair grew.

It distracted Steph for a moment, and that annoyed her even more. "I won't apologize for doing my job. This is what I do, Rae. I use stuff from my life in my routine. If I didn't, I would end up with a string of generic jokes that are about as interesting as watching the home shopping channel."

Rae stormed past her, jerked the fridge open, and pulled out a bottle of water as if she needed it to cool down. "That's bullshit. You had a comedy routine long before you moved in with me. You don't need to humiliate me for other people's amusement."

"Humiliate?" Steph took a mug from the cupboard and slammed it down on the counter with a clunk. "Now you're exaggerating. I poked fun at myself more than I talked about you."

"I don't want you to poke fun at me at all," Rae shot back.

"I didn't. Not really. None of my jokes were really about you. It was just a hook so I could talk about the humorous situations that happen when a slob like me lives with someone who's more of a neat freak. Can't you see the humor in that?"

A growl rose from Rae's chest. "You called me a freak on stage?" She slammed the fridge door shut, whirled around, and took a step in Steph's direction before she was even fully facing her.

Thump!

She crashed into the cupboard door Steph had left open. The edge of the door caught her left temple and sent her sprawling onto the floor, where she sat with a stunned expression.

"Oh God, Rae!" Adrenaline zipped through Steph like an electric shock. "I'm so sorry. Did you hurt yourself?" She dropped to her knees next to her.

"I'm fine," Rae said, but she looked pretty dazed.

When she tried to get up, Steph put her hands on her shoulders. "Stay down. You might have a concussion."

Rae started to shake her head but then winced. "I had a concussion a couple of years ago. This is just a little bump." Despite her protests, she stayed put as Steph leaned closer to examine her.

"Let me see." Steph gently took hold of Rae's chin and turned her head so she could see. The skin wasn't broken, so there was no blood, but an area on the left side of her forehead was starting to swell. Steph winced in sympathy and barely resisted the urge to stroke Rae's cheek to soothe away the pain. She doubted Rae would appreciate that. "Shit. You're starting to get a goose egg. We need to put some ice on it. Wait here."

Rae grumbled but didn't try to get up as Steph went to the freezer. She couldn't find any ice, so she grabbed the first halfway suitable item she encountered.

"Raspberries?" Rae raised her brows, then flinched, probably as the movement tugged on the skin of her forehead.

"They're good for your health." Steph wrapped the frozen berries into a dish towel, knelt again, and gently held them to Rae's forehead.

Rae brushed away Steph's hands and took over applying the improvised cold pack. "Shit. I told you a thousand times not to leave the damn cupboard open."

"I'm really sorry, Rae. But how on earth did you manage to not see it? It was right there."

Rae gave her a dark glare. "Yeah, right there—for someone with two functioning eyes."

They stared at each other. Rae looked as stunned by what she had just revealed as Steph felt.

"You mean you…you don't see very well in one eye?"

"I don't see anything at all on this side." Rae tapped her left eye. It sounded as if she had rapped her fingernails against the hard surface of the kitchen counter.

A spiraling sensation spread through Steph's stomach. She gulped heavily. "Oh my God! You have a glass eye? Why didn't you tell me?"

Rae snorted. "Why would I? So you can use it in your routine too?"

The impact of Rae's words hit Steph like a slap. She fell back onto her ass on the floor. "Jesus, Rae. Do you really think that little of me?"

"How would I know?" Rae mumbled. "Everything seems to be a joke to you, so why would this be off limits?"

Steph's eyes started to burn. *Oh, come on.* She had heard it all before, even from her own sister, and she had always shrugged it off. This shouldn't be any different, but somehow it was. "I would never…"

Rae waved her away. "Yeah, yeah." With one hand still holding the raspberries to her head, she climbed to her feet.

Steph stayed seated on the floor for several moments longer. She felt dazed, as if she had been the one who'd been hit in the head. When Rae moved past her toward her room, Steph quickly jumped up. "Rae, wait!"

Her shoulders so tense as if she were bracing for an attack, Rae turned around.

"Are you sure you don't want me to take you to get checked out?" Steph gestured at the goose egg on Rae's forehead.

"I'm sure." The door clicked shut behind Rae but then opened again not even two seconds later.

Steph looked up with a hopeful gaze as Rae returned to the kitchen. Was Rae ready to talk? Not that Steph knew what to say. The revelation about Rae's eye had caught her off guard.

But Rae only walked up to the plastic water bottle she'd dropped earlier. Before she could bend to pick it up, Steph quickly did it for her.

"Thanks." Without another word, Rae marched back to her room. This time, the door remained shut.

It was three o'clock in the morning, but Steph was wide-awake and pacing around her room. A thousand different thoughts seemed to be bouncing around in her head, keeping her up.

She closed her left eye and tried to imagine what life with one eye might be like. The dresser and the bookcase disappeared from her field of vision.

Now a lot of things she hadn't understood about Rae suddenly made sense: why she sometimes startled when Steph stepped up to her from the left, why she always did a little dance to keep Steph on her right, and why she had seemingly ignored her the day Steph had watched her tossing a tennis ball.

It hurt to think that she might never find out how Rae experienced the world because Rae would refuse to ever talk to her about anything even halfway private again. Was Rae overreacting, or had Steph really crossed a line during tonight's show?

She hadn't thought so at the time, but maybe she needed to take a look at the recording to make sure.

Gabe had recorded her performance for her, but he probably wouldn't upload the video to her YouTube channel before tomorrow. That was why she had recorded the audio so she could go over the set before heading to bed. She crossed the room and dug through her jacket pockets to retrieve her phone. When she couldn't find it, she checked the kitchen and the hall.

Nothing.

She tried to remember when she'd last seen her phone. *Shit.* She had placed it on the stool up on stage to record her set but couldn't remember handling it afterward. In the excitement of the show and then the chaos following it, she must have forgotten it at the club and could only hope that someone from the staff had found it and locked it up securely until she could get it.

Steph flopped down on her bed and stared up at the ceiling. Great. What a shitty end to a shitty evening!

Chapter 11

WHEN STEPH'S ALARM WENT OFF, she let out a groan. She couldn't have slept more than a couple of hours and would have given a kidney to be able to stay in bed. Should she call in sick? The thought was tempting, but she had her first dog-walking appointment of the day at nine and she had promised Penny she wouldn't leave her in the lurch again.

She wouldn't be able to call Penny anyway, since she had left her phone at the club.

Wait a minute! If her phone was at the club, how could the alarm on her cell have woken her up?

She swung her legs out of bed and padded through the apartment, following the sound of her alarm that was still going off.

It was coming from the kitchen, where she found the phone sitting on the breakfast bar.

Steph picked it up, turned off the alarm, and stared at the cell. Had she taken it home after all? No. She had checked the kitchen last night, and the phone hadn't been there.

Rae. She must have found it on stage after the show and had probably forgotten to give it back to Steph once they had started arguing. Or had she purposefully kept it because she was angry with her?

No, that wasn't Rae's style.

Steph checked the counter and the breakfast bar. No note from Rae. The door to her room was open, revealing that her bed was made and Rae gone. Her running shoes were missing from the hall. Had she really gone on a run the morning after taking quite the bump to the head?

The thought made Steph's stomach churn. But even if she had known Rae's preferred jogging route, she had no time to check up on her. It would probably make Rae even angrier anyway.

Steph buried her fingers in her tousled hair. God, when had her life become so complicated? She had always thought she could avoid emotional convolutions if she stayed out of relationships, but apparently, moving in with a woman just as roommates was enough to complicate things.

Rae went all out, racing to beat her own personal record as she hurtled down the hilly path. She had discovered Pan Pacific Park the week after moving in with Steph, and while the loop around the park wasn't a real challenge for her, she still came here every now and then to hit the outdoor gym area.

It was peaceful here if she managed to come at the right time of day. In the center of the park, she couldn't even hear the traffic sounds, and if not for a couple of palm trees, she could almost forget that she was in the middle of LA. Normally, she found the atmosphere soothing, but today, even the third loop didn't help to clear her head, no matter how fast she ran. She slowed as she passed the baseball field and dodged a woman with a stroller.

The fitness equipment had been set up on top of a hill so Rae had a good view of most of the park as she settled down on the ab bench and started doing crunches. A stand of trees blocked her sight of the unheated pool, but she knew it was there and still felt its pull. She imagined gliding through the water, putting her face down, and forgetting everything around her—everything that had happened last night.

But the pool was closed in winter, so the illusion didn't last. She wasn't doing laps—hadn't been for many months—and who knew when she would work up the courage to jump into a pool again? There was no medical reason she couldn't; she knew that. With the exception of fast-paced ball games that required good depth perception, there wasn't much she couldn't do if she put her mind to it. But she wouldn't be able to see if another swimmer crossed into her lane from the left. Worse, what if her prosthesis slipped out? Her ocularist assured her it wasn't very likely, but she'd done some research on a forum for people who'd lost one eye, and it had happened to one or two of them. While her swimming goggles would contain the prosthesis, she wouldn't be able to put it back in while in the pool. Her stomach churned at the thought of other people seeing her empty socket. Rae imagined them staring in horror—just as Steph had stared at her last night.

Her head started to pound at the memory of crashing into the cupboard door. Fuck, that had been so embarrassing, but even worse was that she had slipped up and told Steph about the eye. How the hell had that happened? She had never told anyone, not even by accident. Her boss knew, of course, but her colleagues had no clue, and she wanted to keep it that way.

Now that might not be an option.

She lay back onto the bench and stared up into the hazy sky.

Despite what she had said in anger last night, she didn't really believe that Steph would make up a comedy routine about her one-eyed roommate. But if Steph told her friend Gabe, it wouldn't be long before all the comedians knew, and then it was only a matter of time before the club staff would hear about it. Would her colleagues still trust her to have their backs once they knew she was blind in one eye?

Something cold and wet touched the bare bend of her elbow, nearly making her fall off the bench. She swiveled her head around.

A massive dog loomed in front of her, sniffing up her arm. With its shaggy fur and large head, it looked more like a bear than a canine.

Oh shit. Rae went very still. Who the hell had let that monster off its leash?

The cold, black nose wandered up her arm. Luckily, the dog's body language didn't seem threatening, just curious.

"Hi there," Rae said, keeping her tone friendly and soothing.

The dog stopped its sniffing, tilted its massive head to one side, and studied her. It didn't look as if it were scouting out its next meal.

Just as Rae prepared to carefully sit up, the dog enthusiastically licked her cheek.

"Ugh." Rae quickly sat up and buried her hands in the dog's thick fur to push it back. "Shouldn't you buy me dinner first?"

The dog pushed forward, into her hands, urging her to pet it.

Rae obliged. Wow, its fur was incredibly thick and soft, even though it was on the short side. She scratched behind its floppy ears, and for the first time all day, a smile curved her lips as petting the dog did what even her workout hadn't managed to do: finally relaxing her a little. "You're a big cuddle bug, aren't you?"

The dog let out a contented groan.

Rae looked around for its owner. Someone had to miss this teddy bear of a dog.

Running steps approached from around a bend of the path. "Moose!" an out-of-breath woman called.

The dog's floppy ears perked up.

"Moose, huh?" Rae said. Somehow, it fit the big dog. "I think that's you."

A slender woman barreled around the corner, her blonde hair flying around her head in wild waves. A cloud of sand dust rose up as she skidded to a stop in front of Rae.

Rae's gaze slid up a pair of killer legs in tight jeans, wandered over full breasts revealed by a formfitting V-neck shirt and an open leather jacket—and then froze on the woman's face. "Steph?"

"Rae?"

"What are you doing here?" they said in unison.

Steph couldn't believe it. Of all the people in the park, Moose had escaped to her roommate! Her very sweaty, very sexy, and probably still very angry roommate, who would get even angrier if she noticed Steph ogling the nice curve of her biceps and the way her damp shirt clung to her breasts and shoulders. It took some effort to tear her gaze away.

"I'm working out," Rae said.

"I noticed," Steph murmured. "Um, I mean, yeah, that's pretty obvious." She gestured at the workout equipment.

"What are you doing here?" Rae asked.

Steph pointed at Moose, who had settled his big head onto Rae's knee and was clearly in canine heaven as Rae massaged his ears. "I'm walking this big lug."

"Looks like he's walking you, not the other way around," Rae commented.

Heat climbed up Steph's neck. "I don't normally let him off his leash, but there aren't many people around today, and Moose isn't exactly a sprinter, so I thought it would be fine. But when I got a drink from the water fountain, he made his escape."

Rae squinted down at the dog, never stopping her caresses. "He's not yours, is he?"

Steph laughed. "You think I'm somehow hiding a dog of his size in our apartment?" She shook her head. "I'm a part-time dog walker, and he's my favorite client."

"I can see why." When Rae looked down at the dog, her expression softened in a way Steph had never seen before.

"You like dogs." Steph wasn't sure why she was so pleased at that observation, but she was.

Rae shrugged. "Who doesn't? Most of the time, I like animals better than people." She slid her long fingers through the shaggy fur along Moose's massive neck. "What breed is he?"

"He's a labernard. A mix between a Saint Bernard and a Lab."

Rae's gaze went from the dog to Steph, and again Steph noticed that her left eye didn't move as much as the right. But now she knew it wasn't a lazy eye. She had so many questions. Was she allowed to ask any of them?

When Rae paused in her caresses, Moose jumped up and licked her face to encourage her to continue.

"Moose, no!" Steph clipped his leash back on and managed to drag him away a few inches to give Rae some space.

Rae wiped her face with the sleeve of her T-shirt. "Yuck."

The look on her face made Steph laugh. "Don't worry. He rarely drinks from the toilet."

"Hahaha."

Steph offered her one of the baby wipes she always kept on hand when she walked her canine clients and watched Rae clean her face. Her playful mood disappeared when she noticed the pink-purplish bruise that had formed on Rae's forehead. "Does it hurt?"

"Nah. It's just slobber."

"No, I mean the bruise."

Rae's expression closed. "Not worth mentioning."

"I think it is," Steph said. "I think we should talk about it."

Rae looked as if she would rather be slobbered by Moose again than talk to her. "Nothing to talk about. Just don't tell anyone it wasn't some burly six-foot guy who gave me that shiner." She attempted a crooked smile but didn't pull it off at all. "Being knocked out by a cupboard door would be bad for my street cred."

Steph gave her a look. "Who's making a joke of everything now?" For the first time, she understood why her sister constantly told her how annoying it was. She gently bumped Rae with her elbow. "Come on. You know I'm right. If we don't talk about it, we'll start to tiptoe around each other as if walking on eggshells. I can't imagine you want that either."

Finally, Rae heaved a sigh and got up from the ab bench. "All right." She wadded up the baby wipe and tossed it in the direction of a garbage can. Even though her shooting form was perfect, she missed by a foot.

Was that a side effect of having only one eye? Steph held back the question. Instead, she walked over to the baby wipe, picked it up, and tossed it into the trash.

"Thanks," Rae mumbled.

With Moose happily lumbering along between them, they followed the path. Even though she had told Rae she wanted to talk, Steph now found herself not knowing what to say.

Rae didn't seem to be in any hurry to start this conversation either. She stopped at a water fountain, and Steph tried not to be too obvious about observing her as Rae swallowed a few mouthfuls of water. How in the world could anyone look sexy while doing something so simple as drinking water?

Once Rae had quenched her thirst, they continued.

"Let's sit down over there." Steph pointed at a picnic table and led the way toward it. She flopped down on a bench, then remembered that Rae wouldn't be able to see her if she sat on her left. Quickly, she slid over so she would be on Rae's good side. This would take some getting used to, but she silently vowed to make things as easy as possible on Rae.

Rae gave her the tiniest nod of appreciation and settled down at the other end of the bench, with as much space as possible between them.

Moose looked back and forth between them, then flopped down on a patch of grass in the middle and rested his muzzle on Steph's shoes. His contented sigh filled the silence between them.

Steph waited for Rae to speak, but after a while realized that she would have to take the first step. "So," she cleared her throat and took refuge in the familiarity of flirty teasing, "is this the part where we kiss and make up?"

The corners of Rae's mouth didn't curl up, not even a fraction of an inch. But despite her gruff expression, something changed in her posture—an almost imperceptible softening that Steph probably would have missed a month ago. "You wish."

"Can't blame a girl for trying." Steph sobered and tried to catch Rae's gaze. "But I know I'm to blame for other things. I'm sorry I left the cupboard open. I thought you were being anal about wanting all the cupboards to be closed and everything put away immediately."

"Well, to be fair, my parents would probably tell you I am anal. I've always been a lot neater than them, but for the most part, that's just how I avoid bumping into things on my blind side."

Blind side... The words echoed through Steph's mind, leaving tiny shock waves in their wake. She still couldn't believe it. Even though she had figured there was something not quite right with Rae's eye, she would have never in a million years guessed that she had no sight in it at all.

Rae bent and stroked Moose's side as if not wanting to look at Steph. "Ask," she said in a let's-get-this-over-with tone, never glancing up.

Steph hesitated. It wasn't that she didn't have any questions; she had too many of them. Plus somehow this felt as if she was being tested. If she asked the wrong question, Rae would clam up like an oyster. Finally, Steph settled on the first question that popped into her mind—okay, the second. She sensed that Rae wasn't ready to talk about what Steph really wanted to know: how she had lost her eye. "What do you need from me?"

Rae straightened and faced her for the first time since they had sat down. "Need?" She looked so puzzled as if Steph had asked about her favorite sex position.

Interesting images involving lots of naked skin shot through Steph's mind at the thought. *Focus,* she firmly told herself. "Yeah, need. Other than making sure I close all cabinets from now on, is there anything you need me to do—or not do—to help you?"

"I don't need help," Rae said gruffly.

"Everyone needs help sometimes, Rae. That doesn't make you weak." Great, now she was sounding like her parents or her sister.

Rae shrugged. "I can't think of anything. Close the cabinets and approach me from the right, and we'll be fine."

Steph nodded and waited, but Rae didn't add anything. Was there really nothing else, or did Rae just not want to tell her because she didn't trust her?

"Now can I ask you something?" Rae broke the renewed silence.

"Sure."

Rae gestured at her left eye. "Could you really not tell?"

"That you're blind in that eye?"

"That it's fake."

"No. It looks incredibly real." Steph studied Rae's eyes, comparing the left to the right. They weren't completely symmetrical, with the left one being a tiny bit bigger, but then again, most people's eyes weren't entirely equal. The color of the iris was the same, though, right down to the tiny flecks of amber that Steph had admired before. "Even now I have to think for a moment to remember which one is real and which one is the glass eye."

A near smile brightened Rae's tense features.

Hadn't anyone told her how good the eye looked before? Well, Steph could imagine Rae didn't often let people close enough to study her eye in detail, much less ask questions about it.

"Acrylic," Rae finally said. "Prosthetic eyes are no longer made of glass. They hand-paint the iris to make it a perfect match to the other eye. They even form the blood vessels in the white of the eye with tiny red silk fibers." A hint of fascination shone through Rae's grouchy exterior.

"Wow. Whoever did yours was a true artist."

Rae smoothed her fingers over the pockmark-like scars on her forehead. "Yeah." A visible shiver went through her.

At first, Steph thought talking about her prosthetic eye had brought up unpleasant memories, but when Rae hugged her goose-bump-covered arms to her chest, she realized that Rae was probably just getting cold. Now that she was no longer working out, her body was cooling down. The short sleeves of her T-shirt ended above her biceps, and the breeze up on the hill pressed the damp material to her chest. Steph tried not to notice the way

Rae's hardened nipples poked through the cotton. She shrugged out of her leather jacket and held it out to Rae. "Here."

Rae stared at her without reaching for the jacket.

"You're cold," Steph added.

Rae continued to stare. Then a smile tugged on her lips. "Um, thanks, but I don't think that will fit me. Even if it did, I wouldn't want to get it all sweaty."

"Oh, getting sweaty can be fun." Steph flashed her a grin. Retreating into familiar jokes was a relief.

Rae rolled her eyes...or rather one of them since the left one didn't move all the way up.

Steph was very aware of how overly aware of it she was. She hoped that would lessen with time since she didn't want to make Rae feel self-conscious.

"I think I'll go home before your one-liners become even worse." Rae stood.

"Yeah, it's time for me to get back too. Moose's hour is up." Steph got up and shrugged back into her leather jacket.

With Moose trotting between them, his long, bushy tail swinging from side to side, they left the park. Once they reached Beverly Boulevard, with four lanes of traffic rolling past them, Steph gripped Moose's leash more tightly. They walked several blocks in silence, with only traffic sounds and the soft jingle of Moose's dog tags accompanying them.

Finally, when they stopped at a red pedestrian light, Steph glanced over at Rae. There was one last thing she had to say, as much as she would have preferred to avoid it. "About last night..."

Rae stuffed her hands more deeply into the pockets of her running shorts, as if wanting to hide as much of herself as possible. For someone who was so physically strong, she could appear quite vulnerable at times. "Yeah?"

"Were the roommate jokes I told really that bad?" She had tried to keep them on the tame side, without going into any really personal details.

The light turned green, but Rae didn't move across the intersection. She turned toward Steph and heaved a sigh. "I only listened to one, so I don't know about the rest, but—"

"Wait a minute! You barely even listened, yet you ripped me a new asshole for violating your privacy?" Steph put her leash-free hand on her hip. "What the hell, Rae!"

"Oh no. You don't get to be indignant. You're not the wronged party here."

Steph refused to let herself be intimidated by Rae's glare. "How do you know you are if you haven't heard most of what I said?"

"I heard enough to know I didn't like it," Rae shot back.

Moose let out a low woof as if sensing the rising tension between them.

Steph put her hand on his head, petting him, and tried to soften her stance. "This is getting us nowhere. We're scaring poor Moose."

Rae reached out too, and their fingers brushed as both stroked the same spot behind his ear at the same time. She withdrew and stuffed her hand into her pocket. "Sorry," she mumbled.

Was she apologizing for upsetting Moose or for the accidental touch?

"It's okay," Steph said. "I don't want to argue with you. I just want you to understand. The jokes weren't really about you. They are about situations my audience can relate to, like living with someone who's your total opposite."

"Well, next time you want to talk about that, don't use me. Make something up."

Steph shook her head. "That's not how stand-up works. You've got to be authentic."

Rae faced her without the slightest softening. "Then find another way to be authentic. If there's one thing I hate, it's being made fun of in public." When Steph opened her mouth, she lifted her hand. "I know you think I'm overreacting, and maybe you're right, but I've been teased about my parents and their lifestyle as a kid, and I won't let you do it a second time."

Ah. So that was why Rae had become so defensive. "I'm sorry. I had no idea. If I had known it would bring up bad memories…"

Rae waved off the apology. "It's not just about my parents. Promise not to make me a topic of your routine again."

Steph had never made a promise like that to anyone since she hadn't wanted to restrict her creative freedom. But now that she knew part of why Rae was so strict about putting stuff away in the apartment, she could no longer joke about it anyway. "All right."

"You promise?"

"I promise. Cross my heart and hope to die." Steph ran her thumb across her chest. "Stick a needle in my…" She bit back the *eye* at the last second. "Uh…"

"God, you really suffer from a bad case of foot-in-mouth disease, don't you?" To Steph's surprise, a hint of amusement colored Rae's tone.

Steph hid her overly warm face behind her hand. "Yeah, a pretty severe case. I'm sorry."

Rae shook her head. "I don't want you to have to watch every word you say to me."

"So you want me to watch what I say on stage, not at home?"

"Exactly."

"Okay." But Steph promised herself to be a little more careful with her thoughtless remarks anyway. Her family might think she was incapable of being tactful, but she could be considerate if she wanted to, couldn't she?

They reached the corner where Steph had to turn right to drop off Moose at his owner's place, while Rae needed to continue on to get back to their apartment. Steph slowed her steps and pointed. "Moose lives over there."

Rae hesitated. "Want me to wait?"

Steph considered it for a moment. But she needed to feed Moose and take photos of him to send to his owner along with her daily report. It wouldn't have been fair to keep Rae from her shower any longer. Plus she sensed that Rae probably needed some time alone to recover from the conversation. "No, that's fine. I'll see you at home."

Rae nodded and ran her hand over Moose's head one last time. "You be good, big guy."

He let out a soft whine as if he understood that this was goodbye.

"Rae?" Steph heard herself say before Rae could walk away. She hadn't planned to speak, but at the same time, she knew the question would ricochet through her mind until she finally asked it.

"Yes?" Rae looked over warily. She probably knew what was coming.

"You…you mentioned being…" Steph swallowed against the lump in her throat. "Being shot. Is that how…?"

"Yeah."

Steph had suspected what the answer would be, but hearing it still made a giant fist clench around her stomach.

Rae lifted her hand, either in a wave goodbye or in a gesture to stop further questions. "See you at home." As she strode down Beverly Boulevard, Moose gave a strong tug on his leash, trying to follow her.

Steph hopped to keep her balance and dug her heels in. Her arm muscles strained against his pull on the leash. "Moose, no. We're going this way."

Moose grumbled but plopped his behind down on the asphalt next to her. They both watched Rae's retreating form until other pedestrians blocked their view.

Chapter 12

"Wow. Grandmas sure aren't what they used to be." Rae stared after the elderly lady to whom she had just handed her purse back—minus a big bottle of bourbon Granny had tried to smuggle into the club.

Carlos whistled. "And my *abuela* always insists that in her day and age, women didn't use to drink like men."

Rae shrugged. "It's the twenty-first century. Women can do pretty much everything men can."

"Including getting the shit beaten out of them." Carlos eyed the bruise on Rae's forehead, which, four days later, had darkened to a bluish purple. "Man, I'm always missing all the fun! The one time I take some time off, something like this happens."

"It didn't happen at the club," Rae said.

Carlos waved through several patrons. "Then what happened?"

No way would she reveal how she had gotten that bruise. Rae gave him a pointed look. "I got into a fistfight with the last person who kept asking me questions. He looks a lot worse than this."

"Very funny. You've been living with that comedian for too long. Her sense of humor is rubbing off on you. Oh hey, speaking of the devil… Your girlfriend's here." He jerked his chin toward the crowd lined up in front of the club.

Rae swiveled her head to look in that direction.

Her gaze immediately zeroed in on Steph, who stood toward the end of the line in a pair of curve-hugging jeans and an equally tight-fitting, black T-shirt that had a pink tie painted on it. On most people, Rae would have found the outfit silly, but on Steph, it just worked.

"She's not my girlfriend," Rae said but kept glancing at Steph, who said something to the people in front of her and then slid past them to make it to the front of the line.

Steph stopped slightly to Rae's right so Rae didn't have to turn her head to look at her, but otherwise, she didn't treat her any different than before finding out about the eye, as Rae had first feared.

"What are you doing here?" Rae asked. Steph hadn't mentioned a gig at The Fun Zone.

Steph batted her eyelashes. "Maybe I missed you."

"Yeah, sure."

"Okay, okay. Looks like your MC canceled at the last minute, so Mr. Hicks called me, and I came straight from a nursing home's holiday party."

Rae raised her brows. "Isn't the MC spot considered a step back after being the feature act?" Selling herself under worth didn't seem like Steph at all.

Steph flashed an impish grin. "It is. So I told him I'd only do it in exchange for a chance at another feature spot. One that he'll hopefully watch this time."

Ah. Yes, that seemed more like Steph. Rae gave her a nod of approval.

"So, can I go in, or do you want to search me first?" Steph teasingly spread her arms away from her body.

Rae couldn't help it; her gaze darted to that tight T-shirt again. Annoyed with herself, she wrenched her gaze away.

"I could do it," Carlos piped up next to her.

Rae sent him a glare that promised to turn him into a puddle should he as much as reach for Steph.

"Uh, on second thought, I think we can skip the pat-down this time, seeing as Rae is your roomie and all." Carlos waved her through.

Steph tipped an imaginary hat. "Thanks." She walked past them into the club.

They both turned and watched her for a second.

"She's cute," Carlos commented.

Rae grunted noncommittally. *Yeah, if you go for smart-asses with a sexy grin and hair that always looks like she just crawled out of bed.* Wait a minute... Had she just thought of Steph's grin as sexy?

"If she's not your girlfriend, do you mind if I ask her out?" Carlos asked.

A growl rose up Rae's chest. "Do I look like I'm the manager of her love life? Besides, didn't you say you have a girlfriend?"

Carlos shrugged. "We broke up."

He didn't look heartbroken at all. Did people nowadays really get over failed relationships so easily? When Lise had walked out, Rae hadn't even looked at other women for a year or more.

Brandon joined them at the front door and gave Carlos a pat on the shoulder. "Why don't you help me keep an eye on the showroom before you get yourself into trouble?"

"I'll do it," Rae said before Carlos could answer. She wanted to watch Steph on stage—only to make sure there were no more jokes about roommates, of course.

Not that Steph had a lot of opportunity to do many of her own jokes tonight. She had her hands full making the announcements Mr. Hicks wanted her to make, introducing the other comics, and dealing with a heckler who seemed to have it out for her. The asshole hadn't opened his big mouth at all when the feature act had bombed, but when Steph took the stage again, Rae could almost feel the guy getting ready to interrupt once again.

Too bad that he was in Brandon's part of the room, where she couldn't get to him.

Steph gave the audience a wide-eyed look and gazed at where the feature act had disappeared. "Wow. That was like watching the Titanic sink, wasn't it?"

In the beginning, Rae had been stunned by the way comedians seemed to bad-mouth their colleagues. On the force, cops always stuck up for each other—even for the ones you didn't like. But in her nearly two months at the comedy club, she had learned that it had nothing to do with bad-mouthing. If Steph didn't address her colleague's bombing in some way, the show would become inauthentic—or, worse, the audience would start to expect that this was normal and the following comics would be just as bad.

"Including watching Leonardo die because Kate was hogging the damn door," Steph added.

The audience chuckled.

"Yeah, like you are hogging the microphone," the heckler shouted. "Give it to someone who's funny and original!"

Rae clenched her hand around the walkie-talkie and tried to make out his exact position in the dim light. "Hey, Brandon," she said into the walkie-talkie. "Did you fall asleep? Kick that piece of shit out!"

"And have Steph kill me after the show?" Brandon's voice came through her earpiece. "Cool your jets, and give her a chance to handle him."

Rae knew he was right, but standing back and letting other people handle a problem wasn't her strong suit. She was used to taking control. Under the pretense of getting out of the way of a waitress with a tray, she positioned herself closer to the heckler and watched Steph for any signs that she wanted them to intervene.

But Steph didn't seem intimidated at all. She gazed down at the guy like a preschool teacher talking to an unruly toddler. "Oh, let me guess. You mean someone like you?"

"Hell, yes!"

"I'd invite you to join me up on stage since you clearly need the attention, but honestly, I think therapy might be a better solution for you," Steph said. "If you come see me after the show, I can recommend someone."

The guy let out a roar. "Fuck you!"

"Now who's unoriginal?"

Steph's quick-witted response made laughter ripple through the room. The audience was clearly on her side, and when the heckler realized that there was no glory to gain, he finally shut up.

Rae kept a close watch on him during the rest of the show, but he didn't interrupt again, and Rae even caught him laughing at a joke Steph made. *Not funny, my ass!*

Finally, the late show ended, and the audience filed out.

The guy took his time getting up and wandering to the exit, so Rae hung back too and followed him out into the lobby.

Steph was posing for a photo with the two other comics and a woman from the audience, and the guy headed straight for her.

Adrenaline pounded through Rae's veins. She lengthened her stride to catch up with him and firmly closed her hand around his arm. "The exit is this way, sir."

He swayed a little as he whirled around and tried to jerk his arm from her grip, but Rae held tight. "What the fuck?" From up close, Rae could smell the booze on his breath. "Let go!"

"Just preventing you from slipping and falling on the way out, sir." Rae gave him a grin that she knew resembled a snarl more than a friendly smile.

"I wasn't on my way out. I want a photo with her too." He stabbed his finger in Steph's direction.

Over my dead body. Rae was tempted to grab the offending finger. "Sorry. All out of photos."

Brandon and Carlos walked over and took up positions on either side of Rae. Even though she normally didn't like having someone to her left, it felt good to have backup.

The guy cursed all the way to the front door, but with the three of them towering over him, he didn't have a chance. Within a minute, they had him outside, where the cool night air would hopefully help sober him up.

When Rae went back inside, Steph had finished taking photos and came over to her. "What was that?"

Rae gave her a blank look. "What was what?"

"You're not fooling me for a second." Steph lightly put her hand on Rae's arm, then withdrew as if only now becoming aware of the touch. "Thank you."

"Just doing my job."

Steph looked around the now nearly empty lobby. "I think we can get out of here in a minute. Wanna get something to eat?"

Rae hesitated. She hadn't planned on socializing with her roommate that often, and after Steph had found out about her eye, being around her felt a little awkward, but if she accompanied Steph wherever she wanted to go, at least she could make sure the heckler wasn't waiting for her somewhere. "Yeah, sure."

With her shitty night vision and the potholes in the asphalt, Rae had gotten used to crossing the club's parking lot with care, but Steph grabbed her sleeve and dragged her toward the Mini Cooper convertible. "Come on, come on! We have to hurry."

"Whoa!" Rae wasn't willing to admit that she could barely see a thing, so she tried to keep up with her roommate. "Is whatever place you're dragging me to going to run out of food?"

"No, but they close at one." Steph unlocked the car and had the key in the ignition before Rae had managed to fold herself into the passenger side.

In the interior light of the car, Rae glanced at her wristwatch. "Um, it's a quarter to one."

"Don't worry. We'll make it. I have this down to an art form." Steph started the car and navigated east on Melrose.

Rae had always hated being in the passenger seat. After a dozen years of riding together, Mike had all but given up his attempts to convince her to let him drive every now and then. Now she hated it even more because being in the passenger seat put the driver in her blind spot. But she didn't have a choice right now. She didn't have her car, and even if she had it, driving after dark was stressful at best and dangerous at worst. She slid her seat back and turned as much as possible so she could see Steph. Her hands were pressed to her thighs in an attempt not to grab hold of the door handle.

Steph flicked her gaze over at her. "I'm not speeding, officer."

"I know."

"Then relax. I swear I'm a good driver. I won't kill you in my quest for a Double-Double."

Rae didn't want to focus on how uncomfortable she felt, so she chose to focus on something else. "Of all the places in LA, you're taking me to In-N-Out?"

"Of course. I'm a Californian, so I'm culturally indoctrinated to love them." Steph made a left onto La Brea. "Don't tell me you don't?"

Rae shrugged. "I wouldn't know. I've never had their burgers."

"What?" Steph stared at her as if she had confessed to never having had sex. "We definitely have to remedy that." Within another minute, she pulled into the drive-through lane of the fast-food restaurant and rolled down her window. "Do you trust me to order for you?"

"Um…" Rae knew it was just burgers, not a life-or-death decision, but letting someone else have control, even that little bit, made her uncomfortable.

Steph laughed and held up her hands. "Jeez, okay, order your own. What do you want?"

Rae craned her neck to make out the menu board that was posted in her blind spot. "Guess I'll take a Double-Double and some fries."

"You need a milkshake too," Steph said.

"I do?"

Steph nodded decisively. "Can't have a burger without a milkshake. Try the Neapolitan. That's what I'll be having."

"Neapolitan? What's that?"

"Vanilla, strawberry, and chocolate shake all mixed together." Steph licked her lips. "It's the best."

A shiver went through Rae. She shook herself. "Ugh, no, thanks. I'll stick with vanilla." Before Steph could open her mouth to make the obvious joke about her choice of milkshake, Rae shot her a warning glance. "Don't even think about it."

"About what?" Steph looked back at her with the innocent expression of a choir girl.

"Welcome to In-N-Out," a male voice came through the drive-through speaker. "What can I get you tonight?"

Steph rattled off her order so fast that Rae could barely follow, but the guy didn't seem to have a problem catching everything.

Since they were about to close, it didn't take long before a bag of food was passed through the drive-through window. Steph handed it to Rae and put the two milkshakes into the cup holders between their seats.

When Rae pulled out her wallet to pay, Steph waved her away. "I've got this. You can get it next time."

Rae gave her a quizzical look. "Who said there'll be a next time?"

"Wait until you try the burger."

Rae hadn't referred only to eating at In-N-Out again but also to having dinner with Steph. How had it suddenly become a given that they'd hang out again?

Instead of driving home, as Rae had expected, Steph navigated the car across the parking lot and parked at the far end, away from the two or three other cars. She slid her seat back as if preparing for a big feast. "The fries will get cold if we don't eat them right away."

Rae bit back a sigh. By the time they got home, she would either have a permanent indentation in her thigh from where the middle console pressed into her leg when she turned in her seat, or she'd have a cramp in her neck from craning it so she could see Steph.

"Something wrong?" Steph asked. "Would you rather eat at home?"

"Here is fine." Rae hesitated. But suffering in silence was silly, especially since Steph had realized how uncomfortable she was. "Um, could we switch seats while we eat?"

"Why would you…? Oh!" Steph slapped her forehead. "I'm so sorry. I should have realized." She scrambled out of the car and circled around to the passenger side.

"Thanks," Rae said as they passed each other. She settled into the driver's seat and exhaled quietly. Yes, that felt a lot better.

"No thanks necessary. Next time I don't realize something like this, please tell me." Steph took the paper bag from Rae and opened it.

The scent of sizzling meat drifted up, and Rae's stomach responded with a loud grumble.

Steph laughed and pressed a wrapped burger into Rae's hands. "Here, before you start nibbling on me."

"I don't nibble."

Steph grinned. "Ooh, so you're more of a biter?"

Rae threw her a look but didn't grace her shameless flirting with a reply. She unwrapped her burger, lifted up the top bun, and studied the slice of tomato and the grilled onions for a moment before taking a careful bite. The aroma of juicy meat, the tang of pickles, and the sweetness of ketchup mingled on her tongue. She couldn't help letting out a low moan as she chewed.

Steph paused with her own burger halfway to her mouth. "Good?"

"I've had worse," Rae said as soon as she had swallowed.

"Oh, come on." Steph reached across the middle console and lightly slapped her shoulder.

At least now that Steph sat on her right side, Rae could see it coming and wasn't startled by the sudden touch.

"It's great," Steph said. "Admit it."

Instead of a reply, Rae took a big bite of her burger. It was certainly better than the microwaved piece of cardboard that Mike had sometimes gotten them when it was his turn to pick where they'd have lunch.

Paper rustled as Steph pulled her box of fries from the bag.

Rae lowered her burger and stared over at Steph's food. The French fries were covered in gooey cheese, caramelized onions, and some kind of sauce. "What on earth is this?"

"They call it animal style," Steph said around a mouthful of fries. With a devilish grin, she added, "Not to be confused with doggy style."

Good thing Rae hadn't taken another bite of her burger, because now she would have probably choked on it. Jesus, her roommate was dangerous.

"Want to try?" Steph held out the box of fries.

"No, thanks. I have my own, and I hope they're without all that animal crap on top."

Steph pulled a second box of fries from the bag and handed them over. They were the plain ones, so Rae dug in.

For a few minutes, they ate in silence. Rae glanced over at Steph while she ate her burger. Wow. For someone so slender, she sure could put it away. Well, Rae had always appreciated women who enjoyed their food without counting every single calorie.

Steph finished her meal first and then reached over and stole a handful of Rae's fries. "What?" she said at Rae's look. "I've had a tough night."

Rae slid the rest of her fries across the middle console. "Yeah, the late show seems to attract assholes like that."

Steph took a noisy slurp of milkshake. "You can say that again. Some nights, I don't know why I do this to myself."

"Why do you?" Rae asked before she could censor herself. Usually, she avoided asking any personal questions because most people took it as an invitation to ask questions in return. But she had to admit that she was curious about her roommate. "I mean, you're intelligent, and your family... um..."

"Is stinking rich?" Steph finished the sentence for her.

"Um, yeah. I bet you could have your pick of jobs."

"Oh, and I did." Steph chuckled. "There's not much I haven't done. I've waited tables, I worked at the zoo and in customer service, I starred in commercials, and I was a bartender, and I still sometimes pick up a few extra dollars as an Uber driver…although the last time didn't end so well."

Rae wiped her hands on a napkin. "Traffic accident?"

"No, nothing like that. I always practice my comedy routine while I'm driving alone. Last time, I forgot I had a customer." Steph chuckled. "Pretty embarrassing. Oh, and I was fired as a bartender for doing an impression of the boss. I'm really not cut out for a normal job. Guess I'm destined to be a comic. The first time I tried it, my sophomore year, I was hooked. Dropped out of college to do it full-time a couple of months later."

"What did you major in?"

"Animal science," Steph answered. "When I finished high school, I had no clue what I wanted to do with my life. I just knew I didn't want to become a therapist, like the rest of my family. Since I've always loved animals, I thought why not become a vet?"

"And you gave that up to become a comedian?" Rae tried to keep her voice free of judgment. She knew how it felt to have people disapprove of her job. Her own parents had never liked her joining the force.

"Yep. And I don't regret it for a second. Making people laugh is addictive. Better than sex." Steph paused, then seemed to consider it for a moment. "Okay, it's a close second. Besides, who was I kidding? My grades weren't good enough to get into vet school anyway." She took off the lid of her milkshake and stirred it with her straw. Then she replaced the lid and regarded Rae across the rim of her cup. "How about you?"

"Straight Bs. I have no idea if that's good enough for vet school."

Steph shook her head. "You know that's not what I meant. Do you regret becoming a police officer?"

Did she? Rae wadded her napkin and the burger wrapper into a ball and stuffed it into the empty bag. No one had asked her that before. "No," she said after a while and felt deep in her gut that it was the truth. She had a lot of regrets, but becoming a police officer wasn't one of them.

"Do you miss it?" Steph asked softly.

"Parts of it." She couldn't say what she missed most—the camaraderie, the satisfaction of protecting and helping people, the feeling that she was trained to handle any challenging situation that could come up. But then again, that had turned out to be an illusion. That day, when Mike had been shot, everything had spiraled out of control. Rae tried to flash a grin, but her lips felt stiff. "Not the endless paperwork or spending my days off in court."

For once, Steph didn't smile back or make a joke. "Couldn't the LAPD assign you to a new position? Something you could do with one eye?"

"They did, but I didn't want a desk job. If I could no longer work patrol, I didn't want to hang around and have the constant reminders of what I couldn't do anymore." Rae snapped her mouth shut, amazed at how much she had said.

Steph reached across the middle console, somehow found Rae's hand in the dim light as if by pure instinct, and squeezed softly. Her fingers were cold from the milkshake, but the touch didn't feel as unpleasant as Rae had expected. "I'm sorry."

Rae bit her lip so hard that she tasted the coppery tang of blood. "Not your fault."

"Yeah, but I can still be sorry, can't I? I don't know much about how your life was before or what exactly happened—and I'm not going to ask—but I can imagine you lost a lot." She gave another soft squeeze to Rae's hand.

This time, it felt like too much. Rae pulled away. "Yeah, well, I gained a thing or two too. Now I get to protect the most promising comics in LA from creepy guys, hecklers, and little old grannies who're smuggling bourbon and God knows what else into the showroom."

Again, Steph didn't take the bait. She regarded Rae with a serious expression before reaching over and tapping her shoulder. "You know what? You and I have more in common than I thought."

"Us?" Rae waved back and forth between them with a faux horrified expression.

"Yeah. I've been accused of using humor as a defense mechanism. You do that too."

It was the truth, but Rae didn't want to admit it. "You sound like your therapist sister."

The straw slid out of Steph's mouth, and her eyes widened. "Damn, you're right. Blame it on the sugar rush from the milkshake." She slid the cup into the holder. "Okay, enough deep conversation for one night. I'm usually not one for that either. But if you ever need to talk...you know where I live."

"Thanks," Rae said but already knew that she would never take her up on that offer.

"I know what you're thinking."

Rae looked over at her warily. She had really reached her capacity for today.

Steph's smile changed and became more the carefree grin Rae was familiar with. "You're thinking you need dessert."

A relieved chuckle burst from Rae's chest. "Yeah, that's exactly what I was thinking."

"Great. Let's switch seats and get going. I know a twenty-four-hour diner that makes an amazing waffle sundae."

"Jeez, you're not serious, are you?" Rae clutched her belly. "You're not considering having a waffle sundae after the burger, milkshake, and animal fries you just had?"

Steph opened the passenger-side door and grinned like a pirate about to capture a ship loaded down with riches. "Stick with me and find out."

Chapter 13

THE MONDAY BEFORE CHRISTMAS WEEK, Steph tossed her keys onto the table next to the door. "Honey, I'm home."

No response came from Rae's room.

Steph stepped farther into the apartment. "Rae? Hey, you home? There was a taco truck parked around the corner, so I brought you some tacos. Am I the best roomie ever or what?"

Again, there was no reply from Rae's room.

The door was open, so Steph peeked in.

No Rae.

In the past, when her roommates hadn't been home, Steph had always enjoyed having the apartment to herself, but now she found herself being disappointed. It was just because eating alone wasn't fun, she told herself.

Despite Rae's protests about having a waffle sundae after devouring a burger, milkshake, and fries, she had matched Steph bite for bite at the diner the previous Thursday, and Steph had enjoyed sharing a meal with a woman who wasn't a dainty eater. Well, Rae could have her tacos later, once she got back from wherever she had gone.

Unless I eat hers too. Steph grinned to herself. But first, she'd jump into the shower to get rid of the dog smell she had accumulated on her walks today.

She left the tacos in the kitchen, got a change of clothes from her room, and headed to the bathroom.

As she opened the door, a cloud of steam wafted out. A feeling of reversed déjà vu overcame her. This time, it was Rae who stood in front of the sink completely naked and Steph who'd walked in on her.

Holy moly! Clearly, she was sharing an apartment with a goddess. Steph didn't know how she managed not to drool as her gaze trailed up sculpted calves, strong thighs, and…

Rae cleared her throat. "Enjoying the view?" she asked without a hint of self-consciousness.

"Yes," Steph answered before her brain kicked in. Her gaze snapped up to Rae's face. "Um, sorry, I was—" Then she forgot the rest of what she'd been about to say.

Rae had taken out her prosthetic eye. Her lid had closed three-quarters of the way, but beneath it, Steph could glimpse the pink flesh of her empty eye socket.

"Shit." Rae only now seemed to remember that she'd removed the prosthesis. While she hadn't appeared to care much about Steph seeing her naked, she covered her socket with her hand and glared at Steph with her remaining eye. "Would you mind?"

Steph whirled around so fast that she nearly fell against the doorframe. "I'm really sorry, Rae. I—"

"Out!"

"Sorry. I'm so sorry." Steph fled the room. She closed the door behind her, sank against it, and muttered a litany of four-letter words. God, just when she had gotten Rae to relax around her. Now she had ruined everything. She knew instinctively that Rae wouldn't want anyone to see her like this.

Steph stumbled to the couch and flopped down on it to wait for Rae.

It seemed to take an eternity for Rae to emerge from the bathroom. Was it hard to put the prosthetic eye back in, or was Rae avoiding her? Steph had a feeling it was the latter.

Finally, the bathroom door creaked open, and Rae stepped out.

Her hair was still wet and stuck to her skull, emphasizing her striking features. Her jawline was so tense that her entire face seemed to be carved out of stone. She was fully dressed in her work uniform, and the prosthetic eye was back in. She hurled the darkest of glares in Steph's direction before marching toward her room.

"Rae, wait!" A dozen thoughts tumbled through Steph's mind as she searched for something that would stop Rae's retreat. "I got you some tacos."

"I'm not hungry," Rae said without stopping.

"Please, Rae. There's no need to be embarrassed."

"I'm not."

Steph got up from the couch but held herself back from moving toward Rae, no matter how much she wanted to. She sensed that she'd chase her off if she did. "Then come eat with me."

Already at the door to her room, Rae stopped and turned. An expression Steph couldn't quite identify crossed her face like a cloud trailing over the sun. "I said I'm not hungry. Besides, I would have thought you'd have lost your appetite now anyway."

It would have been easy to miss, and Steph nearly did. But she had grown up in a household where every little gesture, every facial expression, every change of tone was interpreted and discussed to death. For once in her life, growing up in a family of therapists was a good thing because now she caught it: Rae wasn't angry. Not really. She was scared, probably of Steph rejecting her or reacting with disgust.

"Me? Losing my appetite?" Steph made good use of her comedy skills to let out a convincing chuckle. "That never happened before, so why would it now? Because I saw you with your eye out?"

Rae flinched back from the open words, but Steph knew they needed to be said.

"Do you honestly think it would gross me out?" Now she took a step toward Rae and slowly shook her head. "Why would it?"

Rae laughed, but it was a sound full of pain, bare of any humor. "Well, most people can't take out their eye like some…some zombie."

Steph's heart went out to Rae. She bridged the rest of the distance between them but carefully stopped just out of touching distance. "You are not a zombie, and you're not most people. Christ, you survived being shot in the head! This"—she pointed at Rae's prosthetic eye—"is part of survival. I'm not grossed out by it, okay?"

Rae looked at her for several more seconds. Finally, she nodded. "Okay." It came out in a whisper so soft that Steph nearly didn't hear it. Then Rae squared her shoulders, and her usual armor of confidence settled back into place. "What kind of tacos?"

Relief flooded Steph's body, making her knees wobbly for a moment. "I didn't know what you liked, so I got a combination of six different ones. *Carne asada, chorizo,* shrimp, grilled veggies, chicken, and a fish taco."

"Can I have the *carne asada* one?" Rae asked.

"Hmm, depends."

"On?" A bit of wariness crept back into Rae's tone.

God, she was like one of the shy or fearful dogs who backed away from her, watching Steph's every move for the first few times she came to take them for a walk. But Steph had always patiently gained their trust, and she hoped she could do the same with Rae. She flashed her a teasing grin. "On whether you'll continue not to lock the bathroom door when you take a shower so I can accidentally sneak another peek."

Rae stiffened.

"Jeez, I'm talking about a look at that hot body of yours, not your eye." Steph gently elbowed her, then turned and walked to the kitchen. She busied herself putting the tacos on plates and getting two bottles of water from the fridge to give Rae some time to get herself together.

Finally, Rae joined her, wordlessly took the water bottles, and carried them to the couch.

Steph followed, but then, halfway to the sofa, she remembered that she had forgotten to close the cupboard after taking the plates out. Old habits really died hard. She returned to the kitchen, nudged the cabinet door closed, and then took a seat next to Rae. Her stomach gurgled a protest as she slid the plate with the *carne asada* taco in front of Rae.

"Thanks," Rae said.

That one word seemed to encompass so much more than the tacos or remembering to close the cupboard door. Steph gave her a soft smile. "You're very welcome."

Rae rubbed her left eye, then picked up the taco and studied it from all sides as if to decide how to best eat it without it falling apart. "If you continue to feed me fast food, I'll have to up my workout."

"Please." Steph snorted. "I just saw you in all your naked glory. You don't need to up your workout."

Rae let out a noncommittal grunt and took a big bite of her taco. Guacamole dribbled out, and a piece of steak dropped onto the plate.

Steph watched her with a grin.

"What?" Rae picked up the morsel of steak and popped it into her mouth.

"You're eating it all wrong."

"There's a right and a wrong way to eat a taco?" Rae gave her a skeptical look. "Open mouth, insert taco, chew, swallow, repeat. You have a better method?"

"Yeah. Well, not for the chewing part, but I've had tacos with Gabe's family, and they hold theirs like this." Steph pinched the top shut between her thumb, index, and middle finger. "That way, the filling can't fall out. Here, I'll show you." She reached over and guided her fingers into the correct position. Rae's skin was warm and surprisingly soft beneath her fingertips, and Steph's hand lingered for a second.

"Got it. Thanks." Rae held still for a moment but then pulled her hand away by lifting the taco to her mouth. This time, she managed to take a bite without losing half of the filling.

Steph gave herself a mental slap and picked up her fish taco. *Danger, Will Robinson. She's your roommate and a club employee. Look, don't touch, remember?*

Rae finished her first taco, wiped her hands on a napkin, and then rubbed her left eye with the back of her hand.

"Something wrong with the eye?" Steph asked. "You keep rubbing it."

"It's fine." Rae rubbed it again.

Steph kept gazing at her with an I-don't-believe-it-for-a-second look.

"It's irritating me a little today," Rae finally said. "I thought an eyelash got trapped behind it or something. That's why I took it out after my shower to rinse the socket with saline."

"Oh, so you don't...you know...take it out every day?" Steph asked.

A mild smile darted across Rae's face. "What? You thought it's like false teeth that I take out every night and put in a glass of water on my bedside table?"

Steph shrugged. "How was I supposed to know? I've never met someone with a prosthetic eye. At least not that I know of."

"Okay, I'll give you that," Rae said. "In the past, I think doctors told their patients to take it out every day to clean it, but nowadays, the consensus seems to be that you should leave it in as much as possible, unless it bothers you. I only take it out every couple of weeks to clean it."

Steph studied the prosthetic eye. The skin around it was a bit red from Rae's rubbing. "Does it hurt?"

"No. I don't know what's up with it right now. Most of the time, I don't even feel the prosthesis anymore."

"I meant when you take it out and put it back in."

"Doesn't hurt either," Rae said. "It's a bit like putting in a contact, only a lot bigger and thicker."

Steph didn't ask to see it, even though she was curious about how the prosthetic eye would look once it was out. But she didn't want Rae to feel as if she had to take her eye out to amuse her audience, like a magician performing a trick. "I was always thankful to have 20/20 vision. The thought of putting in contacts, much less something bigger... Not sure I could do that."

"You would get used to it. Not like I had a choice. My only alternative was an eye patch."

Steph's mind bombarded her with images of a dashing pirate wearing thigh-high leather boots, a rakish grin, and a billowy, white blouse that was unbuttoned a little too far. She put down her taco to fan herself with both hands. "Ooh, I don't know. I think you'd rock that look."

"I don't even want to know what's going through your mind right now, do I?"

Steph chuckled. "Probably not."

Rae regarded her with a shake of her head. "You're impossible."

"Impossible not to like," Steph added and stuffed the rest of the taco into her mouth.

Rae huffed but didn't object.

Chapter 14

THE HOLIDAY SEASON WAS A busy time at the club, so Rae had worked every night for the past two weeks. On her first day off in what felt like ages, she lay stretched out on the couch, using Steph's Netflix subscription to watch *The Fall*. She'd never watched much TV, but she needed a way to shut off her brain at night, and too much reading on the small screen of her phone tired her eye. Plus she had to admit that the shows Steph had introduced her to were amazingly good—and Gillian Anderson was still sexy as hell.

Steph came out of the bathroom and hopped around the living area on one foot while sliding a high-heeled shoe on the other.

Talk about sexy as hell... Without looking at it, Rae reached for the remote and paused the show. *Wow.* That sure wasn't the jeans, T-shirt, and blazer Steph normally wore when she went to a comedy gig. Her black miniskirt was only an inch or two shy of getting her arrested, and the tight, black top with short, lacy sleeves molded to her every curve.

"What?" Steph, now with both shoes on, paused in the middle of the living room and slid her hands down her skirt, smoothing it down and raising the temperature in the apartment. "Do I have a run in my pantyhose?"

"You're not even wearing pantyhose," Rae muttered. She knew, because damn, it was hard to keep her eyes off those legs.

Steph flashed her a grin. "Why, I didn't know you'd notice."

"I don't." Rae pressed the play button. "Wear whatever you want. Just seems like overkill for a comedy show or going to an open mic with Gabe." Was there still something going on between the two of them? The rumor mill at the club had it that they had shared a short fling before Steph had kicked him to the curb.

"I'm not going to a show or an open mic. I've been booked for a holiday party pretty much every day this month. Now I need a break. I'm going out."

One of the bad things about only having one eye was that Rae couldn't keep watching her out of the corner of her eye while pretending to be focused on her show. "Hot date?"

"Jealous?" Steph gave her a wink.

Oh, come on. Who did that—winking? It should be forbidden for everyone over the age of eighteen. Rae sent her a look until Steph relented.

"I wish. No, Claire and Lana are dragging me out with them, and my sister told me to"—Steph formed quotation marks with her fingers—"dress like an adult."

Yeah, she'd certainly achieved that. "She probably meant not to wear one of your T-shirts with a painted-on tie."

Steph's eyes twinkled. "Oops."

The doorbell rang, interrupting whatever Rae would have said next— not that she knew what to say. Her mouth was admittedly a little dry.

"Oh shit, that's them. Can you open the door while I grab my jacket and put my earrings in?"

"Sure." Rae paused the show again and climbed to her feet. On her way to the door, she and Steph crossed paths, and Rae caught a whiff of Steph's perfume, one she didn't wear every day.

Rae wasn't normally into perfumes and stuff like that, but whoever had created that scent deserved to make a fortune. She shook her head to clear it. Maybe her parents had been right—watching too much TV was messing with her brain.

She strode to the door while Steph disappeared in her room.

Steph's sister and her fiancée were dressed up too. Claire practically wore the tame version of Steph's outfit—a black above-the-knee skirt and a cream-colored silk top, with a black blazer resting over her arm.

But Rae's gaze was drawn to Lana. Her purple wrap top left her arms free and revealed a colorful tattoo of a majestic phoenix stretching its wings above a jagged scar that zigzagged across her left arm above the bend of her elbow.

Rae tried not to stare. Why hadn't she noticed the scar when she had first met Lana on moving day? *Well, probably because you hid out on the balcony half of the time.* It didn't matter anyway. Just because Lana had been injured too didn't make them kindred spirits.

"Come on in," she said belatedly and stepped back to let them in. "Steph's getting her jacket."

Claire and Lana entered hand in hand.

Lana looked around. "Hey, why don't you have your Christmas decorations up yet? It's a week before Christmas!"

Rae shrugged. "I never bother with decorations. I don't even own any."

"Me neither," Steph called through the open door of her room.

"Why didn't you say something?" Claire asked. "We could have given you a box of ours. Now that we live together, we have more than we can use on our tree."

"I don't think we'll be getting a tree," Rae said.

"What?" Lana and Claire said in unison. Lana gave her a puzzled look. "But how will you get into a festive mood without a tree?"

Steph came out of her room, a black leather jacket tucked under one arm. "Festive mood?" She chuckled. "Can you imagine my roomie here in a festive mood?"

Claire and Lana looked at her.

Rae scowled at the three of them. "I'm not cutting down a perfectly good tree to put glittery stuff on it and then toss it out in January." On this one thing, she and her parents were in absolute agreement.

Steph took up a position next to her, and the scent of her perfume trailed over again. "I'm actually with her. No tree. You know I'm not into that Christmassy stuff either."

"Oh yeah?" Claire peered at her younger sister over the turquoise rim of her glasses. "For someone who's not into Christmas, you sure jumped at the chance to go see the lights at The Grove with us tonight."

"Who said I'm coming for the lights?" Steph flashed a toothy grin. "I'm coming for the fancy dinner you said you'd spring for, sis."

"Yeah, sure. You're coming for the fennel salad, the kelp caviar, and the gluten-free, low-fat eggplant lasagna."

Steph let out a cry of protest. "Please tell me we're not going to one of those rabbit food places."

Claire laughed. "I guess you'll just have to wait and see."

"Lana, please tell me we're going somewhere where they actually serve real food on adult-sized plates."

Lana lifted her hands. "I have no idea. Claire made the reservation. I'm just along for the lights and to spend time with my lovely fiancée."

Steph made playful gagging sounds. "Rabbit food and romance. Double yuck." She directed a hopeful look at Rae. "Want to come with us so I don't have to be alone with these two lovebirds?"

Hell, no. Rae backed away. "Sorry, you're on your own. I'm allergic to fennel—and romance."

"Yeah, me too. I'd take a burger and a hot, sweaty—"

Claire covered her sister's mouth with her hand. "I don't think I want to hear that. Let's go before you say something that will put me in therapy."

"Jeez, therapists! Just a bunch of fragile creatures." Once Steph had slipped on her bolero-style leather jacket, she gave a wave and followed her sister and Lana out the door.

For a few moments, their steps on the stairs and their banter drifted back to Rae, then it faded away, and Rae was alone in the silent apartment.

She flopped back onto the couch, stared at the frozen image of Gillian Anderson on the TV screen, and imagined The Grove during the holiday season. The mall would be filled with shoppers and people who wanted to see the largest Christmas tree in LA, annoying holiday music would be piped through the loudspeakers, and the fake snow flurries drifting down during the nightly show would irritate her eye even more. Nope. She wouldn't want to join them for all the money in the world.

So what if she wouldn't get to see how Steph would look with her cheeks flushed from spicy mulled cider? She didn't care about stuff like that, right?

Right. She nodded to herself. Determined, she reached for the remote and pressed *play.*

Good thing Rae hadn't come with them. As much as Steph would have liked to see if any of the holiday decorations or the lights twinkling down from every tree could get a smile out of her grumpy roommate, she knew Rae would have hated the crowd in the mall. She closed one eye to experience The Grove the way Rae would and promptly crashed into someone's shopping bag.

Damn. Navigating with only one eye wasn't easy. Her admiration for Rae grew.

"Are you okay?" Claire asked as they strolled past Santa's workshop and then paused to take in the one-hundred-foot Christmas tree, complete with a lighted Santa and his reindeer streaking across the top.

"Yeah, sure. Why wouldn't I be okay?"

"You just crashed into that guy. Plus you didn't even take a look when we passed Santa."

Steph shrugged. "I told you I'm not into Christmassy stuff."

"But you're normally into bare-skin stuff." Claire pointed over her shoulder.

Steph turned and caught a glimpse of a woman in a Santa costume, if you could call it that. Most of the red velvet and the faux white fur had gone into the hat. The Santa dress was even shorter than Steph's own skirt, and the fuzzy V-neck revealed a very generous amount of cleavage. If they had been in New York or somewhere with a real winter, Santa would have ended up with icicles in some very uncomfortable places.

"Not my type." Steph turned back around.

Claire touched her chest in a gesture of pretend surprise. "Oh, you have a type? I thought you slept with anyone with a pulse and a bad track record."

"Ooh, do I sense some deep-rooted jealousy there?"

"Trust me, your sister doesn't have a reason or time to be jealous," Lana threw in with a grin. "Our love life is—"

"Hey!" Claire waved her hand to get her fiancée's attention. "Could you two stop talking about our love life? That's private."

"You started it," Steph said.

Claire shook her head. "I was talking about your *sex* life, not your *love* life. There's a difference. Not that you would know."

"Jeez, sis. Get off your high horse—or better yet, get off your low-carb diet. It's making you bitchy."

Lana pulled them over to a bench and sat between them, separating them. "Okay, that's enough from both of you. Just for the record, Claire does eat carbs, sometimes even after six." She lightly bumped Steph's shoulder with her own. "So how's the roommate situation working out for you? Are you and Rae driving each other up a wall?"

"Oh, you mean the way you drove me up a wall in the beginning by turning my kitchen into a disaster area every time you entered it?" Claire's voice was affectionate, and she leaned over to plant a soft kiss on Lana's lips.

Lana returned the kiss and trailed her thumb over Claire's cheek. "No, I mean the way you drove me up a wall by hovering behind me with a cleaning rag and taking the dishes out of the dishwasher to arrange them the correct way." She turned toward Steph. "Is Rae like that? She seemed pretty organized with her moving boxes."

"She is. She likes things done a certain way. In the beginning, it felt like living with my dear sis over there."

"But now it doesn't anymore?" Lana asked.

Steph laughed. "No. It's really easy to corrupt Rae into eating junk food. And she doesn't mind dog slobber at all. Can't mistake her for Claire."

Claire leaned forward on the bench, peeked around her taller, more full-figured fiancée, and studied Steph with a look that made her squirm. She wore the same expression their parents always wore when they interpreted something Steph had done. "You like her."

Steph forced herself not to become defensive just because Claire wore her therapist expression. "Yeah, I think I do. She comes across like this big, gruff, antisocial loner, and she can be, but underneath it all, I think she's a lot more complex than that."

"See?" Claire lifted her index finger. "When you're not distracted by having sex with someone and actually talk to them, you can really get to know them." She paused. "Um, you aren't, are you? Having sex with her?"

"No! Jesus, Claire, give me some credit, okay?" Steph reached around Lana and poked her sister's shoulder. "And stop looking at me with that therapist face. You don't want to have anything to do with my job, so keep yours out of my life too."

Claire and Lana exchanged a long look. "Um, about that..."

"About what? Me not liking to be psychoanalyzed?"

"Me not wanting to have anything to do with your job," Claire said. "Lana and I were talking, and maybe...maybe it's time I finally came to one of your shows."

Steph swiveled around on the bench and stared at her sister. In the nearly ten years since she had started doing stand-up, Claire had never expressed the slightest interest in seeing one of her sets. Even when Steph had invited her, Claire had always claimed some work function or another reason she couldn't go. This was big, and she had no doubt that she had Lana to thank for her sister's change of mind. Claire had mellowed out a lot since she had met Lana. "Oh, wow. When?"

Claire looked at Lana again, who gave her an encouraging nod. "I thought maybe the next time you have a spot at one of the nicer clubs."

Was Claire banking on her not getting one of those coveted spots anytime soon? Steph squared her shoulders. Now she would work even harder to get one. "I'll let you know."

Claire nodded and stood. "Ready for some baked jackfruit gyros?"

Steph's jaw dropped open. "You're kidding, right? Please tell me you're kidding!"

Even though Steph had told Rae that she needed a night off from comedy, she had stopped by a bar on her way home to do a five-minute set at an open mic. Now that she knew Claire would come to one of her shows, the pressure was on.

If you can't stand the pressure of having your sister in the audience, how will you handle being on TV, where everyone you know might watch?

She pushed back the thought. She would cross that bridge when she came to it. At the moment, it didn't look as if she would ever have to worry about it. There were barely three months until her self-imposed deadline—her thirtieth birthday in March—and she hadn't even managed to impress Mr. Hicks, much less a booker for a TV network.

Sighing, she let herself into the dark apartment and tiptoed through the living area without turning on the light. It was close to midnight, and she didn't want to wake Rae. She went to the bathroom and got ready for bed, but after the open mic, she was too hyped up to sleep.

She listened to the recording of her set and scribbled down notes on material that had worked and things that hadn't. Usually, that calmed her mind enough that she could sleep afterward.

Not this time. Her brain was still wide-awake, and her stomach was grumbling because she hadn't eaten much at dinner.

She snuck into the kitchen and slid the pizza takeout menu out from beneath the magnet that held it taped to fridge. But then she hesitated. Lately, she had overdone it a little with getting takeout and having food delivered. Not that she had expensive tastes, but it was still adding up. Even though she had made a lot more money this month because of all the holiday party gigs, she had used most of it to pay her part of the rent for January in advance.

Grimacing, she stuck the takeout menu back beneath the magnet and opened the fridge. While she peered inside, faint noises from Rae's room drifted over. Could Rae not sleep either?

Somehow, it was comforting to know someone was in the next room, still awake too.

Steph returned her attention to the fridge. Her part of it didn't hold that many options. But she had eggs, and if Rae was awake, maybe she could ask her if she could borrow an onion and a red pepper so she could make herself some scrambled eggs. She could handle that, right?

Just as she took out the eggs, Rae's door opened, and she stepped outside. "Hey. I thought I heard you out there. How were the lights?"

"Christmassy," Steph said. "But I have to admit it was nice."

"No need to ask how dinner was." Rae pointed at the carton of eggs. "Are you cooking?"

"I don't know if I'd call what I do cooking, but yeah."

"So Claire really took you to a place that served fennel salad and kelp caviar?"

Steph laughed. "No. She wouldn't do that to Lana. I just didn't have much of an appetite earlier. I, um, was a little preoccupied because Claire told me she'll come to my next show at one of the nicer clubs."

"And that's making you nervous?" Rae asked.

"A little." Steph realized she didn't mind admitting it to Rae. "She hasn't seen me do stand-up before, and I'm not so sure she shares my sense of humor, especially if I do any jokes about her or the rest of the family."

Rae's face became shuttered. "Then maybe you should consider not doing any of those jokes."

"I get where you're coming from. Really. But that's like a carpenter not using half of her best tools." Steph didn't want to get into another argument, so she decided to change the subject. "Could I steal one of your onions and a pepper?"

"Go ahead." Rae went to the fridge and took out a bottle of water. Her cut-off sweatpants tightened across her behind.

Steph forced herself to look away. She grabbed a knife from the drawer and started to peel an onion. Two minutes later, she had managed to get the skin off, but her eyes were stinging. She put the onion and the knife down to dab at her eyes. *Shit.* That was why she didn't cook.

A tissue appeared in her line of sight.

"Thanks." Grateful, Steph took it, dried her eyes, and blew her nose before bravely setting out to chop the onion.

"I don't want to interfere with your masterpiece of haute cuisine, but that's a bread knife," Rae said from behind her.

Steph turned and leaned against the counter, knife in hand. "So? There's no such thing as an onion knife, is there?"

"Jesus take the wheel." Rae shook her head and pointed at the breakfast bar. "Sit and let me do this before we end up in the ER because you chop off all your fingers."

Steph gladly relinquished the onion and put the knife into the dishwasher. Instead of sitting at the breakfast bar, she hopped up onto the counter on the other side of the stove, where she could watch Rae cook, and merrily dangled her feet.

Admittedly, she was a bit surprised to see how skillfully Rae handled a knife.

She rested the tip of the knife on the cutting board while just the broader part of the steel rocked up and down in a quick, rhythmic motion. In no time, she had chopped up the onion and the pepper into uniform pieces. Domestic tasks like cooking had never held much appeal to Steph, but watching Rae had something unexpectedly erotic about it.

"What?" Rae asked, wrenching Steph from her trance.

"Um, I thought chopping up stuff might be hard for you. Because it's so visual and precise."

Rae shook her head. "I barely even look down. It's mostly muscle memory." Instead of scrambling the eggs, Rae pulled a steak from her part of the fridge and sliced it up.

"Remind me to give you some money for that once I get paid for my next gig." Steph didn't want to assume that she would get to eat Rae's food for free, especially since she knew Rae needed to watch her money too.

"Don't worry about it. You sprang for the Double-Double and the tacos; now it's my turn to feed you."

Maybe her sister was right. If you actually talked to people and spent time with them outside of the bedroom, they did reveal sides Steph never would have expected. The grouchy recluse she lived with was actually a kind-hearted teddy bear. Who knew?

Rae heated oil in a skillet. While the strips of steak, the onion, and the pepper sizzled away, she sliced a ciabatta loaf lengthwise and put it in the oven for a minute.

Steph's mouth watered at the heavenly scents that started to drift through the kitchen. "Yum. Where did you learn how to cook? Your parents?"

"Kind of," Rae said.

Steph waved her hand at her to keep going. Sometimes, getting Rae to talk was like getting a square to roll. You had to keep nudging.

"My parents were into vegan health food decades before it was a trend, so they had to make everything themselves," Rae said. "They also never stuck to any schedule. There were no set meal times at our house—if we even had a house—so if I was hungry, I made my own food."

"No house?" Steph asked. "You mean you lived in an apartment?"

"No. My parents led a pretty nomadic lifestyle. When I was little, we lived in a commune up north for a while, and before my brother was born, we even lived in an RV and went from one craft fair to the next. I spent most of my childhood running around half-naked and barefoot, without any boundaries."

"Wow. That must have been great. I wish my parents had been more like that. They believed in clear rules, so I spent most of my childhood in my room, grounded." Steph chuckled.

Rae turned off the stove and pulled the ciabatta from the oven. While the bread cooled a little, she leaned against the counter, her strong arms folded across her chest. "It wasn't all sunshine and rainbows, believe me.

149

My parents had this it-will-all-work-out mentality and never planned for anything. There was zero structure. Sometimes, I felt like the only adult in the family, even at twelve."

Steph thought about it for a while. Maybe having so much freedom and getting to make your own decisions at such an early age wasn't always a good thing. She could imagine Rae must have felt adrift in the ocean of life. "Is that why you became a cop? Because it gave you laws and rules and structure to cling to?"

Rae busied herself putting the steak, the peppers, and the onion on the ciabatta and then whipped up a sauce from mayo and mustard that she drizzled over it, along with some chopped-up herbs. Just when Steph thought that she wouldn't get an answer, Rae slid the plate with the sandwich across the counter and said, "I never thought about it that way, but that was probably part of it. Plus it was my way of rebelling against my parents."

"Rebelling by becoming a police officer?" Steph jumped down from the counter and carried the plate to the breakfast bar.

"Yeah, well… Can you think of anything two born-twenty-years-too-late hippies would hate more than for their daughter to become part of the establishment?"

"Right." Steph pressed down on the two halves of the ciabatta to make it more manageable and took a big bite. The juicy meat, the slight sweetness of the peppers, the tang of the mustard, the fresh, peppery taste of the basil, and the crunchy bread blended together in perfect harmony. She let out a long moan. "Oh my God," she said around a mouthful of sandwich, "I think I just had a foodgasm."

Rae rubbed her earlobe. "Um, thanks. I'll take it as a compliment."

"It totally was." Steph licked a bit of mustard sauce off her fingers.

Rae turned away and started cleaning up the kitchen.

Had there been a hint of red on her cheeks for the third time since 1997? *Cute.* Steph grinned to herself but decided not to tease her for once. "Leave it. You cooked; I'll clean…as soon as I'm done with the new love of my life."

After a second of hesitation, Rae set down the cutting board she'd just picked up and climbed onto the barstool across from Steph.

"Um…" Steph looked back and forth between the sandwich and the woman who had prepared it for her. It was a sacrifice but one she was prepared to make. "You want half?"

"No, thanks. All yours."

Steph didn't have to be told twice. She basically inhaled the rest of the sandwich and only slowed down on the last few bites. "So your brother… Is he the same? Craving structure?"

"No. He's great, but we don't have much in common."

"I know what you mean. I love my sister, but sometimes, I can't believe we're related." Steph popped a piece of steak that had fallen off into her mouth. "So what does your brother do? Is he an artist too, like your parents?"

"Kind of. Darrin is a theatrical designer."

"A what?"

"He creates stage sets on Broadway, so we don't see each other a lot," Rae said.

"Oh wow. So you're the only straitlaced one in the family."

Rae glowered at her. "I'm not straitlaced…or straight."

"Or so you keep saying." Steph swiped her finger through the puddle of mustard sauce on her now-empty plate and slid it into her mouth. "Sounds like we were both born into the wrong family. Hey, maybe we should switch. I'll go spend Christmas with your folks, and you join mine. I have a feeling that would be a much better fit."

Rae shook her head. "Wouldn't work."

"Why not?" Steph asked. "Christmas at my folks' is the same procedure every year. My mom has starters on the table at two thirty and the main course at three and not one second later. Lots of structure there. You'd like it."

"Maybe, but the other part of your plan isn't going to work because my parents don't celebrate Christmas. They're not fans of organized religion."

Steph shrugged. "Neither am I, but I still enjoy it for the presents and the food…and even for spending time with my family, though I wouldn't admit that if you try to get me to repeat it to their faces." She studied Rae across the breakfast bar. "So what will you do on Christmas?"

"Work, I guess."

"That's only in the evening. What are you doing before?"

"I don't know." Rae squirmed as if the questioning was making her uncomfortable. "Nothing special."

As much as Steph complained about her family, she couldn't imagine not seeing them on Christmas and spending the day alone. She dabbed at the lone bread crumbs on her plate. Should she invite Rae to join her and her family for dinner? She had never taken anyone home for the holidays, not wanting her current fling to ascribe a level of commitment to the gesture that Steph didn't mean. But she and Rae weren't involved, so it should be okay, right? "Um, would you…uh…?"

"What?" A rare smile crinkled the edges of Rae's eyes. "Make you a second sandwich? You liked it that much?"

"No. I mean, yes, I did, but…um…" *Christ. Out with it. You sound like a teenager asking her crush out.* Steph gave herself a mental kick. "Do you want to come home with me for Christmas?"

Rae arched her brows. "Isn't that taking our fake relationship a little too far?"

This time, Steph didn't join in on the joking. "If you'd rather not, I understand, but I'm actually serious about the offer."

"Oh." The smile on Rae's face disappeared. She rubbed her neck and glanced down at the breakfast bar. "I don't know, Steph. People and I don't usually mix very well."

"They aren't people. They're my family. And you already know Claire and Lana. You're not scared of having dinner with three psychologists, are you?"

Rae looked up and squinted over at her. "Are you trying one of their psych tricks on me by issuing a challenge?"

Damn, was she that transparent, or did Rae know her better than she'd thought already? "Maybe a little." Steph nearly reached across the breakfast bar to squeeze Rae's hand but stopped herself. "But seriously, the offer stands. You don't have to decide now. Just think about it."

"Okay." Rae slid off the barstool. "I'm off to bed now. It's getting late."

"Good night. Sleep well." Steph watched her go. "Oh, and Rae? Thanks again for the sandwich."

"You're welcome." The door closed behind Rae, leaving Steph to wonder if it had been a mistake to invite her. Had she harmed their tentative friendship?

That was what was happening between them, right? They were becoming friends. Since she'd been on the road so much, it had been a while since Steph had made a new friend—and admittedly never someone she was attracted to. Her sister would probably tell her it was a character-building experience.

Steph snorted and went to clean the kitchen.

Chapter 15

TWO DAYS LATER, ON THURSDAY afternoon, Steph waited in the back of a ballroom while the CEO of the construction company that had hired her for their holiday party announced her. There was no stage, but at least the lighting and the sound seemed halfway decent, so she hoped this corporate gig wouldn't turn out as bad as some of the others she had done.

"One more thing before we get to the entertainment," the CEO said into the microphone. "By now, most of you have probably heard about what happened to Jack."

A murmur went through the ballroom.

"For those of you who haven't: He was run over by a dump truck on Monday morning. The driver was backing up and didn't see him. Jack died on the spot. So please, be more careful. No standing around at a construction site while you're taking a cigarette break." The CEO put on a forced smile. "Now let's get to the fun part of the evening. We hired a comedian for tonight's entertainment. Please welcome the very funny Stephanie Renshaw."

Only years of listening to the most messed-up introductions kept Steph's jaw from hitting the floor. This one took the cake by far. They seriously expected her to do stand-up after that announcement? Jeez, and people thought she was tactless!

Barely anyone applauded as she made her way to the front of the room since everyone was busy whispering about what had happened to poor Jack.

Steph took a deep breath and accepted the microphone from the CEO.

Somehow, she made it through the hour-long routine. She even managed to make most of the employees laugh a time or two, but this one wouldn't go down in history as her most successful show.

Why am I doing this again? Oh yeah, that's right. Because it paid ten times the amount she got for a spot at the club. Mentally exhausted but with an envelope full of cash, she made her way back to the car. She climbed into the driver's seat and sat there for a while without starting the engine.

Maybe she should call Penny to see if she wanted to meet up for a drink. She hadn't seen her best friend in a while, partly because she was working her ass off, taking any gig she could get, and partly because she had spent more time at home since moving in with Rae.

Never in a million years would she have thought she would enjoy spending time with someone as reserved as Rae, but she did.

When her phone vibrated, she pulled it from her pocket and glanced at the screen.

Penny.

The first real smile all afternoon formed on Steph's lips. Talking to her best friend always cheered her up, so she swiped her finger across the screen. "Hey, Penny. I was just thinking about calling you. Are you telepathic?"

"Um, if I am, it's a newly developed skill that I'm not aware of."

"Want to meet up for a drink somewhere? I just had the shittiest corporate gig ever."

Penny sighed. "I wish I could. I could really use a drink too, but I'm pet-sitting overnight."

"Want me to pick up a six-pack and come over?"

"No, I'm not at home. I'm at the client's."

"Damn," Steph muttered. "Adulting is no fun, is it?"

Another deep sigh drifted through the phone. "Sure isn't today. Um, listen, Steph, there's something I have to tell you. I didn't want you to find out when you log in to the Unleashed calendar to check when you're booked next week."

Cold crept up Steph's chest. She rubbed her breastbone with her free hand. "Find out what? You're not firing me, are you?"

Penny chuckled, but it sounded nervous. "No, nothing like that. Janine called me earlier today."

"Why? Don't tell me she complained about me! That's ridiculous, Penny. Even when she only books me for half an hour, I always stay with Moose for much longer than that, and I make sure to—"

"Calm down. She didn't complain. She couldn't say enough nice things about you and how great you are with Moose."

Steph let her head drop against the back of the seat. "Oh. It's nice of her to call to let you know how happy she is with our services."

"Um, yeah, but she didn't really call to talk about how wonderful you are. I'm so sorry, Steph. She told me she's moving to Chicago."

The words seemed to echo through the phone, but Steph's brain refused to grasp the meaning. "She's moving?"

"Yes."

"And taking Moose with her?"

"Yes, of course," Penny said. "She wouldn't leave him behind."

"No, of course not." Steph rubbed her forehead. "When?"

"Janine's company is sending her to Chicago at the start of the new year. Apparently, it was all very short notice."

The start of the new year… That meant she had less than two weeks to say goodbye to her favorite canine client.

"I'm sorry. I know how you feel. I lost one of mine last month too." Penny hesitated. "Want to come over and help me dog-sit?"

Aww. Steph knew what the offer had cost her friend. Penny thought it unprofessional to take anyone along while pet-sitting at a client's house and had never before done it, as far as Steph knew. "Thanks, but I think I'll just go home."

"Is Rae home?"

"I don't think so. She's probably at work. December is a busy time at the club." Besides, Rae wasn't really one to give a pep talk or a comforting hug. "Don't worry about me, okay? I'll be fine."

When they ended the call, she dropped the phone onto her lap and leaned her head against the steering wheel. God, what a day. Too bad Rae wasn't home and wasn't the huggy type. She could really use a hug.

The apartment was strangely quiet. Silence had never bothered Rae—just the opposite, she preferred it. In the beginning, she hadn't been sure she could survive life with a roommate for very long. Constantly having someone around, especially someone who was on the talkative side, was her own personal version of hell.

But even though she and Steph were very different, their daily routines meshed amazingly well. They worked the same late hours and most often got up and went to bed around the same time, so Rae had never been kept up by noise from Steph's room. She also rarely had the apartment to herself, and now she found herself roaming the place like a wild animal testing out the borders of its territory.

Just as she stopped in front of the fridge to take stock of her dinner options, a key sounded in the lock. The front door swung open, and Steph trudged in, kicking the door closed with her heel. She dropped her keys on the table as if her fingers didn't have enough strength to hold on to them anymore. "Oh. You're home."

"Yeah," Rae said. "Since I'll be working both Christmas Eve and Christmas Day, Mr. Hicks told me to take the night off."

Steph nodded.

No jokes about Rae ruining her plans for a wild party or inviting people over for an orgy because she had assumed she'd have the apartment to herself? Something strange was going on here. Rae leaned against the fridge and studied Steph. Her gray eyes looked dull, without the usual sparkle that always seemed to light them from within. Normally, Rae wasn't one to notice that kind of thing, but now it seemed obvious to her that something had happened. Should she ask what was up?

Steph plodded over, rooted through the cabinets, and then banged each of them shut.

Well, at least she was closing the cupboard doors. That was progress. Kind of. Rae winced at the loud noise but said nothing.

"Where did all the chocolate go?" Steph muttered.

"Your belly."

Steph abandoned her search and sank against the counter. "Damn."

Any halfway decent roommate would ask if she was okay. Rae knew that, even though she had no clue how to handle the obvious response. She forced herself to ask anyway. "You okay?"

"Moose is moving away," Steph blurted out as if she had waited for Rae to ask. "I mean, his owner is, so Moose is leaving too."

"Oh." Rae didn't know what to say. She had met the lovable giant only once, but even she was a little sad she wouldn't get to see him again, so she could easily imagine how sad Steph must be feeling. "Damn. I'm sorry. That's too bad."

Steph sighed. "Yeah."

"But at least he didn't die or anything, right?"

"Yeah." Another sigh came from Steph.

Rae shifted her weight from her left leg to the right and back. Why was there no book with easy-to-follow instructions on how to handle situations like this? Normally, she didn't bother to even try. Cheering up people wasn't her favorite pastime. She'd done enough of that growing up, when she'd shouldered much of the responsibility for her brother. But the sadness in Steph's eyes pierced her emotional armor. Slowly, she made her way over to Steph and patted her shoulder once. Okay, that was awkward. She patted again, trying to make it less robotic.

Steph leaned in to the touch, soaking it up as if it would chase away the sadness.

That was good, right? She could do this comforting thing. Rae stopped patting and curled her fingers around Steph's shoulder for a quick squeeze.

But Steph took it as an invitation to sink against her side.

Somehow, Rae found herself holding her in a loose embrace, with Steph's head on her shoulder. *Wow.* Rae stood rooted to the spot as if she were holding a fragile newborn that the parents had entrusted her with. She hadn't held anyone for months. Not since trying to be there for Kim after Mike's death. But this felt different. For one thing, she was very aware of Steph's breath warming a spot on her chest and her hands on her back, whereas such details had never registered when she had held Kim.

The weirdest thing, though, was that while this was new and a little awkward, it didn't make Rae as uncomfortable as she had expected.

Steph pulled away first and lowered her head. This time, it was Steph who was blushing. "Sorry. I didn't mean to…" She waved her hand toward the spot on Rae's shoulder where her head had rested a moment ago. "I shouldn't get so upset. Dogs coming and going is part of my job after all."

"It's part of your job to care about the dogs, so you'd be a lousy dog walker if you weren't upset."

Steph looked up into Rae's eyes. The tiniest of smiles tugged at the corners of her mouth. "You're right. Thank you."

Rae wished she had more comforting wisdom to share…or at least some chocolate. But the one rule her parents had when she'd been growing up was no processed carbs, so even as an adult, she tended not to buy any sweets. Should she offer some kind of distraction? She said the first thing that came to mind. "Um, want to go on a little trip?"

"Where?" Steph asked.

Hell if I know. But Rae didn't admit that. "You'll just have to wait and see."

This trip had to be the worst idea ever. Rae realized it before they had even reached the car. It was half past seven, so darkness engulfed them as they left the building. *What was I thinking?*

She looked at Steph, who looked back at her expectantly.

Cheering her up. That's what I was thinking. Sacrificing a bit of her pride was a small price to pay if she accomplished that task. "Um, would you mind driving?"

"Out of gas?" Steph asked.

Rae considered just saying yes, but she didn't want to lie. "No. I… Ever since I…since I lost my eye, my night vision has been total shit. It's probably because there are no shadows when it's dark, and I rely on them a lot to judge depth. Plus the glare of lights from oncoming cars is difficult for me to handle."

"Oh. Sure. I don't mind driving." Steph paused next to their cars. "Is that why you were so eager to find an apartment closer to the club? So you wouldn't have to drive at night?"

"No, it's because you charmed me so much at first sight that I couldn't wait to move in with you."

Steph bumped her.

Rae bumped back, but with her more muscular frame accidentally shoved Steph against the driver's side door. "Oops. Sorry."

"Brute." Steph jingled her keys. "Want us to take your car so you'll have more legroom?"

"Um…" Rae looked back and forth between Steph's convertible and her SUV. She had never allowed anyone else to driver her car.

A chuckle rose from Steph's chest. "God, you're so much like my sister sometimes. Total control freak."

Rae frowned. While she liked Claire well enough, she didn't like being compared to Steph's sister at all. She didn't want to examine the reason for that too closely, though. "Fine. Let's take my car." She tossed Steph the keys.

Steph fumbled and nearly dropped them as if the move had surprised her. "Thanks." She grinned as she unlocked the car. "A Subaru. Such a lesbian stereotype."

"That's not why I picked it." Rae hesitated but then decided to offer more of an explanation. "When I learned how to drive with one eye, I realized that my old car wouldn't work. I needed something with a huge windshield and rear window to reduce the blind spots. So I traded the old one in for this one." She patted the passenger-side door.

"Oh. That makes sense. Sorry. I didn't know, or I wouldn't have made fun of—"

"It's okay." Rae climbed into the passenger seat.

Steph settled behind the wheel and moved the seat up for her shorter height. When she reached out to adjust the side mirrors, she paused. "What's that?"

Rae turned her head to see what Steph was pointing at. It was the small, round mirrors in the upper corner of the SUV's side-view mirrors. "Blind-spot mirrors."

Steph glanced up at the larger-than-usual rearview mirror and then turned in the driver's seat to face Rae. "Driving with one eye must be pretty hard."

Rae's muscles tightened, even though she told herself there was no need to become defensive. "Luckily, my right eye has 20/20 vision, so I can drive fine, at least during the day. I just need to turn my head more than you."

"Still," Steph said. "If you ever find yourself in a situation where you need a driver, let me know, okay? I'm always up for a little road trip."

Rae didn't plan to ever take her up on it, but she appreciated the offer—and the way Steph had phrased it, as if it would be a fun adventure rather than a burden. "Thanks."

Steph buckled her seat belt and started the engine.

Being in the passenger seat of her own car was strange, but Rae had to admit that Steph was a good driver. She smoothly navigated them backward and out of the parking space.

When they reached the gate at the end of the driveway, the car beeped. Steph jumped. "Jeez."

"Sorry." Rae pressed the button to open the gate. "The car comes with a lot of safety features like a backup camera and front sensors. Took me a while to get used to, but now I find them really helpful. I can turn them off."

Steph playfully batted her hand away. "No, that's fine. I don't mind a talkative car. So where are we going? You realize that if I'm driving, you'll have to tell me where you're taking me."

Shit. Rae still had no idea where to take her. It needed to be some magical place that was sure to cheer Steph up. Bonus points for any location that wouldn't annoy Rae with holiday music or large crowds. *Magical... Enchanted. The Forest of Light maybe?*

Steph didn't like holiday lights, but the lighting display in the botanical garden had nothing to do with the holidays. Mike and Kim had tried to drag her there last year, but Rae had refused, not wanting to be a third wheel on one of her partner's rare days off. Her friends had raved about the experience and had even given Rae two tickets for Christmas. She hadn't used them yet.

Were they even still valid, even though the timed-entry tickets had been for January, and could she reschedule for tonight on short notice? It was a long shot, but it was a weekday, so maybe luck would be on her side.

"Hold on." She pulled her phone from her jacket pocket and searched for the email with the tickets. Seeing Mike's name at the bottom of the email made that familiar dark cloud of grief rise up inside of her.

"Rae?" Steph asked softly. "Are you...?"

"I'm fine." Rae realized she'd been sitting there, staring at the email. Quickly, she scrolled down, found the website link, and logged in. *Where is...? Ah. There.* She tapped a few times. *And...bingo!* She sent Steph a triumphant grin. "Just take us in the direction of Pasadena. I'll tell you where to go when we get close."

"Pasadena?" Steph echoed.

"Just drive."

Tonight was definitely the night of bad ideas. Having to ask Steph to drive had been bad enough, but as soon as they got out of the car and headed for the entrance to the botanical garden, Rae realized that walking Descanso Gardens would be as challenging as driving at night.

The gravel paths lay in near darkness, while the tops of surrounding trees were lit up by colorful laser projections. The fact that there were no holiday tunes, only soothing instrumental music, was a small consolation.

A few steps from the entrance, the first display awaited them. Fields of artificial tulips stretched to both sides of the path. Ripples of light in all colors of the rainbow went through them, slowly changing from blue to purple and then from red to yellow as Steph and Rae walked past.

"Wow, Rae!" Steph looked at her with such admiration as if Rae had single-handedly planted the garden and installed the impressive light show. A beam of light danced over her face, revealing the cheerful twinkle that was back in her eyes. "This is beautiful."

Rae had to admit that it was. Just as beautiful as the joy in Steph's eyes. *God, listen to yourself. Must be this overly romantic setting.*

But admittedly, Steph looked good tonight. She had exchanged her blazer for her leather jacket and the painted-on tie T-shirt for a deep red V-neck top that revealed a hint of cleavage.

Soft chimes accompanied them as they moved on to the next display and stepped beneath towering sycamore trees. Columns of light had been erected beneath the sycamores, and as people touched them, the trees lit up in swirls of colors. Each touch produced new hues.

"Ooh." Steph tugged on Rae's sleeve. "Let's see what colors we can make them."

Rae had to smile at her childlike eagerness. She followed her over to the seven-foot columns and stepped up onto the wooden platform—or rather she tried to. In the darkness, she misjudged the height of the step and the tip of her sneaker caught on it. *Shit.* She pitched forward and instinctively raised her hands to break her fall.

Instead of landing on the hard wood, she collided with something soft and warm. Someone soft and warm.

Steph had turned back toward her, either to say something or because she had realized what was happening, and she caught Rae at the last moment.

Arms wrapped around each other, they tumbled across the platform and crashed into one of the columns, which stopped them from falling.

The column and the sycamores lit up in a soft purple.

They stared at each other from only inches away. The glow of the column bathed Steph's face in a succession of pink, green, and orange. Her eyes seemed to shine brighter than the lights.

"Stunning," Rae whispered.

Steph blinked up at her. "Um, what?"

"The lights," Rae said.

"Oh. Yeah. Beautiful." Steph's gaze remained fixed on Rae's face. "You okay?"

Rae gently freed herself from Steph's arms around her. A shiver went through her as their bodies lost contact. It was only because the air was pretty chilly since the garden was up in the hills. "I'm fine. Just didn't pay enough attention." At least not to where she was going. She was paying plenty of attention to the way Steph looked in those magical lights, and that nonsense had to stop right now. She had barely sorted out her life and didn't need any new complications. Under the pretense of wandering over to touch the next column, she increased the distance between them.

But Steph followed her, took hold of her arm, and pulled her around.

What...? Rae didn't want to face her; she needed a minute to gather herself, but her body betrayed her and turned before her brain could stop it.

"God, I'm a jerk." Steph slapped her own forehead. "You can't really see very much here, can you? I should have thought of that. Why didn't you say anything?"

Rae shrugged and opened her mouth to answer.

Steph raised her hand. "Don't say 'I'm fine.'"

Rae closed her mouth.

"Next time, tell me before you break your neck." Steph slid her arm through Rae's, reached over with her other hand, and rested it on Rae's biceps as if to secure her arm against her own and stop her from pulling away. "Come on. Stick close to me."

Resistance was futile; Rae knew that much. She let herself be guided down the wooden platform and along the gravel path that led through the forest and then beneath an arbor arch with glowing stars floating above.

Arm in arm, they walked through a rose garden while soothing music played in the background.

Jeez. This was almost ridiculously romantic. No wonder most of the people walking ahead of them seemed to be couples, judging by their body language.

Steph's fingers on her arm flexed, and she drew them to a stop in the middle of the path. "Oh, damn. I just realized I'm on your left. You don't like that, do you?"

"I don't."

Steph let go of her arm, which instantly started to feel too cold.

"Usually," Rae added. "But with all the other people around..." She gestured toward the lake ahead of them, where groups of people had gathered to watch lights dance on the water. "I'd rather have you on my left than risk bumping into anyone."

Steph's smile was so broad that Rae could see it even in the near dark as the beam of light reflected off her teeth. She gently took hold of Rae's arm again, and they continued their way to the lake.

Waves of light rippled across the water, moving in sync with the soft music.

Steph didn't let go of her arm as they stopped to watch it, as if not wanting to give up the position of trust to Rae's left. Her warmth filtered through the sleeve of Rae's jacket and seemed to engulf her entire body. Usually, she disliked having someone in her personal space, but with the chill in the air, Steph's warmth was actually pleasant, especially since Steph managed not to make it feel as if she was leading her but as if she needed the contact just as much to stay warm.

They continued on together, past a grove of majestic live oaks until they reached a gazebo that consisted of an illuminated frame.

An older couple stepped out of the structure. The woman smiled at them. "Would you like me to take a photo of you two?"

"No, th—"

"Oh, yes, please," Steph said before Rae could finish her sentence. "That would be lovely." She handed over her cell phone and tugged Rae into the gazebo.

The woman waved at them. "Lean a little closer to each other."

Steph slid her arm around Rae's waist. "Come on. I don't bite." She leaned even closer and whispered, "Unless that's a turn-on for you."

Her warm breath fanned over Rae's ear, making her shiver. She put her arm around Steph and used that move to pinch her hip.

Steph jumped but giggled. "Is that a yes?"

Rae pinched her again.

The woman stepped up to them and handed back the phone. "Nice photo."

What? She had already taken the photo? Neither of them had even looked toward her.

"You two are cute together," the woman added and walked away.

Rae stared after her. "She…she thought we're…a couple?"

Steph laughed. "Don't sound so horrified. I'm cute. You're cute…when you stop scowling…so of course we'd be a cute couple too." She finally let go of Rae so she could take a look at the photo. Her laughter stopped as she stared at her phone.

Frowning, Rae leaned closer to see what had gotten Steph to fall quiet.

The photo looked like something out of a fantasy movie—or maybe out of a romance. They stood perfectly centered in the illuminated circle, their arms around each other as if they had embraced a thousand times before. Steph's head was tilted up so she could make eye contact, and she was laughing in that carefree, natural way that made even Rae want to grin in reaction. Rae was looking down at her, not laughing, but her gaze wasn't as fierce as she had imagined. Her expression was indulgent, her mouth soft as if she was close to smiling.

Steph slid the phone back into her pocket without a word. "Let's continue," she said after several seconds of silence. "If we're not moving, it gets cold."

Quite the opposite. Rae felt a little too warm. She pulled the zipper of her jacket partway down as they strolled toward the next display.

Illuminated pathways wound through the grass. Children and adults hopped from one tile to the next, making each one change colors.

"You're not gonna make me hop like a little kid, are you?"

"Can you do it?" Steph asked.

Rae stood a little straighter. "Of course I can."

"No, I mean, with your eye." Steph's tone softened. "I don't want you to slip and get hurt."

Now it was Rae who tugged her over to the walkway. It was lit from beneath, so she could see it just fine. Not that she would have admitted it even if she couldn't. "Watch me."

They raced each other to see who could make the most colors pop up along two loops of the path. It was completely silly, and Rae hadn't done something like that in... Truth be told, she had probably never done something like that. She also hadn't had this much fun in a long time.

When they finally stopped, they were both breathing heavily from the exertion and from laughing so hard.

"I need a break." Steph slid her arm through Rae's again and steered her over toward a glowing bench at the edge of the display. When they passed a little cabin that served as a snack shop, she stopped. "Ooh. They have hot chocolate! Save me a seat. I'll be right back." She was gone before Rae could answer.

Rae walked on alone and sat on the bench. Its color shifted from yellow to orange beneath her. She exhaled and stared out into the near darkness. Somewhere, a sign with the light show's name, *Enchanted*, glowed. Yeah. That's what she felt like. Completely enchanted. Being here, sharing this otherworldly experience with Steph, seemed to have shifted something between them. *Ignore it. It'll go back to normal in the light of day.*

Steph returned in what felt like seconds. She sat on the bench next to her and immediately slid closer until their thighs brushed. "Here." She held out a paper cup and put something down on Rae's lap.

"Thanks." Rae cradled the cup between both hands and looked down at the paper plate on her lap. "What's that?" Whatever it was, it was hidden beneath a heap of powdered sugar.

"Beignets." Steph reached over and picked one up. Powdered sugar rained down as she withdrew it, dusting Rae's jeans. "Oops. Sorry." She put down her hot chocolate and tried to wipe it off.

The warm fingers trailing up her thigh sent a bolt of arousal straight to Rae's core. *Oh, hell.* Her damn libido had hibernated for so long; why did it have to remember now of all times that it existed? She clenched her teeth and trapped Steph's hand beneath hers to stop it from moving. "Thanks," she said, hoping she sounded normal. "I've got it."

When Steph slid her hand out from beneath hers, Rae brushed her hand over her thigh several times, more in an attempt to wipe away the memory of Steph's touch than to remove the powdered sugar.

Luckily, Steph didn't seem to notice anything. She wolfed down her beignet as if she hadn't eaten in days. "Ooh. This is so good. Try it."

Rae picked one up and nibbled on it without much enthusiasm. Afterward, she wouldn't have been able to describe what it had tasted like. *Come on. Don't make this into something bigger than it is. So what if your roommate is an attractive woman and you're not entirely dead?* It didn't have to mean a thing.

That little pep talk helped her put it into perspective.

Once they had finished the beignets and the hot chocolate, they walked on to see the last two displays.

The first one was probably Rae's favorite so far. Discreetly installed fog machines created a mist-filled forest. Blue and green lights filtered through the mist, bathing the tall coastal redwoods, the ginkgo trees, and the ferns in a hazy glow. Nature sound effects drifted over, and tiny spots of light danced around them like fireflies as they wandered through the forest.

"Wow," Steph murmured, her voice low as if she didn't want to disturb this peaceful experience. "I think this is my favorite."

Rae murmured her agreement. Amazing how in tune two people who were so different could be.

Finally, they reached a Japanese garden, where hundreds of red paper lanterns hung in the trees. Their glow reflected off a pond and revealed the contours of a teahouse. Steph led her over an arched bridge across a stream that ran the entire length of the Japanese garden.

From up there, Rae could already see the exit.

Instead of heading back toward the parking lot, Steph pulled her to a halt in the middle of the bridge, probably to gaze into the dark water beneath them.

While Rae couldn't make out anything, she didn't mind letting Steph have a look, so she leaned onto the railing to wait.

But Steph wasn't peering at the gurgling stream. She was facing Rae and gently tugged on her arm. "Rae?"

Slowly, Rae turned until she was looking at Steph. "Yeah?"

Steph moved even closer. "I just...I wanted to say thank you. For all of this." She waved her hand, indicating the Japanese garden and the light displays beyond. "This might actually be the nicest thing anyone's ever done for me." For once, there wasn't even a hint of joking in her tone.

Before Rae could brush her off with a quick "you're welcome," Steph leaned up on her tiptoes and placed a gentle kiss on her cheek, which instantly heated under the touch of her soft lips.

As Steph pulled away, Rae stood in the middle of the bridge and stared at her. Her hand came up as if on its own volition and touched the spot where Steph's mouth had graced her skin.

Steph smiled, and Rae realized she was probably looking like some inexperienced girl who'd never been kissed before, not even on the cheek. Which of course wasn't true. She'd been kissed plenty, even if only by one woman.

She tried to put on a scowl, but it was a struggle. Her face seemed to want to take on only one of two expressions: stunned or elated. Or maybe it was pure terror. Rae wasn't so sure.

"Come on." Steph slid her arm through Rae's once more. "It's getting late. We should head home."

Yes. Heading home, where things would go back to normal, sounded good. Rae nodded decisively, and they walked toward the car.

Chapter 16

STEPH WOKE UP AS THE first rays of the December sun peeked through her window. She stretched contentedly and let out a sound that resembled a low purr. Wow. She hadn't slept this well in weeks.

Then everything that had happened yesterday came back to her, flooding her mind with a slideshow of images: the worst corporate gig ever, finding out Moose would be moving away, and then that magical evening at Descanso Gardens.

Had that really happened? In the light of day, it felt surreal, like a dream...a dream with a decidedly romantic undertone.

She could still feel Rae's arm hooked around her own, the softness of her cheek beneath her lips, and her body pressed to hers as she had prevented Rae from falling. Even now, her body buzzed as she remembered that moment and then that loose embrace as they had taken the photo at the gazebo.

She reached for her phone on the bedside table and unlocked the screen. There it was. The photo stunned her now just as much as it had last night—and just as much as the kiss she had spontaneously planted on Rae's cheek.

Jeez, Stephanie. Why are you making such a big deal out of it? She had kissed more people than she could count, most of them much more passionately than that. A harmless kiss on the cheek wasn't a marriage proposal.

Nothing had changed, right? She still wasn't one for romance or relationships, and Rae wasn't a woman to play around with for a night or two. It was no longer only about Rae being a club employee. She'd been through so much. What she needed now was a friend, not a romp in the hay, and Steph was determined to be that friend for her, even if Rae might not think she needed anyone.

Friends. She resolutely put the phone away, but the memory of how Rae had looked in the glow of the gazebo's lights stayed with her, even as she rolled out of bed and got dressed. Okay, she definitely needed some air and some distance from her roommate, who might wake up any second.

She grabbed her purse and headed out for a walk and a coffee, hoping both would help to clear her head.

But she didn't get very far.

Their landlady—who, as Steph had found out after moving in, lived in the building too—was hauling an armful of grocery bags through the front door.

Steph hurried over to hold the door open for her.

"Thank you, dear," Mrs. Kleinberg said. "How nice to run into you. I was wondering how you and Rae like the apartment."

"We love it."

"Good. I told Harold that we should drop by and make sure everything is all right. I haven't seen much of you since you moved in."

"Everything's wonderful. We just both work unusual hours." Plus they had avoided running into their landlord and landlady, especially when they left the building together, so they wouldn't have to put on a show and pretend to be a couple.

"Oh, yes, of course," Mrs. Kleinberg said. "Well, you'll have to tell me all about it tomorrow."

Steph frowned. "Tomorrow?"

"Yes. You're coming, right?"

Steph felt as if they were speaking two different languages. "Coming? To what?"

Mrs. Kleinberg nodded toward the front door. "Didn't you see? We put the invitation on the door two weeks ago."

Oh. That. Steph had seen it when the sheet of paper had first been taped to the door. The Kleinbergs were having a holiday barbecue in the courtyard, and every tenant in the building was invited to join them. Steph hadn't planned on making an appearance, so she'd forgotten about it. "Yes, of course, I saw it. But as I said, Rae and I both work evenings, even on the weekend, so we won't be able to make it."

"Good thing it's in the afternoon, then. Harold will throw the steaks on the grill around two. I'm looking forward to getting to know the two of you a little better." Without waiting for a reply, Mrs. Kleinberg unlocked the door to her apartment on the first floor and disappeared inside.

Steph was left standing there, her mouth still open to protest. She snapped it shut. Oh well, how bad could it be? They would hang out with their neighbors for an hour and chat with their landlord and landlady. At least there would be actual steaks, not the tofu burgers and slices of eggplant her parents considered appropriate barbecue food.

She stepped out of the building—and froze. *Oh shit.* She had forgotten one little thing: with the Kleinbergs around, they would have to pretend to be a loving couple. So much for keeping her distance from Rae until she had gotten a grip on this damn attraction.

Rae closed the top button on her short-sleeved button-up shirt. But she already felt as if a noose was tightening around her neck, so she popped it open again. "Why can't we just not go and hide out here until the barbecue is over?" she asked Steph through the open bathroom door.

Steph looked up from her attempt to tame her tousled hair. "Because the Kleinbergs will drop by our apartment for a personal visit if we don't show up. At least if we go to the barbecue, there'll be a dozen other tenants to distract them. We'll stay in the background, eat our steaks, and then tell them we have to go to work."

That sounded good in theory, but Rae had the sinking feeling that it wouldn't be that easy. "Yeah, but...we'll have to pretend to be a couple, won't we?"

Steph put the brush down and stepped out of the bathroom. She had dressed up a little, yet in a pair of tan slacks, a white blouse with three-quarter-length sleeves, sneakers, and a black, slim-fit vest, she still looked entirely herself—and she looked good, Rae had to admit. Somehow, the tomboyish look made her appear even more feminine.

"Yes, at least as long as the Kleinbergs are watching." Steph's gaze flickered up to Rae's eyes. "Will that really be so horrible for you?"

Horrible? That wasn't the word Rae would have used. She wasn't a fan of PDAs, but that wasn't what had her worried. She was supposed to let her attraction to Steph die down, not throw gasoline on the fire.

"Wow. I didn't know it was that bad for you," Steph said when Rae didn't answer. Her voice sounded as if she was speaking around a lump in her throat. "Maybe we should just forget about it. I mean, it's not like the Kleinbergs can kick us out, even if they find out we're not a couple."

"No," Rae heard herself say before she had consciously made up her mind. She couldn't let Steph think that pretending to be her girlfriend would be such a horrible experience for her that she'd rather risk the Kleinbergs showing up on their doorstep unannounced. "They might not be able to kick us out, but if they find out we lied to them, it'll make for one hell of an awkward living situation. Forget what I said, okay? I can do this. *We* can do this."

Steph hesitated. The hurt expression lingered on her face. "Are you sure?"

"Affirmative," Rae said. "I'd be honored to be your date for the barbecue. Well, your fake date."

A hint of a smile curled Steph's lips. "Then maybe you should scrub that bit of toothpaste or whatever it is off your face."

Rae walked past Steph to take a look at her face in the mirror above the bathroom sink. Their bodies brushed, and a whiff of Steph's perfume drifted over. *Mmm.* She glared at herself in the mirror. *What are you? A perfume junkie? Cut out that bullshit.* She ran a corner of her towel beneath ice-cold water to clean her face—and maybe cool off a little. "Better?" she asked when she turned back around.

Steph's gaze slowly trailed up and down her body, making Rae's skin heat. "Yes. You look great."

"Um, thanks." Rae smoothed her hands down the outer seam of her black pants and closed the top button on the blue-and-black-checkered shirt again. "Okay, let's go." *Before I change my mind.*

Even though they were on time, loud chatter already echoed through the courtyard when they arrived. Long tables and benches had been set up, and about twenty people were laughing, talking, and apparently having a great time. Dozens of bowls and platters covered every available space on a separate food table. The scent of freshly baked rolls and the smoky aroma of steaks sizzling on the grill hung in the air.

Rae's mouth watered.

"Hey, Steph," one of their neighbors—a guy in a Dodgers T-shirt—called. His gaze went to Rae. "And, um…"

"Hi, Keith." Steph wrapped her arm around Rae's hips, pulled her close, and looked lovingly up at her. "Rae."

While Rae had seen most of her neighbors in passing a time or two, she had never stopped to make conversation or to introduce herself, so she didn't know any of them by name. Steph obviously did.

Keith looked back and forth between them. "Oh, so you two are together? I thought you were just roommates."

Shit. Rae's gaze darted to the grill, where Mr. Kleinberg was flipping the steaks. "Why would you think that? I mean, the Kleinbergs don't even rent to roommates."

"They don't?" Keith shrugged. "Probably because of those assholes who kept blasting metalcore at three a.m."

"Well," Steph said, "we don't like metalcore, and we're definitely not just roommates. We were merely trying to be discreet. You never know how people will react to two women who love each other. Right, sweetie?" She slid her other arm around Rae too and pulled her even closer until they were pressed together from thigh to shoulder.

With Steph so close and her breasts nestled beneath her own, Rae's ability to come up with a brilliant reply was rapidly dwindling. "Um, right."

Keith chuckled. "Oh, you didn't have to worry about that in our building." He pointed at something to Rae's left.

When she turned her head, she caught sight of Mrs. Kleinberg, who was entering the courtyard with a huge bowl. She was wearing a *Love is Love is Love* T-shirt and looked so proud of it as if she were modeling the newest fashion collection of a famous designer.

"Their son is gay," Keith added. "And so are half of the tenants, myself included. The Kleinbergs always pick the LGBT applicants, if there are any. So don't hold back on our account. Unless you rip each other's clothes off and go at it in the middle of the courtyard, no one will bat an eye."

Steph grinned. "Good to know."

"Right," Rae said again and then wanted to slap herself. God, she sounded ridiculous. If the guys from work could see her now, getting all flustered just because a woman was holding her close. This had to stop—right now. She had to take control. But how?

There was no time for strategizing, so she did the first thing that came to mind: she leaned down and kissed Steph.

She had aimed for a short, borderline platonic peck to the corner of Steph's mouth, just a little gesture to confirm their status as a couple in love, but Steph turned her head to say something to Keith at the wrong—or maybe the right—moment, and their lips met.

No way back now. If she wanted this to look convincing, Rae couldn't very well flinch back. Not that she wanted to.

At the first touch of Steph's lips against her own, all thoughts ceased and sensation took over. Steph's mouth was warm and gentle and soft. God, so soft.

A startled gasp vibrated against Rae's lips, and Steph's hands flexed on her hips, then let go.

Just when Rae wanted to back off and whisper an apology, Steph reached up, threaded her fingers through the short hair at the base of Rae's neck, and kissed her back.

Rae's pulse jolted into a wild rhythm. The tender caress of Steph's lips over her own made her body tingle all the way down to her toes. She pressed more tightly against Steph, trying to soak up the feel of her.

Steph swayed toward her, not an inch of space between them now. Her lips parted on another gasp.

Rae was about to deepen the kiss when someone cleared their throat next to them.

It was as if a tub full of icy water had been poured over their heads. Rae jolted out of the haze of desire. She tore her lips away, breaking the kiss.

Steph stumbled back half a step and pressed her hand to her lips. Her pupils were so wide that only thin, gray rings remained of her irises as she stared at Rae.

Oh God. What had she done? Her attempt to take control had backfired completely. Instead of gaining control, she'd lost it completely—along with her sanity.

Keith grinned at them and said something, but the drumming of Rae's heart drowned out his words.

A touch to her elbow startled her.

When she turned, Mrs. Kleinberg stood in front of her, an amused grin on her face. "I'm so glad you could join us...and that you obviously feel right at home in our building."

This time, not even Rae could deny that she was blushing to the roots of her hair. "Um, thanks for the invitation. Do you, uh, need a hand with anything?"

"No, thank you, dear. All done. I think we're ready to eat, so why don't you come with me and pick out two steaks for you and Stephanie?" Without waiting for a reply, Mrs. Kleinberg slid her arm through Rae's and drew her toward the grill.

The tiny hairs on the back of Rae's neck, which had seemed to vibrate with pleasure just a minute ago, now stood on end with discomfort. Like most right-handed people, Mrs. Kleinberg had used her dominant hand to hold on to Rae, which put her on Rae's left side. After her arm-in-arm stroll through Descanso Gardens with Steph two days ago, Rae had thought that maybe she was getting over that feeling of alarm every time someone entered her personal space from the left, but apparently, that had been a one-time thing.

Or a Steph thing, a not very helpful voice in the back of her mind supplied.

She ignored it and tried her best to focus on Mrs. Kleinberg's chatter about salads, salsa, and all the other food she had prepared for the barbecue.

None of it sounded good to Rae right now. Her stomach felt as if a pterodactyl had taken flight in it. That wasn't still from the kiss, was it? She decided to blame it on Mrs. Kleinberg's uncomfortable grip on her left arm.

"Hey." A warm hand slid between Mrs. Kleinberg's fingers and the bare skin of Rae's arm, neatly separating them.

Rae didn't need to turn her head to see who it was. The heat that touch set off told her enough.

Steph nudged in between them and put one arm around each of them. "I don't mean to interrupt, but...um...could I have a piece of halloumi instead of a steak?"

"Oh, are you a vegetarian?" Mrs. Kleinberg asked.

"No. I go through phases, and when I saw the halloumi, my stomach decided that today's a cheese day, so if it's not too much to ask…"

Rae stared at her. That was just an excuse for why she had interrupted them, right? Rae had never heard of a kiss turning anyone into a quasi-vegetarian.

"Of course not. Let's make your stomach happy. You load up on salads, and I'll get you some halloumi." Mrs. Kleinberg gave Steph's belly a motherly pat and then hurried off.

Rae and Steph were left staring after her. They glanced at each other, then away. Now Rae almost wished Mrs. Kleinberg back at her side—even her left side if that meant she didn't have to be alone with Steph.

Steph circled around to Rae's right side and tugged her over to the food table. "What was that?" she whispered and pointed at the spot where Rae had kissed her.

Damn. Of course Steph had no intention of letting it go. Rae would have been happy not to ever talk about it, but Steph was the type to confront situations head-on. Rae began shoveling salads on her plate just so she wouldn't have to face Steph. "I'm sorry," she whispered back. "I didn't mean to go that far. I know kissing wasn't part of our roommate arrangement. I was trying to… I figured any real couple would have at least exchanged a little kiss after Keith gave us the go-ahead, and I intended to make it a peck on the corner of…" Then her brain caught up with the situation. "Wait a minute. Why am I the only one apologizing? You kissed me back!"

Steph squeezed her arm…hard. "Shh. Not so loud. Mr. Kleinberg is already looking at us."

"You kissed me back," Rae repeated in a whisper.

Steph's cheeks took on the color of the tomato salad on Rae's plate. "Um, yeah. I mean, what was I supposed to do? Pull back and let you stand there like a puppy that got caught piddling on the carpet?"

Rae dropped the spoon back into the chickpea salad and straightened to her full height. "Oh, so you only kissed me back to spare me the embarrassment? That little gasp you gave was just…"

"Surprise," Steph said with a straight face.

"Just surprise, hmm?" Rae didn't buy it for a second. The way Steph had threaded her fingers through her hair and pressed her body against Rae's…

Thinking about it made Rae breathless. "Otherwise, it was a completely horrible experience that you just suffered through."

Steph tilted her head as if thinking about it for a second. Then an impish smile stole across her face. "Well, maybe not completely horrible. You're a decent kisser."

"Decent?" Rae echoed. "I've never had any complaints before." Truth be told, she hadn't given many women an opportunity to complain. Steph was only the second person she'd ever kissed. Maybe that should have made this fake kiss feel all wrong, but it hadn't. Nor had it felt fake.

"I bet," Steph muttered.

Rae couldn't help grinning. "Oh, so you admit it was more than decent?"

"Well, under different circumstances, I might have upgraded it to *good*."

"Good? Just good?" Rae reined herself in before she would issue a challenge to repeat that kiss to prove it had been much more than just good. *What the hell are you doing?* That kiss could never be repeated, and here she was, debating the merits of it.

"Hey." Steph lightly touched her arm. "All kidding aside, you can stop looking so guilty. I wanted you to be my fake girlfriend, so it's not like you kissed me against my will. If you want to feel guilty about something, make it the delicious-looking, thick, juicy T-bone steak I gave up to save you from Mrs. Kleinberg."

As if on cue, their landlady bustled over and deposited a piece of halloumi on Steph's plate and a steak the size of a small elephant on Rae's.

Steph looked at Rae's plate with an expression of steak envy and licked her lips.

Stop staring at her lips. Rae wrenched her gaze away.

Mrs. Kleinberg had followed Steph's line of sight and chuckled. "Oh, it's so wonderful to see a woman with a healthy appetite."

Rae looked down. *Oops.* She had gone a little overboard in serving herself food while she had been busy trying not to look at Steph. Towering heaps of half a dozen salads had made it onto her plate.

"It must be a joy to cook for her," Mrs. Kleinberg said.

Steph smiled and leaned her head against Rae's shoulder in a gesture that felt amazingly natural. "Actually, Rae's the cook in our house."

"Aww, what a sweetheart." Mrs. Kleinberg patted Rae's arm. "Enjoy your food, you two. I'll sit with you for a while later, but first, I need to make sure the other tenants have everything they need." She walked off in the direction of the grill.

Steph regarded Rae with an amused grin. "I think our landlady has a little crush on you."

"Does not."

"Does too."

Rae fixed her with a threatening glare. "Do you want half of my steak or not?"

The smirk on Steph's face was replaced with a faux innocent expression. "Crush, what crush?"

Rae nodded. "I thought you'd see it my way." No one here had a crush on anyone else. Nope. No crushes at all.

Chapter 17

GRRRR. THAT GODDAMN EYE WAS driving Rae up a wall. Maybe it was the smoke from the grill earlier. Whatever it was, her left eye—or rather the socket and the lid—felt irritated today, and nothing she did had helped so far. She had even taken the prosthesis out and cleaned it thoroughly after the barbecue, then squirted some saline into her socket to rinse it.

But that uncomfortable feeling remained. For the first time in many months, she felt the prosthesis as if it were a foreign object that didn't belong there. With everything that had been going on between her and Steph, she had ignored that feeling all week. Now the discomfort had reached a level where she no longer could, though.

She clenched her hand into a fist so she wouldn't rub at the eye again and then looked at the line of patrons waiting to get into the club. Maybe once everyone was seated, she could sneak into the restroom and put in a couple of drops of the artificial eye lubricant that she always carried in her pocket. That might help.

Well, at least her eye provided a welcome distraction. It had been at least five minutes since she had last thought of their kiss.

Great. Now the mental slideshow of Steph's lips, her heat, the way she had felt in her arms was starting again. Work was not the place to think about that. Actually, *nowhere* was the place to think about that. She was in no shape to get involved with anyone, especially not with a commitment-phobic woman like Steph.

"You okay?" Carlos asked as they waved through the next group of patrons.

"Just peachy," Rae responded without looking at him. Her attention was on the next guest already. "Sir, I need to ask you to take off your hat please. We've got a strict no-hats policy to make sure everyone can see the show."

Grumbling, the guy snatched his hat off and stomped past her.

Rae rubbed at her eye with the heel of her hand. Damn, now it was tearing. Even though the surgeons had to remove the eyeball, the tear ducts were still intact.

"Your eyes bothering you?" Carlos asked.

"Just allergies."

He gave her a disbelieving look. "In December? Aren't allergies a spring thing?"

"Not if you're allergic to Christmas," Rae answered.

He chuckled. "Yeah, I hear you. *Nochebuena* at our house isn't for the fainthearted."

"Looks like a full house tonight," someone said from behind them.

Both whirled around.

Mr. Hicks stood in front of them, an iPad in his hands.

"Yes, boss." Carlos nodded. "Good crowd tonight."

"Can you handle the rest of the line on your own for a second, Carlos?" Mr. Hicks asked. "I'd like to have a word with Rae."

Rae's heart started to beat in double time. Mr. Hicks had never asked to speak to her alone in the nine weeks since she'd started working for him. Had she done something wrong? Hopefully, it was just about how he wanted her to seat people or something like that. She needed this job, not only because her disability pay was barely enough to cover her living expenses but also because it gave her something she needed even more urgently than the money: a responsibility and the feeling that she was still good for something.

Mr. Hicks paused in the lobby and turned to face her. "I realized you're the doorperson who covers most shifts."

"If this is about overtime, I—"

He interrupted her with an impatient wave of his hand. "It's not. But since you're here almost every night, you've probably seen more comics than any of your colleagues."

Rae tilted her head in silent agreement. Where was he going with this?

"Let's say I needed someone to headline the New Year's Eve show," Mr. Hicks said. "The headliner just checked himself into rehab, and all the other big names are already booked. So I need someone who can do a solid hour on short notice without asking for an arm and a leg. Who would you pick?"

Only one name came to mind, but Rae reined herself in before she could blurt it out. Had Steph's name popped into her head because she'd been thinking about the kiss on and off since it had happened? She mentally compared the snippets of other comedians' routines with what she had heard of Steph's, which was a lot because she often listened to her practice at home. Steph's material and her timing were great. She had made Rae laugh more often than she cared to admit. "Stephanie Renshaw," she said with confidence.

Mr. Hicks narrowed his eyes at her.

Oh shit. Had he heard that they were roommates? Maybe he even thought they were sleeping together. That wouldn't end well because Mr. Hicks had spelled out his rules very clearly on her first day: no involvement with the other staff or the talent.

"You're not just saying that out of female solidarity, are you?" Mr. Hicks asked.

Not that women-can't-possibly-be-funny bullshit again. Rae squared her shoulders and looked him in the eyes. "I'm not recommending her because she's a woman. I'm recommending her because she's good."

"If she's that good, why isn't she already booked for New Year's Eve?"

"I think she mentioned plans with her sister."

Mr. Hicks regarded her for several seconds before typing something into his iPad. He gave her a nod and walked away without another word.

Did that mean that Steph would get the coveted spot, or would he ignore her advice because she was a woman too? She'd better not tell Steph about it yet so she wouldn't get her hopes up.

"Um, Rae?" Carlos called from the front door. "A little help out here? I think I caught a fake ID."

Finally, some action! Rae rubbed her eye once more, then strode to the door. "Coming."

Steph's Saturday evening was going like the rest of her day: not at all according to plan.

A total of four people had shown up for the backyard show one of her friends had organized, and three of them had been girlfriends of the comedians, so the event had been canceled.

Gabe had suggested dropping by The Fun Zone to watch some comedy since they were already out. She couldn't exactly tell him that she would rather stay away from her roommate for the rest of the day, because if she did, he'd immediately want to know why, so she had given in.

Now here they were, in front of the club, with a great view of Rae as she worked, while they slowly got closer to the front door.

As usual, Rae looked stunning in her work suit and tie, and her confident stance as she guarded the club's front door was admittedly hot.

Apparently, Rae and her colleague had just caught a girl trying to get into the club with a fake ID.

"Sorry," Rae said. "I can't let you in without a valid ID. Club policy."

"But I have an ID." The girl waved the fake thing under Rae's nose.

Rae neatly swiped it from her fingers and slid it into the inside pocket of her suit. "No, you don't."

"You can't do that," the girl protested. "It's mine. If you don't give it back, I'll call the police."

Rae folded her arms across her chest and gave her an impassive look. "Go ahead. My former colleagues will be very happy to charge you with possession of a forged document."

"Oh, come on." The girl took a step forward, right into Rae's personal space.

Steph tensed.

The girl put her hand on Rae's arm and batted her lashes. "Or is this your way of trying to get my address? Because if it is, I have to tell you it's fake too. But I could give you my number...in exchange for the ID. Interested?" Her voice was a seductive purr.

Oh Jesus. Steph nearly shoved aside the group of people separating her from the front of the line. Not because she was jealous or anything, of course. She just found it demeaning to see another woman act that way. It gave women everywhere a bad name.

Gabe let out a whistle. "Did you see that? Man, your roomie seems to be a total chick magnet. I don't get it. Women never throw themselves at me like that."

Steph snorted. "You can hardly complain. You get plenty of attention from women."

"Yeah, but not like that. What is it about her that women find attractive?" He looked away from Rae to give Steph his full attention. "Do *you* find her attractive?"

Steph wasn't going to deny it. Why would she? Finding people attractive was an everyday occurrence for her and didn't mean a thing, right? "Oh yeah. She's…" She licked her finger and made a sizzling sound. "And damn, she can kiss."

Gabe stared at her, and Steph stared right back.

Dammit. She hadn't meant to say that out loud, but apparently, the kiss was still on her mind, no matter how much she had tried to forget about it.

Gabe's eyes widened. "You kissed her?"

"Um, technically, she kissed me."

He waved his hand. "Since when do we stand on technicalities with each other? Come on, tell me everything!"

"Don't get overly excited, you perv." She gave him a playful slap to the shoulder. "The entire thing was as fake as that girl's ID. Our landlord and landlady invited us to a barbecue, and we just kissed so they wouldn't suspect that we lied and are only roommates."

"And that required hot kisses? A little hand-holding wouldn't have done it?"

Steph shook her head. "You'd have to have been there to understand it." Not that she fully understood it herself. Well, she did understand the kiss, but not why she couldn't put it out of her mind. She'd kissed dozens of people. Nothing special about that. Except that this one had been.

"So you and Rae are…?"

"Roommates," Steph said firmly. "Christ, Gabe, what do you think? It was one kiss. You know me. That doesn't mean a thing."

"Yeah, I can confirm that." A hint of bitterness vibrated in his tone.

Steph studied him. "You're not still upset because I…?"

"Nah." He grinned. "You're great and everything, but you're hardly the love of my life. You make a much better friend than girlfriend."

"That's for sure, and I told you that from the start." The one time she might have been interested in more than a fling, she had ended up creating a big mess, hurting everyone.

The girl finally stomped away without her fake ID, and soon, Gabe and Steph were at the front of the line.

Rae was rubbing her eye and apparently hadn't seen them yet.

"Hey," Steph said. For probably the first time in her life, she felt a little shy. What the heck? This was ridiculous. She forced herself to look at Rae instead of gazing at her shoes—and did a double take.

Rae's prosthetic eye had slid to the side, and now her iris was right next to her nose instead of in the middle of her eye. She looked back at Steph with her usual poker face. Obviously, she had no idea that something was wrong with her eye.

"Go on in and grab me a seat, will you?" Steph said to Gabe. "I'll be right there."

To her surprise, Gabe entered the club without hesitation—and without even having glanced at Rae. He probably thought she wanted to stay back to talk to Rae about the kiss and wanted to give them some privacy.

Rae's colleague didn't seem to have noticed yet either because he was on Rae's right. But it wouldn't be long before he caught sight of it. Had Rae even told her colleagues that she was blind in one eye and was wearing a prosthesis? Knowing Rae, she probably hadn't. And that meant Steph had to come to her rescue now.

"Rae…" She leaned up on her tiptoes to whisper a warning into her ear.

The pupil of Rae's right eye widened. "What are you…?"

The citrusy scent of Rae's unisex perfume distracted Steph for a second, then she sternly reminded herself of the situation. "Your eye slipped," she whispered.

Rae went pale in a millisecond. She raised her hand and covered her eye while she looked around frantically with the other.

Steph had never seen her usually stoic roommate so panicked. The urge to help her gripped her. *Think! Fast!* "Carlos, do you mind if I kidnap Rae for a second?" she said as calmly as possible. "I need a little help with my… um…bra. The hook got tangled in my shirt."

"Oh. Go ahead. I've got this." Carlos gestured at the remaining people outside. "And I hear Rae's good with bras."

Rae shot him a one-eyed glare while pretending to rub the other so she could cover it with her hand.

Steph slid her arm through Rae's left one and guided her safely around the crowd mingling in the lobby and to the restroom.

They were in luck. One of the three stalls was empty.

Steph dragged her toward it, but Rae dug in her heels and stopped at a sink to wash her hands. "I need a mirror to do this." Her voice cracked with tension. Her gaze darted to the door, then to the busy stalls. "Shit, shit, shit." Her brow knitted, probably as she realized that anyone could walk in or leave a stall and see her.

"I've got one." Steph patted the purse hanging over her shoulder.

"God, I could kiss you."

A nervous chuckle escaped Steph. "Um, I think that kiss earlier was plenty, thanks. Another one would stretch the platonic-roommates limits."

"I didn't mean it literally. I just don't want anyone to see—"

The sound of one of the stall locks being turned interrupted her.

Steph was the first one to react. She tugged on Rae's arm, drew her into the empty stall, and squeezed close so she could shut the door. Only when they were safely behind the locked door did she realize what situation they were in.

Jeez. Had the stalls in the club's restroom always been this tiny? With the toilet, the trash can, and the toilet paper dispenser taking up most of the cubicle, there was barely enough room for two adults. They had to stand so close that only a few inches of space remained between them. Was it just her imagination, or could she feel the heat emanating from Rae's body? It reminded her of how it had felt to press her body to Rae's and caress her amazingly soft mouth with her lips.

Get it together, Stephanie. This wasn't an erotically charged situation for poor Rae. She was still covering her left eye with her hand, and the tension radiating off her seemed to make the air around her crackle.

"All right. We're safe here," Steph said quietly so no one could overhear them. "Now what do you need to do, and how can I help?"

Rae closed her other eye and exhaled as if trying to release some of her tension. When she opened her eye, some of the take-charge attitude was back in her expression. "I need to take the eye out, put in some drops, and then put it back in," she said in a whisper. "For some reason, the damn eye has been bothering me all day. It probably slipped because I wasn't careful when I rubbed it."

185

Steph rifled through her purse until she found the compact mirror that she barely ever used. Good thing she was too disorganized to follow the current decluttering trend. "So I just hold the mirror?"

Rae nodded, her lips compressed to a thin line. "Yeah. And...can you close your eyes?"

"Rae, that's..." Steph stopped herself before she could say *silly*. It wasn't silly at all. She could only imagine how much trust and courage it would take for Rae to let anyone see her without the eye in. "You know I don't mind, right? I can close my eyes if that makes it easier for you, but please don't think you have to protect my delicate sensibilities or anything."

"Just do it, okay? We don't have the time for a long debate," Rae said. "I need to get back, and so do you. Gabe is probably wondering where you are."

Steph flashed her a grin, hoping a bit of humor would ease Rae's tension. "Nah. He thinks I'm in here, having my way with you."

"If anything, I'd have my way with you," Rae grumbled.

Steph snorted. "That's what you think."

Her teasing had the desired effect: Rae seemed to relax a little. "Okay, let's get this over with."

Steph snapped open the mirror, held it up, and closed her eyes. "They're closed."

"No peeking."

"I promise." Steph squeezed her eyes shut more tightly.

Rae's suit jacket rustled. She muttered a string of curses.

"What is it?" Steph whispered. "Do I need to—?"

"No. Keep your eyes closed. I've got it." Rae leaned so close that Steph could feel her warm breath on her face.

A shiver went through Steph, and she struggled to hold the mirror steady. Jeez, this little bit of closeness really shouldn't affect her like that. *She's your roommate. A club employee. A friend.*

"A little higher," Rae said. "Yes! Now more to the right. Yes, exactly like that."

A giggle rose from Steph's chest as she adjusted the position of the mirror. "If anyone hears us, they'll really think I'm having my way with you."

"Then what will they think if I let out a little cheer and tell you it's in?"

Steph nearly choked on her own spit. She chuckled breathlessly. "I don't even want to know. Is it? In, I mean."

"Yes. You can open your eyes."

Steph did. She looked into Rae's amber-flecked irises from only inches away.

Rae's prosthesis was now in the right place again. Her lid and the skin beneath her eye were a little red, but otherwise, her left eye looked like the one on the right. She nervously searched Steph's face. "How does it look?"

"Gorgeous." Steph gave her an encouraging smile and a pat on the shoulder.

Rae blew out a long breath that ruffled Steph's hair.

Steph slid the mirror back into her purse and reached for the door lock, ready to get out of this tight spot.

"Wait!" Rae called.

Steph let her hand drop and turned. "Do you need a minute before we head back out?"

"No, I…" Rae's gaze flicked down to the tiles, then rose to connect with Steph's. Her cheeks were tinged with red. For a woman who insisted that she hadn't blushed since 1997, her cheeks took on that lovely color a lot. "I just wanted to thank you. For holding the mirror and closing your eyes and for getting me in here so fast," Rae said in a rush. "Your quick reaction out there saved my ass."

"No thanks necessary. I know you're the lone wolf type, but I consider myself part of Team Rae."

The hint of red in Rae's cheeks deepened, but a new light seemed to enter her eye—one that appeared tentatively hopeful. "There's a Team Rae?"

Steph nodded firmly. "There is, as far as I'm concerned. And you know, Carlos and the rest of your colleagues… I bet they'd be on the team too, if you let them. Sometimes they take their teasing and their macho lines a little too far, but they're not bad guys."

"I know that."

"Wouldn't it be less stressful for you to tell them about your eye?" Steph asked. "In case something like this happens again."

Rae stared at the floor and scraped her shoe across the tiles. "I don't know."

"This," Steph tipped up Rae's chin with her thumb so she had to look up, then gently touched a spot below Rae's left eye and was grateful when she didn't flinch back, "is nothing to be ashamed of."

"I'm not ashamed. I just…" When Rae shrugged, her shoulders didn't drop all the way back down, revealing how tense she was. "Being the only female doorperson on staff is hard enough. I'm not ready for anyone to know about the eye."

"*I* know," Steph said softly. "And I don't think any less of you because of it. Quite the opposite. It makes me admire you even more."

"Yeah, but that's different. You're…" Rae raised her gaze to meet Steph's, and a new softness gleamed in her eye. "You're Team Rae."

Her acceptance filled Steph with warmth. A lump lodged in her throat, preventing her from speaking. Not that she knew what to say. For once, no jokes came to mind and no words that would express how it felt to be accepted as part of Rae's inner circle, so she didn't say anything at all. Instead, she smiled at her, and in reply, a tentative curl formed on Rae's lips.

Finally, Rae wrenched her gaze away as if she couldn't stand the intensity of the moment anymore. "All right, enough of that," she said gruffly. "Let's get out of here before everyone really thinks I'm taking you up against the stall door."

An image of Rae's strong body pressing her against the door flashed through Steph's mind. Heat suffused her from head to toe. She chased the image away with a shake of her head. "I thought we had established that I'd be the one to have my way with you?"

"You wish." Her old confidence was back in Rae's tone. She reached past Steph to unlock the door. In the cramped quarters of the stall, her front pressed against Steph's body.

Oh God. That damn image of Rae pressing her against the door returned, and her knees felt suspiciously wobbly. As soon as the door swung open, Steph staggered to the sink and turned on the cold water.

Rae followed suit and took the sink next to her. She inspected her eye in the mirror and blinked a few times as if testing whether her lid would close all the way. It did.

"Will you be okay for the rest of your shift?" Steph asked.

Rae nodded. "As long as I don't rub the eye the wrong way again, I should be fine. I hope," she added more quietly. A flicker of vulnerability dashed across her face, then disappeared as she dried her hands, strode toward the door, and held it open for Steph.

Once they had stepped into the lobby, Rae quickly put some space between them. "See you at home."

Steph nodded. "See you." Instead of hurrying to the showroom, she watched Rae cross the nearly empty lobby. She took in Rae's powerful stride and the confident set of her broad shoulders. Rae really seemed okay. No one would suspect what had happened. But Steph knew she would never forget the vulnerability on Rae's face or the way her hands had trembled in the stall.

Finally, when Rae had disappeared outside, Steph slipped into the showroom, where the comedy show was about to start.

It took her a moment to make out Gabe in the dim light. Just as she had thought, he had commandeered seats in the back so he could slip out if he got bored.

She dropped into the seat next to him. "Sorry," she whispered but didn't offer more of an explanation.

"Finally!" He elbowed her. "What took you so long? I was starting to think you had dragged Rae to the restroom to fuck her."

A wave of anger tore through her with a force that surprised her. "Just shut up, Gabe."

"Whoa!" He held up both hands, palms out, and stared at her.

She stared back. *What the...?* She and Gabe had joked about her sex life a million times before, and neither had ever bothered to use PC language, but it rubbed her the wrong way to hear him talk about Rae that way. "Sorry, I..." She pinched the bridge of her nose, where a headache was starting to form. "I think Rae and I..."

His eyes widened.

"Not what you're thinking! We're starting to become friends. We *are* friends. And I don't want you to talk about her that way."

"Okay, okay. I'll rein in my dirty mouth in the future." He nudged her shoe with his. "You know I didn't mean anything by it, right?"

"Yeah, I know."

He leaned closer and squinted. "You okay?"

"Yep. Just fine." But deep down, she was starting to wonder whom she was trying to convince, Gabe or herself?

Chapter 18

RAE CALLED HER OCULARIST'S OFFICE as soon as it opened at nine o'clock on Monday morning. She tapped her fingers against her thigh as the phone rang and rang. Damn, she shouldn't have ignored the problem for so long. Now it was the day before Christmas Eve, and the ocularist might not be able to squeeze her in before the holidays. Was he even open today?

She couldn't afford to let something like that happen again, especially if it led to her squeezing into a tiny restroom stall with Steph and having to take out the eye in front of her. That incident had kept her up for most of the past two nights. She didn't know what to make of the intimacy—not just the physical one of being so close to Steph, but much more so the emotional one. Somehow, even kissing Steph paled in comparison. That one, she could reduce to a spark of attraction, but the episode in the stall had evoked a mix of feelings that was hard to figure out. Or maybe she didn't want to figure it out.

She was wrenched from her thoughts when the phone was picked up on the other end.

"Window to the Soul, this is Ana speaking. How may I help you?"

Rae cleared her throat. "This is Rae Coleman. I'm having some problems with my prosthesis and was wondering if Mr. Kamali can squeeze me in before the holidays."

"Before the holidays?" Ana sounded as if Rae had asked her to turn water into champagne. "I'm afraid that's completely impossible. We're— Oh, give me one second."

Rae tightly gripped the phone while she waited. Muffled voices drifted through the connection.

"Rae?" It was Mr. Kamali's voice. "Ana says you're having problems with your prosthesis. What's going on?"

"The eye has been really irritated for about a week. I took it out and cleaned it several times, but nothing seemed to help. On Saturday night, the eye even slipped to the side." She didn't want to imagine that it could have even fallen out completely and dropped right at the feet of a colleague.

"Hmm. I don't like the sound of that. We'll be closed over the holidays, but maybe this is something with a quick fix, like a repolish. Can you come in today at five?"

Damn. She would have to find someone to cover her shift for her, but that wasn't the real problem. Rae always made it a point to know the sunrise and sunset times, and right now, the sun set at about four forty-five. Which meant she'd be driving in the dark on her way back, all the way from Tarzana to Beverly Grove. But she had no other choice. "Thanks so much. I'll be there."

She hung up and sank back onto the couch until she was lying stretched out, with her feet dangling off the edge. The throw pillow her head rested on smelled of Steph's perfume. Sweet and floral, yet with a gingery kick, the scent was as casual and sexy as the woman who wore it. It was strangely comforting to lie here and breathe it in.

God, maybe you should tell Mr. Kamali to take a look at your head too. She pulled the pillow out from under her head and threw it across the room.

Her phone rang on her lap, startling her. When she glanced at the screen, the familiar feeling of guilt crept over her. Kim. It had been too long since Rae had called her. It wasn't that she didn't care about how her friend was doing. But every time she saw Kim or talked to her, she had to think of Mike…and her role in his death. For a moment, she considered not picking up, but then she dismissed the thought. Maybe Kim needed her.

She swiped her finger across the screen and lifted the phone to her ear. "Hi, Kim. How are you?"

"Hey, stranger." The undertone of admonition was obvious in Kim's voice. "I'm… Well, I won't say I'm great, but I'm getting there. I finally went through Mike's stuff and packed up some clothes that will go to Goodwill."

Rae swallowed. Her throat felt raw with a mix of grief and guilt. "I'm sorry, Kim. I should have been there to help you do it."

"No," Kim said. "I know I could have called if I needed you. But I think this was something that I had to do alone to…to let go a little bit."

Both were silent for a moment, digesting the words.

"That's…that's good," Rae finally managed to say. God, her voice sounded as if she had tonsillitis. She forced herself to ask before she could chicken out. "Have you? Let go?"

For several seconds, only the sound of a long sigh and then Kim's breathing filtered through the phone. "I'm not sure I'll ever be able to completely let go. I don't think I want to. But I also don't want to keep existing in the fog of grief and rage and what-ifs that has surrounded me since March. It isolates me from the people in my life. From the good things in life. Mike wouldn't want that."

"No," Rae said firmly because this one thing she knew for sure. "He wouldn't."

"He wouldn't want it for you either," Kim said quietly.

Rae raised her free hand and pressed her fingers to her temple. Arteries pounded beneath her fingertips. It reminded her of the much-too-fast pounding of Mike's pulse as she had clamped her hands onto the wound in his neck, trying to hold back the flood of blood that squirted out with each weakening heartbeat. Nausea rose. Quickly, she wrenched her hand away. "I know."

"Then please come and have dinner with me and Mike's parents on Christmas Day."

Rae couldn't help feeling blindsided. She curled her lips into a humorless smile at the irony of her mental choice of words. "Kim, I…"

"You always celebrated Christmas with us. You know Dot and Gordon consider you part of the family."

A bitter taste flooded Rae's mouth. She wasn't sure she deserved to be part of the family. If not for her, their son might still be alive and celebrating Christmas with them. "I know, but…"

"But?" Kim prompted.

Rae bit her lip—hard. She couldn't tell Kim that she wasn't ready to face them, especially not today, when Kim probably felt raw after going through Mike's stuff.

"Please, Rae. You already told me no when I invited you to spend Thanksgiving with us. I don't want you to have to spend Christmas alone too."

"I don't have to be alone. Steph invited me to have Christmas dinner with her and her family," Rae blurted out before she had thought it through. The burden of guilt on her shoulders got even heavier. Now she was lying to her friend? Well, it wasn't a complete lie, she tried to tell herself. Steph *had* invited her to Christmas dinner, even though Rae had no intention of accepting the offer.

"Wait! You're going home with Steph for the holidays?"

"It's not what you think. It started out as a joke when Steph pointed out I'd fit in with her family much better than she does and vice versa. But then it turned into a serious offer. I don't even know how it happened."

"She's sneaking up on you, isn't she?" Kim's tone revealed that she was smiling. "You like her."

Rae's first impulse was to deny it. But did she really want to add to the lies and the untold truths between her and Kim? "She's..." How to sum up a person as complex as Steph? "She's different than I thought. So much more..."

"More what?" Kim asked when Rae trailed off.

Rae slid a little higher so she could rest her head against the arm of the couch and stared up at the ceiling. "More...everything. Loyal. Brave. Compassionate."

"Mm-hmm."

"What's that supposed to mean?" Rae asked.

"Nothing. I'm just so happy for you."

Rae sat up. "Hey, I think you're misunderstanding what I'm saying. We're not a couple or anything."

"I know. But you making a friend...letting someone in... That's big."

Had she let Steph in? She considered everything they had shared over the past two months. *Yeah, I think I did.* God, that was scary as hell. Rae sank back onto the couch. "She saw me." Again, the words slipped out without conscious thought. "Without my eye in. Not out of choice. I don't think I'd be ready for that, but... She took it well. I mean, she was surprised, but she didn't flinch or look repulsed."

"Oh Rae. How could anyone be repulsed by it?"

193

How could anyone not be? Rae had needed several months before she could look at herself in the mirror and accept the empty place where her left eye was supposed to be as part of herself. Some days, it was still hard.

"Do you think I'd be repulsed if Mike...if he'd made it home with a missing eye?" Kim asked in a whisper. "I wouldn't have cared, as long as he made it home."

Rae laid her arm across her face. Her eyes were burning, and this time, it had nothing to do with the uncomfortable prosthesis. "I know," was all she got out.

"Please be kind to yourself, okay? And to Steph. Don't push her away just because you get scared."

Rae let out a grunt. "I don't get scared."

"No, of course not." Amusement colored Kim's tone. "Listen, I have to go. I arranged for Goodwill to pick up the boxes so I won't chicken out, and they'll be here any moment. I'll see you the day after Christmas."

"Um, what's going on the day after Christmas?" Had she forgotten a previously arranged get-together?

"You'll come over and help me eat all the leftovers my in-laws will send home with me," Kim said. "And you'll tell me all about your Christmas dinner with Steph and her folks."

Shit. Now she had maneuvered herself into a dilemma. She had to either lie to Kim and make up a detailed story about Christmas with the Renshaws or admit that she'd lied about having dinner with Steph's family—or actually do what she'd said she would do and go home with Steph for Christmas.

It was like the choice between smallpox, Ebola, and the bubonic plague. Once they had ended the call, she thumped her fist against the back of the couch. "Son of a slug!"

"What's wrong?" Steph asked from the door of her room. She rushed over. "Is your eye still bothering you?"

"No. Yes, but that's not..." Rae slid both hands under her neck and massaged it roughly. It didn't help with her tension. Time to choose the best of the three bad choices...even though she wasn't sure which one that was. Probably not lying to Kim again. "So that leaves Ebola and the bubonic plague."

"Um, what?"

Had she said that out loud? God, she was exhausted from everything that had happened today. All she wanted was to crawl into bed and forget about the kiss, her eye slipping, the episode in the restroom stall, and the raw feelings Kim's call had caused to bubble up.

Steph pushed the coffee table out of the way and squeezed sideways onto the edge of the sofa. Her thigh rested along Rae's leg, soft and warm, and her expression was worried as she gazed down at Rae. "What's wrong? And don't try to tell me it's nothing."

"I...I'm wondering..." Rae picked at some loose threads on her cut-off sweatpants. "Does your offer still stand?" There. She couldn't believe she had really said it.

Steph tilted her head to the side. "Which offer is that? The offer to have my way with you?" She lowered her voice to a seductive burr. "Sure. Anytime, darlin'."

Rae gave her a little shove with her knee. "Keep dreaming."

Laughing, Steph took hold of Rae's leg to keep her balance. Even once she had regained it, she kept her hand where it was, probably not even aware of it.

The warmth that touch sent up Rae's thigh and straight to her core was no longer a surprise, but the fact that she didn't mind the casual closeness was. The discovery startled her so much that she needed a minute to realize Steph was looking down at her with a quizzical gaze. "Um, I...I was talking about the offer to have Christmas dinner with your family."

The teasing grin instantly disappeared from Steph's face and was replaced with a genuine smile. "Wow, that... Yes, of course the offer still stands." She bobbed up and down on the couch, jostling Rae. "Great! At least now it'll be three normal people having dinner with three rabbit-food-eating psychologists. That equals things out."

Normal? Rae wasn't sure that description fit her nowadays.

"Hey, don't chicken out now just because I mentioned psychologists, okay?" Steph pointed her finger at her. Apparently, she had misinterpreted the reason for Rae's doubts.

"I won't. You said we can leave anytime and give work as an excuse, right?"

"Anytime. If you're uncomfortable, let me know, and we'll be out of there faster than a greased eel. We can also time it so that we arrive right before dinner, so we'll only be there for a few hours. And don't worry because we might not be back before sunset. I'll drive, so you can have some of my parents' fake vegan eggnog."

Rae shuddered. "No, thanks." Then her mind latched on to what else Steph had offered. Should she ask her if she'd mind driving her to the appointment with the ocularist later today? Steph had offered to be her driver before. But the appointment with Mr. Kamali wasn't a trip to In-N-Out. Maybe she should take an Uber. Sure, it would cost more, but there was something to be said for the relative anonymity of having a stranger drop her off.

Steph tapped Rae's knee, then pulled back her hand as if only now realizing where her fingers rested. "There's something else, isn't there?"

Damn. What had happened to the poker face she had always been able to rely on? Rae wrestled with her mental list of pros and cons for another minute.

"Whatever it is, just tell me," Steph said softly. Amazing how warm and inviting gray eyes could be. "You know I'm on your side."

On my side. Team Rae. Those two simple words tipped the scales in Steph's favor. "I called my ocularist."

"Your…what?"

"My ocularist. The guy who made my eye." Rae pointed at it.

"Right. So could he help with whatever the problem is?"

"He can't say what's wrong without taking a look, so he wants me to come in." Rae swallowed. God, why was this so hard? "Today at five." She let the words hang there, hoping Steph would understand on her own, without her having to ask.

"Great. So he's squeezing you in before the holidays?"

Rae nodded. *Okay, looks like I'll take an Uber after all.* But then another voice piped up, sounding a little like Mike: *Oh for fuck's sake, be an adult and just ask, Coleman!* It was exactly what her partner would have said. And he would have been right. "Steph, um, would you…? Do you by any chance…? The appointment is after sunset. I know you're probably working tonight, but on the off chance that you aren't…"

"I'm not. Working, I mean." Steph moved her hand again but this time stopped and withdrew it before she could make contact with Rae's knee. "Of course I'll drive you."

"Are you sure? Mr. Kamali's office is all the way in Tarzana. It's a horrible drive, without a direct route. I can totally take an Uber if you'd rather not deal with that."

"What, and miss a road trip to Tarzana?" Steph pressed her hand to her chest and put on a horrified expression. "No way!"

"Thank you." Rae hoped Steph would understand that she wasn't only thanking her for driving but also for making it easy for her to ask.

This time, Steph did put her hand on Rae's knee for a second. "No, Rae. Thank *you*. Thank you for not just taking an Uber so you didn't have to ask for my help."

Rae looked away and decided not to mention how close she had come to doing exactly that.

Steph took her hand away and got up. "So what time are we leaving for the eyeball store?"

The irreverent term was so typically Steph that Rae had to chuckle. It made her feel better that Steph didn't make a big deal out of it but made it sound as if they were going to the supermarket to pick up a carton of milk. "Last time I went to his office, it took me an hour."

"Let's leave at three thirty," Steph said. "That way, you're not worried about being late, and if we're early, we can get a coffee or some ice cream."

Rae nodded, still not over how easy this was. If only the same could be said for her appointment with Mr. Kamali.

Steph kept glancing over at Rae while she drove.

Rae was practically vibrating in the passenger seat. Maybe it was a good thing that traffic had been heavy, so they wouldn't have time to get coffee before the appointment. The last thing Rae needed was caffeine that would make her even more jittery.

Now Steph was glad she had called Gabe and asked him to take over her spot in a comedy show in a laundromat so she could drive Rae. A few times, she caught herself taking one hand off the wheel and nearly reaching over to give Rae's knee a reassuring squeeze or to take her hand. *What the hell?* She had never been the hand-holding type, and she was pretty sure Rae wasn't either.

With five minutes to spare, Steph parked in front of the ocularist's office. "Perfect timing."

"Yeah." Rae didn't smile or look relieved.

Steph turned off the engine but didn't get out of the car. "It won't hurt, will it?"

"I doubt it. The last time I was here, he had to take the eye out and put it back in about a thousand times, so it became a little irritated, but that's all."

"Then what has you so worried?"

"I… Nothing."

Steph didn't believe that for a second. She continued to look at her, but Rae hadn't turned her head, and Steph had a feeling Rae kept her in her blind spot on purpose so she wouldn't have to look at her.

But now wasn't the time to force it. Rae was too tense to let down her guard and talk about what worried her.

"Let's go in." Steph got out and pointed at the sign to the side of the door. "Aww, Window to the Soul. That's kind of cute."

"Guess so."

With Rae in the lead and Steph a step behind, they entered the ocularist's office.

Steph looked around while Rae gave her name to the woman behind the reception desk. It looked like a typical doctor's office, with one difference: photos of people covered the walls. When Steph looked more closely, she thought they might be patients who had received an artificial eye. With some of them, she could tell that one eye wasn't real, mostly because the lid was drooping a little, but with others, it was impossible to say which eye was the prosthetic one.

When Rae waved at her, Steph tore herself away from the photos and followed her to the waiting room.

They had just taken a seat when the door opened and a thin man in his fifties entered. "Hi, Rae. I'd say it's good to see you, but I bet you'd rather be elsewhere." His white lab coat swished as he crossed the room and shook Rae's hand, then turned to Steph with a questioning look.

"This is Stephanie Renshaw," Rae said. After a slight hesitation, she added, "My…friend."

Warmth suffused Steph, and she couldn't help beaming. *Friend.* She doubted Rae introduced many people that way.

"Pleasure to meet you. I'm David Kamali." The ocularist took her hand in an enthusiastic grip.

"Nice to meet you too, Dr. Kamali."

He laughed and held up his hand in protest. "Oh, no, I'm not a doctor."

"But clearly, you're an artist." Steph gestured at Rae's prosthetic eye.

With his olive complexion, it was hard to tell, but he seemed to be blushing a little. "Well, yes, it is an art—but an art I don't want people to notice. If I do my job right, my work blends in with its companion eye." He cocked his head at Rae. "Shall we?"

Rae nodded, her expression grim.

Mr. Kamali started to turn, then paused and looked at Steph. "Oh, if you want to come in with her, that's fine with me."

Oh wow. Steph hadn't expected that. Maybe he had taken Rae's slight hesitation when introducing her as a sign that she was really Rae's girlfriend, or he thought Rae could use some support.

Rae had frozen. Her gaze darted back and forth between Steph and Mr. Kamali.

Very likely, whatever Mr. Kamali would do included removing Rae's eye, and that would mean letting Steph see her without the prosthesis. Steph knew Rae wasn't ready for that. She lightly put her hand on Rae's arm. "It's okay. I'll be fine here in the waiting room. I need to catch up on the celebrity gossip in the tabloids anyway."

Rae breathed in and out twice in fast succession, like a diver preparing to dip beneath the ocean's surface. "No. Come in with me."

Steph stared at her. "Are you sure? You don't have to."

"I know."

They looked at each other for several seconds. Steph tried to read Rae's expression. Did she really want her to come in, or was she only trying to avoid hurting her feelings? Emotions flickered across Rae's face too fast for her to read, but she decided to trust her word—just as Rae had shown her trust by inviting her to come in with them. "Okay." Her voice trembled. As she followed Mr. Kamali and Rae down the hall, her heart pounded a rapid beat against her ribcage. *Get a grip. You're here to help Rae calm down, not to freak out.*

She tried to distract herself by glancing around Mr. Kamali's office. It looked like a doctor's office too…or maybe more like a dentist's office, including a chair that resembled a dental chair. The only thing that didn't fit the doctor's office look were the little bottles of paint lined up on one side of an L-shaped, white desk.

Mr. Kamali took a seat behind his desk while Rae sat across from him.

Steph dragged a visitor's chair over so she could sit to Rae's right. She glanced at the huge magnifying glass and a round mirror mounted to the desk.

"So," Mr. Kamali steepled his fingers, "what seems to be the problem?"

"My eye has been really irritated for a while, and on Saturday, it slipped toward my nose." Rae spoke so fast that her words nearly ran into each other. "I guess I rubbed it the wrong way, but still that never happened before, not even when I had a cold. I don't know. It just feels…off."

"Hmm. All right. Let's take a look. Can you lean forward please?" He had her look up, down, left, and right and close her eyes while he followed each movement of the prosthesis. Finally, he reached across the desk and pulled down Rae's lower lid, then—as if it were the most normal thing in the world—let her artificial eye slide out.

Steph wanted to be polite and put Rae at ease by not looking, but the big mirror to Rae's left was angled in a way that it gave Steph a perfect view of her.

For a second or two, the sight of the bare socket took her breath away. Before, when she had walked in on Rae in the bathroom, she had caught only the briefest of glimpses—partly because Rae's very naked body had distracted her. As Mr. Kamali pulled apart Rae's lids to inspect the socket, Steph couldn't help staring at the empty space where her left eye should have been. It didn't look horrible. It would just take some getting used to—provided Rae would let her see the socket with the prosthesis out again—but there was nothing that made her shudder and want to avert her gaze. The pink flesh looked healthy. The color reminded her of the inside of her cheek.

She met the gaze of Rae's remaining eye in the mirror.

Rae looked so serious. Was she even breathing?

To hell with not being the hand-holding type. Steph reached over and took Rae's hand.

Rae's fingers flexed around hers as if she'd been startled, but then she latched on to Steph's hand as if she needed to hold on to keep Steph from fleeing the room.

Steph gave her a reassuring smile. *Don't worry. That won't happen,* she tried to tell her without words.

Mr. Kamali cleared his throat and gave them an amused grin.

Yeah, he definitely thought they were a couple.

"Has your eye been tearing more than usual?" he asked. "Any discharge?"

Rae nodded.

"It might sound like a strange question, but what color was the discharge?" Mr. Kamali asked.

Rae's gaze flicked to Steph, who squeezed her hand to let her know there was nothing to be embarrassed about. "Um, white, I think," Rae said.

"Then it's clearly not an infection. Here's what I think is going on: When they took out your eye, they put in an orbital implant." He looked at Steph and added, "Basically, it's a Ping-Pong-sized ball that they insert to replace some of the lost volume. They attach the muscles of the eye to it and cover it with tissue. The prosthesis sits on top of the Ping-Pong ball so the muscles move it along with its companion eye." He held up Rae's artificial eye.

It was the first time Steph saw it out of its socket. The prosthesis wasn't shaped like an eyeball but more like a curved shell. A black dot graced the white close to the edge of it, maybe to show which side was up or down.

"But the problem is that the tissues surrounding the prosthesis change over time," Mr. Kamali continued, and now he was speaking more to Rae. "The fat in the eye atrophies, and then the shape of your socket no longer fits the back of the prosthesis. Little pockets form, where tears collect, and the salts irritate the eye. The prosthesis also begins to rub on the tissues, adding to the irritation. You might even start to have problems with the eye staying in place because there's now too much room in the socket."

"Yes," Rae said. "I couldn't put my finger on it, but that sounds exactly like what's been going on. It feels like it doesn't fit me anymore."

"Exactly. That's why we tell our clients they need to have their artificial eye replaced every five years—to ensure a comfortable fit."

"Five years? But I've only had it for about seven months."

Mr. Kamali nodded. "I know. But the first year, the socket changes the most. When we first fitted you for the prosthesis, there might have also been some residual swelling from your injury. It can take up to a year for the edema to disappear completely, and that changes the shape of the socket too. So I'm really glad you came in before you ended up with inflammation or a drooping eyelid because the prosthesis started to sit too deep in your socket."

Rae raised her free hand and covered her left eye for a moment as if by pure instinct.

Steph trailed her thumb along Rae's index finger. She didn't know if Rae actually found it soothing, but after a moment, Rae dropped her hand to her lap.

Her grip on Steph's fingers tightened. "That means I need a new prosthesis, doesn't it? And, of course, it won't be done in time for Christmas," she added, as if to herself. "Can I keep wearing this one until the new one is done?"

Steph's breath caught. Christmas? That was what her strong, stoic friend was worried about? She tugged on Rae's hand to get her attention. "You're not worried about what my family will think, are you?"

Rae huffed. "No, of course not. It's not like I'm trying to impress them."

"Liar," Steph said affectionately. "I promise no one will stare or say anything if you show up with an eye patch." She would call each member of her family—and the neighbors or anyone else who might drop by too, if need be—and make sure of that. "Well, I might stare a little, but only because I have a feeling you'll look pretty dashing."

Rae's bunching jaw muscles relaxed a little. "Is that a fetish of yours?"

Steph shrugged and grinned. "It could easily become one."

"Oh yeah?"

Rae's low drawl sent a shiver through Steph. "Mm-hmm." *Christ, would you stop flirting?*

"Um, far be it from me to get in the way of a pirate romance," Mr. Kamali said, "but before you buy an eye patch, maybe let the expert get a word in?"

"Oops. Sorry." Steph gave him a sheepish smile.

Mr. Kamali chuckled. "Don't worry about it. It's great to see that Rae has someone to support her."

"Hello?" Rae waved her hand. "I'm sitting right here. So you are saying I don't need an eye patch? I can keep wearing the old prosthesis for a while?"

"Even better," Mr. Kamali said. "The change of your socket isn't so drastic that we need to start over with a new eye. At least not yet. It will probably become necessary at some point, but for now, we just need to enlarge the prosthesis a little by adding some material to the back."

Rae beamed as if he had said her eye would be growing back.

Steph couldn't help staring. Even during the first week of living together, when Rae had scowled at her most of the time, she had thought Rae was attractive in a brooding sort of way. But a beaming Rae, radiating happiness, made her chest expand as if her heart had suddenly doubled in size.

Rae picked up the prosthesis from the desk and held it out to the ocularist. "Well, what are we waiting for, then? Get to work."

Laughing, Mr. Kamali took it. "Is she always this bossy?"

"Pretty much."

"Then let's get started. I'll have you out of here in an hour, tops."

They actually made it out in forty minutes, and as they walked out of the ocularist's office, Steph realized that Rae hadn't let go of her hand the entire time.

"Um, you're going in the wrong direction." Rae had been deep in thought, checking out the license plates of oncoming cars—a habit that always soothed her—so it had taken her a while to realize Steph was heading west on Ventura Boulevard instead of turning east, toward Hollywood. That in itself was startling. Normally, she paid close attention to everything the driver did if she was in the passenger seat.

"No, I'm not." Steph pulled into the parking lot of a strip mall. "I thought after a day like this, you deserve some—"

"Alcohol?"

Steph chuckled. "That too. But no. I mostly mean this." She pointed to one of the stores, with tiny, colorful tables out front.

Rae could make out the words *Italian ice* on the glass door. "Ice cream?"

"Yes! Or would you rather go straight home?" Steph looked over. "Damn, I should have asked. I bet your eye hurts."

"Nah, not really. Just a little sore." Mr. Kamali must have taken out and replaced her prosthesis more than a dozen times as he added layers of wax and then clear acrylic until it fit. "I'm not used to so much in and out."

Steph burst out laughing and pressed her hand to her mouth. "Sorry, sorry. I'm not laughing at your eye. Replay what you just said."

Rae craned her neck so she could shoot Steph a pretend disapproving look. "I'm probably not the first to tell you that you've got a one-track mind."

"It's been mentioned a time or two." Steph stopped laughing. "But seriously, how do you feel?"

"I'm fine. The fit feels a bit tight right now, but Mr. Kamali said that will stop on its own in a day or two."

"I know," Steph said. "I was there."

"Yes, you were."

The words hung in the air between them, heavy with meaning. They looked at each other, and an unfamiliar warmth rose up Rae's chest.

This time, Steph was the first to look away. "So ice cream?"

"Ice cream." Rae could definitely use something to cool down.

"Then come on!" Steph jumped out of the car.

Rae followed at a slower pace and entered the ice cream parlor after her.

Blackboards on the yellow walls listed a huge selection of Italian ice and gelato flavors, while another one said, *Trust the magic of ice cream.*

Trust somehow seemed to be the motto of the day. Rae still couldn't believe she had invited Steph to come into Mr. Kamali's exam room with her. No one but her doctors and her ocularist had seen her with the eye out, not even Kim, so that decision had made her stomach cramp. But she needn't have worried. Steph had taken the sight of her empty socket in stride. Toward the end of the appointment, Rae had been able to turn toward Steph and face her without stiffening when Mr. Kamali had left them alone to take the prosthesis to his lab next door. Steph had continued to chat as if it made no difference to her whether the eye was in or out.

Amazing. Rae's gaze followed Steph, who had discovered a wall of retro candy in the back of the store. In the beginning, she hadn't liked Steph's cavalier attitude, the constant jokes, and offhand comments, but now she was starting to appreciate Steph's approach to life. Maybe some of Steph's ability to enjoy herself in the moment and let go of things she couldn't change would rub off on her if she kept hanging out with her—and that was something she definitely wanted to keep doing.

"Rae! Look at this," Steph called from the back of the store. She swung a yard-long bubble gum stick as if it were a baseball bat, then held an oversized pair of wax lips up to her mouth and made kissing sounds in Rae's direction.

Rae pretended to cover her face in embarrassment when the man behind the counter looked at them, but secretly, she couldn't help laughing at Steph's antics. She joined her in front of the candy shelf. "God, I can't take you anywhere. You're like a kid in…um, a candy store. Literally."

Steph gave her an unrepentant grin and pointed at a colorful candy necklace. "Oh, we had these when we were little. Did you?"

"No. My parents didn't allow candy, remember?"

"Right. Thank God my parents weren't as strict back then. Come on, I'll buy you one." Steph reached for the necklace.

Quickly, Rae held on to her arm. "Buying me jewelry, even candy jewelry, isn't in the roommate contract."

Steph pretended to pout. "But we're definitely getting one of these." She grabbed a Peppermint Pig that came with a little hammer to break it up into pieces. "Lana loves them. Apparently, it's an East Coast thing, and she grew up in New York. She'll be happy if I give her one as a bonus Christmas present, and if my parents insist on feeding us kale and beets, at least she'll have something to eat."

Christmas presents. Oh shit. Rae had been so busy worrying about her appointment with Mr. Kamali that she hadn't had time to think about what having Christmas with Steph's folks would mean. She grabbed the remaining two Peppermint Pigs and marched to the counter.

Laughing, Steph followed her. "Are you discovering your sweet tooth?"

"No. They're for Lana, and you need to tell me what to get for you and the rest of your family. If I'm crashing your Christmas dinner, I can't show up empty-handed."

Steph took hold of Rae's right arm and tugged her around. "You don't need to get us anything. You being there—that's gonna be my Christmas present."

Oh Christ. How sappy. Now it was Rae's turn to wrinkle her nose.

Steph lightly bumped her with her hip. "Oh, don't pretend. Deep down, you're just a teddy bear."

"Mm-hmm. More like a grizzly."

"Yeah, right. Come on, Grizz. Ice cream first, freak-out about presents later." Steph pulled her to the counter, where two glass cases held dozens of different flavors. Her gaze went back and forth between various Italian ice buckets and tubs of gelato, and she started nibbling on her pinky like a little kid facing the impossible task of deciding on a favorite flavor.

The look should have appeared ridiculous on an adult woman, but on Steph, it was simply cute. Instead of studying the ice cream, Rae observed her with a smile.

"Let me know if you'd like to try some of the flavors before you decide," the man behind the counter said.

Steph's face lit up. "Ooh, that would be great."

That was the beginning of the longest ice-cream-decision-making process Rae had ever witnessed. The man—who was apparently the owner—kept handing over new samples. Steph tried them all willingly, even questionable choices like wasabi or root beer. After each sample, she declared it her new favorite, only to change her mind with the next one she tried.

Finally, she narrowed it down to her top five and then chose two of the most decadent gelatos, while Rae needed only seconds to decide on strawberry Italian ice.

They carried their selections to one of the tiny tables in the front, and Steph immediately steered toward the chair with its back to the door, leaving the chair in the corner for Rae.

"Thanks." Rae settled back and stretched out her legs, only now realizing how tense she must have been all day. Her muscles hurt as if she'd completed a high-intensity workout. But she forgot her discomfort as she watched Steph dig into her gelato.

Steph swirled the little plastic spoon through the soft mass, then slid it between her lips. She closed her eyes, leaned her head back, revealing her elegant neck, and let out a moan that was much too sensual.

Rae shoveled several spoonfuls of her strawberry Italian ice into her mouth, hoping it would cool her down. It was refreshing as it slid down her throat, but it did little to lower her body temperature or to distract her from the sight of Steph enjoying her gelato.

Steph slid another spoonful into her mouth, her eyes still closed. "God, so good."

Christ, sounding so damn sexy while eating should be a crime. Rae squirmed in her seat. "Well, it'd better be good after it took you an hour to decide." She tried to pretend it was the cold Italian ice that was making her voice sound a little strange. "I thought you'd go through his entire inventory."

Steph opened her eyes and shrugged. "What can I say? I like to sample a lot of different flavors."

"Yeah, so I heard."

"Do people at the club really say that about me?" Steph looked more curious than insulted.

Rae sobered. "No. Not when I'm around," she said firmly. "They know I wouldn't let them talk about you that way."

"I don't care what they say about me, you know?"

"I do."

Beneath the table, Steph touched her foot to Rae's. "Thank you." She regarded Rae with an uncharacteristically serious look until Rae glanced away. "Here, try this vanilla apple crisp." Steph slid her paper cup across the table. "I swear it tastes like my grandmother's apple pie. Well, the apple pie she had her staff bake. Grandmother Katherine wouldn't have been caught dead with her hands in pie dough. She was posh as hell. No one was allowed to ever mention how her husband—my grandfather—made his millions."

Millions? Rae swallowed. The more she heard about Steph's family, the more she doubted she would fit in with them. "Which is? Was he a con artist? A mafioso? A drug lord?"

Steph laughed. "You're such a cop. Yeah, I guess you could say he was a drug lord—kind of."

"How can anyone be *kind of* a drug lord?"

"His company produced a legal kind of drug: laxatives."

That was the last thing Rae had expected her to say. Her jaw dropped open.

Laughing, Steph stretched her arm across the table and slid a spoonful of apple crisp gelato into her mouth.

Chapter 19

IT WAS HALF PAST EIGHT by the time they made it back to the apartment. Steph flopped down on the couch as soon as they walked in. Now that the sugar rush from the gelato had worn off, she felt as if all energy had been sucked out of her. She could only imagine how beat Rae must be, so she wasn't surprised when Rae didn't take a seat but remained standing halfway to her room.

"Thanks again." Rae looked at her with an intense expression. "For driving. And everything else."

"Anytime," Steph said, meaning it.

Their gazes caught, then Rae gave her a nod and quickly disappeared into her room.

Steph stared after her. Was she imagining it, or had something between them shifted? Sure, she had been part of Team Rae before, but now it felt different.

She shook her head at herself. It was probably just that moment when Rae's gaze had met hers in Mr. Kamali's mirror. The naked vulnerability in her eye must have triggered some primal protective instinct, like a mother protecting her child.

Yeah, sure. She snorted. Stephanie Renshaw having maternal instincts! No one would believe that for a second.

The word *maternal instinct* reminded her that she still hadn't called her mother to tell her she had invited Rae for Christmas dinner. *Oh damn!* She scrambled for her phone and went to her room while it rang.

"Hi, honey," her mother said as she picked up the phone. "How are you?"

In her parents' house, that wasn't only a meaningless phrase used as a greeting; they actually expected an answer—and *I'm fine* didn't cut it. "Hi, Mom. I'm a little tired but otherwise great. Still no exciting news on the comedy front, though."

"That's too bad," her mother said. "Do you really think that will change at some point?"

Steph wasn't in the mood for that discussion, which usually ended with a subtle nudge encouraging her to go back to college. "If I keep at it, I'm sure it will. But that's not why I called." She closed the door behind her and sank onto her bed. "I know this is very late notice, but would you mind if I bring someone with me for Christmas dinner?"

For several seconds, she didn't hear anything, not even her mother's breathing.

Steph lowered the phone and glanced at the screen to confirm that they hadn't accidentally been disconnected, then moved it back to her ear. "Mom? Are you still there?"

"Sorry. Yes, I'm here. I just needed to process that for a second. I'm a little surprised, to be honest."

"Me too," Steph muttered.

"Pardon me? I didn't catch that."

"It's not what you think, okay? Rae and I... We're...we..."

"Oh, you're bringing your roommate?" her mother asked. "Your sister mentioned meeting her."

Steph wondered what else Claire had told their parents about Rae. "Yes. I know it sounds like the college kid thing to do, but we...we've grown kind of close."

"Is that a euphemism for sleeping with her?" her mother asked.

"No! Why does everyone keep thinking that?" Steph took several calming breaths. "Okay, don't answer that. I know why everyone keeps thinking that. But this time, it's really not like that, Mom."

"All right," her mother said in that careful therapist voice Steph hated. "Bring her. I'd certainly like to meet the woman who's so different. And so would your father."

"Mom..." Steph lowered her voice to a low growl, channeling Rae. "I'm warning you. No psychoanalyzing her. I'm serious."

"Believe it or not, honey, but *psychoanalyzing* people, as you call it, is not what therapists do in their spare time."

Steph snorted. "Yeah, right. The way you didn't psychoanalyze Elyse when Claire first brought her home."

Her mother was silent for a moment.

Damn. Steph bit her lip. Why on earth had she brought her up?

"Well," her mother finally said, "as it turned out, I was right when I suspected she had some issues she needed to work through. I mean, who seduces her ex's sixteen-year-old sister just to—"

"That's not what happened, Mom. I told you that a million times. Besides, we were talking about your constant psychoanalyzing."

"Is that why you never brought anyone home?" her mother asked, again using that damn therapist voice.

"No." At least it wasn't the only reason. "Bringing someone home to meet the family implies a level of commitment that I don't want. That's why I don't do it, if you need to know."

"Until now." Steph could practically hear a smug grin spreading across her mother's face.

"I told you, this is different." Wasn't it?

"Of course. So does your friend have any special dietary requirements?"

"Food," Steph said firmly. "And by that, I mean food intended for human consumption, not a pile of rabbit food."

Her mother sighed. "We're having dinner catered again. Claire insisted on a honey-baked ham with a sweet potato casserole and bread stuffing for Lana. You and your friend can have that too."

"Oh yum." Steph's stomach rumbled. "I knew there was a reason I liked Lana so much."

"The food will be delivered around two. Try to be on time, okay?"

Steph flicked her gaze upward. *Jeez, be late once and you'll hear about it forever.* "We'll be there before two. Rae is super reliable, so she'll probably be raring to go at one."

"Good. See you on Christmas, then. Oh, and please send me an email with a couple of suggestions for a little something your dad and I could get your friend for Christmas."

"Will do." Steph's annoyance faded. For all her flaws, her mother had her good sides too. "Um, Mom?"

"Yes?"

Steph hesitated. She hated asking her parents for money with the passion of a million suns. But if she bought Rae the present she had in mind, she wouldn't have enough money left for her share of the utility bills. "If you don't have a Christmas present picked out for me already, um… money's always good, you know?"

Her mother made a resigned sound, as if she hadn't expected any better from Steph. "Tomorrow is Christmas Eve. Of course we have a gift picked out already."

Yes, of course. It was only Steph who left the gift shopping until the last minute. Maybe Claire was right, and she really should become a little more organized.

"But if you need money, why don't you just say so?" her mother added.

Steph bit her knuckles until her teeth had left two rows of indentations. The urge to say, *Never mind,* and end the call was overwhelming. But then she either had to stick Rae with her part of the utility bills or show up to Christmas dinner without a present for her. She swallowed her pride. "I…I need money."

"How much?" her mother asked in that disappointed-parent tone that Steph hated even more than the therapist voice.

Steph quickly calculated how much Rae's present would cost. "Two hundred, if that's okay. I'll pay you back next month."

"I can send you more," her mother said.

"No, thanks. Two hundred is enough."

"All right. I'll transfer it right away."

Steph struggled not to let her humiliation show. "Thanks."

They ended the call, and Steph tossed the phone to the foot of the bed. *God, the things we do for love. Um, not love. Friendship,* she firmly corrected herself. But she knew Rae was worth it. She could hardly wait to see her face when she unwrapped her present.

At half past one on Christmas Day, Rae clutched the two bags of presents, hers and Steph's, on her lap. Why on earth had she agreed to join the Renshaw family dinner? She would stick out like a sore thumb among these rich people who were probably all very much in touch with their feelings. But now it was too late to change her mind because they were already in the car, on their way to Beverly Hills.

Without warning, Steph pulled over into a gap between two parked cars on Rosewood Avenue. "You know what? This is silly."

The sinking feeling in Rae's stomach became a spiraling sensation. She craned her neck to make out Steph's expression. "Um, what's silly?" Did Steph regret inviting her along for Christmas dinner?

"Me driving," Steph said. "It's still light out, so why don't we switch, and I'll drive home later? I know being in the passenger seat makes you nervous."

Was it so obvious that she was nervous? "Thanks, but your Mini has blind spots the size of a whale. Besides, um…" Should she admit it? Rae gave herself a mental nudge. "It's not being in the passenger seat that's making me nervous."

"Oh. Despite everything I might have said, my parents really aren't that bad, you know?"

"They won't think I'm your girlfriend, will they?" Rae asked.

Instead of reassuring her immediately, Steph pulled back into traffic. "Would it be so bad if they did?" she asked quietly.

"No, of course not. I didn't mean it like that. Any of your future partners should consider themselves lucky." The thought of Steph with some woman or man made Rae grip the bags of gifts more tightly.

Steph let out an unladylike snort. "We both know that's bullshit."

Rae turned in the passenger seat as much as possible so she could see her better. Since the weather was gorgeous, Steph had put down the top of her convertible, and now her hair blew in the wind. Rae couldn't help admiring how carefree and beautiful she looked. For a moment, she nearly forgot what she'd been about to ask. "You keep saying you suck at relationships, but you know what? I'm beginning to doubt that."

"That makes one of us," Steph muttered. "Why would you think that?"

"You're considerate, loyal, and fun." Rae struggled not to blush at handing out compliments. That wasn't usually her strong suit. "Not that I'm a relationship expert or anything, but I'd think those are traits people want in a partner."

Steph shook her head. "Trust me, all those traits go right out the window once I'm in a relationship. I'm really not a good girlfriend."

"Have you even been in a relationship?"

"Define *relationship*," Steph said.

"That's a no, then."

Steph shrugged. "It's hard to sustain a relationship when you're on the road all the time."

Rae looked at her, knowing there was more.

Steph made a right onto Beverly Boulevard before she answered. "Yeah, okay, I didn't really try. It was fun to be free to hook up with whoever I wanted while I was touring the country. I didn't even need to make up excuses for why I wouldn't call, because they knew I'd be off to a new city the next week."

"Was there never anyone who made you want to call?" Rae found herself asking. She wasn't usually one for relationship talk, but the urge to understand Steph better was unexpectedly strong.

"No," Steph said immediately. "The people I had flings with on the road met me as a comedian. That was mainly what they saw me as, and that's all I tried to be with them. They wanted to be with the entertainer who cracked jokes all the time, so that's what they got."

"Hmm." Rae smoothed out a wrinkle in one of the bags on her lap. That sounded kind of lonely. The people who hadn't seen the complex woman behind the act didn't deserve her.

Steph braked at a red light and looked over at her. "What about you?"

"I don't want you to crack jokes all the time," Rae said, deadpan.

Steph reached across the middle console and flicked Rae's thigh with her index finger. "I know that. Don't avoid the real question." She rubbed her face and chuckled. "Christ, I sound like my parents. Just pretend you're already in their house and answer anyway."

Rae stared at the license plate of the car in front of them. "Yeah, I've been in a relationship."

"*A* relationship?" Steph echoed. "Singular?"

The driver in the car behind them started to honk as the light turned green and Steph didn't clear the intersection.

She flipped him off and stepped on the gas. "You don't mean you've only been in one relationship...do you?"

Rae's defensive instincts rose. "There's nothing wrong with that."

"No, of course not. Sorry. I didn't mean to imply otherwise. It fits you. You're clearly a one-woman woman." There was something like admiration in Steph's tone...or maybe even a hint of longing or envy. "I bet you were together for quite some time."

"Fifteen years."

Steph glanced at her with wide eyes, then back at the road. "Wow. That's..." She whistled quietly. "What happened? You don't just walk out after fifteen years together...do you?"

"Yeah, you do. At least Lise did." Rae couldn't stop a bitter tone from entering her voice.

"Lise," Steph repeated as if tasting the name. "Did she cheat?"

"No. Nothing like that. She..." A hard knot formed in her stomach.

Steph reached over and softly touched her knee.

Rae realized that it had been quite some time since any of Steph's touches had startled her, even when they came from the left. It was as if her body had lowered its shields around her and accepted her hand as part of itself. *Okay, now you've officially lost it, and you haven't even tried her parents' vegan eggnog yet.*

"You don't have to talk about it if you don't want to," Steph said.

"It's okay. I'm over it." And maybe, for the very first time, that was the truth because she realized she hadn't even been thinking about Lise right now. "Lise moved out four years ago."

"Just like that?"

"No. We talked a lot...argued a lot the year or two before. Well, she talked. That's the thing. She said she couldn't be with me anymore because I didn't talk to her."

Steph frowned. "But she must have known you weren't exactly a chatterbox when the two of you got together."

"She said I was different then," Rae said. "That my job changed me."

"Do you think there's some truth to that?"

"Yeah. I mean, like you said, I've never been a chatterbox, but I'm sure being a police officer enhanced that tendency."

"How so? I mean, don't cops have to be good at talking to people?"

"Sure. I was fine talking to people as part of my job. But talking about myself and my feelings..." Rae shook her head. "Cops see that as a weakness. Lise never understood why I didn't talk about how my day was. I wanted to keep her away from all the ugliness I saw at work, and I guess in the process, I stopped talking to her altogether. I forgot how to open up and talk about my feelings, and Lise got sick and tired of having to drag things out of me. I don't blame her."

Steph looked over, then returned her attention to driving as she made a left onto Santa Monica Boulevard. "Hey, don't be so hard on yourself. It's obvious you've worked on yourself. You've got no problem talking about your feelings right now."

Rae opened her mouth to reject that notion, then snapped it shut. *Damn.* Steph was right. She was talking about her feelings—without having to be dragged into the conversation screaming and kicking. When had that happened?

Steph laughed. "What's going through your head? You should see your face! You look like you just found out you have a kid you didn't know about!"

Before Rae could come up with an answer, Steph turned right onto a quiet street lined by tall palm trees. Stylish mansions and sprawling one-family homes were set back from the street behind iron gates and towering hedges. One of the gates stood open, and Steph navigated her Mini Cooper up a long driveway flanked by cone-shaped bushes.

For the second time in as many minutes, Rae was speechless. She stared at the snow-white two-story mansion rising up in front of her. "This is where you grew up?"

"Yep."

It couldn't have been more different from the RV and the tiny houses in which Rae had grown up. There had never seemed to be enough space for all the people who moved freely in and out of her parents' home, while the Renshaws' mansion looked as if you could get lost on the way to the bathroom.

"Don't worry." Steph chuckled and took one of the bags from her. "I know my way around. You won't need to leave bread crumbs to find your way out," she said as if guessing Rae's thoughts. "Just stick close to me."

That was exactly what Rae was planning. She clutched her bag as they climbed out of the car and made their way to the portal-like front door.

When Steph rang the doorbell, it was her sister who opened the door. "Merry Christmas." Claire tapped her elegant silver wristwatch as if it had stopped working. "Wow, alert the media! Stephanie Renshaw is on time."

"I'm actually early, sis. Merry Christmas." Steph bumped her sister aside and pulled Rae into the house.

Rae tried very hard not to stare slack-jawed at the chandeliers on the high ceiling. A stately staircase with garlands wrapped around the banister led to the second floor, and Rae wouldn't have been surprised to see Steph's parents descend in a silk ball gown and a formal tux. She smoothed her hand over her navy chinos and light blue dress shirt. She hoped she wouldn't misjudge the distance and knock over any of the expensive-looking porcelain statues, vases, and mostly hideous Christmas decorations that filled the foyer.

Steph discreetly circled around to Rae's left and slid her hand onto her arm. "Am I okay on this side?" she asked so quietly that her sister couldn't hear.

Rae exhaled. "Very okay. Thanks."

With Claire trailing behind them, Steph led her into a huge dining room with a table long enough for ten. Silverware and gold-rimmed china sparkled beneath another chandelier, but no one was sitting at the table, nor was there any food to be seen.

Lana uncurled from an armchair and walked toward them with a welcoming smile. In a flowing, chocolate-brown skirt and an ivory-colored wrap top that emphasized her ample curves, she was dressed nicely, yet comfortably. She was also barefoot, Rae noticed, which immediately put her a little more at ease.

"Hey, you made it." Lana embraced her future sister-in-law warmly and then tugged on Steph's T-shirt with the painted-on tie. Since Steph had to head to her gig directly afterward, she was wearing her comedy outfit. "Cool shirt. I would steal it from you, but I don't think it would fit me." She chuckled, apparently not at all self-conscious about her full figure.

Rae had instantly liked that about Lana the first time she had met her.

Lana turned toward Rae and gave her a slightly shorter hug, ignoring the bag that Rae kept pressed to her chest as a shield. "Hi, Rae. Good to see you again."

Rae stood still and patted her back once. "Um, hi."

"Oh, Stephanie, you're here already."

Rae took the new voice that filled the room as an excuse to take a step back from Lana. She watched as Steph greeted the woman who could only be her mother. The resemblance between her and her daughters was uncanny. They all had the same slender figure, gray eyes, and blonde hair, but Dr. Renshaw wore hers in an elegant chignon. In a lavender pantsuit, she looked as if she were about to head out to a business meeting or a therapy session, not spend Christmas with her family.

How could the irreverent, casual Steph possibly come from such a posh family?

"And you must be Rae. Merry Christmas." Steph's mother studied her with an intent gaze, then lightly took hold of Rae's shoulders to greet her with air kisses.

Rae somehow managed not to squirm out of her grasp. "Merry Christmas. Nice to meet you, Dr. Renshaw. Thanks so much for having me."

"My pleasure. I've heard so much about you, I couldn't wait to meet you."

Rae arched her brows and looked at Steph. What had she told her mother?

Steph held up her hands and sent her sister an accusing glare. "Not from me. I didn't tell her a thing."

"It was more what you didn't say that was so interesting," her mother said.

"Mom, it's Christmas. Leave the psychobabble at the office."

"I wasn't about to…" At her daughter's gaze, Dr. Renshaw nodded. "Well, then you'd better call me Diane, Rae."

Rae bit her lip. She wasn't sure she was ready for that, but she nodded politely.

"Where's Dad?" Steph asked. "Sneaking some ham in the kitchen while no one's looking?"

"Your father doesn't eat meat; you know that," her mother said. "Besides, the food isn't even here yet. He's outside, lounging by the pool. Why don't I take this," she took the bags of presents from them, "and you go keep him company? I'll call you when the food arrives, which should be any second."

Of course the Renshaws would have a pool—and it was large enough to swim laps, not just splash around a little. The sun sparkled on the turquoise water. As Steph led her through a set of French doors into a resort-like backyard with a beautifully landscaped garden, Rae felt an instinctive pull toward the oval pool. God, if she had grown up in this house, she'd have never gotten out of the water.

"Good thing I'm holding on to you." Steph laughed and squeezed Rae's arm. "You look like you want to jump right in. You could, you know? If you're not too full after dinner, that is."

Rae tore her gaze away from the pool. "Nah. I didn't bring a swimsuit."

Steph flashed her a wolfish grin. "Oh, I wouldn't mind at all if you'd wear just your birthday suit."

"I bet."

"Seriously, I'm sure you could borrow a suit, or we could come back if you ever want to have a swim in a private pool. You look like you swim." Steph brushed her hand along Rae's shoulder.

The fleeting touch made Rae tingle all over. Her cheeks warmed. "I used to, every day before work, but it's been a while."

"Not since…?" Steph gestured toward her left eye.

Rae nodded.

"Would it harm you if chlorinated water got into your socket?"

"No. It's not that. I would wear goggles. But I… I'm not ready. Maybe someday."

"Any time."

They continued toward a poolside pergola that shaded a glass table surrounded by double lounge chairs on three sides.

A tall man in his sixties stood from one of them. He wore black dress pants and a crisp, white shirt, but his sleeves were rolled up to his elbows, revealing a golfer's tan that stopped at his left wrist. With his black hair, silver-tinged at his temples, and his tanned face, he didn't resemble Steph at all, and Rae looked forward to discovering what—if anything—Steph had inherited from him.

Dr. Renshaw gave Steph a hug and then took Rae's hand in a strong grip, sizing her up as he shook it. At least he didn't try to embrace her.

"Rae, this is my father, James. Dad, this is my friend Rae."

My friend. The simple introduction warmed Rae to the core and made her feel less insecure, reminding her that she was in this luxurious mansion because Steph wanted her here.

"Welcome and Merry Christmas." Steph's father nodded at one of the two-person lounge chairs. "Please take a seat and make yourself comfortable. The food should be here any minute."

Claire and Lana had joined them outside and were already cuddling close on one of the chairs, and with James settling back on his chair, that left only one for Rae and Steph to share.

"Come on." Steph tugged her toward the remaining lounge chair. "Let's share. I don't bite. Unless…"

Rae vividly remembered how she had finished that sentence when they had leaned close for a photo in the gazebo in Descanso Gardens. She sent Steph a warning glance, not wanting her to repeat it in front of her father.

Steph grinned. She kicked off her shoes and made herself comfortable on her half of the lounge chair, one leg curled under her as if she didn't care one bit if her slacks got wrinkled.

Rae sat next to her and put her hands flat on her own thighs in an attempt not to fidget.

"Relax," Steph whispered.

"So, Rae," James said, making Rae stiffen even more, "what is it that you do for a living?"

In the past, Rae had always been proud to tell people she worked for the LAPD, but now she wondered what he would think of her job.

Steph leaned into her in silent support. Her shoulder warmed Rae's side.

Rae glanced at her, then looked Steph's father in the eyes. "I work security at The Fun Zone, one of the comedy clubs where Steph occasionally works."

"Security?" James repeated.

Rae couldn't interpret the undertone in his voice. Was he judging her or admiring her? "Yes, sir."

"James, please. So you're one of the people who keeps my daughter safe?"

Rae straightened. She liked that description of her job. "Yes, s—James."

"She's the best," Steph said firmly. "I never have to worry about the audience being seated the wrong way or a heckler getting out of hand when Rae is on duty."

Lana sighed. "Where were you the one and only time I tried stand-up? I could have used someone to save me from the heckler who kept making fun of me."

Claire gave her a sympathetic kiss on the cheek. "Aww. Poor sweetie. I'm sure you were great."

"God, no." Lana laughed. "I was horrible. The heckler was actually funnier than me. Stand-up isn't as easy as it looks."

"I'm sure it isn't," James said, but it sounded like an empty phrase, not a statement made out of conviction.

Silence descended on them. Neither Claire nor her father seemed to have much to say about stand-up comedy, and Steph had gone strangely quiet too. As far as Rae knew, no one in Steph's family had ever been to one of her shows, and Lana seemed to be the only one who respected what Steph did for a living.

Steph stood, reached for Rae's hand, and tugged her up with her. "I'm going to show Rae around before dinner." Without waiting for a reply, she dragged Rae away from the pergola. Instead of taking her inside to show her the house, she steered them toward the edge of the property, as if she wanted to get as far away from her family as possible.

Rae didn't question her. She was very aware that Steph still hadn't let go of her hand as they strolled along a row of apricot and plum trees.

Steph paused at one of the older trees and touched a small, uneven heart that had been carved into the trunk, along with *S&C*.

"Stephanie and…?"

"Hmm?" Steph looked at her as if she'd been lost in thought.

Rae gestured at the tree. "What was the name of your sweetheart? Constance? Curtis? Chester? Clementine?"

Steph shook herself and laughed. "Where did you get those names from? *The Book of Old-Fashioned Baby Names*?"

Mission accomplished. Rae smiled to herself. She had made Steph laugh and distracted her from whatever sad thoughts she'd been thinking. "Who's the tree girl or boy? Clarence? Cornelius? Clytee?"

"You made that one up!"

"No, I swear." Rae raised her free hand as if taking an oath. "I once arrested a woman with exactly that name. So?"

"There is no sweetheart. Claire and I carved the heart when we were little."

Rae stared across the pool toward Claire, who sat on her lounge chair with a perfectly straight back, not a wrinkle in her tailored slacks or her silk blouse. "Claire carved something into a tree?"

"It took me a week to talk her into it. She didn't want to get in trouble with our parents."

But she had done it, just because her little sister wanted to have their heart on a tree. "Were you close growing up?" Rae asked.

Steph's gaze roved through the garden as if she was replaying scenes of her childhood. "Yeah, kind of. As close as two siblings can be when they're as different as Claire and me."

"What happened?"

Steph shrugged and looked away. "The usual, I guess. Puberty. Growing up. Not that Claire thinks I ever grew up."

Was that really all? Rae waited but didn't ask, in case Steph didn't want to talk about whatever had happened.

"I slept with her ex, okay?" Steph tugged her hand free, turned on her heel, and marched toward the detached guesthouse at the other end of the pool.

For a moment, Rae stood frozen and stared at her retreating back before hurrying after her. "Steph! Wait, please." She gently gripped her elbow and forced her to slow down. "I'm not judging. I'm sure there was a good reason for it."

Steph sat in the grass in front of the guesthouse. "Not really. I was sixteen, and it seemed like a good idea at the time."

Rae eyed the grass but then sat next to her, best pair of pants be damned. Her knee lightly brushed Steph's, but she didn't move away. Both were silent for a while, just sitting together.

"When I was little, I always wanted to live out here." Steph pointed at the guesthouse with a glass front that faced the pool. "My parents didn't understand it, especially since I had the biggest, most impressive bedroom you can imagine."

"Impressive isn't your thing," Rae said. "Didn't your parents understand that?"

Steph sighed. "They thought they understood more about me than I did. They insisted there was an unconscious reason for every little thing I did, and of course they always knew what it was. Like me being late meant I didn't really want to be here." She made a face. "Okay, guess they were right about that one sometimes."

"So you did a lot of stuff for no good reason at all, just to prove them wrong?" Rae asked.

Steph turned to face her more fully, which made her knee slide along Rae's thigh.

A shiver went through Rae, and she clutched a handful of grass.

"Damn. I think you're right." Steph laughed, but it sounded mostly startled and bitter. She tapped Rae's knee. "*You* should be a psychologist."

"Hey, no insults, or you're not getting your Christmas present!"

They laughed together, and this time, there was no bitterness in Steph's laughter. Finally, she sobered. "Claire assumed I did it to hurt her. But that's not true. Elyse—her ex—was great. Smart and really beautiful. And she listened to me. She never treated me like her girlfriend's annoying baby sister. I guess I had a little bit of a crush on her." Her cheeks took on a pinkish hue.

It was like a puzzle piece that had been missing to help Rae see the full picture. Maybe this was the reason Steph avoided relationships. The one time she might have wanted to be someone's girlfriend had ended in a huge family drama and everyone involved getting hurt.

"Sounds like you had more than a little crush," Rae said quietly. "Maybe you had a reason after all."

"Maybe." Her hand still on Rae's knee, Steph looked her in the eye. "Thank you for not judging."

"No thanks necessary. I'm Team Steph, okay?"

A soft smile drove the last hints of sadness from Steph's face. Their gazes held as she leaned toward Rae. Her heat seemed to engulf Rae, along with the irresistible scent of her perfume.

Rae's heart hammered against her ribs. *Calm down. She's just going to give you a thank-you kiss on the cheek.* Steph had done that before. But she wasn't looking at Rae's cheek. Steph's gaze darted to her mouth as her face drew closer. Her warm breath caressed Rae's lips, a harbinger of what she would do with her soft mouth in a second.

"Honey, I think we have a problem." Diane's voice right next to them made them both jerk back.

Rae nearly fell back into the grass as the eye contact with Steph was interrupted, as if a lifeline had been cut.

Steph pressed her hand to her mouth as if she had actually kissed her and could still feel Rae's lips on her own. "Um, what?" She blinked up at her mother.

"We have a problem," Diane repeated. "I just called Foodtopia to see why our delivery is delayed, and it turns out our order isn't in their system. Apparently, someone forgot to enter it."

Her husband, Claire, and Lana walked over, and the Renshaws exchanged helpless gazes.

"Can't they whip something up and send it over?" James pressed a hand to his belly. "I'm starving."

"They offered, but they have a lot of customers today, so they said it would be at least an hour and a half," Diane answered. "That would mean Stephanie and Rae have to wolf down their food and rush out the door. I'm so sorry. I thought we had plenty of time, or I would have had you over earlier in the day."

"You couldn't know there'd be such a delay, Mom," Claire said.

Lana wrapped one arm around Claire and lovingly trailed her hand over the sleeve of her silk blouse. "Why don't we order pizza?"

The Renshaws looked at her as if she had suggested eating the neighbor's dog.

Rae got up and pulled Steph to her feet too. "Or we could just cook something." That earned her a look as if she had suggested eating the neighbor's *kids*, but Rae didn't let that stop her. After that near kiss, she needed something to distract herself. "There's a kitchen in the house, right?"

"Yes, of course," Diane said. "But—"

"Then let's go. I'll be the chef, and you can be my armada of helpful sous-chefs. We'll have dinner on the table in no time." Rae marched toward the house and waved at the others to follow.

Steph stayed back and stared after Rae, who had taken charge as if she had been cooking for the Renshaws for years. But that wasn't the most surprising thing.

She touched her mouth again, trailing her index finger along her bottom lip, where she could still feel Rae's warm breath. There was no doubt in her mind that they would have kissed if her mother hadn't interrupted—and would probably still be kissing.

This time, their landlord and landlady hadn't been around, so she couldn't blame it on needing to convince them they were a couple. Was this one of the spontaneous things that she did just to prove that her parents were wrong and she didn't always have a reason for doing what she did?

No. She might not be a psychologist, but she knew herself, and she knew she had nearly kissed Rae for one reason only: because she wanted to. God, did she want to. It was almost like a physical ache. But it was more than merely physical. She liked Rae. Really liked her.

"I like her."

Her father's voice echoed her thoughts, wrenching Steph from her near-kiss haze.

"Dad…" She put a warning into her tone. "We're not a couple."

"I can still like her, can't I? Besides, the way the two of you look at each other… Well, I might only be an organizational psychologist, not a couples therapist like your sister, but I lived with a roommate or two before I met your mother, and none of them ever looked at me the way you and Rae look at each other." He patted her shoulder. "Now you'll have to excuse me. I don't want to miss your mother's first and probably only attempt to help with cooking."

When he walked off, Steph stayed behind and sank back down into the grass.

Her parents might not always understand her or know what was really going on inside of her, but that didn't mean they were always wrong. She had never looked at any of her roommates the way she looked at Rae. Hell, she had never looked at *anyone* the way she looked at Rae. It made her feel elated and nervous all at the same time because what if she messed this up? With her track record, that was likely to happen. In the beginning, she had decided to ignore her attraction to Rae because she was her roommate and an employee in one of the biggest clubs. But now losing the apartment or even her gigs at The Fun Zone was the least of her worries. Losing Rae's friendship would be so much worse.

But what if…? She chewed on her lip. No, she couldn't let herself think like that. Rae was a one-woman woman. Someone who had only ever been in one fifteen-year relationship. She didn't do casual, and Steph wasn't sure she had what it took to do anything but. Walking out when she got restless or things got serious had always been her modus operandi, and she couldn't do that to Rae. It was what Lise had done, and Rae deserved better than that.

She wasn't sure how long she'd been sitting in the grass, brooding, but loud voices drifting over from the house finally shook her from her thoughts. Quickly, she jumped up and rushed inside.

God, what had she been thinking to leave Rae alone with her family? She knew Rae wasn't comfortable around people most of the time.

One step from her parents' usually pristine kitchen, she came to an abrupt halt.

Rae had taken up position in front of the enormous six-burner gas range like a captain on the bridge of a ship, and she was ordering everyone around.

What was even more amazing was that her helpers—even Steph's mother—jumped to do her bidding, getting pots and ingredients and anything else Rae asked for.

Steph took a careful step closer, feeling as if she would wake up from this very strange dream any second. "Um, do you need any more help?"

Rae looked up, and their gazes connected. "Well, I would say you can cut the onions, but I've seen you try, so…"

Lana laughed. "Is she as bad as Claire?"

"Hey, I can cook," Claire protested. "I just prefer dining out—or having my talented fiancée cook for me." They paused in whatever they had been doing and exchanged a short, sweet kiss in the middle of the kitchen. "Even if I have to practically renovate the kitchen afterward," Claire added when the kiss ended.

Lana playfully stuck her tongue out at her.

Steph tried to peer around them and catch a glimpse of whatever was cooking in the giant pot in the back of the range. "What are you making?"

"Spaghetti with fresh tomato sauce," Rae answered.

Steph burst out laughing. "We're having spaghetti for Christmas dinner?"

Rae shrugged. "Well, we were a little limited in our options because your parents have the biggest nearly empty walk-in pantry I have ever seen."

"Spaghetti sounds great," Steph said. "Beats the tofu turkey with apple stuffing we had a few years ago. I'm just surprised you got my mom to agree to eating carbs."

"Hush," Steph's mother said. "I do eat carbs on special occasions. Now give me the onions, Rae. I can chop them…I think." She walked up to Rae from the left. Before Steph could stop her, she plucked the onion Rae held from her hand.

Rae jumped and stumbled backward against the stove. Water sizzled and hissed as it sloshed over the edge of the pot and onto the gas flame.

"Okay, everyone!" Steph shouted over the chaos in the kitchen. She struggled against the impulse to hurry over to Rae and make sure she was all right. "This is clearly a case of too many cooks in the kitchen. How about you all go back outside while I help Rae?"

"It's okay, Steph," Rae said quietly.

Steph looked at her and mouthed, *Are you sure?*

Rae nodded.

"What happened?" Steph's mother studied Rae with a look as if she was mentally flipping through her copy of the *DSM-5* to come up with the right diagnosis for her.

Gritting her teeth, Steph took the onion from her mother and plopped it down on the other side of the huge center island, a safe distance from Rae. "There. You can cut it here." She gave her mother a warning look. "And don't use a bread knife."

Apparently, her mother got the message. She closed her mouth and took the knife Lana handed her.

Dinner had been a lot better than Rae had feared—not only the food, but the conversation too. While she hadn't contributed much, preferring to stay in the background and listen, she had enjoyed watching Steph and her family interact.

She had to give the Renshaws credit. They had adjusted to the catering service snafu with ease and had dug into their plates of spaghetti as if Rae's simple creation were a meal at a five-star restaurant. Maybe they weren't as posh as she had thought.

Once everyone had finished eating, Diane stacked the empty plates. When Rae rose to help, Steph's mother waved her back down. "You cooked. We'll clean the kitchen. Steph will stay and keep you company."

As the rest of the family cleared out, Steph and Rae sank back onto their chairs and looked at each other.

Rae's gaze veered away. Should she say something? Talk about what had happened…or nearly happened…earlier? But she had no idea how to approach that conversation. Would Steph even think it was worth mentioning? With her more casual approach to her love life, a simple kiss might not mean as much to her as it did to Rae.

What would it have meant? Steph was a good-looking woman; Rae had known that from their very first meeting. Still it had been relatively easy to ignore the short flashes of attraction she felt when Steph was close or paraded around the apartment in one of her spaghetti strap tops. But this… this bond that was growing between them…that was more than physical attraction, wasn't it? It also wasn't nearly as easy to ignore. That kiss would have meant something—at least to her.

Finally, it was Steph who was brave enough to break the silence. "How are you doing with all this?" She waved her hand in a vague gesture.

"I'm…" Rae bit off the rest of the sentence before the habitual *fine* could slip out. No, she wasn't fine, and Steph deserved to know that. "I'm not sure. It's all a little jumbled." She tapped her head, then, after hesitating for a second, her chest. "A lot jumbled actually." That was as much as she was willing to say. Even that felt as if she was making herself much too vulnerable, and the only reason she had said it at all was because Steph was still Team Rae. Whatever happened, she trusted that Steph wouldn't hurt her, at least not on purpose.

Steph put her hand on top of Rae's and clutched it tightly. "You didn't hurt yourself, did you?"

"Hurt myself?" Rae slid her chair around to be able to study Steph's expression more fully. What was she talking about?

"Earlier." Steph pointed in the direction of the kitchen. "When you crashed into the stove."

Oh. Was that what Steph had been talking about? The little episode in the kitchen, when Diane had stepped up to her from the left? Rae bit her lip. "I'm fine."

"What did you...? Oh!" Steph's eyes widened. "You thought I was talking about—"

"All done." Diane returned to the dining room along with the rest of the family, dusting off her hands as if they had gotten dirty. "Let's go over to the den and open the presents before Stephanie and Rae have to head out."

Rae didn't know whether to be glad or disappointed at being interrupted.

Steph again hooked her arm through Rae's left one, protecting her from knocking over any of the expensive decorations as they followed Diane into the den.

Rae instantly decided that this was her favorite room in the house. Two large bay windows extended out of the wall, letting in plenty of sunlight and offering a panoramic view of the garden and the sparkling pool. Cozy window seats curved along the three panels of each window. A stone fireplace gave the room a relaxing feel, and a fully decorated Christmas tree twinkled in one corner.

Carefully, Rae moved aside one of the silk throw pillows and sat on one of the window seats next to Steph. The curved shape of the seat naturally made them sit close, and Rae was overly aware of the way Steph's shoulder rested against her own.

"Don't get too comfortable, Stephanie," Diane said. "Handing out the presents has always been your job."

Grumbling, Steph heaved herself up. Her hand brushed Rae's shoulder. She made quick work of handing out the Christmas gifts, as if she couldn't wait to be back at Rae's side.

When Steph was done, Rae stared down at her lap full of wrapped packages. She hadn't expected this. Good thing she had gone shopping yesterday and hadn't been too proud to ask for advice from the salesladies. She had bought two bottles of red wine for Steph's parents, and as soon as they unwrapped them, they were already debating which one to open later. Claire instantly put on the turquoise silk scarf that matched the frame of her glasses, and Lana let out an enthusiastic squeal at discovering the Peppermint Pigs in her package.

Steph leaned even closer. "Wow, Rae. You did great." Her breath tickled Rae's ear.

"Really?"

"Yes! Look!" Steph pointed at Lana, who swung the little hammer and then playfully fed Claire a piece of the Peppermint Pig. "They love their presents."

"What about you?" Rae asked quietly and nodded down at the unopened gift on Steph's lap.

Steph had unwrapped her other presents—an *I'm a comedian, what's your superpower?* T-shirt from Lana, a silk robe and an envelope with some money from her parents, and a Pressed Juicery subscription from Claire— but left Rae's for last. She slid her finger beneath the tape so carefully as if afraid that the package would hold the same type of well-meant, but not-really-Steph gifts she had gotten from her family.

Rae prayed she had made a better choice.

Finally, Steph set down the bow and paper and lifted the gift from its padded box. "A mug?"

"It's the same as mine—because you seem to like it so much that you're stealing it every morning."

Steph blushed. "Guilty as charged. I love that mug. Thank you."

"Wait. The real gift is in the mug."

Steph peered inside the big mug and fished out the rolled-up envelope.

Rae tried not to fidget as Steph opened it and read the card. God, she hoped Steph didn't think this was boring or sappy or—

Steph put the card down and threw her arms around her.

Instantly, Rae's eyes fluttered shut, and all her worries evaporated like snow in LA as she hugged Steph back and breathed in her scent.

Countless moments later, she realized that the room had gone quiet, and she quickly pulled back.

"That must be some gift," Diane said. "What is it?"

Steph held up the certificate with a broad smile. "A year-long membership for Descanso Gardens."

"The botanical garden in La Cañada Flintridge?" James's forehead wrinkled as if he was wondering what the draw was for her.

"Yes." Steph nodded eagerly. "When I had a rough day, Rae took me to see their lighting display. It was amazing."

Claire stared at her. "You went to see the lights? You?"

"They're not holiday lights. It's…special. I'd love to go again."

"You can," Rae said. "The membership not only includes free admission for two but also discounted presale tickets for the Forest of Light."

Steph's gaze searched Rae's. "For two?"

"Mm-hmm. That doesn't mean you have to take me, of course."

"Are you kidding?" Steph gently nudged her. "Of course I'm taking you!" Then she seemed to become aware that she had kind of picked Rae over her family, who were all listening intently. "Um…"

Her mother laughed. "Don't worry. We weren't expecting you to take your boring parents."

"Or your boring sister," Claire grumbled.

Rae squirmed on the window seat. "Um, if you wanted to go, you could—"

"Relax. I was kidding. It's fine if Steph wants to take you." Claire's reassuring smile seemed genuine. "I'm glad she has someone to cheer her up after a rough day."

"Jeez, would you all stop talking about me as if I'm not sitting right here?" Steph tapped the presents on Rae's lap. "Your turn."

Very aware of everyone's attention on her, Rae peeled off the tape and opened the first present, with a tag that said it was from Steph's parents. She held up a black-and-silver silk tie and admired the rainbow clip attached to it.

"I asked Steph for some gift ideas, and she said you wear ties at work," Diane said.

Steph leaned over and slid her fingers over the smooth material. "Ooh. Nice choice, Mom."

A shiver went through Rae as if Steph had caressed her fingers instead of the tie. "Yeah. Very nice." Her voice came out a little hoarse. "Thank you so much."

"It's not too long, is it?" Diane asked.

"It should be just f—"

Rae's words caught in the back of her throat when Steph took the tie from her, looped it around Rae's neck, and tugged her down a little.

For a moment, Rae halfway expected her to kiss her, but of course all Steph did was tie a knot. Her traitorous body reacted as if she'd been kissed anyway, her heart hammering so hard that she was afraid everyone in the room could hear it.

"There," Steph said, her voice sounding a bit rough too. "It's perfect."

Rae looked down and touched the rainbow clip. "Perfect."

Lana and Claire traded amused glances, and Rae wasn't sure she wanted to know what they were thinking.

She quickly reached for the next gift, an envelope from Claire and Lana. When she opened it, a gift certificate fell out. "Paddleboard lessons. Wow. This is too much."

"Don't worry about it," Lana said. "A friend of ours does them on the side, so we got them at a great price. She's a stuntwoman and a wonderful teacher. Even Claire had a great time when we did it in June. We thought you might enjoy it too."

"I'm sure I will." As soon as she had worked up the courage to take up swimming again. Maybe this was exactly the encouragement she needed.

Steph leaned in to her as if sensing what she was thinking.

The next present revealed a USB stick. Rae held it up and gave Lana and Claire a questioning look. "Something else from you? You already gave me the paddleboard lessons."

"This is just a little something extra," Lana said. "Copies of all the audiobooks I have narrated so far. Claire insisted that you would enjoy them."

"Anyone with taste would enjoy them," Claire said.

Rae gave Lana an impressed look. "You're an audiobook narrator?"

While Claire beamed proudly, Lana shrugged. "Mostly. I also do some acting on the side, but I discovered I really enjoy narrating books."

"On the side!" Claire gave her a loving nudge. "She's being modest. She'll start shooting with Grace Durand next month!"

Rae gave a low whistle. "Wow. Grace Durand! She's—"

"Hot," Steph said with a grin.

"That too. But I was about to say 'a great actress.'"

"Last one." Diane pointed at the remaining present on Rae's lap.

For some reason, Rae was a little hesitant to open Steph's gift in front of everyone. It wasn't that she thought it might be something embarrassing; it just felt like a private thing between the two of them. But since everyone was waiting, she removed the colorful gift wrap from the rectangular, relatively flat package. "Wow. An e-reader." She opened the box and pulled it out.

"It has an E Ink display, so you don't get any glare, even in bright sunlight, and it's much easier on the eyes than your phone or a tablet." Steph gave her a meaningful look.

Aww. Steph had noticed her struggle with reading on her devices. Rae swallowed down the lump in her throat and decided not to rebuke her for spending so much money. "Thank you."

"You're very welcome."

They looked into each other's eyes, and again that strange gravity set in and seemed to pull her toward Steph.

"Um, far be it me to spoil the mood or to kick you out, but didn't you say you have to leave at five to make it to work on time?" Diane asked.

Rae tore her gaze away from Steph and glanced at her wristwatch. *Oh shit.* It was a little after five. How had that happened? Before coming here, she had been afraid of every minute crawling by painfully slow.

They jumped up, collected their gifts, and said their goodbyes.

Again, Lana gave Rae a hug, but this time, Rae knew it was coming and patiently waited until it was over.

Claire limited herself to a warm pat to Rae's arm. "Thanks again for cooking. You were a lifesaver."

"No problem." Rae shook James's hand and then turned to Diane, while Steph said goodbye to her sister. "Thanks so much for having me."

"It was my pleasure—and I mean that." Diane didn't lean in for air kisses this time, as if the little episode in the kitchen had made her unsure about how much physical closeness Rae could tolerate. "If you ever need anything—any help—give me a call."

Rae stared down at the card that Diane had slipped into her hand. *Dr. Diane Renshaw, psychodynamic therapist and professor of psychology, USC,* it said. It also listed Diane's work numbers. *What the...?*

"I can't take you on myself," Diana added, her voice pitched low, "but I know a lot of great people who do trauma-focused work."

Trauma? Did Diane think she had PTSD, because she had startled her in the kitchen? Rae's fingers tightened around the card, and she had the sudden, uncomfortable feeling that Diane was looking right at her left eye.

When Steph walked over to hug her mother, Rae quickly slipped the card into her pocket. If Steph saw it, she would probably kill her mother, and Rae didn't want to cause family drama, especially not on Christmas.

Then they were finally out the door and headed toward the Mini Cooper. She was so focused on the business card that it took her until she reached for the seat belt to realize that she was now alone with Steph, without a clue what to say about their almost kiss...or if she should say anything.

Chapter 20

"YOU KNOW WHAT?" RAE SAID as Steph turned left onto Santa Monica Boulevard. "I think it's faster if you drop me off at work. I have a change of clothes there."

Steph looked over at her. Had Rae suggested that because she was afraid of being late or because she didn't want to be alone with her any longer than necessary? For once, she couldn't read Rae's expression. "Sure."

She sped up to make it across an intersection before the light turned red.

For a while, they were both silent.

Oh hell. This is ridiculous. Steph opened her mouth to say something… anything.

"Steph?"

"Hmm?" Her heart beat faster, and she was no longer sure she was ready to talk about it. Maybe there was something to be said for ignoring the elephant in the room.

"Um, thanks for inviting me," Rae said quietly. "I had a wonderful time."

"Really?"

"Mm-hmm."

"Great," Steph said. "I would have hated for my family to scare you off."

"I don't scare easily."

"Oh really? Could have fooled me." The words were out before Steph could stop herself. God, Claire was right. She really had no filters sometimes.

"What's that supposed to mean?" A scowl darkened Rae's face, but the time when Steph might have been intimidated by that was long over.

"It means that you are just as much of a chickenshit as I am." Again, her mouth seemed to answer without consulting her brain first. But maybe that was a good thing because if she waited for Rae to approach the topic, she might die of old age before that happened. "We're both tiptoeing around each other...around what's happening between us."

When no reply came from Rae, Steph glanced over.

A look of pure panic flashed across Rae's face.

It made Steph's belly clench in response. Rae had probably faced down armed criminals without losing her cool, but she clearly had no armor when it came to more tender feelings. And that scared Steph in return because she had a talent for fucking things up, and she didn't want to hurt Rae.

"I..." Rae cleared her throat. "We...we nearly kissed, right?"

"Yeah. Truth be told, I've been wanting to do that for a while now. For real, I mean, not just to trick the Kleinbergs." Steph glanced at Rae again to see her reaction. *Damn.* A car was not the best place to have this conversation, but they didn't have the time to stop somewhere and talk while being able to look at each other. She caught a glimpse of a blush dusting Rae's cheeks.

"Me too," Rae said quietly. "Did you want it the same way you wanted to kiss...and do other stuff...with U-Haul Girl?"

"U-Haul G... Oh!" Steph had nearly forgotten about her, and that kind of answered Rae's question for her. "No. This is different."

Rae turned in the passenger seat as much as possible. "How?"

"I don't know." Steph took one hand off the steering wheel to rub her face. She wasn't ready to put a name on it, because with that came a huge responsibility that she had avoided all her life. "I just know that it is." Steph tried to flash a grin, but it felt a bit wobbly. "For one thing, if we slept together, I couldn't kick you out the next morning, because it's your apartment too."

Rae was quiet as they crossed another intersection.

Steph glanced over.

Rae had slid back around to face forward. She sat with her hands flat on her thighs and her teeth digging into her bottom lip, staring straight ahead.

Oh fuck. She was already messing up, hurting her. *Make it right, asshat.* "I'm sorry, Rae. That was me being a chickenshit, hiding behind jokes. I told you I suck at relationships."

Rae's head whipped around. "Is that what you want? A relationship… with me?"

Steph white-knuckled the steering wheel. Was there a hint of hope in Rae's voice? Did she want her to say yes? But Steph couldn't do that. If they were to have any chance of staying friends, much less becoming lovers, she had to be completely honest. "I…I don't know. I never wanted one before. But now… I don't know. The only thing I know for sure is that I don't want to hurt you or lose our friendship."

"I don't want that either. I'm not saying I want us to jump into anything headfirst." Rae sighed. "Most days, I'm not even sure I deser—"

"Shit, hold on!" Steph had nearly missed the turn into the club's parking lot. She stepped on the brake and swung the wheel to the right.

The Mini Cooper bumped across the curb and then neatly slid into one of the few remaining parking spaces.

"Sorry." Steph loosened her death grip on the wheel and turned off the engine. "You were saying?"

Rae rubbed the pockmark-like scars on her forehead. "Let's talk later, at home. I have to go. Mr. Hicks is waving me over."

Steph glanced toward the club's front door.

Mr. Hicks stood at the entrance with Brandon and made a "come here" gesture.

God, their timing really sucked. Why were they constantly being interrupted? But maybe that was a good thing. She needed to think this through. For once in her life, something was too important to make any hasty decisions. "Okay. We'll talk later." She reached across the middle console and lightly touched Rae's arm. "Be careful please. The late show on Christmas can get a little rowdy sometimes, maybe because people are happy to have escaped their families and want to let off some steam."

Rae put her hand on Steph's as if wanting to keep it resting on her arm for a moment longer. "Will do. Good luck with your gig, and please drive carefully. No more stunt maneuvers." Her tone was fierce, but her fingers on Steph's were gentle.

"Aye, aye, officer."

Neither of them moved for several seconds, then Rae sighed, climbed out of the car, and closed the door. Through the glass of the passenger-side door, their gazes met.

Rae raised her hand, and when Steph returned the gesture, she nodded and walked away.

Steph slumped forward and rested her forehead on the steering wheel. *Oh my God. What am I doing?*

A knock on the driver's side window made her jerk. She straightened and looked up, expecting to see Rae. The mere thought made her heartbeat speed up.

But it was Mr. Hicks who stood in front of her car. He waved his index finger in a circle.

Steph pressed the button to roll down the window. "Hi, Mr. Hicks. Merry Christmas."

"Merry Christmas." He bent to peer through the window and gave her a disgruntled look. "Didn't you see me waving at you?"

"Oh. I thought you were waving to Rae."

"No. I've been meaning to talk to you, but the holiday season keeps me busy at the club. So I was wondering… Do you still want that chance you've been begging me for?"

"Of course I do!" Somehow, Steph managed not to stammer. "When?"

"Are you free on New Year's Eve?" he asked. "I need someone to headline the late show."

Oh my God! Steph struggled not to bounce up and down. She had made plans to spend New Year's Eve with Claire and Lana, but they would just have to understand. Headlining one of the biggest shows of the year at The Fun Zone was a once-in-a-lifetime opportunity. Maybe Claire could finally make good on her promise to see one of her shows. "Yes!"

"Are you sure you can handle it? New Year's Eve can get pretty rough."

Steph knew he was right. People were drinking more, and for many of them, it was their first visit to a comedy club, so they had no idea how to behave. She looked him in the eyes. "I'm not a shrinking violet. I can handle it."

"All right. I'll email you the details." He walked away without waiting for a reply.

"Yes!" Steph managed to pump both fists in the cramped space of the driver's seat.

Mr. Hicks turned around. "Did you say something?" he called back to her.

Shit. She had forgotten that the window was still down. "Um, no. Nothing at all." She sent him a hopefully professional, not over-the-top elated smile and rolled up the window. Once he had disappeared into the club, she bobbed up and down several times.

New Year's Eve was big. If the show was a success, it would open doors for her in other clubs. Maybe she would even manage to get a TV booker's attention. This might lead to the breakthrough she'd been waiting for.

After a while of sitting there, grinning like a lottery winner in the middle of the parking lot, the wave of euphoria ebbed away. Steph sank against the back of her seat and blew out a long, jittery breath. Wow, what a day! It seemed as if the universe was conspiring to see what all it could throw at her. None of the things that had happened today were bad, but what were the odds of them happening at once? It left her mind spinning like an out-of-control carousel.

Could she really handle it? Not the comedy show. She had trust in her skills as a comedian. But her romantic relationship skills were a different matter altogether. Comedy had always been her true love, and none of the women or men she had been with had ever been able to compete. She had never expected or wanted them to. Now that her career might finally be taking off, shouldn't she focus on that instead of letting herself be distracted by something that might never work out anyway? What would happen if she got her big breakthrough and had to travel? Wouldn't that mean her tentative relationship with Rae was doomed?

The silence in the car held no answers.

Sighing, she turned the key in the ignition and started the engine.

Adele's voice drifted through the speakers, singing some heartbreak ballad. Of course.

Steph turned off the radio and drove to her gig in silence.

Steph hadn't been kidding when she'd said the late show on Christmas could get rowdy. Rae scowled at the waitresses and door staff members who had gathered around her, but the expression was rendered less effective by the ice pack she held to the spot above her left eyebrow. "For the hundredth time, I'm fine. Go home, people. Nothing to see here."

Mr. Hicks pushed through the circle of people surrounding Rae in his office. "Give her some space, everyone."

Finally, they dispersed, leaving behind only Carlos and Mr. Hicks.

"I'm so sorry," Carlos said for what felt like the hundredth time too.

"Not your fault." Rae knew she had only herself to blame. Her head hadn't been in the game all night. In her mind, she had replayed every little touch and every word she and Steph had exchanged today, and she'd been thinking ahead, to what would happen when she got home later.

Would Steph say that it was a bad idea and they should stay friends instead of trying for something they were both not ready for? Or would she—Rae—be the one to say it?

Those thoughts had accompanied her all through the early show and most of the late one.

She'd been glad when the headliner had signaled for them to step in and remove the heckler in the back.

At first, the guy had followed them, docile like a puppy, but as soon as he caught sight of the front door, his eggnog-dampened brain seemed to get that they were about to kick him out, and he started to resist.

In the ensuing chaos, Rae had been focused only on him, and when she and Carlos had tackled him at the same time, she had taken an elbow to the face.

"Are you up to filling out the accident report?" Mr. Hicks asked.

Rae lowered the ice pack. "Do we really need a report? This is just a little bump. It's not even bleeding."

Mr. Hicks shook his head. "That's not how I run my business, you should know that by now."

"All right. Where's the paperwork?" She wanted to finally get out of here—and home, where Steph was probably waiting.

It seemed to take ages for Mr. Hicks to find the correct form and for her to fill it out, all while Carlos hovered next to her.

Finally, she handed over the filled-out report and heaved herself up from the short couch in Mr. Hicks's office.

But instead of dismissing her, Mr. Hicks looked at Carlos. "Can you give us a minute?"

"Sure, boss. I'll wait outside and drive her home when you're done."

Rae shook her head, glad when it barely hurt. "I don't need you to—"

But Carlos was already gone.

Jesus. Every bit of control seemed to slip through her fingers today.

Mr. Hicks waved her back down onto the couch and lowered himself onto the edge of his desk. "Listen, Rae. I want you to be completely honest with me. I know you and Carlos both said it was an accident, and I don't doubt it, but…"

Rae gritted her teeth. She knew what was coming—the same bullshit she had heard from LAPD brass when they had told her she wasn't fit for patrol duty anymore and offered her a goddamn desk job instead.

"…are you sure you are up for the job with only…you know?" He gestured at her eye.

Rae's fingernails drilled into her palms. "You hired me back in October. Isn't it a little late for these doubts?"

"I'm not doubting. I'm asking."

"The answer is yes. I am up for the job." Rae labored to keep her voice calm and professional. "Or have there been any complaints?"

"Not at all. You're pretty no-nonsense, and the guys respect that. Even the comics, jaded as most of them are, seem to like you." He paused, then added, "One of them in particular, or so I hear."

That unexpected direction of their conversation hit Rae like a punch to the gut. Did he know anything? Were people talking about her and Steph? She didn't want to lie and deny it. *Not that there is anything to deny yet.* But she knew that wasn't quite the truth. There was undeniably something going on between Steph and her, even though they hadn't yet figured out where it was headed. So she snapped her mouth shut and waited for what he would say next.

"I don't know what's going on between you and Ms. Renshaw." He lifted both hands. "And frankly, I don't want to know. But whatever it is, keep it out of the club, or one of you walks."

Rae had expected a wave of panic at his threat but instead felt only a quiet determination not to let herself be distracted by thoughts of Steph at work again. A couple of months ago, she would have been desperate to keep her job because it was all she had left. But somewhere along the way, she had regained the trust in herself that she had lost. If Mr. Hicks fired her, she'd just move on and look for a new job, probably something bigger and better. She now trusted herself to do more, even with one eye. "Understood, sir."

"And one other thing." He leaned forward, and his gaze drilled into hers with an intensity that reminded Rae of her former lieutenant. "If I find out you recommended her because the two of you are—"

"I recommended her because she's good," Rae said more sharply than she had intended.

"She'd better be. If she bombs on New Year's Eve…"

Did that mean he would give Steph the coveted spot? "She won't," Rae said firmly.

He fixed her with his sharp gaze for a few moments longer before finally nodding. "All right. Take the day off tomorrow, and if you have any problems, go see a doctor."

"Yes, sir." She made a beeline to the door and didn't break her stride as she passed Carlos in the lobby. If he insisted on driving her home, she would let him. The sooner she got home, the better. She couldn't stand this uncertainty one second longer.

Steph had been pacing the apartment since she had gotten home from her gig. Every time she sat down, that restless energy buzzing through her body made her jump back up and resume her pacing. Half a dozen times, she had reached for her phone to call Penny or Claire and ask them for advice, but then she had put it away again. What if they talked her out of it…or into it?

She wasn't sure which one would be worse.

One a.m., the time she had expected Rae to return, came and went. No Rae. Was she roaming the neighborhood, trying to clear her mind and figure out what she wanted instead of going straight home?

Finally, the sound of a key being slid into the lock made Steph freeze in the middle of the living room. She turned and came face-to-face with Rae.

They stared at each other like a hippo and a lion who had run into each other at the watering hole and didn't know whether to carefully approach or to turn tail and run.

Then Steph's gaze fell on a red, swollen area above Rae's left eyebrow. "Oh my God!" She rushed to her and reached out to tenderly touch the bump but then pulled back at the last second, not wanting to hurt her. "What happened?"

Rae offered her a crooked smile. "I zigged when I should have zagged."

But Steph's sense of humor deserted her at the moment. She gave Rae a look that demanded a real answer.

"We had to kick out a guy who didn't want to be kicked out."

A roaring started in Steph's ears. She curled both of her hands into tight fists. "Did he hit you?"

"No. This," Rae tapped the bump with two fingers, "is courtesy of Carlos's elbow."

"Jesus! That could have been really dangerous with your prosthesis and all." Steph slung her arm around Rae's hips to support her and slowly walked her over to the couch.

Rae laughed. "Steph, I can walk just fine." But she didn't pull away from Steph's supportive grasp.

As soon as Rae was safely seated, Steph rushed to the fridge, pulled out the first frozen item she could find—a package of peas—and hurried back to her side with the peas and a dish towel.

"I'm fine. I already put some ice on it at the club."

"Humor me." Steph sat next to her and wrapped the peas in the dish towel.

Rae held still as Steph pressed the improvised ice pack gently to her forehead. "Looks like we're making a habit out of this."

"Yeah." Steph swiped a strand of dark brown hair out of Rae's face with her free hand. "And it's always the left side of your face. Can we do something about that? Maybe there's something that would help. You know, like the blind-spot mirrors on your car."

"Nah. All the blind-spot mirrors in the world wouldn't have prevented this," Rae said. "I wouldn't have seen Carlos's elbow coming, even if he had been on my right. I wasn't…um…as focused tonight as I usually am at work." She ducked her head, but it didn't keep Steph from seeing the blush rise up her neck.

Aww. So Rae had been unable to stop thinking about her—about them—too. Heat swirled through Steph's body, and she had a feeling she was blushing right along with Rae. Tenderly, she traced the path of Rae's blush with one fingertip, along her strong jaw, the corner of her mouth, which twitched like a cat's whiskers beneath her touch, and then an incredibly soft cheek until she cradled Rae's entire face in her palm.

Rae leaned into the contact.

They looked into each other's eyes from only a few inches away.

"I just don't want you to get hurt," Steph whispered. Was she talking about Rae bumping into things on her left or…?

"I'm not hurting," Rae murmured. Her right pupil was wide, the amber flecks around it dancing like flames that drew Steph in, closer to that tempting heat.

"No?"

"No. Quite the opposite." Rae brought up her own hand and touched her fingertips to Steph's cheek in a gesture mirroring hers.

Steph wasn't sure she was still breathing. She didn't care whether she was. All she could hear was the heavy thumping of her own heart. Or was it Rae's?

The frozen peas dropped to the floor as they leaned toward each other at the same time.

Steph's hand came to rest on Rae's hip, and her fingers curled into her shirt, drawing her closer until their breaths mingled…and then their lips brushed, light as a feather.

Both paused before their lips met again, this time in a longer caress.

Steph's eyes fluttered shut. It was the gentlest kiss she had ever experienced, yet it burned her with its passionate intensity too. Rae's lips were warm and soft, and they moved against her own in a slow, languid exploration that made Steph sink against her as all her muscles turned into a wobbly mush.

A soft moan escaped Steph.

As if in answer, Rae made a raw sound in the back of her throat and gave the corner of Steph's mouth a little flick with the tip of her tongue that felt more tentative than teasing.

God, yes. Steph's lips parted.

Rae took the invitation and stroked her tongue along Steph's, sending a tug through her belly.

Steph slid her hand around to Rae's neck, threaded her fingers through her short hair, and angled her head to deepen the kiss.

Their tongues caressed, retreated, then met again, taking their time familiarizing themselves with each other.

Rae's taste, her scent, the heat emanating from her made Steph light-headed. As Rae continued to caress her with her lips and her tongue, the world around her faded to white noise, the only thoughts on her mind *so good* and *more*.

Quivers started at the base of her spine and radiated outward, rushing along every nerve ending. She wanted to sink onto the couch and pull Rae on top of her, but she tamped down the urge. *Slow,* she told herself. But she did allow her hands to wander a little, mapping out the planes of Rae's strong back.

When she couldn't stand the sweet torture any longer, she gave one last nibble on Rae's bottom lip before pulling away.

Rae stared at her, her breathing as ragged as Steph's. Her right hand still rested on Steph's cheek while her left one was bunched into the fabric at the back of Steph's T-shirt.

Somehow, it felt good to know that she wasn't the only one struggling for control.

Rae licked her lips, which immediately made Steph want to kiss her again. "We…we kissed."

The rasp in Rae's voice did funny things to Steph's insides. "Oh yeah."

"What now?" Rae asked. For a woman in her midthirties, a former cop who'd seen and been through so much, she sounded amazingly innocent and vulnerable.

Renewed shivers went through Steph, and this time they were equal parts desire and uncertainty. Part of her wanted to run, but she fought the impulse. "More kisses?" She forced a lightness to her tone she didn't really feel.

Rae trailed her hand down Steph's cheek, along her neck, and down to her collarbone. Just when she was about to brush the swell of Steph's breast, she seemed to realize what she was doing and pulled her hand away. "Don't tempt me. We need to talk, and if you kiss me again, I'll lose all self-control and won't stop until I have you moaning naked beneath me."

A jolt of heat went straight to Steph's core. "Jesus, Rae. You make it so damn hard to see anything wrong with that scenario."

Rae slowly shook her head as if needing to get rid of the images dancing through her mind. She looked Steph in the eyes. "I don't want to be just another notch on your bedpost."

Steph firmly shook her head. Rae could never be just that; Steph already knew that. Even though her body cried out its protest, she slid to the side a little, away from Rae, so she could think more clearly. "What is it you want?"

Rae leaned her elbows on her thighs and rubbed her face with both hands, then winced when her fingers brushed the bump on her forehead. "Hell if I know," she mumbled from behind her palms. "I guess I...I want what everyone wants."

"Which is?"

"To live my life instead of going through the motions. To stop having to force myself out of bed every day."

Her words stabbed at Steph's heart. She wanted that for Rae with an intensity that scared her even more. Rae wanted to be happy—she deserved to be happy—but could Steph really be the one to give her that? The weight of responsibility pressed her into the cushion. "I don't know if I'm the right person for that. Unless you count between the sheets, I haven't ever made anyone happy."

"I'm not asking you to." Rae roughly bunched her fist into her hair, twisting it to the side and revealing a very narrow strip of scalp where no hair grew. "Some days, I'm not sure I deserve to be happy when Kim..."

"When Kim...what?" Steph asked when Rae fell silent.

Rae bit her lip and looked away.

Steph decided to take a guess. "When she lost her husband? It's tragic, and I'm very sorry he died, but that has nothing to do with you and me."

"It has *everything* to do with me." The words burst out of Rae. "It's my fault he's dead."

The self-loathing in her voice cut Steph deeply. "I'm sure that's not true." She tried to take Rae's hand, but Rae pulled away.

"It is. If you knew..."

"Then tell me." Steph reached for Rae's hand again, and this time, she didn't allow her to withdraw but held it with steady pressure, silently letting Rae know that she would be here, no matter what she was about to say. "Please, tell me."

Rae closed her eyes as if she couldn't risk the possibility of seeing any disgust on Steph's face. Or maybe she was focusing on the images in her head. She hesitated for quite some time before she finally said, "Mike and I rode together for twelve years. In the LAPD, that's a very, very long time."

"Like dog years?" Steph asked.

A hint of a smile tugged on Rae's lips. "Kind of. Most partners only last a couple of years before one of them is transferred—or they request a new partner because they can't stand each other. If you're cooped up in a squad car with someone you don't gel with, it can be hell."

"But you and Mike got along great, right?"

"Yeah. At first I didn't think we would. We were just so different. Mike had a mischievous streak a mile wide, always making jokes during roll call. When we first got assigned to the same unit, I was prepared to hate him. But somehow, we just...worked. We got each other without words."

Steph threaded her fingers through Rae's. "Sounds kinda like us."

Rae blinked as if she had never considered that before. "Kinda, yeah."

"Minus the kissing."

Rae wrinkled her nose. "Ugh. Yeah. Minus that. He and I had the kind of relationship I always wanted to have with my brother but never managed. Our captain tried to break us up several times over the years because he wanted each of us to train new partners, but we resisted. The last time that happened was less than a month before..." She swallowed. "...before he was killed. If only he had gone along with the captain's request, he would still be alive."

"You don't know that."

"Yes, I do," Rae said.

"What happened?"

Rae was silent for so long Steph thought she would refuse to answer. Finally, she said, "On March 4, Mike and I responded to what sounded like an armed robbery in a restaurant. When we arrived on the scene, it turned out to be something else entirely. One of the waitresses had broken up with her boyfriend, so he had marched into the restaurant to get her back—with a shotgun."

Steph bit down on her lip hard when she started to suspect where this was going. Her grip on Rae's hand tightened.

"He had dragged the waitress outside, probably to get her in his car. We couldn't let him take her, so I decided not to wait for backup. I could always talk people down in situations like that, and I thought I could do it this time too. God, I was so full of myself. I didn't doubt myself for a second."

"I don't think cops are supposed to, are they?" Steph asked, but Rae didn't seem to hear her.

"I really thought I had done it this time too. He had started to lower that damn shotgun. I could almost hear it clatter to the ground. But then backup arrived. He panicked and pulled the trigger."

Steph couldn't hold back the gasp that escaped her. "He...he shot you...in the head?"

"Yeah. I caught a few pellets." Rae's hand trembled as she fluttered it over her eye, the two or three pockmark-like scars on her forehead, the spot on her head where no hair grew, and the top of her left shoulder. "But he wasn't even aiming at me. Mike took most of the blast. His vest caught some of it, but one pellet..."

Steph wrapped her other hand around Rae's too. "You don't have to say it."

"Yes, I do. One of the pellets hit his...his carotid artery." Rae clutched her own neck as if she could feel the hot lead piercing her flesh. Her gaze was hazy, reaching into the past. "There was blood everywhere. So much blood." A shiver went through her. "I tried to stop it. I tried to... But he b-bled to death within minutes, right there in my arms." She looked up, and her gaze latched on to Steph's in desperation. "H-he died, and it's all my fault."

"Oh Rae. It wasn't your fault. It was no one's fault but that guy with the shotgun." Steph pulled her forward by their joined hands until Rae slumped against her and buried her face against Steph's shoulder. Her body shook violently, like a dam holding back tons of water, about to burst. "Let it go, Rae. You have to let it go. Let go."

Warm tears hit the skin where Steph's neck met her shoulder. She wrapped both arms around Rae, her fingers buried in her hair, holding Rae's head against her and wishing so much she could soak up all that pain and guilt.

Rae clung to her and sobbed without making a sound.

Each sob felt like a painful squeeze to Steph's heart.

Finally, Rae stilled against her until just an occasional tremor ran through her body. She loosened her tight grip on Steph's back, pulled away, and ran her shirtsleeve over her face. Her cheeks were blotchy from crying and her eyes a little swollen.

To Steph, she had never looked more beautiful.

"I'm sorry," Rae said without looking at her. "I didn't mean to cry all over you. Probably not how you imagined this night to go."

"Not exactly what I had in mind when I thought about you getting me wet," Steph said with a soft smile. "But you needed it, so it's totally okay. I think if you want to be happy, you need to make room for it here." She put her hand on Rae's upper chest, where Rae's heart hammered a rapid beat against her palm. "You won't be able to do that if you hold on to all that guilt."

Rae visibly struggled to put a crooked smile on her face. "You sound like—"

"My sister or my parents. I know." Steph groaned. "I won't admit it around them, but every once in a while, they are actually right. You had no control over your backup arriving at the wrong moment—or over where that guy was aiming. You are a victim as much as Mike was. If that pellet had penetrated a little deeper…" A wave of nausea rushed over her, and she clamped her mouth shut, refusing to finish the thought.

"But it didn't. It was Mike who died. Not me."

Was it selfish of her to be glad about that? "That doesn't mean you are to blame. It's not like you traded your life for his."

"I wish I could. If it would bring him back, I would—"

"I know." Steph didn't want to hear the words. "But you can't. All you can do is live your life instead of wasting it on could-have-beens."

"I want to," Rae whispered. "For the first time since March, I want to."

They sat in silence for a while, and Steph knew Rae was too drained to talk more tonight. "Come on." She stood and pulled Rae up with her.

"What are you doing?" Rae asked when Steph dragged her past her room and toward Steph's.

"Taking you to bed."

"Um, I don't think I'm up for that."

Steph chuckled. "Get your mind out of the gutter. I just want to hold you."

"Oh."

"That is, if it's okay with you," Steph added.

Rae looked away. "I… It's been a while."

"Hey, it's okay. If you're not comfortable with it, I can just—"

"No." Now it was Rae who tugged her the last yard to the bedroom. "I think it would be really nice to hold you."

"And to be held," Steph added. "This is going to be an equal relationship, not one where you have to be strong all the time."

Rae pulled them to a halt in the doorway. "Is it?"

Deliciously trapped between the doorframe and Rae's muscular body, Steph struggled to think clearly. "What?"

"Is this," Rae waved a finger back and forth between them, "going to be a relationship?"

Oh shit. She had said it, hadn't she? She gathered all her courage to push through the fear. "I think I'd like it to be. I just don't know if I have what it takes."

"Me neither."

"You've had a fifteen-year relationship," Steph said.

"That ended because I couldn't communicate worth a shit," Rae replied. "Plus that was before…before I lost Mike and my job. Your mother clearly thinks I'm a mental case, and she's probably right. I mean, you saw my little breakdown…" She pointed toward the couch.

"What I saw was a strong woman who finally allowed herself to grieve," Steph said firmly. "My mother would never use a word like that. What gave you the idea she would think that about you?"

Rae pushed her free hand into her pants pocket. "She…um…gave me her card and offered to get me in touch with one of her colleagues."

"What? You've got to be kidding!" Steph looked around for her phone, not caring that it was nearly two in the morning. She wouldn't allow her mother to interfere with her life—especially not when it came to Rae.

But Rae tightened her grip on Steph's hand and kept her in the doorway. "Don't. She was trying to help, probably because she was worried about you getting involved with someone like me."

"We don't need her help. You and I can manage on our own just fine."

Rae tilted her head. "So you think we can do it? Maybe…figure it out together?"

Steph decided to forget about her mother's little intervention for tonight. She smiled at Rae. "The blind leading the blind?"

"More like the one-eyed leading the blind," Rae said.

A wave of...affection welled up deep in Steph's chest. "We could just date and see where it goes. Avoid bumping into things by going slow."

"Sounds like a plan. I'd like that." Rae placed two fingers on Steph's cheek, dipped her head, and kissed her, just a tender brush of her lips against Steph's.

Before Steph could react and deepen the kiss, Rae put some space between them and ducked out of the room.

"Hey, where are you going?"

"Getting something to sleep in," Rae said over her shoulder. "I'm not going to tempt fate by sleeping with you naked."

Steph stared after her. "Bummer."

"I heard that," Rae called before disappearing into her room.

Steph slumped against the doorframe. *Oh God. We're doing this. Dating. Sleeping together. Just sleeping.* Both were definitely a first for Steph. Never before had she taken someone to bed without having sex with them.

Rae passed Steph's room on the way to the bathroom, shirt already unbuttoned and tie dangling around her neck. The almost shy smile she gave her made Steph weak in the knees.

"Lord, give me strength," she whispered. "Don't let me mess this up."

Rae paused at the bathroom door. "Did you say something?"

"Um, I was asking if it's okay if I sleep in this?" Steph waved at the T-shirt and the loose cotton shorts she had changed into when she'd gotten home.

"Is that what you normally sleep in?"

A chuckle rose up Steph's chest. "No. My normal sleepwear is a lot sexier than this."

Rae's gaze traveled up Steph's bare legs. "Sexier than that? Really? What do you sleep in—lacy lingerie?"

Was that what Rae considered sexy? Steph filed it away. "Nope. Most of the time, I sleep in the buff."

Rae gulped audibly and waved at Steph's T-shirt and shorts. "This seems fine. For now." Her voice dropped to a husky rasp on the last two words.

Now it was Steph's turn to gulp as she watched Rae disappear into the bathroom.

She had already brushed her teeth while she'd waited for Rae to get home, so she was ready for bed. She walked to her queen-size bed and pulled back the covers, then hesitated. Which side would Rae prefer? With other bed partners, she had never bothered to ask. There wasn't usually much sleeping going on anyway.

Finally, she decided to take the side of the bed that would enable Rae to still see her if she really curled up against her and let herself be held. Steph settled down on her back and pulled the covers up to her chin. *Christ.* She probably looked like a scared virgin. She pushed the covers down to her hips.

Rae seemed to take forever in the bathroom. Usually, she was a lot like Steph in that regard—she liked minimal fuss and was in and out of the bathroom within ten minutes, max. But not now. Was she in there, staring at herself in the mirror, having second thoughts?

The bathroom door creaked open, and Rae's footsteps came closer in a slow, hesitant pattern.

Shit. She *was* having second thoughts.

"Steph?" Rae asked from the doorway.

Steph clutched the covers. "Yes?" Even she could hear the tension in her voice.

"Um, I…"

"If you'd rather not sleep with me…next to me, that's okay," Steph blurted out before Rae could say it.

"No, that's not it." Rae was still speaking from across the room, not moving any closer. "My eye isn't used to all that crying, so it feels a little irritated now, and with the new prosthesis… I was wondering if you'd mind if I leave it out tonight."

Steph sat up. "Why would I mind? I've seen you without your eye."

"Yeah, but… I don't know. Maybe it's different now that we… I mean, this," Rae waved toward the left side of her face, which was dipped in shadow because she hadn't fully entered the room and the light was off in the hall, "isn't exactly sexy."

Steph patted the bed next to her. "Come here."

Rae hesitated, then padded across the room and perched on the edge of the bed with her right side toward Steph.

Steph shoved the covers aside and knelt next to her. Gently, she took hold of Rae's chin and directed her head around so she could see her entire face in the light of the lamp on the bedside table.

Rae gulped but didn't try to resist. The prosthetic eye was out, and what Steph could see of the socket beneath the drooping lid looked indeed a little tender.

"Everything about you is sexy," Steph said firmly. "Do you hear that? Everything. Now come to bed, and don't force me to say more sappy stuff."

Rae barked out a laugh. "God, you're something else."

"Is that a good thing?" Steph asked.

"A very good thing."

They stretched out on their sides next to each other, close but not touching.

Steph looked her in the eye. "You don't ever have to hesitate to take off anything you want around me—and that includes your prosthetic eye."

"Thanks." Rae's voice was husky.

"So," Steph said after a while, "are you a cuddler?"

"Nah. Not really."

"Me neither."

They looked at each other.

"Want to make an exception since I promised to hold you and all?" Steph asked.

Rae smiled and nodded.

Steph rolled onto her back and opened her arms.

Rae slid down a little, wrapped one long arm around her, and settled her head on Steph's chest. Then she lifted it again, laid it back down, and repeated the entire process about two or three times, shifting against her.

The slow slide of Rae's warm body against her own sent tingles down to Steph's toes. When Rae's chin rubbed along her nipple, Steph dug her teeth into her bottom lip to keep from moaning and wrapped both arms around her to hold her still. There was only so much temptation she could resist. "What are you doing?"

"Just trying to get comfortable. I'm not used to being held. With Lise, I was the one holding her most of the time."

"I'm usually not one for rules, but can we have one dating-Steph-101 rule? No talking about exes while in bed with me."

Rae lifted her head off Steph's chest to peer down at her. "Are you jealous?"

"No, of course not." She'd never been jealous in her life. Why would she start now? Steph reached out and turned off the lamp on the bedside table, throwing them into darkness.

Rae chuckled, sending warm puffs of air across the bit of skin that Steph's V-neck shirt revealed. "You totally are."

"Am not." Steph combed her fingers through Rae's hair. "Let's try to sleep. It's been a long day."

"Oh yeah. Is it really still the same day?"

"Well, technically, it isn't. But it feels like it's still Christmas." The sappy part of Steph—the one she usually hid away behind a layer of sarcastic humor—insisted that the best Christmas present of all was right there, in her arms. She trailed her hand along Rae's strong back in soothing strokes.

"This is kind of nice," Rae murmured, "but I don't think I'll be able to fall asleep like this."

"That's okay. We can switch in a minute." Steph continued her gentle strokes along Rae's back, and it took all of ten seconds for Rae's breathing to ease into the soft, regular pattern of sleep.

Steph grinned into the darkness.

Chapter 21

Steph woke up overheated. She had always suspected that sharing the bed with Rae would be hot and sweaty, but this wasn't quite what she'd had in mind. Rae's powerful body beneath hers radiated heat in waves. God, the woman was like a heater—a sexy five-foot-ten heater.

Groggily, Steph lifted her head and realized they had somehow traded positions during the night. Rae was now sprawled out on her back, both arms wrapped around Steph, holding her close. One of her hands had slipped beneath the waistband of Steph's shorts and was now resting on the swell of her buttock.

That discovery didn't exactly help to cool Steph down. She struggled not to press her hips against Rae.

Normally, she would have woken up her bedmate for a quick round of morning sex before slipping out of bed—and out of their life. But with Rae, that wasn't an option.

She looked down at Rae's face, which was relaxed and looked younger in sleep, with all the brooding lines gone. The swelling on her forehead had nearly disappeared, but a reddish bruise had formed.

Protectiveness flared through Steph. Maybe she needed to have a word with Carlos and tell him to be more careful where he stuck his elbow next time.

She continued to watch Rae sleep, taking advantage of being able to study her unobserved. How different she looked when her lips weren't set in a grim line that warned people to stay away. Steph was tempted to trace the contours of Rae's full lips with her finger, but she didn't want to wake her. After her breakdown last night, Rae needed all the sleep she could get. Her left eye wasn't all the way closed, which was a bit spooky, but Steph knew she'd get used to it if they… Her breath caught. If they kept doing this. Whatever this was. The thought still scared her. Could she really do this without ending up hurting Rae…or being hurt in return?

Rae stirred beneath her, her arms around Steph flexing, which made her fingers on Steph's butt slide a little lower.

She shivered and squeezed her eyes shut.

"You awake?" Rae whispered. Her voice rumbled under Steph's ear.

"Not sure," Steph murmured into the fabric of Rae's shirt. "It's possible that I'm still asleep and having a very erotic dream."

Rae sucked in an audible breath. "Is this your idea of taking it slow?" Her voice was rough with the remnants of sleep and a hint of desire. "Telling me about your erotic dreams?"

"Hey, you started it."

"Me? I was asleep up until a second ago. How could I have started anything?"

"Take a look at where your right hand is."

"My h—? Oh shit." Rae snatched it away. "God, I'm sorry. I didn't realize…"

Steph stopped her apology by lightly kissing her on the lips. "I didn't say I minded, did I?"

Rae stilled beneath her. "No, you didn't." She moved her hand to a safe spot on Steph's hip.

Steph propped herself up on one elbow and looked down at her, which made Rae squirm as if she was afraid her eye was leaking or something.

"How do you feel?" Steph asked.

"Fine," Rae said immediately. She stretched her broad shoulders. "Slept like a log." Steph kept studying her until Rae added, "A little weird. I'm not used to crying in front of people, for one thing."

"I'm not people," Steph said softly.

Rae smiled. "No. You're Team Rae."

The familiar term had taken on a new meaning. Steph swallowed and nodded.

"Is that…is it a two-person team?"

Steph had no idea what Rae was asking, so she gave her a questioning look.

Rae swept one of Steph's probably very tousled strands of hair behind her ear. "I mean…dating…taking it slow…" She stared over Steph's shoulder. "Does that mean you'll be seeing other people too?" She flicked her gaze to Steph's face, then away again. "Because to be honest, I'm not sure I can do that."

Oh God. Emotional discussions before coffee. Steph wasn't sure she could do *that*. But more importantly… Could she do what Rae was asking? She had never promised monogamy to anyone. She rolled to the side until she'd created a bit of space between their bodies and could think more clearly. "You don't have to worry about that." She tried to keep her voice light, but that didn't help to soothe the erratic beat of her heart. "I have a feeling I'll have my hands full with you anyway, with no energy left over for other people."

Rae didn't smile. "So does that mean we're exclusive?"

Steph's throat was too tight to speak, so she nodded. No big deal, right? It didn't mean they were now married and stuck with each other forever.

"If you change your mind, let me know, okay? Don't just—" Rae bit her lip.

Cheat? Walk away, like Lise? Steph shook her head. "I won't." She didn't need the same promise from Rae. Rae was in this now, one hundred percent, and that was as scary as it was reassuring.

"Thank you," Rae whispered.

"No problem." Steph put on a grin and rolled back, half on top of Rae, hovering over her until their lips were only inches from each other. "Now that we have that covered, any idea how we could kill some time until I have to leave for my last walk with Moose?"

"Ah, that's today? I'm sorry."

"I'm trying not to think about it," Steph said. "Maybe you can think of something to provide some distraction."

"Hmm, let's see…" Rae looked around as if trying to come up with a promising distraction. Then her gaze paused on the alarm clock, and she stiffened beneath Steph. "Oh shit. It's nearly eleven! How on earth did that happen?"

Steph shrugged. "We went to bed late, and you needed the rest after… after everything. Is that a problem?"

"Yes." Rae slid out from beneath her without the kiss Steph had hoped for. "I promised Kim I'd be over for lunch."

"Want me to drive you?"

Rae was already at the door. "No, thanks. It's light out, and I won't stay late, so I'll be fine."

When she disappeared into the bathroom, Steph let her head sink onto the pillow. It smelled of Rae.

Oh no. She wouldn't bury her head in the pillow and sulk at not getting to spend more time in bed with Rae. This was what she had wanted—keeping things between them light, not instantly jumping into that joined-at-the-hip-can't-function-without-you stage that she had always wrinkled her nose at. Right?

Right. She rolled out of bed. But that didn't mean she would let Rae leave without a kiss.

Rae squeezed a little bit of baby shampoo onto a gauze pad and cleaned off any traces of mucus still clinging to the corners of her eye. She stared at herself in the mirror above the sink. God, she couldn't believe she had cried in Steph's arms last night. But she did have to admit that it had helped to finally voice what had been on her mind every day for nearly ten months. While she would probably never be at peace with what had happened and her role in it, the choking weight that had sometimes kept her up at night now didn't feel so heavy anymore. She had slept like a baby in Steph's arms.

That had been another surprise. One of many last night.

She and Steph were dating! The thought made her pulse speed up with equal parts excitement and panic.

After losing first Lise, then Mike and her job and by extension all of her comrades on the force, she hadn't thought that she'd ever let anyone close again, but Steph had somehow managed to push her way past the walls Rae had built around herself. No, not push. More liked sneaked through, without Rae noticing until it was too late to keep her out.

But now was not the time to process that. She had to get going, or she'd be late for lunch with Kim.

She studied her eye socket in the mirror. Luckily, it was back to normal, no longer puffy or irritated. She cleaned the prosthesis with baby shampoo, then rinsed it thoroughly before dabbing at it with a tissue. Once it was dry, she lifted the upper lid with her index finger, slid the top edge of the prosthesis beneath it, and then pulled the lower lid down so it would slide in.

There. Everything looked normal now, exactly how she preferred it when visiting Kim. She didn't want any unnecessary reminder of what they had lost that day.

Hastily, she got dressed and closed her belt buckle on her way to her room, to get Kim's Christmas present.

When she returned, gift in hand, Steph was in the kitchen, still wearing the T-shirt and the shorts she had slept in. The shorts Rae's hand had slipped beneath earlier. Heat gathered low in her belly, and she gave her head a rough shake to clear it.

Come on. No lingering. Get going.

"Here." Steph pressed a travel mug into her hand. "It feels almost a little too domestic, like the dutiful housewife making breakfast, but I thought you could use some coffee."

Rae had longed for a cup but knew she didn't have the time. "God, I could kiss you."

"Nope. Not *could*—you will. I'm not letting you go without a kiss."

"Oh, is that so?" Rae drawled. "Another dating-Steph-101 rule?"

"Guess you could call it that." Steph took another step closer, right into Rae's personal space. "So?"

The physical closeness made Rae's body buzz in a way that all the caffeine in the world couldn't. She had to grin at Steph's playful demand. Nothing meek about this woman. If she wanted something, she went after it, no matter if it was a spot in a comedy show or a kiss. "Well, as a former cop, I guess I'd better follow the rules, hmm?" She tucked the travel mug beneath one arm with Kim's gift so she could wrap the other around Steph and draw her closer.

"Yeah," Steph murmured, sounding a little breathless, "you'd b—"

Rae lowered her head and kissed her.

Steph's curves pressed against her as she clasped the nape of Rae's neck and kissed her back. There was something so damn sexy about the way she threaded her fingers through Rae's hair and drew her closer. She teased the corner of Rae's mouth with the tip of her tongue, then dipped inside.

Electric sensations sparked through Rae's belly. She lost herself in the softness and damp heat of Steph's mouth and had no idea how much time had passed when she found herself flush against the counter, with Steph's body molded to hers. "I need to get going," she murmured against Steph's lips.

"Mm-hmm." Steph placed one last, soft kiss on her lips and smoothed her hands down Rae's shoulders before stepping away.

"Hey." Rae caught her hand and drew her back. "I know it'll be tough to say goodbye, but I hope you have a good walk with Moose."

Steph sighed. "Thanks."

Rae hesitated, not sure what to say to cheer her up. Maybe she shouldn't have brought it up. God, this communication stuff was hard.

"You need to go, or Kim will worry."

"I know." Rae didn't move. "Mr. Hicks told me to take the day off. Want to...I don't know...do something tonight?" She tried to make it sound casual, not like a date, even though it would feel like one to her.

"Ah, normally, I'd love to, but I want to hit an open mic or two to make sure I'm ready for... Oh, wait, I haven't told you about that yet. Your boss is letting me headline the New Year's Eve show!" Excitement lightened the color of Steph's eyes to a silvery gray.

So Mr. Hicks had indeed followed her recommendation. Rae had worried that he would change his mind now that he knew they were involved. She decided not to let on that he had asked for her opinion, not wanting Steph to think she had gotten the spot only because of her. As far as Rae was concerned, Steph had earned it. "Oh wow. That's wonderful! Congratulations!"

"Thanks." Steph gave a happy little hop.

So cute. Rae couldn't help grinning. "Is your family coming to see you?"

Steph's bright smile dimmed. "Maybe Claire and Lana. Unless Claire changes her mind."

"What about your parents?"

"Nah. They don't like stand-up."

Rae bit her lip. Couldn't they get over themselves for one night to support their daughter? "That's what they said when you asked them to come?"

"I didn't ask. I already know the answer." Steph waved her hand as if to dismiss the topic. "Are you working on New Year's Eve?"

"Yes, I am." If necessary, she would bribe her colleagues so she would get to cover the showroom during the late show, just to make sure all would go smoothly.

Steph's smile returned. "Great."

For a moment, Rae considered suggesting that she join Steph at the open mic, but then she rejected the idea. If Steph had wanted her there, she would have asked. Maybe Steph needed a little space so she wouldn't get overwhelmed and run for the hills. She swallowed down her disappointment at not getting to see Steph all day and said, "Well, then, have a good open mic. Guess I'll see you tomorrow."

Steph hesitated. Was she thinking about asking her to come along after all? But then she nodded. "See you tomorrow. Tell Kim 'hi' from me."

As Rae finally hurried to her car, she reached into her pants pocket for the car keys but encountered the business card Steph's mother had given her. She drew it out and stared at the number.

If she didn't leave now, she really would be late. She opened the driver's side door and climbed into the Subaru.

Oh, fuck it. She reached for her phone, sent Kim a short text to let her know she might be a few minutes late, and typed in the cell phone number. It rang and rang...and rang.

Just when she thought the call would go to voice mail, Diane answered. "Dr. Diane Renshaw."

The formal answer drove home the fact that she had given Rae her number as a therapist, not as Steph's mom.

"Um, hi, Diane. This is Rae Coleman. I'm sorry to bother you, especially on your work phone. I didn't have any other number for you, or I would have used that."

"Don't worry about it," Diane said. "I gave you my card so you could call—and I'm happy you did. I didn't think you would."

If not for Steph, she wouldn't have.

"So have you thought about what kind of therapist you'd like to see?" Diane asked. "Cognitive processing therapy and EMDR have a good success rate with PTSD patients, but there are other options as well."

Rae tightened her grip on the phone. "That's not why I'm calling. I don't have PTSD."

"Listen, Rae. I know it's hard to face—"

"I don't have PTSD." Rae's voice echoed through the SUV. *Shit.* She'd spoken more loudly than she had intended, probably confirming Diane's assumption that she was in denial. "You just startled me. That's all."

Diane sighed. "Rae…"

She wouldn't let it go; Rae sensed that. Steph had probably inherited her stubbornness from her mother. She swallowed against the lump lodged in her throat. "I'm blind in one eye."

Diane went so quiet that Rae wondered if she had hung up. Then she cleared her throat. "Oh. So that's why I startled you when I walked up to you. You didn't see me."

"Yeah." Rae rubbed her eye with her free hand. God, she hated telling anyone. It made her feel so exposed and defenseless. Already, she was dreading the next time she saw Diane, knowing Steph's mother would stare at her prosthetic eye. She took a steadying breath and forced herself to face her fears and be completely honest. "Listen, Diane, I know I have some stuff to work on, and maybe one day I will ask you to recommend a colleague, but that isn't why I'm calling today. This is about Steph."

"Does she know? About your eye."

"Yes."

"Good," Diane said. "I know she likes to come across like a flippant person who never takes anything seriously, but that's just her way of keeping people at arm's length to avoid getting hurt. She has it in her to be a wonderful friend…or more."

The little hairs on the back of Rae's neck prickled with unease. Even though Diane meant well, Steph wouldn't appreciate being analyzed like that behind her back—or being nudged into a relationship. "Um, I actually called to see if you have plans for New Year's Eve."

Diane chuckled. "Is Steph planning to ring in the New Year with some big announcement about the two of you?"

"No!" Christ, she was messing this up royally. "Steph is headlining the New Year's Eve show in the club where I work. That's a big deal, and I know it would mean a lot to her if you came."

"Then why isn't she calling us?"

"Because she's afraid you'll say no...again." Rae didn't quite manage to keep the reproachful undertone from her voice, but she didn't care.

Diane was quiet for several seconds. "I didn't know it was that important to her to have us there. Last time she asked, I had a conference to attend and told her I couldn't make it. She shrugged and said we would have cramped her style anyway."

Jeez. For a therapist who had just pointed out Steph's defense mechanisms, she was remarkably oblivious to them at times...or she hadn't tried too hard to see through them because it was more convenient.

"I know what you're thinking." Diane sighed. "And you're probably right. If you text me the time and address, we'll be there."

Rae exhaled. "Thank you."

"No, Rae. Thank *you*."

When they ended the call, Rae threw the phone onto the passenger seat and took a big sip of her coffee as if it were schnapps. Her capacity for human interaction was more than reached, and she hadn't even made it to Kim's yet. Groaning, she started the car.

Rae's stomach churned as she got out of the SUV and made her way toward Kim's front door. The garden gnome Mike had put on the lawn as a joke was still there, as if Kim couldn't bring herself to remove it.

Kim swung open the door before Rae could ring the bell. "Hi." She greeted Rae with a warm hug, then drew her into the house.

Rae braced herself for the onslaught of memories being in Mike and Kim's house always brought. Even though Kim had put some things away, every room still held reminders of Mike. Sometimes, she even imagined catching a whiff of Mike's aftershave in the air. God, how could Kim stand to live here? Or was being surrounded by memories of Mike a comfort to her?

Kim led her to the kitchen, where various bowls and platters were already lined up. "Mind if we eat in here, since it's just the two of us?"

"No, that's fine." More than fine, actually. At least then she wouldn't have to think of last Christmas, when she and Mike had played tug-of-war over where to put up the Christmas tree in the living room. Did Kim even have a tree this year? "Anything I can help with?"

"No, thanks. Dot did all the hard work yesterday. I just have to heat everything up." Kim put a dish into the microwave. "She and Gordon send their best."

"Tell them 'hi' from me next time you talk to them."

"You could call them yourself," Kim said quietly. "They'd love to hear from you."

Rae put her present down on the counter so she had an excuse to turn her back to Kim. "I will give them a call sometime." Just not anytime soon. Her head already felt close to exploding with all the new things she had to process.

Thankfully, Kim let it go and didn't pressure her to call Mike's parents.

Rae sat at the breakfast bar and watched Kim walk back and forth between the counter and the microwave. In a pair of light blue jeans and a short-sleeved, black turtleneck, Kim looked great. She seemed to be gaining back some of the weight she had lost.

"What?" Kim asked as she took out the stuffing and put the gravy into the microwave.

"Nothing. Just...you look good."

Kim turned and smiled at her. "Thanks. So do you." She tilted her head and regarded Rae across the breakfast bar.

Rae fidgeted beneath her perusal and slid from the stool. "Let me get that for you." She carried the stuffing to the breakfast bar.

Finally, they sat down to eat, and Rae dug in with gusto since she hadn't eaten since yesterday afternoon.

"What did you have for Christmas dinner?" Kim asked. "Turkey too?"

Rae laughed. "Spaghetti with tomato sauce."

Kim lowered her forkful of roasted butternut squash back to her plate. "You had spaghetti for Christmas dinner? Sounds like Steph's family is as unconventional as she is."

"Not really. There was a mix-up with the catering service they ordered from, so we ended up cooking, and the only thing in their pantry was spaghetti."

"But you still had a good time?"

Rae thought of sitting in the grass with Steph...and nearly kissing her. "Yeah, I did."

"I can tell. Your eyes are sparkling."

"That's because I saw my ocularist on Monday," Rae said. Had that really been only three days ago? So much had happened since then. "He gave the eye a polish."

"Oh, did he polish the right one too?" Kim asked with a grin. "Because there's a sparkle there too."

"Nonsense," Rae muttered. "I don't sparkle."

"Uh-huh. Come on, Rae. I've known you for twelve years. Something is different about you, and I think it's the good kind of different. What is it?"

Rae drew a pattern through the cranberry sauce on her plate, then put her fork down. Her appetite was gone.

Kim set her cutlery down too. "Why won't you tell me?"

A groan bubbled up from deep in Rae's chest. How could she tell Kim about that tentative kernel of happiness growing inside of her when Kim might be alone for the rest of her life?

"Rae, please. Don't shut me out."

The pain in Kim's voice pierced Rae's armor. "I don't want to." She reached across the breakfast bar and took Kim's hand. It felt fragile against her broader palm. "It's just… I don't want to hurt you."

"Hurt me?" Kim echoed. "How could your happiness hurt me?"

Rae hung her head. "I…"

Kim slid from her stool and dragged Rae into the living room, where she had indeed set up a Christmas tree. She pressed her down onto the couch and handed her a gift-wrapped present. "I think you need to open your present."

"Now? We haven't finished eating."

"I don't think either of us would have eaten another bite anyway."

Rae lowered her gaze to the gift on her lap. A heavy weight settled in the pit of her stomach. Almost afraid of what she would find, she fumbled with the tape until the gift wrap finally fell away, revealing a beautiful wooden picture frame. When she turned it around, she discovered that it already held a photo.

At the sight of it, all air rushed from Rae's lungs as if she'd been punched.

The picture showed the three of them—Mike, Kim, and her—arms around each other, with Kim in the middle. It had been taken on Kim's birthday, a couple of weeks before the shooting. Rae and Mike were in uniform. Mike's mother, Dot, had snapped the photo just before they had headed out to work. All three of them were laughing at something, without a clue that this would be the last photo they ever took together.

Rae's thumb swiped over the faces beneath the glass. She didn't look away from the picture even as Kim sat next to her. Maybe it was for the best that Kim had settled down to her left. At least that way, Rae didn't need to see the grief on her face when she regarded the photo.

But when Kim touched a trembling finger to the glass, it wasn't Mike's features she traced. It was Rae's. "This," she said, her voice raw. "This is the Rae I want to see. If something happened to get you there, why would you think it would hurt me?"

"Because...because Mike..."

Kim took the picture from her tight grasp and gently set it down on the coffee table before taking Rae's hand with both of hers. "Don't you think he'd want you to be happy?"

"He'd want to be here with us...with you. And I messed that up." She bunched her fist into the comforter next to her. Steph's voice, warm and firm, echoed through her mind. *It wasn't your fault. It was no one's fault but that guy with the shotgun.* "At least I think I did," she added.

Kim gripped her hand more tightly. "What? Why would you think that?"

"Because I walked into that situation without backup."

"Mike was your backup, and you were his."

Rae hunched her shoulders. "Yeah, but..."

"I watched the video," Kim said quietly.

Shock zapped through Rae. She whipped her head around to stare at Kim. "You...you watched it?" She hadn't been able to watch the recording from their squad car's camera.

"I had to. I kept thinking he'd walk through the door and greet me with that grin of his. I needed to see." On the last word, Kim's voice broke.

Rae wrapped both arms around her in a sheltering embrace. When Kim pressed her head to Rae's shoulder, Rae leaned her cheek against her and whispered, "I'm so, so sorry."

Kim grasped her almost painfully tight. "That's just it, Rae. You've got nothing to be sorry for." She pulled back and looked at her. Tears glittered in her eyes. "Nothing."

"But I should have—"

"Done what? Stayed in the car until that asshole drove off with the waitress, doing God knows what to her? You think Mike would have let that happen any more than you did?" Kim fiercely shook her head. "Shot him, even though he had already lowered his weapon? What should you have done, Rae?"

"I...I don't know. Something. Anything."

"You were shot. You came this close to dying." Kim held up her shaking hand, thumb and index finger half of an inch apart. "You had a shotgun pellet in your eye and were bleeding profusely. I don't know how you even managed to stay conscious. But you didn't even try to stop the bleeding or get help for yourself. Your entire focus was on Mike."

"I tried to save him." Rae hung her head, unable to look her in the eyes. "I tried, but...I failed."

Kim took her face in both hands. With unexpected strength, she guided her head up until Rae had to look at her. "You didn't fail. No one could have saved him. I had to accept that, and so do you. None of it was your fault. Nobody ever thought that. Not Dot, not Gordon, and not me."

"I do...did." Part of her still couldn't help thinking it, even after both Steph and Kim had reassured her that she hadn't done anything wrong.

"Oh Rae." Kim lightly shook Rae's head, which she still held between her hands. "You've got to let it go, or it'll eat you up inside. Mike wouldn't want that. He would kick your ass if he were here now."

A tired smile crept onto Rae's face. "I know. I...I'll try."

"Good." Kim stroked her cheek, then let go and gave her shoulder a friendly nudge. "Now tell me what put that sparkle in your eye...and don't pretend it was the ocularist."

Rae hesitated only for a second longer. Deep down, she was bursting to tell someone about this unexpected turn her life had taken. "Steph." Saying her name made her lips want to curl up into a smile. "It was Steph."

Kim stared at her. "Wait, you mean, she and you...? Didn't you just tell me on Monday that you weren't a couple?"

"We weren't. This...us... It just happened yesterday. You were right. She did sneak up on me."

A smile spread over Kim's face until she was beaming in a way Rae hadn't seen in months. "That's great. I'm so happy for you."

Rae held up her hand. "We're not ready to buy monogrammed towels or anything. Just dating for now. Steph hasn't been in a relationship before, so we're taking it slow."

"You mean, with a woman?"

"With anyone." Rae tried to sound unconcerned. "She only had casual hookups so far."

A wrinkle formed between Kim's brows. "But that's not what…?"

"No."

"Good," Kim said firmly. "Because you deserve to have it all. The real deal."

Rae leaned forward and studied the photo on the table, the way Mike and Kim had their arms wrapped around each other. "When you and Mike first started dating, how did you know that things would work out between the two of you?"

Kim snorted. "I didn't. I questioned my sanity for agreeing to go out with him."

Rae's mouth gaped open. "What? Why?" As far as she was concerned, they had been the perfect couple.

"Because he was such a player back then." Kim shook her head with a fond smile. "That man could charm the panties off any woman without even trying."

"Mike? Our Mike?"

"Oh yeah. Just ask any of the guys who knew him in the academy. They could tell you some wild stories."

Rae swiped her hand through her hair. "I had no idea. All he ever talked about was you."

A sad smile darted across Kim's face. "Are you worried things might not work out the same way for you and Steph?"

"No."

Kim poked her in the ribs.

"Okay, yeah, maybe a little. Steph's so…independent. She doesn't need me. Not the way Lise did. What if she gets bored with me or decides a relationship would get in the way of her comedy career?"

"Then I'll hunt her down and give her hell," Kim said with her most intimidating expression—which, admittedly, wasn't very intimidating at all.

Rae burst out laughing. God, she'd needed that.

"But seriously, Rae. If being a dating consultant has taught me one thing it's that a successful relationship isn't about needing someone."

"It's not?"

Kim shook her head. "It's about *wanting* someone. About choosing someone over everything else—not because you can't live without them, but because you don't ever want to."

That made sense. Kind of. Rae scratched her head. "Huh. Why does everyone else seem to know so much about relationships and how they work, while I feel like a totally clueless beginner, even though I was in one for fifteen years?"

"Because you never had to work at it," Kim told her. "You and Lise fell into it when you were...what?"

"Seventeen."

"Jeez, you were a baby."

"Was not," Rae grumbled.

Kim waved her protest away. "Seriously, I hope this works out for you. Please don't ever hesitate to come to me for advice, a shoulder to cry on, or just to let me know that you're deliriously happy, okay?"

Rae released a jittery breath. "Okay."

Kim got up from the couch. "Now tell me: Does Steph like sandwiches?"

Thank God. The emotional part of this conversation seemed to be over. She could talk about sandwiches. "She loves them. Why?"

"Because we've got a ton of leftover turkey, and I don't think we should warm it up again, or it'll become dry." She pulled Rae up from the sofa. "Come on, let's go make some sandwiches."

With one last glance at the photo on the coffee table, Rae followed her back to the kitchen.

Chapter 22

THIS WAS TURNING OUT TO be one of the shittiest days of Steph's life. Except for how the day had begun, of course. Waking up in Rae's arms had been surprisingly nice, but everything had gone downhill from there.

First, she had chickened out on asking Rae to join her at the open mic. She had assumed that Rae got enough comedy at work, so she wouldn't want to listen to more of it on her night off, especially not the amateurs and weirdos at an open mic. Rae hadn't asked if she could come, and Steph had taken that as a confirmation, but now she wondered if Rae had been waiting for an invitation.

Damn, this communication thing was hard. Just as hard as saying goodbye to Moose had been earlier today.

And now, to top it all off, she was bombing badly. As soon as she took the mic from the guy who'd gone up before her, she blanked. She stared into the bored faces of the comics in the audience, and it took her a second to remember her opening joke.

Jesus. When had that last happened to her?

Finally, she remembered and delivered the joke. She even got a laugh from someone at the bar, but she wasn't sure if they laughed at the joke or at her weak delivery. What on earth was up with her? She stammered her way through a bit she'd done perfectly a hundred times before.

Just when she finally found her rhythm, her five minutes were up and she had to surrender her spot on the stage.

Warren, one of the comics she sometimes hung out with, formed a megaphone with his hands. "Boo! That was about as funny as a bad case of the clap, Steph!"

"You'd know," Steph shot back. She walked past him and slid back onto her barstool next to Penny.

"What was that?" Penny raised her voice to be heard over the rambling of the guy who had the mic now. He wasn't faring any better than Steph had, so the audience was booing.

"Hell if I know." Steph took a big swig of her beer and made a face. It had gone flat.

Penny leaned closer. "I didn't think you'd take Moose moving away so badly. I mean, I knew you'd be sad, but losing your focus up on stage? That's not like you."

Steph put her arm on the bar and buried her face in the crook of her elbow. Moose wasn't to blame. It had been mostly thoughts of Rae that had thrown off her focus. "I know." She lifted her head. "I hope I'll get it together before New Year's Eve. This is my last chance to make it in stand-up, Penny. If I mess it up…"

"You won't," Penny said. "This was just a fluke. You'll be back to your usual hilarious self by then."

"Let's hope so. You're coming, right?"

"Wouldn't miss it for the world."

A guy in his late twenties, who'd been waiting for his drink next to them, turned toward Steph. "Hey, you were just up on stage, weren't you?"

"Yep. Me and most of the people here." As usual at open mics, the audience consisted mostly of comedians waiting to go up.

"Yeah," he said. "But unlike most of them, you were good."

"And you are full of shit."

He burst out laughing, his very white teeth flashing against his tan. "Well, you were good toward the end." His gaze went from Steph to Penny and back. "What are you ladies drinking? Can I buy you another round?"

Steph hesitated. She did want a new beer, and with his twinkling blue eyes and California-surfer-type good looks, the guy was kind of cute, but if she accepted the drink he offered, he'd take it as an invitation to flirt his ass off. Was some harmless flirting okay if you were in a relationship?

God, she was in a relationship! She still couldn't believe it.

The bartender came over. "What can I get you?" he asked the guy.

"Another beer?" The cute guy gave Steph a questioning look.

"No, thanks," Steph said. "I'm good."

"Just a beer for me, then," the guy said to the bartender. When he received it, he turned back to Steph. "If you change your mind, I'll be over there." He pointed across the room.

"Good to know." Steph gave him a friendly, but not too friendly smile.

Penny stared after him, then gave Steph a wide-eyed look. "What just happened?"

"Hmm?"

"First you bomb, then you turn down a drink from a guy who's obviously into you. What's going on with you?"

Steph stared at the puddle of water that had formed beneath her beer bottle. "I've turned down drinks before."

"Yeah, from assholes, but he seemed nice." Penny reached over and felt Steph's forehead. "What's up? You're not sick, are you?"

Laughing, Steph swiped her hand away. "I'm fine. I just... I'm in a relationship now, so letting someone else buy me a drink might not be—"

"Wait, wait, wait!" Penny tapped her ear. "Can you repeat that? It's so loud in here that I thought you said you're in a relationship." She laughed.

Steph took a sip of her lukewarm beer. "Yeah, that's what I said."

Penny's laughter stopped abruptly. She grabbed hold of the bar with both hands. "You? In a relationship? You're kidding, right? This is like the fake relationship thing you and Rae had going on, isn't it?"

"No," Steph said. "There's nothing fake about it. It's the real deal."

"Christ on a bike! How did that happen?"

Steph let out a nervous chuckle. "I have no idea."

"Who?" Penny still looked as if she was about to slip from her barstool. "Oh, wait, don't tell me. It's Rae, isn't it?"

Now it was Steph's turn to take hold of the bar. "How did you guess?" She hadn't been that obvious, had she?

"Easy. You cared a lot about her opinion of you, even as you were complaining about her cramping your style."

"But...but..." That had been nearly two months ago, when they had first moved in with each other. Had there really been a kernel of something between them even back then?

Penny laughed. "God, you should see your face. I never thought I'd get to see you this way."

"What way?"

"In love!"

"Whoa!" Steph held up both hands. "I never said that."

"So you're saying you're not in love?"

"I'm saying we're taking it slow." Steph looked away. Her heart was racing. "I...I care about her, and I don't want to mess this up and hurt her."

"Now I get it! That's why you were so distracted on stage. You're having feelings other than lust for someone for the first time, and you're freaking out a little."

Steph pushed the bottle of beer away. "I'm not freaking out."

Penny raised her brows at her.

"Well, not much anyway."

Penny's eyebrows lifted even higher.

"Okay, I'm scared shitless. I mean, you just said it yourself. I rarely reject a hot guy or a beautiful woman who's up for a little flirting...or more. What if I'm not cut out for a relationship? What if I can't be monogamous?"

Penny's mop of hair quivered as she laughed.

"Thanks a lot," Steph grumbled. "I'm baring my soul here, and you're laughing at me?"

"Hey." Penny stretched her five-foot-one frame to wrap her arm around Steph. "I'm not making fun of you. It's just... When was the last time you had an 'or more' with anyone?"

"What?"

"You always text me when you're going home with someone, in case the person turns out to be a creep."

Steph shrugged. "Yeah. So?"

"I just realized it's been months since I got a text like that. Unless you went home with someone without telling me, you haven't been with anyone since the day you moved in with Rae."

Steph's foot slid off the rung of the stool. "Holy hell." Penny was right! She hadn't slept with anyone since U-Haul Girl, and she hadn't even noticed! How on earth had that happened? She lifted her bottle and gave the bartender a desperate wave. She really needed another beer now.

Penny laughed and squeezed her hip. "See? You're basically already monogamous."

Steph needed a few seconds to make her vocal cords work. "I guess you're right. Want to know the weirdest thing? I don't miss hooking up with other people. I always thought I'd get bored if I let myself be tied down by one person."

"What's different with Rae?" Penny asked.

"I don't know." Steph took a sip of the beer the bartender slid in front of her. "She just...she gets me. Even the parts that I don't usually show people. And at the same time, she doesn't let me get away with anything."

Penny leaned her head on Steph's shoulder. "Aww. Sounds great. I always wanted that for you. Hold on to it with both hands, okay?"

"How do I do that?"

"Sounds like you're already doing it," Penny said. "Keep doing what you're doing, and you'll be fine."

Could it really be that easy? Steph gave her a skeptical look.

Penny burst out laughing.

"Jesus, you'll give me a complex if you keep doing that. Why are you laughing now?"

Penny pressed a hand to her mouth, but little giggles still slipped through. "Sorry. I swear I'm not laughing at you. Not really. I just remembered that old joke. What do two lesbians bring on their second date?"

"I'm bi, not a lesbian."

"Fine. What do two women-loving women bring on their second date?"

"A U-Haul." Steph flicked her gaze upward. "Oldest joke in the book. What's so funny about that?"

"You and Rae really did."

Steph paused with the bottle halfway to her lips. Laughter bubbled up, and soon they were both bent over, gasping for breath.

When Steph let herself into the apartment, it was close to midnight—late for most people, but not for her and Rae, who never made it home from work any earlier than that. But when Steph stepped into the hall, everything was dark and quiet. Hadn't Rae returned from her visit with Kim? She'd said she would make it home well before sunset.

Concern stirred in her belly. She flicked the light on.

Rae's keys were on the table in the hall, next to a beautifully framed photo.

Steph picked it up to study it.

Her gaze took in Kim and a handsome man who was probably her late husband, then immediately zeroed in on Rae. God, she looked hot in her uniform...and she looked happy. Her head was thrown back, and she was laughing, eyes flashing with unrestrained mirth. Steph longed to hear her laugh like that.

Gently, she put the photo back down and laid her keys next to Rae's.

Everything remained quiet in the apartment. No light came from beneath Rae's door. Apparently, she had gone to bed already.

A quiet sigh escaped Steph. She trudged past Rae's door on the way to her own room. *Oh come on. You are the one who was always afraid of feeling smothered in a relationship, and now you're disappointed because Rae didn't wait up for you?*

But she couldn't help it. After the day she'd had, all she wanted was to crawl into bed with Rae and forget about everything but Rae's comforting warmth. Could she just do that? She had no idea what the protocol was now that they weren't only roommates anymore. Did Rae expect them to share the bed from now on, or had last night been an exception? Did Rae want to wait until they were ready to have sex? Or would they play it by ear and decide on a night-to-night basis?

Damn. Dating someone was hard, and already living with the person you dated made it even more complicated. Should she knock and ask?

But she didn't want to wake Rae or come across as clingy. Besides, what if Rae preferred to sleep alone for now and said no? That would make things awkward.

Steph plodded to the bathroom and got ready for bed. In a T-shirt and a pair of panties, she tiptoed to her room. She paused in front of Rae's door and listened.

Still no sound or light coming from her room.

Sighing, Steph flicked off the light in the living room.

Before she could head to her room, a board creaked and then the door swung open. A warm body collided with Steph's, and a gasp of surprise echoed through the darkness.

"Just me," Steph called quickly before Rae could mistake her for a burglar and knock her out. She grasped Rae's arms to keep them both upright.

"Jesus, Steph!" The light flared on. Rae stood in front of her, wearing a pair of boxer shorts and a faded LAPD T-shirt. "What are you doing?"

"Um, going to bed."

"In front of my door?" Rae frowned, then her lips formed a silent "Oh." She cleared her throat. "Did you want to...you know?"

"What?"

Rae pointed over her shoulder. "Sleep with me? In my bed, I mean."

"That's not why I was in front of your room." Steph could have slapped herself the moment she said it, but she didn't want Rae to think she was too needy.

"Okay." Rae walked past her to the kitchen, where she got herself a glass of water.

Steph watched her take several big sips but couldn't interpret the expression on Rae's face. Was she disappointed, or was Steph just projecting her own feelings onto her? God, she really needed to stop overthinking everything. She was starting to sound like her parents.

Half-empty glass in hand, Rae stepped past her on the way back to her room.

Steph stopped thinking and let herself react. She grabbed a handful of Rae's T-shirt and tugged her to a halt. "I do want to. Sleep with you. In your bed. Can I?"

A smile transformed Rae's brooding good looks into something that took Steph's breath away.

"Of course. Come on." Rae reached for her hand and led her into her bedroom, where she lifted the covers up for Steph to slip beneath.

Steph crawled into the warm nest, immediately surrounded by Rae's scent and her body heat, even before Rae climbed in next to her. A pleasant shiver went through her as Rae's bare legs slid along her own.

Rae rolled onto her back and pulled Steph into her arms.

Mmm. Steph cuddled closer. The feel of Rae's body against her own was addictive. She couldn't believe she had nearly missed out on this just because of...what? Pride? It took her hazy brain several seconds to realize she was lying to Rae's left. "Do you want us to switch sides?"

"Nah. Seeing is overrated." Rae trailed her hand over Steph's back, then, as if deciding that she needed closer contact, slipped beneath her T-shirt and caressed her bare skin.

Steph's eyes fluttered shut. Seeing was definitely overrated. Every nerve ending in her body was focused on feeling.

"Is this okay?" Rae whispered.

"Mmm, very okay." Steph arched into the touch.

"Even if...?"

Steph forced her eyes open, but it was too dark to make out Rae's face. "Even if what?"

"Even if it's all we're doing?" Rae sighed. "My body is giving me other signals right now, but I'm really not up for more than this tonight."

Steph felt around in the darkness until her fingertips made contact with the soft skin of Rae's cheek. "Listen. I love sex. I never made a secret of that, and I don't think it's much of a secret either that I'd love to have sex with you."

Rae's groan rumbled through Steph since she was pressed against her body. "God, I want that too." Her voice came out husky. "But..."

"But if you need a hug or a cuddle more than you need multiple orgasms, that's totally fine," Steph said.

"Multiple..." Rae sucked in a breath. "God, you'll be the death of me."

Steph chuckled. "Yeah, but what a way to go." She sobered and caressed Rae's cheek. "Seriously, though. I know I don't have the best track record. Hell, I have *no* track record when it comes to relationships. But please believe me when I say that this isn't just about sex for me." Maybe that was why she was totally fine with not having sex for now—because she knew that for the first time in her life, it would be much more than merely sex. God, that was a scary thought. It made her feel like a nervous teenager who had no clue what she was doing.

Rae wrapped her arms around her more tightly and held her as if she couldn't find the right words.

Steph settled her head on Rae's shoulder and buried her nose in the soft fabric of the old LAPD T-shirt. It smelled deliciously of Rae. "You said you're not up for more tonight. Did something happen while you were at Kim's?"

"We...we talked. About Mike. About what happened."

Steph put her palm on Rae's upper chest and spread her fingers. Rae's heart beat much too fast beneath her hand. "Oh Rae. That must have been tough. Are you okay?"

"Mm-hmm. Getting there. She said the same thing you did. That it wasn't my fault."

"It wasn't," Steph said firmly.

Rae was silent for a while, as if she needed some time to let that thought sink in. "How was your day?"

Wow. She was suddenly part of a couple who asked each other how their day had been! Steph had always considered that boring and predictable, but now she found it unexpectedly nice to have someone care enough to ask. "Not great, but definitely not as bad as yours."

"Hey, this isn't the suffering Olympics." Rae trailed her hand down Steph's back once more. "I know saying goodbye to Moose was hard for you. Want to tell me about it?"

"Moose was his usual sweet self, totally excited to see me and head out for a walk. He didn't know it was the last time, and that made it even tougher. And then I bombed in front of Penny and about a dozen comics I know."

"Bombed? You?"

"Yeah, royally." Steph groaned. "By tomorrow, half of LA's comedy scene will know. I hope Mr. Hicks doesn't hear about it and change his mind about the New Year's Eve show."

"Nonsense. Every comic bombs at an open mic every now and then. Even I know that." Rae drew soothing circles between her shoulder blades. "Probably just jitters before the big show. You'll do great when it really matters."

"Great," Steph repeated. "What if that's not enough? There's plenty of great comics out there, but only a handful of them ever have their big break. Sometimes, I wonder if my parents might be right and I should consider other—"

A soft squeeze stopped her midsentence. "Close your eyes."

Steph chuckled. "They closed the second you started caressing my back."

"Good. Then imagine you are up on stage. Not at an open mic. At a real club, with a great sound system and nice brick walls. The room is packed, and you can practically feel people's anticipation as you walk up to the mic. Then you launch into your first joke, and everyone bursts out laughing. How does that feel?"

Steph imagined the scenario. She could almost feel the mic in her hand, the heat of the spotlight shining down on her, and the first wave of laughter rippling over her. "Right," she whispered without opening her eyes. "It feels right. Like I'm exactly where I want to be."

Rae resumed the soft touches to her back. "See? You were born to do stand-up. You just need a chance to prove it. Don't doubt yourself."

"Hmm." Rae's reassurance soothed the anxiety that had plagued her since her last birthday. So far, she had worried about their relationship holding her back and making a breakthrough even more unlikely, but now she began to wonder whether being with Rae might actually even be good for her career. She slid her thigh across one of Rae's and cuddled closer. Rae's question and her own answer ricocheted through her mind. *It feels right. Like I'm exactly where I want to be.* It was the same feeling that swept through her right now, while she lay in Rae's arms. *Oh God. Penny was right. I think…I'm in love with her.*

No, that couldn't be…could it? It was too much, too fast. They had only just started dating. They hadn't even had sex, for Christ's sake, nor had they gone on an actual date. And yet that feeling of elation and belonging was unmistakable.

"Hey, I can feel your heart racing." Rae sounded alarmed. "Are you okay?"

"Yeah, just thinking." Panicking was more like it.

"About?"

"Uh…" She couldn't tell her. Rae would think she was out of her mind. Hell, Steph herself thought she was out of her mind. She latched on to the first thing she could think of. "Just wondering what happened in 1997. You know… The infamous blushing incident."

"Oh. That. Nothing important. Silly teen stuff."

"I'd like to hear it." Maybe the story would distract her from the startling realization that she might be in love for the very first time in her life.

Rae shifted beneath her. "Okay, I'll tell you. But no laughing."

"I'll try my very best. So, what happened?"

"When I was fourteen, I was on the swim team, and so was Lise."

"Your Lise?"

"Mm-hmm. Well, she wasn't my Lise back then. She barely knew I existed."

How could anyone not notice Rae? Steph didn't get it. "But you had a crush on her?"

"Oh yeah. God, it was embarrassing. I didn't even know if she was interested in girls, but I knew I liked her, so I set out to impress her."

Steph smiled. She could easily imagine how cute teenage Rae had been. "What did you do?"

"One day, during practice, we were swimming in the same lane, and I decided to show off my speed. But Lise thought I was trying to race her and sped up too, without me noticing. I ended up accidentally slapping her in the face."

Steph struggled to be true to her word and not burst out laughing. "Well, I guess you could say you left an impression."

"Literally. It left a red mark on her cheek for the rest of the day." Rae groaned. "And she wouldn't even look at me for a year afterward."

"Wow. How did you get her to even consider dating you?"

"I stopped trying to impress her and just adored her from afar for the next three years," Rae said. "Apparently, that did the trick. Seems I'm more irresistible from a distance."

"Oh, I don't know. You seem pretty irresistible close-up too." Steph lifted up on one elbow and placed a kiss on Rae's lips. She had intended for it to be a sweet peck, but the second their lips touched, *sweet* went out the window.

Rae's mouth moved against hers with a sexy hum, while her hands continued to trace Steph's back beneath the T-shirt, leaving behind trails of fire on her bare skin.

The kiss deepened, and Rae's tongue slid sensuously over her own.

Steph tangled her fingers into Rae's hair and pressed herself against the heat of Rae's body beneath hers.

On the next swipe up, Rae's hands grazed the sides of her breasts.

Steph tore her mouth away, turned her head, and pressed her forehead to the pillow, gasping for breath. *Slow, dammit. Slow.*

"Sorry," Rae said, her voice husky. "I know I said I wasn't up for anything like this tonight. Talk about sending mixed messages, huh?"

Steph willed her erratic heartbeat to slow down. "You don't have to apologize. I'm not sure I'm up for more either, no matter what my body says." Rae had only ever been in love with one woman—had only ever shared herself with one woman. Getting to be the second wasn't something to take lightly. And while Steph had never been shy about sharing her body, she had never shared her heart. This wasn't something to rush.

Rae resumed her soothing caresses along Steph's back. "Steph?" she whispered after a while.

"Hmm?" Steph's heart sped up in anticipation.

"I..." The covers rustled. "Thank you for getting me to talk about Mike. If you hadn't, I wouldn't have had the guts to talk to Kim."

A warmth of a different kind spread through Steph, drowning out the hum of arousal still coursing through her. "No thanks necessary. You did the hard part."

Rae said nothing. She rolled onto her left side, which Steph was starting to recognize as the position she usually slept in.

When Steph did the same, Rae immediately spooned her from behind, curving her arm around Steph's waist. Even though Rae was three inches taller, their bodies molded together in a perfect fit.

Steph reached for Rae's hand, pulled it up to her mouth, and pressed a gentle kiss to her palm before resting their clasped hands against her chest.

Her day had definitely gotten a lot better. She could get used to this—and that thought was only scaring her a little now.

Chapter 23

STEPH STARED AT THE EMAIL on her phone. The Chinese restaurant that had booked her for tonight's comedy show had canceled. *Damn.* The New Year's Eve show was in two days, so she probably wouldn't get another chance to try out the newer parts of her routine on a real audience instead of just comics at an open mic.

But maybe it wasn't all bad. Since she'd found out she would get to headline the biggest show of the year, she had spent nearly every waking moment either on stage, in traffic, or in her room, perfecting her material. She and Rae had barely gotten to see each other—except for very late at night, when they fell asleep in each other's arms.

Maybe instead of trying to find another gig, she could finally spend some time with Rae or even go out on their first real date.

God, a date. Steph hadn't been on one in ages, except for the casual "hey, want to grab a beer?" evenings that had occasionally ended in someone else's bed. While she certainly wouldn't mind ending up in Rae's bed, she wanted more than that with her. She wanted to do something special for Rae. The question was, what?

She had never planned a date, so she had no idea. Was a candlelight dinner at a nice restaurant too stereotypical and sappy? In the past, she had certainly thought so, but with Rae, it might actually be fun.

Her phone rang in her hand before she could come up with an idea.

For a second, she thought it might be the restaurant, calling to tell her the show wasn't canceled after all. Disappointment flared through her at the thought, and that surprised her. She wanted time with Rae more than time up on stage.

But the caller was her mother. Exhaling, she lifted the phone to her ear. "Hey, Mom. What's up?"

"I thought I'd check in with you. Your sister always calls on Sundays, and since you don't…"

Not that good-daughter-bad-daughter stuff again. Steph gritted her teeth. "Claire has a normal weekend. I don't. I'm working today."

"If I'm keeping you from something important, I can—"

"No, it's fine."

"If you're sure," her mother said. "So tell me. How are you?"

Busy. Nervous. In love. But Steph wasn't ready for her feelings to be analyzed and dissected. What she felt for Rae was too new and fragile. "I'm fine. What's new with you and Dad?"

"Not much. I finally got your father to take dancing lessons with me."

"Oh, nice." Dancing… Was that an option for her date with Rae? She dismissed the idea. A crowded dance floor was probably not Rae's idea of a good time. "Um, Mom? What did you and Dad do on your first date?"

Her mother chuckled. "We went to a talk on social psychology."

Steph groaned. "God, no wonder I don't have a romantic bone in my body if you both thought that's a great thing to do on a first date!" At least she had always assumed she didn't have a romantic bone so far. "Second date?"

"I think we went to the movies."

Hmm, movies. That was a classic, wasn't it? And Rae liked movies. She would just have to make sure it wasn't a 3-D movie because she'd read somewhere that those didn't work for people with monocular vision. But would Rae really want to spend their first date in a dark, crowded room full of people?

"Why are you asking?"

"Oh, just curious," Steph said.

"Are you looking for something to do on a date with Rae? You two are dating, aren't you?"

Was she that transparent? So much for keeping it between her and Rae for a while. "Um, yeah. We are."

"I knew it!"

God, Steph hated that all-knowing tone of voice. She fought the impulse to say something that went against her mother's expectations. That would mean denying her relationship, and Rae deserved better than that. "Listen, Mom. Rae is special to me. I don't want you to put our relationship under your shrink microscope, okay?"

"What makes you think I'd do that?" Her mother sounded deeply insulted. "Can't I just be a mother who's happy her daughter is finally ready to open her heart?"

"I don't know. Can you?" Steph shot back. "Handing out business cards isn't what mothers do."

Her mother sighed. "So she told you about that. Well, at least you two seem to have established good communication."

"Mom! You are doing it again."

"Sorry," her mother said. "I'll try to rein in my inner psychologist, okay? I really am happy for you. Sometimes I just seem to have problems expressing that."

Her mother had admitted to being the one at fault. That was a first. "Thanks. I have to go. Talk to you soon."

"Have a wonderful date," her mother said before they ended the call.

Wonderful date... Yeah, but first, she'd have to find the perfect date activity for them. She opened the browser on her phone and started her search.

Rae opened yet another tab on her browser, scanned the recipe, and then discarded it. None of the meals she'd seen so far seemed special enough for what she had in mind. While she knew Steph didn't have the time for an elaborate date right now, she at least wanted to surprise her with a special dinner at home before work tomorrow.

The battery icon flashed across the iPad screen, warning her that she needed to plug in the device.

She reached out and pulled open the drawer on her bedside table.

But instead of the power cord, she encountered something else. When she withdrew her hand, she held her swimming goggles. How had they ended up in there?

She dropped the iPad onto her bed and rubbed her thumb over the plastic lenses. On impulse, she carefully placed them over her eyes and tightened the elastic. With the goggles on, she crossed the room and peeked outside.

The door to Steph's room was closed, signaling that she was still preparing for tonight's show.

Rae went to the bathroom and glanced into the mirror above the sink.

She wasn't sure what she had expected to see. The goggles looked perfectly normal. They created suction around her eye, pulling down the lower lid the tiniest bit. Would that be enough to make the prosthesis slip out? She shook her head—up, down, left, right.

The eye stayed in place. But would it hold up to a flip turn or a plunge from the edge of a pool?

Rae exhaled and stared at the hand-painted iris. She wasn't sure she was quite ready to try, but for the first time since March, she felt that a little nudge of encouragement was all it would take.

"Hey, gorgeous. Are you up for a little adventure?"

Steph's voice from behind startled her. Damn. She hadn't closed the bathroom door. Quickly, she reached for the goggles to pull them off. Then she paused. Hiding the goggles so she wouldn't have to talk about her feelings was what she would have done in the past. But she didn't want to hide anything from Steph. She braced herself with one hand on the sink and slowly turned.

Steph blinked. "Looks like you have your own little adventure planned already. Are you going swimming?"

"No. Not yet." Rae took the goggles off so she could see her better. "But maybe you and I could go together...at some point."

Steph came closer and trailed her index finger lightly along Rae's skin beneath her left eye, where the goggles had rested. "I'd like that. Whenever you're ready, just say the word."

Rae leaned forward, bridging the remaining space between them, and kissed her gently. "I will. Thank you."

They looked at each other.

A ball of complex emotions filled Rae's chest. She shifted and cleared her throat. "So what kind of adventure did you have in mind?"

"I thought maybe we could..." A hint of pink dusted Steph's cheeks. "We haven't actually...you know..."

Rae tilted her head. Was Steph talking about sex?

"I mean, I'm not normally one to put a lot of thought into stuff like this, but…well, I thought, maybe it would be nice if we, um…"

Rae couldn't help smiling. She hadn't expected Steph to be so shy about it. After all, Steph had been with more partners and normally didn't hesitate to go after what she wanted. She decided to help her out, even though Steph's blush was decidedly cute. "You want us to sleep together. And this time, do more than actually sleep."

"No! Yes. I mean, of course I want that, but that's not what I…" Steph huffed out a breath as if losing patience with herself.

Rae cupped her face and caressed Steph's cheek with her thumb. "Just say it."

"How would you like to go to the movies with me?" Steph blurted out.

Aww. "Are you asking me out on a date?"

Steph nodded. "Yes." Her voice was a little croaky.

Rae found it thoroughly charming. "I'd love to go on a date with you, but we're both working tonight."

A more confident grin flashed across Steph's face. "Nope."

"We're not?"

"My show got canceled, and I called Carlos and asked if he would cover your shift for you. He owes you for that elbow to the eye."

Rae couldn't help laughing. "You guilt-tripped him into covering my shift?"

Steph shrugged. "I'm a woman on a mission. So are we going?"

"We're going." Rae didn't have the heart to tell her that she hadn't been to the movies since losing her eye. Just finding her seat in the dim light of a movie theater was a challenge, and if the movie Steph had picked was a 3-D film, it wouldn't work for her. But none of that mattered. She would still enjoy herself if she could cuddle up to Steph and maybe sneak a kiss or two.

"This is the weirdest movie theater I've ever been to," Rae muttered as the elevator doors closed behind them and Steph pressed the button for the top floor.

Steph nudged her. "Just trust me."

"I do." Rae linked her fingers through Steph's, and when the elevator doors opened, she let Steph guide her onto a rooftop terrace.

Eight rows of white-and-blue-striped deck chairs had been set up in front of a huge screen. The setting sun dipped the high-rise buildings surrounding them in orange hues. The scent of popcorn trailed on the air, mingling with the mouth-watering aroma of frying burgers.

"Wow." Rae looked around. "A rooftop movie theater?"

Steph nodded. "I thought you'd be more comfortable out here than cooped up in a dark room with a hundred other people."

"Definitely." She tugged Steph closer by their joined hands and gave her a short but heartfelt kiss. "Thank you. This is great. How did you find out about it?"

"I did a comedy show up here last year, and I remembered that they show a couple of movies a month even in winter." Steph handed over her phone with the online tickets. "If you grab us headphones and pick a seat, I'll get us some food."

As Steph walked toward the concession stand, Rae paused for a moment and watched her get in line. Steph said something to the guy ahead of her, gesturing animatedly and making him laugh. Rae couldn't hear what she had said, but she couldn't help smiling. God, she was one lucky woman. Being with Steph had brought an unexpected—and much-needed—lightness into her life.

When the young woman handing out the headphones smiled at her, Rae realized that she was still smiling too. Maybe there was something to be said for not scowling at people, even though it was an effective technique for keeping strangers out of her personal space and avoiding small talk.

She took the wireless headphones and the cozy blankets the woman handed her and picked a double deck chair in the last row. Thankfully, so far only about thirty people had found their way to the outdoor movie theater, so they'd have plenty of space.

"Um, Rae? Help!" Steph said from behind her.

Rae dropped their headphones onto the deck chair and turned around.

Steph was struggling to carry two sodas, burgers, and a huge bucket of popcorn toward her.

Quickly, Rae relieved her of the sodas. "I thought you wanted to get *some* food, not *all* of their food. Look at the size of that popcorn! And burgers! God, you are so bad for me."

Steph cocked her head. "Am I?"

Rae let her grin fade away and looked her in the eyes. "No. Just the opposite."

"Ditto." Steph smiled softly, then shook herself. "Ugh. We're getting sappy again." Without being prompted, she settled on the side of their seat that would put her to Rae's right.

Rae loved that about her.

As they ate their burgers and watched the previews, the sun sank beneath the horizon until only a faint orange glow remained. The stars came out, twinkling down on them along with the city lights. The temperature dropped, and Rae spread both of their blankets over their laps.

When Steph cuddled up to her, Rae quickly finished her burger so she could wrap her arms around her. *Mmm.* Steph smelled even better than the food. *Best date ever.*

Steph poked her. "Hey, the movie is starting. You need to watch."

Rae directed her attention to the giant screen, where a magician was performing coin tricks. Then Richard Gere appeared, talking on the phone. She threw Steph a disbelieving look. "*Pretty Woman?*"

"Oh, don't pretend you're not into it. I saw it on your Netflix watch list."

Rae's cheeks heated. "Damn. Guess it's impossible to maintain an air of mystery when you're dating your roommate."

Laughing, Steph scooped up a handful of popcorn and stuffed it into her mouth without caring how it looked.

That was another thing Rae liked about her.

Despite her claim that Steph had bought too much food, they managed to finish off the popcorn not even halfway through the movie. The popcorn was hot and fresh, but what Rae enjoyed even more than the buttery treat was the way their hands brushed whenever they reached into the bucket at the same time.

Her face heated even more as she watched Steph lick a bit of melted butter off her fingers, and she took a big gulp of her cold soda. It was Coke, which she didn't normally drink. She looked from the extra-large paper cup to Steph. "Christ, that's enough caffeine to kick-start a herd of elephants. Are you planning to keep me up all night?"

Steph's eyes seemed to smolder in the near darkness. "I am," she whispered, her voice low and intimate.

Her words and the timbre in her voice sent shivers through Rae's body.

Then, with a sigh and a rueful smile, Steph added, "But not tonight. I'll have to get up super early tomorrow, and once we…you know…nothing short of an earthquake will make me leave the bed for at least twenty-four hours."

"Twenty-four…" Rae gulped down more soda.

"Possibly more," Steph said with a comical leer.

"Now you're just showing off," Rae muttered.

"Shh!" someone in the row in front of them hissed.

Steph shot Rae a sultry look and leaned even closer to whisper in her ear, "You'll just have to wait and see."

Her warm breath made goose bumps trail down Rae's body. "I will," she whispered back. "I definitely will."

Chapter 24

Rae had asked Carlos to cover the early show on New Year's Eve so she could stay home with Steph until it was time to leave for the club. She was glad she had asked him for the favor because she had never seen Steph so nervous.

Steph had been pacing their apartment with her set list in hand for most of the day, running through her material again and again. Rae had left her alone for the most part, only interrupting her to make sure she ate at least a little.

Now it was finally time to go. She slid the rainbow clip the Renshaws had given her for Christmas onto her work tie and threw one last glance into the mirror to make sure her prosthetic eye looked normal and her hair covered the scar on her head.

God, you'd think you are the one having to go up on stage! But she couldn't help it. This was a big day for Steph, so Rae couldn't pretend it was just another day at work. She hoped everything would go well and the show would be a smashing success, but at the same time, she couldn't help worrying about what would happen if it was really the start of Steph's big break. Would Steph leave LA…leave her? If she went on a countrywide tour, would she view their relationship as something that would only hold her back?

Cross that bridge when you come to it. She stuck her head into Steph's room. "Ready?"

Steph looked up from her set list. Instead of the blue jeans she usually wore when she had a gig, she had chosen a pair of black slacks for today, but she had stayed true to her style by combining them with one of her T-shirts with a painted-on pink tie and a blazer.

Rae smiled at her. "You look cute."

"Cute?" Steph gazed down at herself. "I think the words you are looking for are *stylish* and *hot*."

"That too." Rae walked up to her, slid her hand onto Steph's hip beneath the blazer, and drew her close for a quick kiss. Steph's perfume was fast becoming an aphrodisiac for her, or maybe it was the way Steph always threaded her fingers through Rae's hair when they kissed. She forced herself to keep the kiss light and short anyway. "Hot as hell. Come on. Let's walk to the club. It might help you get rid of some of that nervous energy."

They left the apartment and set off toward Melrose.

After a couple of steps, Steph reached over from the right and slid her hand into Rae's. "Okay?"

"Of course." Rae gave her fingers a soft squeeze, and they continued hand in hand. Her colleagues would probably tease her mercilessly if they saw them walk up like this, but Rae didn't care.

Soon, the club came into view. The parking lot was packed, making Rae glad they had left the car at home. She hoped the Renshaws had factored in enough time to find a parking spot nearby and wouldn't be late—if they even came.

She glanced over at Steph, who was unusually quiet.

Rae could tell she was running over her material in her head. Had she done the right thing by asking Steph's family to come, or would their unexpected presence throw Steph off and mess up her focus? *Shit.* She should have thought of that before. Maybe she should tell her now. But if Steph got her hopes up and then her family didn't show after all, it would break her heart. Steph might pretend not to care, but Rae knew better.

At the edge of the parking lot, Steph stopped abruptly, as if she had run into an invisible wall. "Oh my God. Look at that!"

Rae craned her head to see what she was looking at.

Stephanie Renshaw shone in bright lights on the marquee outside the club.

Rae's throat tightened, and she had to swallow a couple of times before she could say, "You'd better get used to it. After tonight, I have a feeling you'll see your name up there a lot."

"Let's hope so." Steph turned away from the marquee to face Rae. "Can I have a kiss for good luck?"

"Of course. But you won't need any luck—you've got skills." Rae kissed her gently and then, instead of letting go, pulled her into a tight embrace and held her for a moment. "You'll be great."

Steph rested against her for several seconds, then she squeezed once and stepped back. "See you after the show."

"I'll see you *during* the show," Rae said. "Don't worry about hecklers, okay? The minute someone opens their mouth, they'll be out on their ass."

"Thanks, but I can handle them." Her usual confidence was back in Steph's tone.

"I know. I just…" Rae shrugged, not knowing how to explain that overwhelming need to protect her.

Steph smiled and brushed her lips against Rae's a second time. "See you later." Then she strode toward the club's entrance and past Carlos, who was covering the door.

When Rae joined him, he grinned and slapped her on the back. "So you and Steph, hmm? I could see that coming from a mile away!"

"That makes one of us," Rae muttered. Not in a million years would she have imagined ending up with this smart-ass, carefree comic. But she had never in her life been so glad to be wrong.

Steph peeked through the short, hidden hallway leading to the stage. Laughter drifted back to her. The showroom was jammed tonight, and the crowd seemed great. When some of the tables in the back had gotten a bit rowdy earlier, Rae and her team had quickly gotten them to settle down.

The house lights had been dimmed, but Steph could almost sense that Rae was somewhere down there, waiting to watch over her. Instead of making her feel smothered and patronized, as she had assumed in the past, it gave her a warm feeling in the pit of her stomach, calming her pre-show jitters.

The door to the greenroom swept open, and Gabe burst in. "Hey, guess who I just ran into in the lobby?"

"Scarlett Johansson?"

"Hahaha. Keep your jokes for the stage. No. Your mother."

"What?" Steph shook her head. No, that was impossible. Her parents were most likely at some fundraiser or ringing in the new year with friends, most of whom were psychologists too. "You haven't even met my mother, so how would you know what she looks like?"

"Oh, come on. She looks exactly like you and Claire."

Steph shook her head. "It's probably just someone looking like her."

"Yeah, that must be it. Just some woman looking like your mother, now sitting in the first row, next to Penny, Claire, Lana, and a guy who probably looks a lot like your father."

Steph stared at him. "You're shitting me?"

He pressed a hand to his chest. "Would I do that?"

"In a heartbeat."

"Okay, I would, but I'm not. They are here. I swear."

Steph flopped down onto the worn couch along one wall. "Holy… That's…wow." It had to have been Lana. She must have talked her parents into coming. Steph made a mental note to give her future sister-in-law the biggest hug when she saw her after the show.

The door to the greenroom was opened again, and Rae stuck her head around the doorjamb. Her gaze went to Gabe, then to Steph. "You're up in three."

Steph's mouth went dry. She clenched her hand around the set list in her pocket. "I just found out my family is here."

A smile inched across Rae's face. "That's great…isn't it?"

"It is." Then it hit her. "Or maybe not. Shit. Half of my material is about them!" Quite vividly, she remembered the heated argument with Rae when she had told a few jokes about her on stage. Her family would probably react the same way. She dug out her workbook and flipped through her jokes in search of something to replace her family-related bits with.

Gabe snatched it away from her. "What are you doing? Switching up your material at the last moment never ends well; you know that. Besides, you never gave a shit about what your family thought before."

He was right, but a lot of things had changed in the last couple of months. Steph's gaze went to Rae. "What do you think?"

Rae touched the tiny, round scars on her forehead as she seemed to think about it for a few moments. "It might sound strange coming from me, but I think you should go with the routine you had planned. If you had asked me a couple of months ago, I probably would have had a different response, but now that I know you and the comedy business better, I have a slightly different view. I mean, you keep saying that's all they're meant to be—just jokes, right?"

Steph stared at her. She hadn't expected Rae to say that. Of course, Rae's reply probably would have been different if Steph had planned to do any jokes about her. But it still felt good to have her support. "Right."

"Besides, no one in your family has supported your career, so they shouldn't get a say in it now," Rae added.

"Hell, yeah," Gabe said. "They'll just have to wear their big-girl-and-boy undies and not make such a big deal out of a couple of jokes."

Steph exhaled and squared her shoulders. "Okay, I'll do it."

"Go up and kill 'em. You can do it." The utter confidence on Rae's face was like a cloak of calm settling over Steph.

One last glance back at Rae, then Steph slipped through the hidden hallway and onto the stage, just as the MC announced her name.

Thunderous applause echoed around her, and as Steph took the mic, the last of her jitters faded away. This was what she had worked toward for the past ten years. She was ready.

With the biggest smile ever, she stepped up to the edge of the stage.

Damn, Gabe had been right. Her parents, Claire, Lana, and Penny were right there in the very first row. Even Rae's friend Kim had come, and they were all looking at her with expectant gazes.

No pressure or anything.

She gave a merry wave and waited for the applause to reside. "Hey, everyone…and a special hi to my family, who has come out to see me for the very first time tonight."

The audience clapped politely.

"That's actually a bit of a surprise. Up until now, we seemed to have an unspoken agreement: they don't go to my job, and I don't go to theirs." She used her foot to push the cord out in front of her so she wouldn't drag it along as she moved along the stage. "Well, I still won't show up at their work, because all three of them are," she lowered her voice to a whisper as if she were speaking about something scandalizing, "psychologists. Yeah, yeah. I know what you're thinking. But you seem so normal!"

Laughter rippled through the showroom and echoed back from the brick wall behind her, as Rae had described it last night. Steph didn't pause to check if her family was glaring at her or laughing along with the rest of the audience. Holding her head up high, she launched into her next joke. "Can you imagine what my childhood was like? It gave new meaning to the phrase, 'Honey, I shrunk the kids'!"

Normally, there was no place Steph would rather be than up on stage, but as the show ended right before midnight and the comedians gathered to lead the countdown, all she wanted was to jump down and find Rae so she could spend the first seconds of the new year with her.

But she was the show's headliner, so she had to stay where she was. "Ten, nine, eight," she shouted into the mic.

Her fellow comics and the audience counted backward with her.

At "five," the house lights came back on.

Steph's gaze flew over the audience in search of Rae.

"Four, three, two..."

She found her just as everyone chanted, "One." Shouts of "Happy New Year!" rolled over her, and cheers erupted from the crowd. Steph barely heard them.

Rae had taken up position at the back of the room, where she could see everyone, but her gaze was on Steph alone. She was the only one standing perfectly still in an ocean full of movement, hugs, and kisses. In her black suit and tie, she took Steph's breath away. Slowly, a smile lit up Rae's serious features.

Steph lifted the glass of sparkling wine someone had pressed into her hand and mouthed, "Happy New Year" over the heads of the audience.

Rae's smile broadened, and she mouthed back the words.

A warm feeling spread through Steph's entire body, even though she hadn't taken a sip of her sparkling wine yet. God, she wished they were home, where they could welcome the new year with a kiss.

The DJ Mr. Hicks had hired for the after-party started playing "Auld Lang Syne," and Steph listened to the lyrics for a second. Rae wasn't an old acquaintance; they had only known each other for a couple of months, but already she didn't want to imagine her life without her.

She groaned at herself. Christ, when had she become such a sap?

A party horn shrieked next to her, making her jump. "Gabe!" She snatched it away from him and stuffed it into the pocket of her blazer, which she had tossed over her shoulder.

He pulled her into an exuberant hug, and she got the feeling that he'd emptied a few glasses of the sparkling wine already. "Happy New Year!"

"Happy New Year." Steph pulled away from him to rub her ear, which was still ringing.

"Great show!" He high-fived her. "I loved how you improvised that new opening about your family."

"Thanks. Let's hope they'll think so too."

"You're about to find out." He pointed at something behind her. "Your sister is headed in your direction, and she looks like a woman on a mission. I guess I'd better leave you alone." He patted her back and slipped away, into the crowd.

"Thanks, traitor." Steph braced herself and slowly turned around. Time to face the music.

Claire walked up to her. In a knee-length skirt and a formfitting, pink sweater, she looked stylish but more casual than Steph had expected. Before meeting Lana, she probably would have shown up in one of her work power suits.

"Hey, you came." Steph gave her sister a hug that felt a little stiff. "Happy New Year."

"Happy New Year. Of course I came. I promised."

Claire wore her therapist mask, as she often did in public, so Steph had no idea what was going on inside of her. Was she secretly seething with anger, feeling as if Steph had made her into a laughingstock?

"Where's Lana?" Steph asked because she didn't know what else to say—and because Lana often felt like her only ally in the family.

"At the bar, getting Mom and Dad a glass of champagne."

"Did she enjoy the show?"

"Oh yeah." A loving smile broke through Claire's therapist mask, giving her face a happy glow. "A few times, she was laughing so hard that I could barely hear the end of your punch lines."

"That's great." Steph stared down at Claire's pumps as she tried to gather the nerve to ask what Claire and their parents had thought of the show. God, when had she become such a chickenshit?

A touch to her arm made her look up. That glow was still on Claire's face. "So did I."

"Um, you did what?"

"I enjoyed the show," Claire said.

Steph nearly dropped her flute. "You did?"

Claire nodded slowly. "I enjoyed it a lot, actually."

"Even the bits about…well, you?"

Claire sighed. "I admit that I would have enjoyed them more if they'd been about someone else's sister. But since Lana came into my life, I've learned to relax and not take myself so seriously all the time. So yeah, I might have laughed a time or two…even about your take on the way I put the dishes into the dishwasher."

Wow. Her future sister-in-law was a miracle worker. *Love* was a miracle worker.

Claire chuckled at Steph's slack-jawed expression, then sobered. "I know we weren't always as close as we could have been, but I want you to know that I really admire you for never giving up on your dream, no matter what Mom and Dad or anyone else said. I admit I didn't fully understand why you clung to that dream, but seeing you up there…" She swept her hand toward the stage. "I think I understand it now. I should have come to see you sooner, and I'm sorry I didn't. I'm really proud of you."

Tears welled up without warning. She clutched her sister to her in a second, tighter embrace, and Claire curled her arms around her just as fiercely. "Thanks," Steph choked out. "And thank you for talking Mom and Dad into coming too."

Claire let go. "That wasn't me."

"Well, then tell Lana—"

"It wasn't her either. Apparently, your friend Rae called Mom and asked her to come and bring the rest of the family."

"Rae…" Steph searched the back of the room but couldn't spot her now that she no longer had her vantage point up on stage.

"Although Mom indicated that she is more than a friend." Claire studied her closely. "Are you…?"

"Yes."

Claire shook her head. "You didn't even let me finish my question. I was about to ask if you're serious about her."

Steph swallowed. "Yes," she said again. "Very."

"You are?" Now it was Claire's turn to stare slack-jawed.

"I know you didn't think I had it in me. Hell, *I* didn't think I had it in me."

"Actually, I had a feeling you had it in you," Claire said. "Ever since you gave me that 'happiness can't be planned like your retirement fund' speech."

Steph squinted at her. "I did?"

"Yeah. When you pointed out that my feelings for Lana weren't so fake after all. You told me to put my heart on the line and hope for the best."

Steph wrinkled her nose. "Yeah, I guess I said that. But it sounded so much better when it was about you, not about me. That putting-my-heart-on-the-line thing is scaring me shitless."

Claire wrapped one arm around her. "Welcome to the club, sis."

"What club?" their mother asked as she walked up to them with Lana.

"The club of best comedians in LA," Claire answered.

Steph gave her a grateful nod. She wasn't eager to discuss her new relationship with her mother again.

Lana handed Claire a glass of champagne and gave Steph a warm hug. "In the entire country," she corrected. "You were great."

"Thanks." Steph accepted a hug from her mother too, who hadn't said anything yet. That wasn't like her at all. "What did you think, Mom?" she asked quietly.

"I won't lie. It was a little strange at first to hear you talk about us like that." Her mother shrugged. "But humor has always been your coping mechanism."

"Mom, can you please stop the psychobabble for once and just tell me what you thought?"

"Well, your father couldn't stop laughing at that Freudian slip joke."

Claire snorted. "Dad. Sure. That's who was giggling at that joke."

"All right." Their mother finally broke into a grin. "I might have laughed a little too. Don't tell the APsaA."

"APsaA?" Lana asked.

"The American Psychoanalytic Association," Steph, Claire, and their mother said in unison.

Her mother slid one arm around Steph's hips. "Don't worry, honey. I got over myself quickly. Mostly, I was in awe. I couldn't believe it was my daughter up there, dazzling an entire roomful of strangers with her brilliant jokes."

"Um, thanks." Steph peered at her mother, waiting for a *but*. It took her a while to realize it wasn't coming. That would take some getting used to. "Where's Dad?"

"He went to the lobby with your friends Penny and Kim," her mother said. "There's a table where they're selling your DVD."

Steph hung limply in her mother's half-embrace. After ten years of her job not being taken seriously, it felt great to finally get some praise. But at the same time, she couldn't help being angry. Why hadn't her family managed to be so supportive from the start?

"Hi, everyone." Rae strode up to them, her broad shoulders clearing a path through the crowd.

The sight of her was a relief. Steph struggled to stay at her mother's side. Her body wanted to gravitate toward Rae like a piece of iron drawn to a magnet.

"Sorry to interrupt," Rae said. "Do you have a minute, Steph? Mr. Hicks would like to talk to you."

"Oh, sure. I'll be right back, guys." Steph slid her arm through Rae's left one to help her navigate through the crowd as they walked off in the direction of Mr. Hicks's office. But truth be told, she needed that connection just as much.

Rae tugged her past the office to the greenroom and closed the door behind them.

"Um, Mr. Hicks wants to talk to me here?"

"No," Rae said. "He didn't really tell me to get you. I only said that because you looked pissed off, so I thought I'd give you a chance to get away from your family."

Steph rubbed her face. "Was it that obvious?"

"It was to me. What happened? Didn't they like the show?" Rae let out a growl. "Fuck them. You were great."

Her passionate defense made Steph's anger melt away. "No, they liked it. They're suddenly buying my DVD and telling me how proud they are. I mean, it feels great, but at the same time, it's a little late. I could have used that kind of support ten years ago."

"I know. I'm sorry." Rae wrapped both arms around Steph and drew her against her body. "You deserve better. But better late than never, right?"

Steph slid her arms beneath Rae's suit jacket and buried her face against her shoulder, breathing in her soothing scent. "Right. I hear I have you to thank for that." When Rae stiffened in her arms, she squeezed her softly. "Don't worry. I'm not angry. I'm very grateful." She looked up at her. "Oh, by the way: Happy New Year."

Rae chuckled. "Happy New Year."

Finally, Steph got to do what she had wanted to do since she had started the countdown to the new year. She curled one hand behind Rae's neck and pulled her down for a kiss.

Their mouths melded together in a perfect blend of passion and tenderness.

Steph made a humming sound of pleasure in the back of her throat. Just as she was about to deepen the kiss, the door to the greenroom swept open.

They both quickly pulled away from each other. *Damn.* If Mr. Hicks or one of his assistant managers caught them making out in the club, Rae could get in trouble, or he might refuse to ever let her take the stage again, no matter how great she had been tonight.

But it wasn't Mr. Hicks who stood frozen in the doorway, staring at them.

"Shit, Steph." Gabe shook his head at her. "What happened to no flings with club employees?"

Steph looked him in the eyes. "That rule is still firmly in place."

"Cut the bullshit. I saw you two—"

"What you saw isn't a fling." Steph reached for Rae's hand and held it firmly. She looked at Rae, who gave her a nod. "Rae and I...we're in a relationship."

Gabe laughed, then stopped abruptly when Steph didn't join in. "You're serious?"

"Dead serious."

"But you don't do relationships."

The steady pressure of Rae's hand around hers gave Steph the courage to say, "I do now."

Gabe crossed the room and plopped down onto the couch as if his legs refused to carry him any longer.

Rae squeezed Steph's hand. "Do you two want to talk alone?"

That was probably a good idea. Steph reluctantly let go of Rae's hand.

But before Rae could leave or Steph could walk over and sit next to him, the door opened again.

This time, it was Mr. Hicks who stuck his head into the greenroom. "Ah, there you are." He crooked his finger at Steph. "Can I talk to you for a minute?"

Shit. His timing couldn't have been worse. Now she'd have to leave Rae alone with Gabe, who was still looking pretty upset. But she didn't have a choice, so she forced a smile. "Sure." She looked over at Gabe. "I'll catch you later, okay?"

"Whatever."

Ouch. As Steph walked to the door, she threw a regretful gaze at Rae. If Gabe hurt her because he was angry with Steph, she would kick his sorry ass.

The door closing behind Steph sounded awfully loud.

Rae moved to follow her. "I'd better go back to work. It's not fair to let my colleagues do all the work of securing the club."

"Oh, but it's fair to drop that bomb on me and then leave?" Gabe shot back.

Damn. Rae turned back toward him. Her throat tightened as she saw the hurt look on his face. She hated situations like this.

"How long has this...thing between you two," Gabe waved his hand back and forth, "been going on?"

His tone made the little hairs on the back of her neck stand on end. "It's not a *thing.*" She struggled to speak quietly. "I know you and I barely know each other, but you could at least show some respect for Steph."

He slumped against the back of the couch and crossed his arms over his chest. "Yeah, like she's respecting me by sneaking around instead of telling me what's going on between the two of you."

"We aren't sneaking around. We just... This is new, okay? Very new."

Gabe stared off into space for a while. Finally, he directed his gaze back at Rae and shook his head. "Steph Renshaw is in a relationship. How the hell did you manage that when she wouldn't even let me stay for breakfast the next morning?"

Rae tried not to think about what had gone on between him and Steph. There was no reason to be jealous. Whatever they'd shared was in the past and didn't matter anymore. "I wish I knew." If she did, she could do more of it. "Just lucky, I guess."

He sighed.

Rae studied him. Was he hurt because Steph hadn't told him sooner, or was there more going on?

"What?" he asked.

"Nothing." She didn't want to get into this topic with him.

"Come on." He waved both hands at her. "Spit it out."

Shit. No way out now. "Well, you know, the way you're acting makes me wonder... You're not still in love with her, are you?"

"Nope," he answered without hesitation. "But you are, aren't you?"

The question made her stop breathing for a moment. Was she? The answer rose from deep inside of her, where, if she was honest with herself, it had lurked for some time. She couldn't pinpoint the exact moment when it had happened, but she knew without a doubt that it had. She was in love with Steph. Her mind spun with a mix of giddiness, joy, and panic. She took two shaky steps and plopped down at the other end of the couch.

He looked at her with an expectant gaze.

Rae didn't want to reveal her innermost feelings to a guy she barely knew, especially since she hadn't even told Steph, but neither did she want to deny it. "Yes." Her voice was barely more than a rasp, so she looked at him and repeated a little more firmly, "Yes, I am."

He gaped at her as if he hadn't expected that answer. Then he gave her a grudging nod. "At least you had the guts to admit it to her. I didn't back then."

Rae stared at the mess of chips crumbs and bottle caps on the table. "I haven't, um, told her yet."

"Yeah, you'd better not. It'll make her run."

Would it really? Fear crawled up the back of her neck. She swallowed against the lump that had lodged in her throat.

"To answer your question," Gabe said. "I got over her a long time ago."

Rae gave him a disbelieving look. How could anyone get over a woman like Steph?

"Really," he said. "Yolanda and I are a much better fit. I admit that it rankles a little that Steph jumped into a relationship with you so quickly, while she wouldn't even consider it with me, but that's all. I'm her friend, nothing more." Gabe's voice became more forceful. "And as her friend, this is the moment where I tell you that I will pull your guts out through your nostrils if you hurt her."

Rae knew she could have him on the floor, struggling helplessly against her grip, in two seconds, but that wasn't the issue. She gave him a respectful nod. "I'll do whatever I can to not make that happen."

"Good."

"And speaking of hurting Steph... Please don't give her a hard time about not telling you sooner."

"All right." He got up and went to the fridge. "Beer?"

"No, thanks. I need to get back to work." As she walked to the door, her legs still felt a little rubbery. Would Steph really run if she told her she loved her?

When Mr. Hicks handed her the envelope with her payment, Steph took it, but instead of opening it and counting the money, she just held on to it and gave him a questioning look.

"What?" He leaned back in his desk chair. "What else are you waiting for?"

She faced him across the desk. "Maybe a 'well done'?"

He gave her a you're-a-pain-in-the-butt look but nodded grudgingly. "All right. Well done. I admit you're funny."

Steph knew she shouldn't say it, but she couldn't help herself from adding, "For a woman."

"Let's get one thing straight, Ms. Renshaw. Despite whatever you might have heard, I have nothing against women—in general or in comedy."

Steph knew there was a *but* coming even before he said it.

"But because there are fewer women in comedy, some of them are given spots in a lineup before they're ready, just as the token lady, not because they're good."

Steph stood her ground. "Then maybe we need to work on encouraging and supporting female comics to get more of them into stand-up...and to keep them."

"Well, I hired you, didn't I? And you turned out to be good, so it's a moot point." He cracked a smile. "Looks like I won't have to fire Rae after all."

"Fire Rae?" Steph echoed. What the hell? "Why would you want to fire her? She's great at her job!"

He shrugged. "That's what she said about you too when I asked her opinion."

"Wait. Are you saying...?" Steph bit her lip. "You only booked me because Rae recommended me?"

"Why wouldn't I? My door staff sees more comics than anyone else. If anyone knows who's good, it's them, and I freely admit that Rae was right."

It made perfect sense, but still Steph wasn't sure how she felt about getting her biggest gig of the year because of the recommendation of someone she was involved with. One more reason why she had avoided flings with club staff.

Yeah, but with Rae, it's not just a fling, that new voice inside of her said. With other people, she might have wondered if they had only recommended her to get her into bed, but she knew Rae had done it because she believed in her. The warm glow she still hadn't gotten used to spread through her chest again.

"You okay?" Mr. Hicks laughed. "Getting a compliment from me didn't stun you into silence, did it?"

"No. I'm fine." More than fine, actually. For the first time in her life, everything seemed to be going right instead of her barely keeping things together. She shrugged into her blazer and slid the envelope into the inside pocket. "I'll call next week to talk about the next show I could headline."

He gave her an impassive look. "What makes you think I'll let you headline again?"

"Women's intuition," Steph said. "And my math skills. I talked to several people who said they'd come back to see me again, so it's not like you're losing money on me."

"Get out of here." It sounded as if he was suppressing a grin, though.

Steph walked to the door with a bounce in her step, ready to go rescue Rae from Gabe and go home.

Chapter 25

AFTER STEPH HAD BRIEFLY TALKED to Gabe and they had said goodbye to Steph's parents, Claire, Lana, Penny, and Kim, it was after two in the morning when they left the club.

Rae paused in the parking lot to deeply breathe in the night air and to give Steph a chance to circle around to her left side, which Steph promptly did.

Her right hand found Rae's left one without losing even a second.

Rae squeezed her fingers. Amazing how natural and right it all felt. She had never thought that she'd have this again…if she'd ever really had it, at least to this degree.

"Careful." Steph pulled her a little to the side and steered her around a pothole when Rae misjudged its distance.

A few months ago, it would have made Rae feel helpless, angry with herself, and determined to work harder to not need that kind of assistance. Now she didn't waste any energy on thoughts like that.

She kept glancing over at Steph, trying to make out her face in the light of the streetlamps they passed. Was it possible that Steph returned her feelings and was just as scared to say anything? This pull between them wouldn't be so strong if this were one-sided, would it?

Steph caressed the back of Rae's hand with her thumb. "Everything okay?"

"Hmm, yeah."

"Gabe didn't give you a hard time, did he? I think he had a bit too much to drink. Not that it's any excuse for being an ass…if he was."

Rae returned the caress to Steph's hand. "Nah. He was fine."

"What is it, then?"

Damn. Steph knew her too well already. Rae's heartbeat thudded so loudly that she didn't even hear the sound of their steps along the sidewalk anymore. A cold prickle of sweat broke out along her back as Gabe's warning echoed through her mind: *It'll make her run.*

But what if it didn't? Gabe hadn't expected Steph to ever be in a relationship either. What if he was wrong? Rae had promised herself not to endanger what she had with Steph the same way she had destroyed her relationship with Lise, by not talking about her feelings. She took a steadying breath and decided to trust that kernel of hope in her belly. "I…" Her voice didn't sound like her own, so she cleared her throat. "There's something I need to tell you."

Steph soothingly rubbed her hand. "I already know."

Rae's head jerked around. "Y-you do?"

Steph smiled and nodded.

Oh. She knew and she was still smiling? That was good, wasn't it? The kernel of hope expanded to fill her entire chest. "So…what do you think?"

"It's okay. Actually, scratch that. It's more than okay. It feels really good."

Relief flooded Rae with such intensity that it made her light-headed. "It does?" God, she sounded ridiculous, always echoing Steph's statements.

"Yeah. At first, I was a little… I don't know. I guess it hurt my ego a bit."

What the…? Rae stared at her. How could knowing Rae loved her hurt her ego?

"Don't worry. I'm over it," Steph said.

"Over it?"

Steph nodded. "I realized it's actually wonderful to have you believe in me like that. I know you risked a lot."

Hell, yeah. She was risking her heart here. But somehow, she got the feeling they were talking about two different things. "Um, what do you mean?"

"You recommending me to Mr. Hicks, of course." Steph peered at her. "Isn't that what you were talking about?"

Rae hesitated. She could still tell Steph, right? But now her courage had left her, and the words wouldn't come. "Oh, no, no, I mean, yes, that's what I meant."

Steph chuckled. "Anyway, thank you." She drew them to a halt and placed a short but tender kiss on Rae's lips before setting them off toward home again.

Dazed, Rae touched her lips. "Um, you're welcome. By the way, I recommended you to Mr. Hicks before we got together. If it makes any difference."

Steph opened her mouth, then closed it again. A smile slid over her face. "You know what? I thought it would, but it doesn't. So what if you might not be completely objective? If I want an unbiased opinion, I could ask any of the strangers in the audience tonight. From you, I'd rather have your slightly biased support."

Rae trailed her finger along Steph's wrist. Her throat felt a little tight as she said, "You'll always have that."

They had reached their apartment building and paused to look at each other.

Should she try again to tell Steph how she felt?

A loud rumble from Steph's stomach interrupted the moment.

Rae laughed. "You should have eaten more before the show."

Steph rubbed her belly with her free hand. "I couldn't. Too nervous."

Rae unlocked the front door and pulled her up the stairs. "Come on. I'll make you something yummy. Can't have the..." She stopped herself before she could say *woman I love*. "...star of the evening go hungry."

"Are you sure you want to cook?" Steph asked. "It's two in the morning. I can just eat some cereal or something."

Rae unlocked the door to their apartment and held it open for Steph. "No, I don't mind." She took off her suit jacket, removed her tie, and rolled up her shirtsleeves. "I'm wide-awake anyway."

"Yeah, me too."

While Rae got a bowl of strawberries from the fridge, Steph hung her blazer on the back of a chair and hopped up onto the counter.

Rae smiled and snuck a look at Steph's long legs as she dangled them. She felt Steph's gaze follow her around as she heated up a skillet and slathered peanut butter onto tortillas.

"What on earth are you making?" Steph asked from her perch.

"Patience. You'll find out in a minute." She walked over to Steph's side of the kitchen to get a knife so she could cut up the strawberries, but Steph's legs were blocking the drawer. "May I? I need a knife."

Steph's eyes twinkled. "Oh, do you?" She crooked her finger. "Then why don't you come here and get it?"

Rae's lips curled into a grin. Challenge accepted. She stepped between Steph's parted legs and slid her index finger along the outside of Steph's thigh from knee to hip in a slow line, enjoying the sensual feel of the satin-like fabric and the heat of Steph's leg beneath. "Knife?" Rae whispered into her ear.

A visible shiver went through Steph. "What am I getting in exchange?" she asked, her voice hoarse.

Rae swallowed against her dry mouth. "What do you want?"

"You. I want you."

They stared into each other's eyes. The temperature in the kitchen appeared to climb, and it had nothing to do with the skillet heating on the stove.

Steph's smoky-gray irises seemed to smolder. She hooked her fingers through the belt loops of Rae's dress pants, tugged her closer, into the cradle of her thighs, and kissed her.

Their mouths connected with a passion that both had held back so far.

Rae nipped at Steph's lips, then urged them apart.

Steph buried her fingers in Rae's hair in that way Rae loved.

The warm glide of Steph's tongue against her own made Rae's head spin. As they continued to kiss, she let her hands drift down Steph's back and onto the soft swells of her ass.

Gasping, Steph dug her fingers into Rae's scalp. Without breaking their kiss, she wrapped her legs around Rae's hips and drew her closer.

Her heat filtered through the thin fabric of her slacks. Both moaned as Steph pressed herself against Rae's lower belly.

Desire spiked through Rae. She tore her lips away from Steph's just long enough to ask, "How hungry are you?"

"Very," Steph rasped. She nipped the sensitive spot below Rae's ear. "Turn off the stove."

Rae wasn't ready to give up the heady feeling of having Steph pressed so intimately against her. She slid both hands under her thighs and lifted her up from the counter.

Steph let out a gasp. She curled her arms around Rae's neck, and her legs squeezed around Rae's middle. "What are you doing?"

"Carrying you to the bedroom to make love to you." The words slipped out before Rae could think about their implication.

But then Steph's lips were back on hers, and she stopped thinking altogether. She stumbled over to the stove and managed to turn it off without dropping her precious cargo or breaking the kiss. Then she carried her to the nearest bed, not caring whose it was.

Steph had imagined what it would be like to make love to Rae a couple of times—okay, a couple dozen times. In her fantasies, they had always undressed each other slowly, savoring the experience, but now taking it slow was the furthest thing from her mind. Her entire body hungered for Rae's.

When Rae put one knee on the bed and lowered her to the mattress, Steph tugged her down until Rae's body covered hers and their lips met again. God, Rae's weight on her felt heavenly.

Rae trembled against her as she slid one hand down Steph's hip and beneath her T-shirt to caress the sensitive skin of her side.

An answering tremor went through Steph's body. All her thoughts scattered except for one: more. She needed to feel all of Rae. Already breathing hard, she broke the kiss and sat up beneath her.

Rae rose up on her knees to give her space and used that moment to switch on the bedside lamp.

Her gaze heated Steph's skin as she grasped the hem of her T-shirt, pulled it up over her head, and tossed it aside.

Rae's fingers stilled on the top button of her own shirt. Naked hunger and awe mingled on her face as she stared at Steph. Her gaze slid up Steph's body, pausing on her belly button piercing, then trailing higher. She swallowed audibly and traced the edge of Steph's black lace bra with one fingertip.

Goose bumps raced down Steph's chest. Her nipples hardened against the cups of the bra.

"Do you have any idea how sexy you are?" Rae whispered.

"You have a thing for lace, don't you?" Steph asked with a grin, trying to insert a bit of playfulness into the situation. The intensity of what she felt—not just arousal, but more importantly, love—was almost overwhelming.

But Rae didn't smile. Her blazing gaze remained fixed on Steph. "I have a thing for you."

Before Steph could ponder what exactly that meant, Rae leaned down and placed a string of heated kisses down her throat, then nibbled a path along her collarbone and down her cleavage. With shaking fingers, she found the front clasp of the bra and twisted it open. Still kneeling, she drew the straps down Steph's arms and gazed at her. "Gorgeous." Softly, she trailed her fingertips along the outer curve of one breast.

The tenderness of her touch made Steph's body ache and her heart melt. "Rae," she groaned out.

As if in reply to the unspoken plea, Rae slid down and lowered her head.

Steph's breathing sped up in anticipation, and she threaded her fingers through Rae's hair to draw her down.

Rae didn't resist the light tug. She kissed the valley between Steph's breasts, caressed the soft swells with her lips, and then licked a sensual circle around one nipple.

Steph writhed beneath her and tightened her grip on Rae's hair. God, if Rae already had her so worked up, she could only imagine—

A jolt of arousal shot down her body as Rae closed her mouth over her nipple and sucked lightly.

Steph gasped and arched up beneath her. "Jesus, Rae," she got out thickly. "If you keep this up…"

"Mmm, I'm planning to," Rae murmured against her damp nipple.

"Not like this. I want to see you…feel you too."

With obvious reluctance, Rae moved her mouth away, sat up, and started to unbutton her shirt, fumbling slightly.

Too slow. "Let me." Steph brushed Rae's hands away and reached for the buttons. Her fingers weren't any steadier, though. A growl escaped her.

Jeez, why can't I...? Finally, she gave an impatient yank that made the last few buttons fly everywhere.

Rae stared down at her, then a slow, sexy grin spread across her face. She wrenched her arms free of the sleeves and tossed the shirt on the growing pile of clothes next to the bed.

Steph's gaze went to Rae's broad shoulders, then to the soft curve of her breasts, cradled in a black sports bra. God, she couldn't wait to feel them—to feel all of Rae. "My turn." She pushed against Rae's shoulders until she got the hint and rolled over, taking Steph with her.

"Is this okay?" Steph indicated their reversed position.

Rae nodded. The mix of raw vulnerability and desire on her face took Steph's breath away.

Steph cupped her cheek with one hand and kissed her, softly at first, then with escalating passion. She reached between them with her other hand, found Rae's belt buckle, and tugged on the leather. Finally, the belt fell open, and she fumbled for the button of Rae's dress pants. The rasp of the zipper filled her ears.

Rae willingly lifted up her hips as Steph eased the pants down, along with her boxer shorts.

When Steph stood for a moment to get rid of her own slacks, Rae took the opportunity to pull her sports bra up over her head.

Steph's slacks dropped from her hands as she stared down at Rae, who lay before her, now completely naked. "Wow. Now who's the gorgeous one?" There was something incredibly appealing about this mix of strong muscles and subtle curves. Steph hoped she wasn't drooling. Impatient to feel all of her, she reached for her own panties to tug them down.

But Rae sat up and covered her hands with her own, stopping her. "Let me," she said, her gaze smoldering.

The heated forcefulness in her tone sent a thrill through Steph. She took her hands away. "Be my guest."

Rae slid to the edge of the bed and pulled Steph into the V of her powerful thighs. She trailed her fingertips up the outside of Steph's legs, as she had done earlier, in the kitchen. But now, with no fabric between them, the touch was so much more intense that Steph groaned out loud.

When Rae reached Steph's hips, she dipped her fingers beneath the elastic, but instead of finally drawing the panties down, she slid her hands around and caressed Steph's butt.

Steph would have teased her about being a butt woman, but she needed all of her focus to stay on her feet.

Keeping eye contact, Rae slowly eased the panties down.

Her hands left trails of fire along Steph's skin. When she swayed, Rae grasped her hips, lowered her to the bed, and rolled over her. Now she was back in the top position.

"Smooth," Steph whispered, "very—" Her sentence ended on a gasp as Rae's strong thigh slid between hers, pressing against her wetness.

Rae bent her elbows until they were touching all along their lengths, Rae's breasts nestled against her own, their heartbeats racing in tandem.

The skin-on-skin contact was the most delicious thing Steph had ever felt. The little sounds of need vibrating through Rae's chest made Steph's entire body tighten. She arched her hips up against her.

"God," Rae whispered against her lips. "You make my head spin." She trailed her hand up and down Steph's hip and side as if she didn't know where to touch first. After a few seconds of sweet torture, she cupped her breast and rasped her thumb across one stiff nipple.

Pleasure rushed down Steph's body. She hooked her leg around Rae's and pressed herself against her until Rae made that strangled sound again. Her hands slid restlessly over Rae's back. "Rae…"

"Hmm?" Rae let her lips follow the path of her hand over the swell of Steph's breast.

Steph's heart thumped hard beneath each caress. When Rae sucked her nipple into her mouth, Steph buried her fingers in Rae's hair and bucked her hips upward.

Rae nipped lightly on the underside of her breast, then pressed openmouthed kisses to the planes of her belly. At Steph's pierced navel, she paused. Her warm breath fanned over Steph's skin, making her quiver. Gently, Rae traced a circle around the piercing.

Just the brush of a single finger over her skin made Steph arch up for more contact.

Rae touched her fingertip to the small stud. "Does this hurt?"

"No," Steph got out. "The only spot on my body that is aching is farther down."

Rae chuckled against her belly. "Don't worry. I'll get to that spot." She flicked at the stud with her tongue, sending another bolt of pleasure through Steph. "Eventually."

Steph grazed her fingernails down Rae's muscled back until she drew a groan from her. "Now."

The need in her voice seemed to wash away the last bits of Rae's self-control. Her eye smoldered with desire as she kissed a path back up her body until she captured her lips in a demanding kiss.

Steph moaned into her mouth, then had to pull away to gasp for breath as Rae slid her hand down her belly. With two fingers, she combed through the trimmed curls between her thighs, then slid deeper.

Moaning, Steph struggled not to come at the first touch. Her eyes half closed as Rae drew slow circles. Shivers coursed up her spine and down her thighs.

"Like this?" Rae asked, her breath teasing Steph's lips. "Tell me what you like."

Speech was quickly becoming a thing of the past, so Steph tilted her hips upward in a silent request, inviting more.

Rae looked her in the eyes as she slowly slid inside.

Steph's gasp turned into a long moan as Rae withdrew, then came back with another finger. She added the pad of her thumb, now stroking her inside and out.

Their gazes held as they moved with each other, and the heady desire on Rae's face matched her own.

The rhythm Rae set was perfect, and Steph gave herself over to her touch. She dug her fingers into Rae's back and her heels into the mattress to feel her even deeper.

Rae's mouth found hers again, and she kissed her with fierce intensity, mirroring the movements of her fingers with her tongue, until Steph had to wrench her mouth away to suck in a series of ragged pants. Each of Rae's thrusts made her nipples brush over her own, and the added stimulation was almost enough to send her over the edge.

No. Not yet, not yet. She struggled to hold back and enjoy every second.

Rae nipped the rim of Steph's ear, then sucked lightly on her neck, while she curved her fingers at just the right angle.

"Yes! There!" Steph's hips surged off the bed. Her muscles started to shake. Pleasure cascaded through her body. With a guttural moan, she clawed at the damp, quivering muscles of Rae's back and arched up beneath her one last time. White spots burst in her vision, and the only reason she didn't scream was because she didn't have enough air left in her lungs.

The next thing she knew, Rae was covering her face with soft kisses.

Steph let out a breathless sigh. Her hands, which had been clutching Rae's back, flopped to the mattress.

When the last aftershocks of pleasure ebbed away, Rae eased back her fingers with another kiss.

A shiver went through Steph. Her entire body felt heavy and sated, but she managed to lift one hand and traced her fingertips over Rae's shoulders and back to see if she'd left any marks. "Shit," she got out, her voice raw. "I hope I didn't hurt you."

"Hurt me?" Rae let out a dazed laugh. "God, no." A smile curled up her lips. Somehow, it managed to be blazingly hot and sweetly shy at the same time. "Like you said earlier, the only spot that is aching is a lot lower than that."

"Don't worry. I'll soothe that ache…as soon as I can move properly."

"I'm not in a hurry," Rae said, even though her voice was husky and her hips strained against Steph's, perhaps without her even noticing. "I love seeing you like this. All flushed and beautiful and satisfied." She combed a damp strand of hair back from Steph's face, her expression so tender that Steph's heart melted.

"Very satisfied." Steph slid her hand up, into Rae's hair, and pulled her down. She had intended for it to be a thank-you kiss, but as soon as Rae's lips met hers, new desire stirred, and the kiss turned urgent.

Rae let out a helpless little groan and pressed herself against Steph's thigh.

The warm wetness against her skin made Steph moan along with her.

"Jesus, Steph." Rae's hot breath tickled her ear. "You make me feel like I'm about to come apart at the seams."

"I want to see that. And then help you put yourself back together." She trailed her hands down Rae's back, enjoying the silky slide of her skin, and then gripped her hips. "Roll over. I want to touch you everywhere."

Rae shook against her as they rolled together, their bodies never losing contact.

Steph braced herself on her elbow and lay half on, half off Rae so she could admire her in the light of the bedside table. God, she was gorgeous—her wide swimmer's shoulders, the gentle rise of her breasts, the neat patch of curly hair at the juncture of her powerful thighs. That wasn't what made Steph's breath hitch, though; the complex mix of love and passion that flooded her was. She had always taken what she wanted—what both she and her bed partner for the night wanted—but never had she wanted to give so much, to please anyone so much, touch anyone's body, heart, and soul.

Slowly, she ran her hands over Rae's strong arms and traced two small, round scars on her left shoulder. A bump rose beneath her fingertips, probably where a shotgun pellet had lodged deep beneath Rae's skin. Steph swallowed down a wave of emotions and placed a whisperlike kiss onto the spot.

When she looked up, their gazes met, exchanging so much without either of them saying a single word.

Steph caressed Rae's collarbone, her sides, the arc of her ribs, taking the time to learn what made her suck in a breath or groan out Steph's name.

It stunned her how easy it was to please Rae. Everywhere she touched got her an instant reaction. Heat came off Rae's body in waves. "God, your skin is on fire."

"Yeah." Rae's voice was thick with arousal. "That's what you do to me."

"Let's see what else I can do to you."

When Steph cradled one small breast in her palm and stroked it with her thumb, Rae tilted her head back and let out an almost tortured groan.

Steph immediately took the offer, nibbling a path along her jaw and then down her neck.

A bead of sweat trickled down between Rae's breasts, and Steph slid lower to follow its path with her mouth. God, Rae tasted delicious, of salt and passion. Steph instantly wanted more. She licked around Rae's firm breast, making each circle smaller and smaller until she twirled her tongue over her hardened nipple.

Rae's hips bucked up beneath her. The sheets rustled as she fisted her hands around them.

The way she fought for control was hot, but seeing her lose it would be even hotter. Steph closed her mouth over the stiff nipple and sucked gently, while she rubbed the other nipple between her fingers.

Rae muttered a string of helpless words that sounded like curses.

Smiling, Steph flicked her thumb across her nipple one last time before she teased her fingers down Rae's belly.

Taut muscles tensed and twitched beneath her touch.

Steph took her time as she slid her hand down her hip and explored her powerful thighs, stroking down along the outside and up along the inside, where the skin was even softer. She loved the sound of Rae's breathing getting more and more ragged as she trailed her fingers higher.

They both moaned as Steph combed through moist curls.

Rae caught her bottom lip between her teeth. The amber spots in her brown iris flickered like an all-consuming fire.

Steph kept her gaze on Rae's face, raptly watching her expression as she slid her fingers through the heat between Rae's legs.

Rae's entire body jerked. "Steph. God, Steph." She let go of the sheets and clung to Steph, her strong hands gentle.

Steph stroked her softly at first, then with slightly more pressure, following the rhythm of Rae's hips.

All too soon, Rae's legs began to tremble.

The sight of Rae with her head flung back, cheeks flushed, moving against her with abandon, sent a rush of heat between Steph's thighs. She reached up with her free hand and rubbed Rae's hard nipple between her fingers again.

A shout vaguely resembling Steph's name tore from Rae's throat.

The sound and feel of Rae's climax nearly made Steph come a second time. She clenched her thighs together and watched in awe as pleasure washed over Rae's face. Steph gentled her touch and caressed her through it until Rae covered her hand with her own.

When Rae stilled against her, Steph buried her face against the curve of her neck and gently kissed the damp skin. Rae's pulse thudded a fast rhythm against her lips, then, eventually, slowed to a more normal pace.

Steph cuddled against her, her usual urge to get some distance completely absent.

Rae blinked and looked as if she had trouble focusing her eye. Weakly, she lifted one hand and caressed Steph's hair. "Sorry." Her voice was hoarse, and she cleared her throat before continuing, "I'm usually not that loud."

"Are you kidding? Why would you apologize for that? I loved making you moan and shout." She flashed Rae a mischievous grin. "Plus if any of our neighbors still doubted that we're really a couple, we just convinced them otherwise."

Rae's chest vibrated beneath her as she burst out laughing. "God, you're such a comic. But you're m—" She bit her lip.

Steph's heart started beating faster. Had Rae really been about to say what she thought she would say? She swallowed and forced herself to say it. "But I'm your comic?"

Rae stilled beneath her. A combination of hope and insecurity flitted across her flushed features. "Do you want to be?" she asked quietly.

Steph's throat closed, and all she could do was nod. "But only," she finally got out, "if you'll be mine too. I mean, not my comic, obviously." Shit, she was babbling. "Just…mine."

"Does that mean you…?"

Denying it was futile. Her feelings were probably written all over her face. Not that Steph wanted to deny it, as scary as saying it out loud was. "Yeah," she croaked out. "I…I love you."

Rae closed her eyes, and when she opened them again, they gleamed with tears. She dashed the balls of her hands across them. "Damn. Sorry. I didn't mean to—"

Steph drew her hand away. "No apologies." She leaned down and kissed first the corner of Rae's right eye, then, even more tenderly, the left one.

Rae wrapped both arms around her as if she didn't intend to ever let her go. "I love you too, in case you didn't guess already."

Their lips met in a lingering kiss.

Steph felt incredibly light, as if she would have drifted away if not for Rae's hold on her. Even being up on stage couldn't compare. "How long have you felt like this?"

"I have no idea. A while, I guess, but I can't tell you when exactly." Rae kissed her nose, the corner of her mouth, then her lips again. "Completely blindsided me."

"Blindsided, hm?" Steph smiled and traced Rae's features with her fingertips. Just when she leaned down to kiss her again, a loud rumble from her stomach interrupted them.

Rae laughed, slid her hand between them, and caressed her belly, instantly causing a hunger of a different kind to flare up. Despite Steph's protests, she rolled out of bed.

"Hey! Where are you going?"

"Getting you something to eat. You gotta keep your strength up because I'm not done with you." On the last few words, Rae's voice lowered to a sexy burr.

Steph shuddered and rolled onto her side so she could watch Rae walk to the door in all her naked glory. God, she had to be the hottest woman alive...and what was more, she was all Steph's.

Chapter 26

Rae woke up in the wrong room—Steph's, she realized only now—but in exactly the right spot. Steph was curled up in her arms, her bare thigh across Rae's and one arm loosely slung across her hips. The trimmed curls between Steph's legs tickled her skin, and her warm breath washed over Rae's nipple with every peaceful lift and fall of Steph's chest as she slept.

Need curled in the pit of her belly. God, how could she want her again so soon? They had made love until the sun had come up, starting the new year in the best way possible and leaving Rae pleasantly sore.

Her body buzzed with awareness at Steph's closeness, but for the moment, she was content to just hold her.

More than content, actually. A feeling of belonging filled her—something she hadn't felt since she had left the LAPD.

For a moment, the old guilt crept up. Did she have the right to be this happy when Kim might cry herself to sleep every night and wake up alone every morning?

She pushed that thought aside. Clinging to her misery wouldn't bring Mike back or help Kim. Mike would want her to be happy. He would like Steph; she was sure of it. Rae smiled at the thought of the mischief those two would have gotten into had they ever met.

Steph stirred and then stretched against her with the cutest little sound.

The slide of her warm skin against her own sent ripples of sensation up and down Rae's body.

"Good morning," Steph said, her voice rough with sleep.

Rae smoothed a strand of Steph's wildly tousled hair behind her ear. "Morning."

"Mmm." Steph cuddled even closer. "I like waking up like this. With you."

"Yeah? No regrets? I mean, we went from 'just date and see where it goes' to 'I love you' pretty fast." Being able to say it out loud still made warmth spread through Rae's chest. "I don't want you to get scared and..."

"Run?" Steph shook her head so firmly that her blonde hair became even more of a sexy mess. "Excuse me for breaking my own rule by mentioning an ex in bed, but...I'm not Lise, Rae. I admit that this," she put her hand on the slope of Rae's breast, where her heart was thudding, "still scares the living daylights out of me, but I figure that's only because it matters so much. *You* matter so much to me."

Rae kissed her gently. "Ditto."

"Besides," Steph added, a mischievous smile curling her lips, "as Penny pointed out, we both showed up with U-Hauls the third time we ever saw each other, so moving fast seems to be our thing."

A belly laugh chased away the remainder of Rae's fear. "So if I do this..." She rolled them over and trailed her fingertips down from Steph's cheek, along her neck, to her breast, where she drew sensuous circles and watched Steph's nipple harden, even though she hadn't touched it yet. "You won't think it's too fast?"

Before Steph could answer, a phone started to ring from beneath the pile of clothes next to the bed.

Steph let out a frustrated groan. "Sorry. I think that's mine."

Reluctantly, Rae moved her hand away from Steph's soft breast.

"Hey!" Steph tried to draw her hand back to where it had been. "Let it ring. I promised you twenty-four hours in bed, and I'm a woman of my word."

It was tempting. Very tempting. Rae struggled to let reason prevail. "It could be Mr. Hicks, wanting to book you again."

Steph's gaze went back and forth between the floor and Rae.

The phone stopped ringing.

Steph looked up at her with a triumphant smile. "Now, where were we?"

"I think somewhere around here." Rae stroked her thumb across her nipple, and when Steph arched up beneath her, Rae forgot about the phone and everything else for the next couple of hours.

It wasn't until three o'clock in the afternoon that Steph finally checked her phone.

The need for food had finally made them get out of bed, and she smiled at the sounds of Rae whistling in the kitchen as she stretched out on the wrinkled sheets. She loved knowing Rae was happy—and that she was the source of her happiness. Half of her attention was still on the doorway as she lifted the phone to her ear to listen to her voice mail.

"Ms. Renshaw, this is Dwight Ribbard with Universal Television. Would you give me a call at your earliest convenience?"

Television? Oh wow! Steph scrambled for something to write with as he repeated his phone number. She tried not to expect too much. If Mr. Ribbard were someone important, he probably wouldn't be working on New Year's Day, right?

Still her fingers trembled as she reached for her T-shirt next to the bed and pulled it over her head. She couldn't call a TV network rep naked. Not that he could see her. She tried to calm her breathing as she typed in the number. The phone seemed to ring forever.

"Mr. Ribbard, this is Stephanie Renshaw, returning your call," she blurted out as soon as a male voice answered.

"Thanks for calling me back. Listen, I'm supposed to be on vacation, so I'll keep this short. I'm an entertainment producer for *The Tonight Show*."

The phone nearly slid from Steph's grasp. Good thing she was already sitting down. "*The Tonight Show*?" her voice came out in a squeak.

"Yes." Amusement colored his tone. "As I said, I'm on vacation in LA right now, and I saw you at The Fun Zone last night. I loved your routine, so I looked you up and found your YouTube channel. Long story short, we'll be doing a week of shows at Universal in March, and we're looking for up-and-coming local talent to mix things up a little. Would you be able to do a five-minute set on the show?"

Steph pressed her bare feet to the floor to keep herself grounded. She would be on *The Tonight Show*…and in March of all months, right when her self-imposed deadline ended! Was she really awake, or had she fallen into a sex-induced slumber, and this was just a dream?

"Ms. Renshaw?"

"Oh, sorry. Yes, of course I can do a set on the show." It took all of her self-control not to shout out her elation.

"Great. My assistant will contact you next week with the details, but from what I saw on YouTube, your material is exactly what we're looking for."

Yes, yes, yes! She struggled to hold back a giddy laugh.

"Your roommate jokes in particular could be a hit with our audience," Mr. Ribbard added.

A chill slid over her. She paused in her internal victory dance. *Oh shit.* She had totally forgotten that Gabe had posted the video on her YouTube channel. "Um, the roommate jokes?"

"Yeah. They will resonate with the younger, urban audience we want to reach. I definitely want you to do them. Is that a problem?"

"No," she said quickly. "Not a problem, but...I have a lot of great material your audience would love. I'd be happy to send you links to—"

"That won't be necessary. Your roommate bits were perfect. But let's talk about it later. I'm calling from the hotel pool, and if my husband catches me working, I'll be in the doghouse."

Steph might have answered and politely said goodbye, but she wasn't sure. She dropped the phone to the bed, sank back onto the mattress, and covered her eyes with her arm. God, the world was cruel.

Here it was—the breakthrough she had always wanted. She had worked for ten years to get to this point, and now her big dream was finally within reach. But it came with a price. She would have to break her promise to Rae that she would never use her up on stage again.

Cold sweat broke out along her spine as she jumped up and started to pace the room. Could she really do that? Hurt Rae that way?

Two months ago, she would have done everything for this once-in-a-lifetime chance. But now there was one thing she wasn't willing to sacrifice for her dream. Her promise to Rae was just as important as her career, especially now that she knew why Rae had reacted so strongly to being made the butt of jokes.

Goddammit! She stopped her pacing at the shelf with her comedy books and pounded her fist against it. She wouldn't be able to talk Mr. Ribbard into letting her use different material; she could sense that. He was used to getting what he wanted, and what he wanted was the roommate jokes.

Of course she could reject his offer, but if she did that, her career would be toast. The gatekeepers of television comedy all knew each other. Word would get around quickly, and no one would book her a second time. This was her one chance, and she wanted to grab hold of it with both hands.

But that would turn Rae and their relationship into a laughing matter, and they were everything but to her.

She leaned against the bookcase and pressed both hands to her chest, feeling as if this impossible choice was ripping her apart.

She couldn't hurt Rae by doing the roommate jokes on national TV, but how on earth was she supposed to let go of her decade-old dream?

Rae whistled as she slid the eggs onto plates and placed them onto the tray, where coffee, toast, and jam already waited to be delivered to the bedroom. She loved being able to spoil Steph with breakfast in bed. Well, more like brunch in bed. A grin tugged on her lips as she remembered what had made them skip breakfast…and lunch.

Steph's voice drifted over from the bedroom, probably as she returned that phone call from earlier.

Rae hoped it wasn't someone about to lure Steph out of the apartment. Neither of them had to work today, and she intended to make the most of their time together.

Barefoot and dressed just in a T-shirt and a pair of boxers, she carried the tray to Steph's room and paused in the doorway to admire Steph's form.

But Steph wasn't resting peacefully or greeting her with a smile. She had gotten out of bed, put her T-shirt back on, and was leaning against the bookcase, both hands pressed to her chest as if she were in pain.

Rae's stomach twisted itself into knots. She raced over. The mugs and plates clinked as she set down the tray on the floor and gently put her hands over Steph's. "What happened?"

Steph straightened and gave her a smile that, for the very first time, wasn't genuine at all. "Nothing. Everything's fine."

"Don't try that with me." Rae's gaze went to the phone that lay discarded on the bed. "Bad news?"

"No. Yes. I'm not sure. It could have been great news, but..." Steph clutched the back of Rae's T-shirt with both hands and buried her face against her shoulder.

Rae wrapped both arms around her and held her tightly. "Tell me what happened."

"That call earlier... That was a producer for *The Tonight Show*."

Rae drew back a little to stare at her. "Are you serious?"

Steph nodded.

"Do they want to book you? For *The Tonight Show*?" Rae's voice came out a little squeaky.

Again, Steph nodded.

A dozen different thoughts and emotions bounced around Rae's mind like out-of-control billiard balls—pride and happiness for Steph, but also her own fears and doubts about what a big breakthrough would mean for them. Would Steph leave LA...leave her? Would their relationship survive if Steph toured the country for months? Few comics on the road had successful relationships; she knew that. God, she had lost so much already. She couldn't lose Steph too.

In the end, she discarded all but one thought: Steph wanted this. She deserved this. She had worked tirelessly for ten years to get to this point. No way would Rae destroy her dreams just because of her own insecurities. They would find a way to make it work.

"Wow, Steph!" She sent her a proud smile. "That's wonderful!"

But instead of beaming and cheering, Steph looked as if she had gotten the worst news of her life.

Rae rubbed her back. "Hey, don't worry. We'll make it work somehow. I'm not giving up on us just because you might be on the road for part of the year."

"That's not it. At least that's not all." Steph hung her head. "I don't think I can do it."

"What? Of course you can! You're going to be great!"

"That's not what I mean." Steph pressed her face against Rae's shoulder again and whispered, "They want me to do the roommate jokes."

Tension flooded Rae's body. "Oh." She had to swallow twice before she could continue. "How does *The Tonight Show* even know about them?"

Steph looked everywhere but at her. "Gabe posted the video on my YouTube channel, and I forgot to take it down." She peeked up. "I'm so sorry, Rae. I'll delete it right away."

But, of course, the damage was already done.

Damn. It took some effort to unclench her teeth. "Well, it can't be helped now. What did you tell them?"

"I tried to offer him different material, but he wasn't interested. I got the feeling it's the roommate jokes or nothing."

Rae's stomach churned. "Shit." A roaring filled her ears. It sounded like the laughter of the audience when Steph had told those jokes about her. Could she live through those moments of feeling exposed again?

"Maybe I could rewrite the roommate jokes so they aren't about you anymore," Steph said, her tone hesitant. "I could make up a fictional roommate."

"What about authenticity? You said good comedy is based on real life, not just making stuff up."

Steph looked her in the eyes. Her gaze was sad, but fierce. "Me protecting you is very authentic."

Warmth spread through Rae, settling her queasy stomach a little. "But what if he insists on the original jokes?"

"Then I'll tell him no. It might not be worth it anyway," Steph said. "This isn't the 80s anymore, where one appearance on *The Tonight Show* would have made me a star overnight."

"It would still be a big step, wouldn't it?"

"Yeah." Steph forced a brave smile. "But maybe I'm not ready for what would come after *The Tonight Show* anyway. Jokes about my bad taste in bedmates were a big part of my comedy routine. Now that I'm with you, I'll have to come up with new material."

Silence stretched between them.

No matter what Steph said to make Rae feel better, they both knew that this was probably the big break Steph had been hoping for, and she should grab it with both hands. Rae had expected her to. She realized now that part of her had been waiting for the other shoe to drop and for Steph to choose comedy over her. Maybe she still wasn't completely over thinking she didn't deserve happiness. But Steph believed she did—and she was even willing to sacrifice her dream for it.

A wave of love and gratefulness swept over Rae, driving back her fears. Her throat felt raw as she said, "I want you to do them. The roommate jokes. In a revised version or the original one. It doesn't matter."

"What? Of course it matters! I promised you not to use them on stage again."

"That was before. I'm no longer just your roommate, so strictly speaking, those jokes won't even be about me." Rae let her hand trail down to Steph's hip and squeezed gently. "Tell them you'll do it."

Steph's expression was pained. "God, I want to. But I also want to avoid hurting you by bringing up bad memories from your childhood."

Each word felt like a healing caress to Rae's patched-up heart—and made her more determined not to let Steph sacrifice her dream for her. "It wasn't only my childhood. I'm starting to understand that those jokes hurt mostly because of the shooting."

"The shooting?" Steph echoed. "But I'd never joke about that. Never!"

"I know. It's not about you. It's about the press. In the weeks after the shooting, I couldn't escape all the news reports. Again and again, they brought up everything I had lost…my eye, my job…Mike. They exposed it all to the public at a time when I felt most vulnerable. But the worst thing was that they made me out to be a hero, and that made me feel even worse because I thought I was to blame for Mike's death."

"You're not," Steph said firmly.

"I get that now. And that's why I think I would be fine with you doing the roommate jokes. I'm in a different place now than I was two months ago. I no longer feel so raw. You taught me that I have no reason to fear being exposed or to hide in shame, not for my eye and not for anything I did the day of the shooting. I can deal with a couple of jokes, just like your family did."

"Rae…" Steph's voice was thick with emotions. "I can't ask that of you."

Rae lightly stroked her cheek with her fingertips. "You're not asking. I'm offering. I trust you. I know you'll find a way to tell those jokes in a way that is authentic yet won't make me feel bad."

"I will." It sounded like a solemn oath. "But before we make that decision, we should really think this through."

"What's there to think about? You want this, don't you?"

"Of course I do. But I want you too. I want us. And if I do *The Tonight Show* and my career takes off, I'll probably be traveling all over the country. Maybe even all over the world." Steph raised her gaze to Rae's, despair written all over her face. "I'd have to leave you behind."

Just the word *leave* made every muscle in Rae's body tense. Her barely healed heart felt as if it would shatter into a million pieces if one more person left her—especially if that person was Steph.

"Unless…" Hope vibrated through Steph's voice. "I'm getting way ahead of myself here, but if I really manage to become a bit of a celebrity, won't I need a bodyguard? And you know, there's really only one person I'd want to guard my body." A hint of playfulness made its way into Steph's voice.

Rae kissed her lightly. "And you know I'd guard that gorgeous body with my life, but I don't think that's the solution. There's a reason why I had to give up being a police officer. I have a huge blind spot, and that would put you in danger if I were your bodyguard. I won't risk that."

Steph sighed and held on to Rae more tightly as if not ready to let go.

"But maybe you're on to something with that thought. If I could find a way to make a living while traveling with you…" Rae played with a strand of Steph's hair.

For a while, they clung to each other while trying to come up with an idea.

"What if you…?"

"What if I…?"

They spoke at the same time, then stopped and laughed.

Steph gestured at her to go first.

"There's a security guard training company in Burbank that is looking for instructors. They have facilities in multiple states, and some parts of the guard training are completed online. Maybe I could freelance for them."

Steph studied her. "Is that something you'd be interested in?"

Rae nodded. "Back in October, when I first started working at The Fun Zone, I wasn't ready to take on the responsibility of teaching other people." Her chest expanded under a deep breath. "But now I am. I just don't know if they'd have enough work for me to make a living from it. At least not at first."

"Well, if you freelance, you could do other things on the side."

"Such as?"

"Lana is going to work with Grace Durand, who recently established her own production company. And since Lana is now on Team Rae too, I bet she'd be willing to introduce you."

A chuckle escaped Rae. "Um, sorry to burst your rose-colored bubble, but I don't think I meet Hollywood's beauty standards."

"Pah, what do they know?" Steph cupped her face in both hands. "You are beautiful. But I wasn't actually suggesting that you become a movie star. I know producers are always looking for people with a police background. Maybe you could set yourself up as an adviser to film sets, and I could try to do shows close to wherever you are working."

Rae would have never thought of something like that in a million years, but it definitely sounded interesting. Maybe she could do a bit of both. "That sounds great. God, I love you."

"I love you too."

All remainder of tension drained from Rae's muscles as their lips met in a long, tender kiss.

Untold minutes later, Steph pulled back slightly. Her nose twitched like a dog's catching a scent trail. "Is that coffee and toast I smell?"

Rae laughed. "You've got a one-track mind."

Steph had slipped her hands beneath Rae's T-shirt while they had been kissing, and now she lightly scraped her fingernails up and down her back. "You've got no idea."

Rae shuddered. "You could always remind me."

"And I will," Steph said, her usual confidence back in her voice. "After coffee and food."

Laughing, Rae picked up the tray and followed Steph back to bed.

Epilogue

RAE PUT THE SWIMMING GOGGLES on and looked at herself in the mirror of the Renshaws' guest bathroom. The suction from the rim pulled down her left lower lid a little, emphasizing the difference between her eyes. Slowly, she turned toward Steph, who leaned against the closed bathroom door and watched her. "What do you think?"

"Hot." Steph grinned and made a sound as if she were striking a match. Her gaze trailed up and down Rae's body. "You look totally hot."

Rae couldn't help chuckling, and part of her tension eased. "Ditto." The sight of Steph in her black bikini—cut high at the hip so her killer legs appeared even longer and sexier—made her wish they had stayed home instead of spending the day with Steph's family. They hadn't spent a lot of time in their apartment in the past two months. Since Steph's set on *The Tonight Show*, she had been booked by several big clubs in New York, while Rae had trained future security guards there. Now they were back, Steph for the comedy festival and shows at The Improv, The Comedy Store, and The Fun Zone and Rae to work on the set of *Central Precinct*. "But I wasn't talking about the bathing suit. I meant the eye."

"That's part of you, so it's hot too." Steph pushed away from the door and wrapped her arms around her.

Her warm skin touched Rae's, making her think of much more pleasant things than her eye.

Steph stroked slow circles between her shoulder blades. "Even if your eye pops out—and I don't think it will—I promise no one will stare at you. But if it would make you more comfortable, I can tell my family to get lost while we use the pool."

Rae shook her head. "Thanks. But I think I can do this." Truth be told, she had felt ready months ago, but with everything that had happened since then—preparing for *The Tonight Show*, the anniversary of the shooting and Mike's death, Steph's birthday, and starting a new career—she hadn't made it into a pool yet.

"You can." Steph squeezed her softly, then stepped back. "Let's go. I can't wait to see you swim."

"It's not that interesting. Doesn't compare to watching you on *The Tonight Show* or in all of those big clubs." Rae was still bursting with pride.

"We'll have to agree to disagree on that. Watching you power through the water, those sexy muscles bunching..." Steph let out a little growl. "Maybe I should tell my family to get lost. They can have the pool back in August, when the two of us are back on the road."

Rae chuckled. "Nah. It's okay." Deep down, she knew that getting over her fear of the prosthesis slipping out and people catching a glimpse of her socket was as important as getting back to swimming. "They're your family, so that means they're Team Rae too, right?"

"Right."

Hand in hand, they made their way through the Renshaws' house and across the patio. There wasn't a cloud in the sky, and May Gray had long since dissipated, so the shiver that went through Rae had nothing to do with the temperatures as they made their way toward the pool.

Steph's parents were sitting beneath the poolside pergola, chatting with Claire and Lana, who had recently returned from their honeymoon tanned and with happy smiles. Now they were cuddled up together on one of the double lounge chairs.

When Steph and Rae approached, they all looked up, acting so casually that Rae knew Steph had instructed them not to stare, no matter what might happen.

Everyone but Lana was heeding orders. Steph's sister-in-law playfully raked her gaze up and down Rae's body. "Hot."

"Hey!" Steph and her sister said in unison.

Claire bumped her wife with her shoulder, but Rae could tell that she was teasing, not truly jealous.

"What?" Lana said. "Just because I'm happily married doesn't mean I can't appreciate a good-looking woman in a bathing suit."

"What a happy coincidence. Look what I'm wearing." Grinning, Claire gestured at her own bathing-suit-covered body.

"Oh, I noticed. Believe me." Lana's gaze was a lot less playful and a lot more sensual as it slid over Claire.

Steph groaned. "Guys, you'll put Mom and Dad into therapy if you don't cut it out."

"You're one to talk," Claire shot back. "It took you five minutes to get out of the car because you couldn't stop kissing."

It had really been a pep talk from Steph, interspersed with kisses, but Claire didn't need to know that.

Steph shrugged. "Come on." She tugged on Rae's hand. "Let's get in the pool." At the edge of the pool, she turned to face Rae and gently kissed her. "Ready?"

Rae nodded.

"Then have fun." Instead of walking down the steps and wading into the water, Steph sat on the edge and dangled her legs into the water.

Rae tilted her head and gave her a questioning look through the lenses of her goggles. "Aren't you coming in with me?"

"Nope. I might drown because I'm too busy ogling you."

"I'd rescue you."

"I'll join you in a second." Steph shaded her eyes with her hand and looked up at her. "But I think you need to do this yourself first."

She was right, and Rae loved her for intuitively understanding. She nodded and turned toward the pool.

The May sun glittered on the turquoise water. It looked so inviting that Rae could no longer understand what she had found so threatening about this situation. She checked the fit of her goggles one last time and tightened the elastic. One last glance back at Steph, who nodded encouragingly, then she waded into the pool and dove in.

The water embraced her like the hug of an old friend she hadn't seen in a long time.

She kicked her legs and cut through the water in steady overhead strokes. Her body immediately remembered the familiar rhythm and took over until she didn't have to think about finding the right angles anymore. Four strokes, breath, four strokes, breath.

When she got closer to the other end of the pool, she hesitated. Should she try a flip turn? But what if she did it too hard and the goggles slipped off and the prosthesis—? She stopped herself. So what if that happened? No one here would respect her any less if they caught a glimpse of her empty eye socket.

An arm length from the wall, she ducked her head and curled her body. Both of her feet hit the tiles and propelled her forward. *Yes!*

It wasn't the most elegant turn ever, but she had done it, and neither her goggles nor the prosthesis had slipped.

Water churned as she kicked it up a notch, her arms and legs catapulting her through the pool. She did lap after lap until her muscles burned.

When she finally stopped and floated on her back, Steph's head bobbed up next to her. Her normally tousled hair was slicked back, emphasizing the beautiful lines of her face. "How was it? The goggles look like they held up pretty well."

Rae reached up and touched the left lens. "They did. The last few laps, I even forgot to worry about them."

"Great. I hoped that would happen. You looked really awesome. Tell me again why you're not competing in the Olympics?"

Both treading water, they had reached the deep end of the pool, away from the Renshaws.

Rae turned her back toward the tile wall and faced her. "Because I like my life exactly the way it is."

Steph gripped the edge of the pool on either side of her and leaned in to her until Rae felt the heat emanating off her body even through the water swirling around them. "Yeah?" she whispered, her mouth only inches from Rae's.

"Yeah," Rae murmured, her voice hoarse. She glanced from Steph's lips to the pergola and back. "We'll really put your parents into therapy if we don't stop this."

Steph gave an impish grin. "So what? They have great connections in the therapy world."

"Hmm, true. Well, in that case..." Still treading water, Rae bridged the gap between them and kissed her but kept it short and tender. This was a thank-you and an *I love you*. There would be time for passion later. Hopefully, not too much later.

If you enjoyed *The Roommate Arrangement*, check out Jae's romance *Just for Show*, the book in which Steph's sister Claire hired struggling actress Lana to be her pretend fiancée...and ended up falling in love with her.

About Jae

Jae grew up amidst the vineyards of southern Germany. She spent her childhood with her nose buried in a book, earning her the nickname "professor." The writing bug bit her at the age of eleven. Since 2006, she has been writing mostly in English.

She used to work as a psychologist but gave up her day job in December 2013 to become a full-time writer and a part-time editor. As far as she's concerned, it's the best job in the world.

When she's not writing, she likes to spend her time reading, indulging her ice cream and office supply addictions, and watching way too many crime shows.

CONNECT WITH JAE

Website: www.jae-fiction.com
E-Mail: jae@jae-fiction.com

Other Books from Ylva Publishing

www.ylva-publishing.com

Just for Show
Jae

ISBN: 978-3-95533-980-7
Length: 293 pages (103,000 words)

When Claire, an overachieving psychologist with OCD tendencies, hires Lana, an impulsive, out-of-work actress for a fake relationship, she figures the worst she'll have to endure are the messes Lana leaves around. It's only for a few months anyway. And it's not as if she'll enjoy all those fake kisses and loving looks. Right?

A lesbian romance where role-playing has never been so irresistible.

Who'd Have Thought
G Benson

ISBN: 978-3-95533-874-9
Length: 339 pages (122,000 words)

When Hayden Pérez stumbles across an offer to marry Samantha Thomson—a cold, rude, and complicated neurosurgeon—for $200,000, what's a cash-strapped ER nurse to do? Sure, Hayden has to convince everyone around them they're madly in love, but it's only for a year, right? What could possibly go wrong?

Contract for Love
Alison Grey

ISBN: 978-3-96324-086-7
Length: 301 pages (97,000 words)

Sherry lives in a trailer park with her son, trying to make ends meet.

Madison's life couldn't be more different. Her only goals are partying and bedding women.

When her grandmother threatens to disinherit her, Madison has to find a way to prove that she's cleaned up her act.

After a chance encounter with Sherry, Madison comes up with a crazy idea: she wants Sherry to play her fake girlfriend.

Chasing Stars
(The Superheroine Collection)
Alex K. Thorne

ISBN: 978-3-95533-992-0
Length: 205 pages (70,000 words)

For superhero Swiftwing, crime fighting isn't her biggest battle. Nor is it having to meet the whims of Hollywood star Gwen Knight as her mild-mannered assistant, Ava. It's doing all that, while tracking a giant alien bug, being asked to fake date her famous boss, and realizing that she might be coming down with a pesky case of feelings.

A fun, sweet, sexy lesbian romance about the masks we wear.

The Roommate Arrangement
© 2019 by Jae

ISBN: 978-3-96324-279-3

Also available as e-book.

Published by Ylva Publishing, legal entity of Ylva Verlag, e.Kfr.

Ylva Verlag, e.Kfr.
Owner: Astrid Ohletz
Am Kirschgarten 2
65830 Kriftel
Germany

www.ylva-publishing.com

First edition: 2019

Credits
Edited by Robin J. Samuels
Cover Design and Print Layout by Streetlight Graphics

Printed in Great Britain
by Amazon